The International KISSING CLUB

The International KISSING CLUB

ivy adams

Walker & Company ☀ New York

First published in the United States of America in January 2012
by Walker Publishing Company, Inc., a division of Bloomsbury Publishing, Inc.
www.bloomsburyteens.com

For information about permission to reproduce selections from this book, write to
Permissions, Walker BFYR, 175 Fifth Avenue, New York, New York 10010

Photograph credits: "Cassidy" © iStockphoto/Knape, "Piper" © iStockphoto/Lauri Stone,
"Mei" © Shutterstock/Layland Masuda, "Izzy" © iStockphoto/
Tom Fullum; author photograph © Sherry Thomas

Library of Congress Cataloging-in-Publication Data
Adams, Ivy.
The International Kissing Club / by Ivy Adams.
      p.   cm.
Summary: Best friends Piper, Mei, Izzy, and Cassidy of Paris, Texas, spend a semester studying
abroad and track their romantic escapades on a Facebook fan page.
ISBN 978-0-8027-2318-5 (paperback) • ISBN 978-0-8027-2358-1 (hardcover)
[1. Foreign study—Fiction. 2. High schools—Fiction. 3. Schools—Fiction. 4. Dating
(Social customs)—Fiction. 5. Facebook (Electronic resource)—Fiction.
6. Online social networks—Fiction.] I. Title.
PZ7.A2146Int 2012   [Fic]—dc22   2011005225

Book design by Regina Roff
Typeset by Westchester Book Composition
Printed in the U.S.A. by Quad/Graphics, Fairfield, Pennsylvania
2 4 6 8 10 9 7 5 3 1 (paperback)
2 4 6 8 10 9 7 5 3 1 (hardcover)

For Deanne Hutcherson: your wit and warmth and, especially, your friendship are deeply missed

The International KISSING CLUB

Prologue

She couldn't believe she was doing this.

Seriously. Couldn't. Believe. She. Was. Doing. This.

Had she completely lost her mind? God knew her friends certainly seemed to think so.

Cassidy had teased her, had asked if she was wearing a dress or a peach lace parachute.

Izzy had wondered aloud how many children had labored in sweatshops to sew on the thousands of crystal beads and sequins.

And Mei, Mei hadn't said anything. She'd simply bitten the inside of her cheeks so hard she looked like a fish that had just had liposuction. Somehow, Mei having to work so hard not to laugh only made standing here in this ridiculous designer dress that much worse. Her nose itched and she gave the dress a discreet sniff. How many perfume sprayers had her mother walked by at Neiman Marcus when carrying the thing, anyway? And when had vanilla gotten so popular?

As the Cotton Princess float—a pink-and-white monstrosity that was the biggest in Cotton Festival history—pulled up in front of the town-square gazebo, Piper Douglas lined up along the front of it, next to Germaine Stewart and her posse of Cotton Queen wannabes. Though Piper smiled and waved at the crowd just like the others, all she really wanted to do was run, or, barring that, beat her head against the ground until she slipped into blessed unconsciousness.

Because if she passed out, then she wouldn't have to go through with this whole ridiculous farce. Right? Right.

As the Cotton Festival noise rose to a deafening crescendo—one that meant the band, and the rest of the parade, had finally made it back to the town square after their tour through the streets of downtown—it was a measure of her desperation that Piper really did consider knocking herself out, despite the ugly bruise it was sure to cause.

But in the end, she just couldn't do it. Not because she was afraid of a little pain, but because every time she closed her eyes to psych herself up, she saw her mother's glowing face.

For the first time since she'd been born, practically, Piper was doing something to make her mother proud.

So what if it was making *her* miserable? If it kept her mom sober for a few days—and softened her up enough to get Piper the new oil paints she wanted—then it was all worth it. Even this ridiculous, stinky excuse for a dress.

Besides, after years of being an embarrassment to her parents, who ruled her with an iron fist in an effort to keep her from doing things they considered bizarre, it was kind of nice to have her mother look at her like she wasn't a total waste of space. It was even nicer to be the focus of positive attention for once, instead of standing by and watching her mother praise her thirteen-year-old sister, Savannah, before heaping a bunch of criticism on Piper.

Sure, she knew it was stupid to be this concerned with making her mother happy. After all, they were two totally different people, and being a Cotton Princess wasn't going to change that. But at the same time, it was kind of cool that one weekend could so completely change the dynamics in her house. Suddenly, her mom was listening to her instead of reaching for the bottle of vodka whenever Piper walked into the room. For once, she didn't feel like an alien someone had dropped on her parents' doorstep shortly after birth.

It was a good feeling.

True, her nomination to the court had seriously pissed off

Germaine, which was never a good thing. Piper had had years to learn that an angry Germaine was a dangerous Germaine. But Piper's mother, a former Cotton Queen herself, had called in a ton of favors to get her on the float, and Piper was determined to make her proud.

As she and the other princesses descended from the float, the music waned and so did the cheers, which meant it was almost time.

Almost time to hear her name announced for the entire town to hear.

Almost time for her to walk to the dais set up in the center of the town square and get the silly little tiara she was supposed to wear to this afternoon's barbecue and tonight's square dance.

Almost time for her to curtsy and join the rest of the court for copious pictures.

And then this whole thing would be over and she would have a little breathing room, at least until the barbecue.

Nervous, and more than a little freaked out, she scanned the crowd for her best friends' familiar faces. It took her a minute, but she finally found them at the top of the bleachers set up across from the dais, and they were all looking straight at her.

Cassidy shot her a thumbs-up sign, Izzy gagged at the blatant dumb-assery, and Mei smiled an encouraging you-can-do-it grin that helped put Piper at ease like nothing else could. No matter what happened today—no matter how ridiculous she looked in the pale peach atrocity her mother had bought for her in Dallas—her friends would still be there. They might be propping themselves up as they laughed hysterically, but they would be there.

As the court was introduced, the first person called was Germaine, who was Cotton Queen for the second year in a row, despite being only a junior. And yes, even here in Paris, Texas, everyone knew that the Cotton Queen was supposed to be a senior, but Germaine's mother ruled the town the same way Germaine ruled Paris High School, and neither of them was willing to let Germaine take second place to *anyone*.

After Germaine was crowned queen, and her boyfriend, Tanner

Colt—who she *so* didn't deserve—had been crowned Cotton King, the announcements began for the rest of the court. There were four princesses, and Piper waited impatiently for her name to be called. She was the last on the court and the sooner she got up there, the sooner this whole debacle would be over and she could get out of this stupid dress. Which she couldn't wait to do, as it was really starting to itch. Not to mention that the funky vanilla scent seemed to be getting stronger the longer she wore the thing.

Finally, her name came over the loudspeaker and she began the long trek up the red carpet. As she headed toward the center of the square, where the rest of the Cotton Court was waiting, she scanned the crowd for Jackson Grosbeck, center for the football team and a total jerk. Much to her disgust, she'd gotten stuck with him as her escort onto the makeshift stage.

She finally spotted him, but he wasn't walking down the stretch of red carpet opposite her, as they'd practiced earlier that morning. Instead, he was coming from the side of the town square closest to the parade route, and he was pulling something behind him.

Unsure of what to do, Piper kept walking—no way was she going to be the first princess in the history of the Cotton Festival to screw this up and thus earn everlasting shame—but the closer Jackson got, the more uneasy she became. And as the crowd parted, she finally figured out what he was dragging behind him. It was a very large, very ugly, *very* agitated pig. And it was dressed in a swine-sized version of the same tuxedo Jackson was currently wearing.

Piper stopped uncertainly, not wanting to get any closer to the angry-looking thing than was absolutely necessary, Cotton Court or no Cotton Court. It wasn't the first pig she'd seen up close by any means—this was farm country, after all. But it must have been one of the 4-H kids' pigs, because while it wasn't fully grown, it was still big enough that Jackson could barely control it.

She didn't want the drooling, seething animal anywhere near her.

What is Jackson doing, anyway? she wondered frantically. Germaine would kill him for destroying the ceremony, and if *she* didn't, the festival director, Mrs. Rand, certainly would. She'd been in charge of the festival for fifteen years. It was her life. No one had ever before risked her wrath, and Piper couldn't believe Jackson was going to be the first.

But Jackson didn't seem to care, as he kept dragging the reluctant pig through the now-hushed crowd. At the last minute—when he was only a few yards from Piper—he let go of the rope wrapped around the pig's neck. The thing headed straight for Piper at a dead run.

For one excruciatingly long moment she was frozen in shock and fear. And then instincts she didn't even know she had took over and she started to run. She didn't get far, however, before her high heels got tangled in the hem of her dress and she went down hard.

Within seconds, the pig was on her, squealing loudly as it snuffled its snout all over her dress and face. And in that strange, surreal moment, she finally figured out what the weird scent from her dress was: vanilla wafers.

They'd learned last year in biology that the sweet cookies were pigs' favorite treats.

Someone had obviously hidden them somewhere on her dress, because the beast was going crazy looking for them, nudging her with its snout and even licking her wherever it could. Piper tried desperately to shove it away, even grabbed onto its minituxedo and tugged, but the thing outweighed her by a good thirty pounds, and it was as determined to find its treat as she was to get out from under it.

As Piper scrambled backward, she heard her dress rip but didn't pay any attention to it. All her focus was on eluding the vanilla wafer–crazed pig.

Clambering toward safety, with the pig following her every move, Piper became aware that the entire crowd was staring at her with mouths wide open. Except Mrs. Rand, who stood on the dais, screaming, as she took in the fiasco her beloved cotton crowning had become.

Even worse, a chant had started among the football players, one that was growing louder with every second that passed.

Kiss the pig.

Kiss the pig.

Kiss the pig.

Piper's cheeks flamed and her heart felt like it would burst right out of her chest. *This can't be happening,* she told herself. No way had she gone through with this whole Cotton Festival thing just to be humiliated by a giant *pig.*

Only it *was* happening, the chant growing louder with each second that passed. And then, as if it understood what the words meant, the pig chose that moment to run its cold, wet, disgusting snout down one of her cheeks, across her mouth, and over her chin.

Piper clamped her hands on her face in a meager attempt at protection that was too little, too late and prayed for the ground to open up and swallow her whole. She prayed for an earthquake, for a five-alarm fire, for anything that would make this nightmare end.

Finally, someone managed to pry the pig away from her—she glanced up and realized Tanner had grabbed the rope and was wrestling the animal back across the square—and Piper scrambled to her feet.

It took a minute, but the entire gathering fell silent once again. As she looked up at the bleachers and wondered half-hysterically what she was supposed to do now, she realized Mei, Izzy, and Cassidy had been frantically making their way down the crowded stands to reach her. As they got to the bottom, Izzy looked up, straight at Piper, and her already pale face drained of color. Then she started to run, directly toward Piper.

Following Izzy's horrified gaze, Piper looked down and realized her struggle with the pig had ripped the front of her dress clear off.

She was standing in front of Tanner, her classmates, and a large percentage of Paris, Texas, bare from the waist down except for the ridiculous pair of Spanx her mother had forced her, under duress, to wear.

Laughter once again replaced the football players' silence, though Piper realized a number of adults were crowding into the square—including the high school principal, Mr. Callahan, and the town's mayor, Mr. Hunter. But they were too late. The damage had been done.

She looked around for her mother, finally spotted her on the ground about thirty feet away. Her father and sister were crowded around her mom, fanning her with their Cotton Festival programs, but she wasn't stirring. For one fleeting second, Piper wondered if she'd finally done it. If she'd finally embarrassed her mother so badly that her mom had done what she'd always threatened to do: died of shame.

It was the last straw.

As her world caved in, Piper turned to flee and ran straight into Germaine, who was grinning widely as she used her iPhone to click picture after picture of Piper's humiliation.

The last thing Piper saw before she made a beeline for her car was Cassidy's fist connecting with Germaine's face.

Despite her complete and total humiliation at Germaine's hands, Piper couldn't help smiling as she imagined blood gushing from the head cheerleader's nose. One thing was for sure—this year's Cotton Festival was going to be one nobody ever forgot . . .

Chapter 1
Piper

"Are you sure this is a good idea?" Piper asked as she tentatively picked her way through the field toward the huge barn about three hundred yards away. Even from this distance she could hear the loud music and raucous laughter of her classmates. Which would normally mean she and her friends were going to have a kick-ass time. It was the biggest party of the year, after all. The say-good-bye-to-summer blast they'd been looking forward to for what seemed like forever. This year, since they were finally upperclassmen, they wouldn't get razzed for attending.

But that was before the Cotton Festival.

Before the Kiss the Pig incident.

Before she had become a YouTube, Facebook, and Twitter overnight sensation.

God, it had gotten so bad that she could hear the oinking in her sleep.

The thought had Piper stopping in her tracks, her feet refusing to move one step closer to the party. So what if it was at Mike Jenkins's ranch? So what if he was Tanner Colt's best friend, thereby guaranteeing that Tanner would be there? So what, even, if she'd had a crush on Tanner forever? Nothing was worth the humiliation of being chased around by drunken losers making pig noises. *Nothing.*

"I can't do this," she said, her voice sounding way too high, even to her.

"Oh, come on, Piper. It's going to be fine." Mei reached out and squeezed her hand, her dark, almond-shaped eyes filled with sympathy. "It's been months since the video of the Cotton Festival hit the Internet. They've probably forgotten all about it by now."

"They'd be the only ones who forgot," Izzy commented under her breath before saying out loud, "I can't believe—"

She stopped in the middle of her sentence, and from the sudden, harsh inhalation she took, Piper could only assume it was because Cassidy had stepped on her foot.

"Even if they haven't forgotten, you're going to have to face them sometime," Mei said, taking over smoothly, logical as always. "School starts on Monday."

Piper groaned. "Don't remind me."

"Yeah," Cassidy joined in, "and since the party's already been going for a couple hours, everyone in there is probably too drunk to care about what happened at the beginning of the summer."

"I'm not so sure about that." Piper eyed the barn doubtfully, even as she allowed her friends to drag her closer to it. "They'd have to be pretty drunk to forget that the whole world knows me as the Kiss the Pig girl."

"Not the whole world," Izzy said, with a comforting pat on her shoulder.

"Yeah. Just all of North America." Piper's stomach clenched as she remembered the back-to-school shopping trip to Dallas she and her mother had made a few days before. She'd been so excited to get out of Paris and away from all the strange looks and pig snorts that she hadn't considered that her troubles could follow her.

Ten minutes in the Neiman Marcus juniors department had disabused her of that notion as she'd been asked—three times—if she was the YouTube pig girl. By the time the fourth person approached her, she had given up trying to deny it and had shouted loud enough for the entire floor to hear that "Yes, I kissed a pig!"

Too bad the person approaching had been the saleswoman, who'd looked at her like she was insane. Then again, she probably was. Especially since within minutes of her outburst her mother's hand had crept into her purse for her omnipresent bottle of little white pills. If Piper had just kept her mouth shut, she wouldn't have spent the rest of the day steering her stoned-on-Xanax mother from one store to the next and then driving her home through rush-hour traffic.

None of that would have been so bad—after all, her mother had been so out of it that Piper had managed to cop some really hip clothes that normally she never would have had a chance to buy—but when she got home, her father had been furious with her for upsetting her mom. Again.

Of course, she'd tried to explain that her mother got upset if Piper so much as climbed out of bed in the morning. But her father hadn't appreciated her humor or her honesty. Especially not with Savannah, the pageant princess and perfect daughter, fanning the flames of his annoyance by acting like their mother was one step away from the grave instead of simply bombed out of her mind.

Piper had tried to explain her side of the story, but in the end it hadn't mattered. Savannah's fawning attention to their mother had gotten her curfew extended by two hours, while Piper's "attitude" had merely gotten her grounded. Which was why she and her friends were so late to this stupid party. She'd had to wait for her parents to go to bed so she could sneak out.

As the sounds of a Brad Paisley song drifted toward them, accompanied by a loud chanting that could only mean someone was doing a keg stand, Piper couldn't help thinking that being grounded hadn't been so bad, after all. She turned to head back to Izzy's car.

"Come on, girl. Suck it up." Cassidy grabbed her arm and propelled her forward. "Let them have their fun. A couple minutes of oinking and they'll lose interest, especially if you just ignore them."

Easy for Cassidy to say, Piper thought a few minutes later as she weaved her way through the throng of gyrating bodies that had turned the barn's main room into one big dance floor. Cassidy had been here five minutes and she was already deep in conversation with the basketball team about some new play their coach had introduced that morning at the first practice of the year.

Izzy had locked onto River, and the two of them were currently making out in one of the unused stalls. Admittedly, Piper found that kind of odd—she'd thought they were on a break, since River was heading to college in a few days—but obviously she'd been mistaken. At least judging by the way they had started going at it the second they'd seen each other.

Mei was still hanging with her, but as the pig sounds worked their way up to epic proportions, Piper wasn't sure that was such a good idea. Especially when she knew her best friend would object if she tried to drown herself in one of the ice chests set up against the back of the barn.

Snort. Snort, snort, snort, snort. Snooooooort.

Piper ducked her head, ground her teeth together, and did her best to be as invisible as possible—which normally might not have been a problem, but it was when every guy she passed had a pig noise to make.

Of course, it could be worse, she thought, trying to console herself. *Someone could let loose with the dreaded—*

"Suuuuuuuuey!"

And there it was. Big surprise. It wasn't like her classmates were rolling in originality or anything.

"That's it," she told Mei, heading for the door at the back of the barn. "I can't do this."

"Come on, Piper." Mei tugged at her arm. "I know it's bad, but you can't hide in your room forever."

"Wanna bet?" Homeschooling was looking better and better. So what if it was junior year and she'd been looking forward to finally taking art with Ms. Hannebaker, one of the coolest artists and teachers in Paris? Missing her choice elective was a small price to pay for keeping her sanity.

"Let's go get a drink," Mei said, gesturing to the row of ice chests Piper had moments before been contemplating for a very different reason. "That'll make you feel better."

"Nothing will make me feel better except the complete and total annihilation of Germaine the Stain."

"That's the spirit." Mei laughed, and even Piper had to grin.

There was just something about besmirching Germaine's name that made everything okay. Or if not okay, at least a little better. It might be juvenile, but they'd been doing it since eighth grade and some traditions were worth preserving.

"Come on, we'll get a wine cooler and plot the downfall of the Wicked Witch of Paris, Texas."

"Now, that's a plan I can get behind," Piper said as she followed Mei through the crowd.

It took only a couple of minutes for them to grab two bottles of Smirnoff Ice—so much better than the peach-flavored wine coolers filling two of the ice chests—and then head into one of the few stalls not currently being used for make-out sessions. As they settled on the ground, Piper got her first glimpse of Tanner through the open stall door and her heart did a little shimmy in her chest, especially when his eyes met hers across the crowded room and he smiled.

She smiled back, her stomach unclenching for the first time since she'd gotten to the party. Maybe the night wouldn't be a total bust.

"You might want to wipe up the drool running down your chin," Mei said with a laugh. "I hear guys don't go for that."

"Yeah, it's the drool keeping them away, not my spectacular career as a YouTube joke."

"Aww, Pipes. It could have been a lot worse." She wrapped her free arm around Piper's shoulders in a quick hug.

"Shh! Don't say that too loud. You don't need to give Germaine any other ideas." She took a long sip of her drink. "Besides, if things got any worse, my mom would have to add Prozac to her daily cocktail of tranquilizers and vodka. My father would kill me."

"Good point." Mei nodded toward Tanner. "Why don't you go talk to him? He's obviously happy you came."

"Are you kidding? And lose my primo hiding spot? I don't think so."

"Are you ever going to tell him how you feel? You've been mooning over that boy since ninth grade!"

"Yeah, but I can't talk to him when the other guys are all making fun of me." Piper shook her head emphatically. No way was she going out there right now—not when the cries of "*Suuuuuuuuey*" were still ringing in her ears.

"Besides, he's dating Germaine the Insane—God only knows why—and we've already seen what she can do when she's mad. If she thought I was trying to steal her boyfriend . . ." Piper shook her head. "Remember, this whole stupid thing started because Johnny Michaels kissed me instead of her at summer camp."

Up until seventh-grade art camp the five of them had all been friends. But after the Johnny incident, Germaine had gone from being their BFF to the WWW (Wicked Witch of the West).

"Yeah, well, that was four years ago. It's about time Germaine learns that she can't have everything she wants in life. I'm so sick of her crap."

"*You're* sick of it?" Piper pretended to choke herself. "At least you're only on the periphery. She's had me in her sights for years now. I'm sick of always losing to her."

"Which is why you should go talk to Tanner!" Mei shoved at her shoulder a little. "He's obviously not as into her as everyone thinks if he's looking at *you*."

Piper's breath caught at the implication that Tanner might be even a little interested in her, but just as she was beginning to contemplate following Mei's advice, Germaine looked up from the conversation she'd been having with one of the other football players and shot Piper a death glare.

Piper settled back against the wall. Yeah, right. Who was she kidding? Germaine would never let her within ten feet of Tanner—at least not without humiliating Piper all over again. And really, she just didn't think she had it in her to kiss any more swine.

"Or maybe not," Mei said. "God, how does she make her eyes do that? I swear, I expect lasers to shoot out of them any minute now."

Piper laughed, like she knew Mei had wanted her to, before taking another sip of her drink. Maybe if she got drunk enough, she wouldn't care what everyone was saying about her or what evil plot Germaine was hatching even now. But using alcohol to escape was her mother's favorite game, and it was one Piper wasn't particularly interested in playing. She put her Ice down before stretching her legs out in front of her.

"Your toes look cool," Mei said. "I like that color."

"'Crimson and Clover,'" she said with a toe wiggle. "If it's good enough for Joan Jett—"

"Then it's good enough for us!"

"Exactly. You can borrow it if you want."

"I just might. But only because of the cool name. I can wear it when I'm practicing 'I Love Rock 'n Roll' on my Fender Strat."

"Right, of course. We wouldn't want anyone to think you were turning country if they saw you without your black nail polish."

"Damn straight." Mei took another sip of her drink, then coughed.

Piper patted her on the back. "God, don't die on me now. I'm not sure I could face this party without you."

Mei didn't answer, and when Piper followed her gaze, it was easy to see why. Germaine and her unmerry band of malicious minions were working their way over to the stall where Mei and Piper were sitting. Of course they were. Because really, the snorts and pig grunts hadn't been enough to ruin her night—she needed a close encounter with her own personal nightmare to really make the evening complete.

"Ignore her and she'll go away," Mei said. "She just wants to get a rise out of you."

Piper nodded, knowing Mei was right. She wouldn't react this time, wouldn't even acknowledge Germaine's existence. It would be almost impossible, but Piper refused to give Germaine any more ammunition. That girl could turn the most innocuous comment into a way to make fun of her enemies. It was a gift Piper would kill to have, at least at times like these.

But as Germaine stopped a few feet away from Piper's hiding place, Piper realized her archnemesis had a new brand of torture in mind.

"Sorry to drag you guys back to the losers section," she said to her friends with a pointed look at Piper and Mei, "but I had to get away from Tanner for a few minutes. I swear that boy is *way* too clingy. Every five minutes he's telling me how beautiful I am and how much he *loves* me."

Piper's hands curled into fists. She was going to lose it if she had to sit here and listen to how much Tanner adored the cruelest skank ever to walk the halls of Paris High. Piper would do anything to be with Tanner, and he barely knew she was alive. Germaine did nothing but talk badly about him and he was crazy about her.

"Ignore it," Mei whispered again, and Piper tried. She really did. But it was so hard to sit by and listen as her worst enemy made fun of the guy she'd wanted forever. Of course, Germaine knew that. It was why she'd stationed herself next to Piper and Mei to begin with.

"You're lucky," sighed Rosemary, Germaine's best friend and one of the fawning minions. "He's so cute, he could have any girl here. It's awesome that he wants *you*."

"Who else would he possibly want?" came the scathing retort. "Besides, cute isn't everything. He's about as exciting as a piece of toast—without the butter. I'm not sure how much longer I can keep pretending to like him."

"Well, you could break up with him," suggested Elizabeth, another of the cheerleaders. "It's not like you'd have trouble finding another boyfriend."

Germaine laughed, a cold, calculating sound that made Piper shiver despite herself. "Of course I wouldn't. But, really. Who else would I date? Tanner may be pathetically dull, but he's the best Paris High has to offer. Even if he does kiss like a dead fish." Piper shook her head in disbelief. Every time she figured Germaine had reached a new low, every time she decided Germaine couldn't get *any* worse, she did something to make Piper change her mind.

How could she say those things about Tanner?

How could she call him pathetic when he *so* didn't deserve it?

It wasn't like he was just any guy, after all. He was the smartest, hottest, nicest guy to ever grace the halls of PHS—not to mention the best wide receiver their team had ever had. He'd even scored the winning touchdown at state last year, and that was saying something, as they were a tiny little school in the middle of nowhere.

Not that Piper had been surprised. She'd known that Tanner was amazing and wonderful and exceptional—even before he'd pulled that hideous pig off her. That had just been the final bit of proof that he was as close to perfect as any guy could get, except, of course, for his one glaring flaw: he was dating Germaine the Vain.

It *so* wasn't fair.

How could he not see what a total and complete jerk Germaine was to everyone around her? Especially since she'd spent most of the last four years making up vicious rumors about anyone who wasn't under her spell—which included Piper and her friends.

Plus, she was totally responsible for the pig incident, even if she'd never been questioned about it. More than once Piper had heard her bragging at the Dairy Queen about pulling it off and about what she'd done to "persuade" Jackson to take the fall for her. Manipulative witch.

"So, how does Tanner feel about your views on his kissing talents?"

asked Lisa, another one of the minions. "I mean, if I went around telling people Jimmy kissed like a fish, he'd be really pissed."

Wow. Piper shot Lisa a look of respect. Finally, a Paris cheerleader with a brain. It was the same question Piper had wanted to ask ever since she'd realized Germaine was dissing her boyfriend like he was some kind of loser.

But it would take more than a challenge from a tiny little nobody like Lisa to throw Germaine off her game. Her grin faded, only to be replaced by what Piper and her friends liked to refer to as her "oh, bless your heart" look, usually reserved for imbeciles, non–Dallas Cowboy fans, and those people who weren't born in Paris, Texas.

"Obviously, it's not like I say it to Tanner's face." Germaine's voice cut like broken glass. "And who would be stupid enough to tell him what I said?" The warning in her eyes promised retribution of the Germaine kind if anyone even dared to think about betraying her.

The cheeseburger Piper had eaten during her earlier trip to Dairy Queen with Mei, Izzy, and Cassidy gurgled in her stomach and threatened to crawl back up her esophagus, but Piper womanfully held it back. Still, could Germaine get any more obnoxious?

"That's a good point," agreed Michaela, who usually held a spot on the food chain right below Rosemary. "I mean, what Tanner doesn't know won't hurt you, right?"

"Exactly," Germaine said. "But enough about Tanner." She eyed her friends critically. "I swear y'all gained ten pounds over the summer. If we're going to be ready for Nationals, you need to work out extra hard for the next few weeks. Plus, if you go around looking like that, Piper might mistake you for a pig and try to kiss you."

And there it was, the comment Piper had been waiting for. It was as close to acknowledging her presence as Germaine would get. Her entire group laughed, and since Germaine had timed her comment to slip into the brief silence that fell between songs, so did most of the barn. Piper felt Mei tense beside her. Knowing her friend was about to confront Germaine—and attract the WWW's ire onto herself—Piper sprang to her feet before Mei could talk herself into the same miserable position Piper had held for four long years.

"What is your problem, Germaine? Don't you think this whole vendetta thing has gotten a little old?" As Piper spoke, she was conscious of Mei standing behind her, lending her silent support.

Germaine didn't even seem to notice Mei as she focused directly on Piper for the first time, her eyes so coldly mocking that Piper grew nervous despite her resolve. But in typical Germaine fashion, she waited for the music to start again so that the other partygoers wouldn't hear her response.

"Old?" she asked icily, as if she'd never heard of the word. "Piper, I've barely gotten started."

"You've humiliated me in front of half of North America. Surely that's enough to satisfy even *your* vanity."

Germaine smiled nastily. "I look at it more as my duty to society, weeding out the weak members of the herd. It is survival of the fittest, after all."

"This isn't the jungle, you know. It's a town."

"Oh, no, Piper. This isn't just *a* town. It's *my* town. And as long as you live here, it'll never be over. The pig thing was just the beginning." And then she turned and walked away, her minions trailing in her wake as if Piper was no longer worth their interest.

But as her words echoed in Piper's head, she knew Germaine's lack of concern was just an act. The last four years had been miserable and the next two would be just as bad.

"Piper." Mei rubbed a comforting hand on her back, but Piper shrugged her off.

"I need some fresh air."

"I'll go with you—"

"No, stay here. I'll be fine. I just need a few minutes by myself." Leaving her friend behind, Piper weaved her way through the crowd, trying her best to ignore the new chorus of snorts and oinks that followed her.

By the time she got outside, Piper was shaking so badly that she wasn't sure how much longer her legs would support her. Sinking down onto the hard, parched ground, she leaned her head against the barn and dashed away the frustrated tears rolling silently down her cheeks. Behind her the party was still going on. She didn't want anyone to see her this upset, but her efforts didn't seem to matter—new tears spilled over, and the more she told herself not to cry, the faster the tears came. Her lack of control infuriated her.

For the first time since this whole stupid thing had happened, Piper felt hopeless.

Like things really weren't going to die down.

Like she really would spend the rest of her life being pointed at, laughed at, and made fun of.

Turning her head, Piper saw Germaine work her way through the crowd that had gathered in front of the barn's entrance. Everyone fawned over her or ran from her—just as she liked it—and as Piper watched, she knew that Germaine was right.

As long as she stayed in this stupid backwoods town, it would never be over. She would be at Germaine's mercy forever.

Chapter 2
Cassidy

The tardy bell rang just as Cassidy slid into the back row of homeroom.

"Thanks for saving my seat, Izzy." She set her backpack on the floor between their desks. Mei and Piper took up the other two seats in the row. Every year the four of them finagled getting "C" Class homeroom—it was the only period their disparate schedules allowed them to be all together.

"How's it going, Piper?" she whispered down the line. Talking was not allowed during homeroom, but Cassidy saw it more as a guideline, really.

Piper shrugged and gave her a little smile to say she was hanging in. "Atta girl," Cassidy said.

"Shhhh," Mei scolded her.

"That librarian impression is really coming along, Mei, but you need to learn to shush with a lot more authority—really engage those core muscles."

"Some of us have actual studying to do, Cassidy. That's what homeroom is for."

Cassidy rolled her eyes. "It's only the second day of school, Little Miss Valedictorian. I'm pretty sure your GPA is not at stake at this very moment."

"Ignore her," Izzy said. "She's freaking out because Mr. Canales asked her to lead the first lab practical in her AP Chem class on Friday."

"You academic types are way too uptight. You need more exercise to relieve your stress. That's why I stick to athletic pursuits."

"I seem to recall that last year, right before the district basketball playoffs, you threw up all over your Nikes, Cassidy Barlow, so don't lecture me on being uptight," Mei said.

Piper giggled, the first time Cassidy had heard her do that in at least a week. "Meowww. Mei, I didn't know you had it in you," she said.

Cassidy was about to follow Piper's comment with a smart-ass retort of her own when the lights went dark in the room.

"Your attention, please, boys and girls," said Ms. Vogel as she bustled up to the front of the class, a box in her arms. "Now, I know you all have studying to be doing"—Mei shot Cassidy a little self-righteous smirk—"but I need a few minutes of your time."

The entire classroom began to glow a hazy blue as cell phones were whipped out of hiding the second the overhead lights dimmed.

"Cell phones away, everyone," Ms. Vogel said, her honey-blond ponytail bobbing back and forth, her bright overexaggerated smile beaming like she was still leading cheers at a pep rally. "Boys and girls, I need your undivided attention."

Cassidy and Izzy snickered. Ms. Vogel had graduated from Paris High School six years ago. This was her first school counselor position out of grad school, and at twenty-four, the former head cheerleader was all of seven years older than the students, so calling them "boys and girls" was a little condescending, to say the least.

The projector turned on, blaring the words "Broaden Your Horizons" across the pull-down screen.

"Have you ever thought about what it would be like to live somewhere else?" asked Ms. Vogel. *Only every day of my life,* Cassidy thought.

Ms. Vogel flipped the slide to a collage of pictures of American-looking teenagers laughing and hanging out in front of Buckingham Palace, beneath the Eiffel Tower, listening to mariachis, taking pictures of the Taj Mahal.

"How about another *country*? Becoming a foreign exchange student could give you the opportunity to travel, to learn about a different culture, or perhaps even become fluent in another language."

In her peripheral vision Cassidy saw Piper sit up in her seat and lean forward, hanging on every word coming from Ms. Vogel's lips.

The next slide: kids sitting outside on a green lawn listening raptly to an Asian teacher.

"For ten weeks you can go to school . . ."

A picture of a Hispanic family having dinner together, laughing, an American boy at the table with them.

". . . live with another family . . ."

A shot of Buddhist monks holding lit candles in their hands, praying.

". . . learn about different cultures . . ."

The last slide was an American girl dressed in a beautiful sari, dancing at a festival.

". . . you could see a different way of life, be a different person."

It actually sounded pretty awesome to Cassidy. She'd take any one of the places in those pictures. Just imagine: ten whole weeks away from Paris, Texas, with its small-town ways and its small-minded people; a whole semester in a place where no one knew her, her mom, or their whole sordid family history—because even though Cassidy empathized with Piper's ordeal, she had really only been suffering a few months. Cassidy had been a walking scandal her whole life.

She glanced down the row, past Izzy, who was checking her phone surreptitiously under her desk, and Mei, still bent over her chemistry textbook, to look at Piper. From the far-off look in Piper's eyes, Cassidy could tell she wasn't the only one ready to blow this pop-stand town.

The lights came back on, warranting a collective groan from the class.

"Do you have any questions, boys and girls?"

One hand went up in the front. "If I go to Sweden, can I live with a family that has twin daughters?" Jackson Grosbeck asked. The guys all snickered appreciatively.

Ms. Vogel pursed her perfect bow-shaped mouth and froze Jackson with an obviously oft-practiced glacial stare. *Brrr.* Germaine had some serious competition for ice queen of Paris High.

"Any *real* questions?" she followed up. "If anyone would like more information on placement as a foreign exchange student, there are brochures in the box or you can come see me. But you need to hurry if you want to be placed for the spring semester."

Having lived in the same small town her whole life, in the same house, on the same street, and gone to school with the same kids since pre-K—which was pretty much the story for every one of the kids in this room except Izzy—Cassidy's only question was, Where did she sign up? But coming from a single-parent household meant your vacation was to Papa and Memaw's leaky fishing cottage on the Texas coast, where you avoided tar balls, seaweed, and red tide— the highlights of the so-called Redneck Riviera—and not ten weeks on the real one in Europe.

Oh, well. She'd already spent almost seventeen years in Paris, Texas—what was another two? And yet, Cassidy couldn't help but think that if she did have the money, she'd sign up for one of those trips in a heartbeat, and spring couldn't come soon enough.

After school, the girls ended up at Yogurt Worxx to rally Piper, who needed the extra encouragement. Yogurt Worxx wasn't that much closer to school than the Dairy Queen, but Izzy liked it because, as she was always saying, it was more urbane. Plus, it had fewer calories. Not that watching her weight concerned Cassidy much—she spent too many hours running drills up and down the basketball court for it to matter. She descended on the toppings buffet as if it were her last meal on death row.

"Today wasn't too bad, right, Piper?" Cassidy asked, coating her mixture of birthday cake, tart green apple, and island banana froyo with Cap'n Crunch, strawberries, and white chocolate chips. "I really only heard an oink or two, and I shut those down pretty quick. Piper?"

She glanced over to see that Piper was planted facedown on her notebook at their usual table by the window.

"Think about it this way, Pipes," Izzy said around a mouthful of blueberry granola and plain yogurt, "there's only seventy-one more shopping days till Christmas vacation."

"Sixty-eight if you don't include Thanksgiving break. Come on, Piper, have some iced chai; nonfat, just how you like it. You know you want to." Mei swirled the drink on the table next to Piper's triple-pierced ear.

Piper finally sat up and shook her head, oblivious to the L-shaped indentation the corner of her notebook had pressed into her forehead. Cassidy bit her cheek to keep from smiling, while Mei looked away and Izzy allowed herself to get distracted checking her phone again. Because if Piper knew, this pity party would go till long after dark and they all had homework to do.

"I'll never make it that long, y'all. Never." She sagged in her chair. "It's like . . . like . . . I'm drowning in a vat of Germaine's venom. I've got to get away from this town. It's the only way." She exhaled a woe-is-me breath with silent-film-star expertise.

"Okay, take it down a notch, drama queen," Cassidy teased, eliciting a mock bite-me glare from her best friend. "Where you gonna go? Even if you transfer to North Lamar or Chisum High—which you aren't—it wouldn't change anything. They're not far enough away to make a difference."

"No, but this is." Piper unrolled the paper she'd been clutching in her fist and put it on the table. It was one of Ms. Vogel's brochures.

"France?" the other three said in unison, staring at the picture of the Eiffel Tower. It looked just like the one that stood on the outskirts of town, only this one didn't sport a cowboy hat on top.

"You're not going to France, Piper," Cassidy said. *'Cause nobody's leaving here without me.*

"Why not? Think about it. I could go to Paris, the *real* Paris, and study French and art and drama—"

"Which you study here," Izzy pointed out.

"But I wouldn't have to hear any oinking or smooching sounds or see Germaine's smug face for an *entire* semester. It would be heaven! And maybe by that time there'd be a new Internet sensation and everyone would stop focusing on my pig-kissing exploits."

"Let me get this straight: you want to go all the way to Paris, *France*, to get away from Germaine?" Mei asked incredulously.

"You can't do that," Izzy protested. "She'll think you're running away."

"It *is* running away," Cassidy said. Not that she could blame Piper. They all knew that Germaine—as bad as she was—was only half of Piper's problem. When it came to tormenting Piper, her mom was nearly as bad as the Wicked Witch of the West. As much as it sucked to be poor, Cassidy knew that her own mom would do anything for her. Of course, that kind of devotion could be almost as stifling as the town's low expectations of her.

"You can't let Germaine win," Mei insisted.

Piper stared at her in disbelief. "She *has* won. The girl made me kiss a pig and turned me into a laughingstock in front of the entire country. Do you know how many fans the Kiss the Pig fan page has on Facebook?" When no one answered, she continued, "Over *three million*!"

"Still. If she thinks she's won, it will only get worse."

"Really, Mei? Worse? Tell me, please, exactly how do you think it's possible for things to get *worse*? Today even the lunch ladies had it out for me—they served bacon cheeseburgers and I'm pretty sure I heard one of them oink."

Mei's lips pinched together and she didn't answer. Cassidy knew it was because she couldn't. Cassidy had seen Germaine the Mundane at work for four years, and she knew nothing could top this. She glanced down at the tiny white scar on her middle knuckle, the one that had connected with Germaine's once-perfect nose and caught on one of her vampire fangs—oops, she meant teeth. It had *so* been worth the three stitches.

Silence stretched among the four of them, and with every second that passed Piper seemed to grow more agitated. Obviously she'd expected her friends to be more enthusiastic, and after everything Piper had been through in the last couple of months, Cassidy couldn't leave her friend hanging.

"I think it's a great idea."

"You do?" Piper gave her a broad smile of relief; Mei and Izzy just looked confused.

"I do. Getting away from all this would totally rock. After a few months in France, everything will look better." In fact, the more she thought about this exchange thing, the more kick-ass it sounded. And not just for Piper . . .

"But what about Germaine?" Izzy protested. "We still have another year of school after this to live through. If she believes she was able to push Piper out of the country, think what she may plan for the rest of us; she'll be unbearable!"

"Not necessarily," Cassidy said carefully, the plan coming together in her head. "Not if we all go, too."

Mei and Izzy stared at her like she'd spoken rooster. Piper clapped and squealed.

"Really? Y'all would go with me? Then it wouldn't be just about me running away, it would be like we'd planned this all along: a world-wide adventure to broaden our horizons, to experience indigenous cultures, to—"

"Yeah, right . . . 'cause our parents are just going to let us go jet-setting around the globe to save Piper from Germaine. No way." Izzy snorted.

"Well, obviously we can't sell it to them like that. We'd be going to school, too," Piper argued. "There are tons of places in these bro-chures." She reached into her hot-pink Poppy purse and pulled out a stack. "We could go anywhere we wanted."

"We can't just take off." Mei shook her head. "What about school here? And the SAT? I'm taking it in March."

"Shouldn't life be about more than just the SAT, Mei?"

"Sure. After we've rocked it, Piper. But even then, life shouldn't be all about avoiding embarrassment, either. No matter how much Germaine sucks."

Cassidy was barely listening to any of them anymore, the possibilities buzzing through her as her gaze scanned the fan of brochures. What if she *could* get the money? She knew a trip like this was expensive—certainly more than her mom could afford working at the hospital lab. And Cass's after-school job at the dry cleaners three afternoons a week wasn't going to cut it, either.

There was another option. But she knew it was one she shouldn't really consider, since it could seriously damage the tight relationship she had with her mom. The problem was, now that she'd thought of it, Cassidy found she couldn't give it up. Not if it meant there was even the slimmest possibility she could go on the trip.

"I'm going," she said. Mei and Izzy turned their shocked gazes to her. "Why wouldn't I want to?" she responded. "It's only *the* thing we've imagined doing every day since we were kids, right?"

"When we go away to college, of course," Izzy said. "But not in the middle of junior year."

"Yeah, that's the plan for you guys, Izzy, but we all know that's probably not going to happen for me."

"You'll get a scholarship, Cass; there's not a women's basketball coach in the country who wouldn't want you," Mei said.

"And if it doesn't happen, y'all will be gone and I'll still be here at Paris Junior College, hanging out at Dairy Queen, since I won't have you to drag me to Yogurt Worxx because it's more urban."

"Urbane," Izzy said with a smile.

"Whatever. Maybe this is my one chance to get out of town before I'm stuck here forever."

"Jeez, Cassidy. Don't you think we've had enough drama around here lately?" Izzy asked.

"I'm not saying y'all have to go, too—live and let live—but maybe

Piper's right. This could be a good thing for all of us. Let's at least consider it."

She sifted through the pamphlets. "Look, Mei, here's one for China. You could go and find out all about your heritage and learn Mandarin. Think how impressive *that* would look on your MIT application. And Izzy, you could go to the rain forest." Cassidy handed her a brochure for a school in Costa Rica. "You could actually help save some endangered tree frog or something instead of just writing articles about recycling for the school newspaper."

Izzy scrutinized the glossy jungle photos, her eyebrow cocked dubiously, but Cassidy could see she'd struck a chord.

"Guys, listen to Cassidy. This could be awesome, the experience of our lives!" Piper gushed, capitalizing on the moment. "There're a ton of great places out there to visit. Like I said, I'm going to Paris. The brochure talks about this amazing art academy there that takes exchange students. I'm going to paint, and see the Louvre, dye my hair, and drink coffee in quaint bistros on the Seine. And pretend the last four months *never* happened."

"What about you, Cass? Where do you want to go?" Mei asked.

"The farther away the better, but someplace where they speak English—I don't have a flair for language," she said with an exaggerated redneck Texas drawl, making them all laugh. At the bottom of the brochure pile was one with a cheesy picture of a koala in a graduation cap sitting on top of Ayers Rock.

Australia.

Cassidy grinned. You couldn't really get any farther than the whole other side of the world.

She held it up for the girls to see. "This is it; this is where I'm going."

Izzy took it out of her hand and flipped it open. "It's eighty-nine *hundred* dollars, Cassidy. If you're worried about paying for college, how are you going to afford this?"

Cassidy kept her face deliberately blank, hiding her shock. Eighty-nine hundred dollars was more than triple what she'd guessed it might cost. "I'll have to figure something out," she said, more to convince herself than her friends.

"Maybe you don't have to go so far, Cass," Mei said, rifling through the brochures.

"No," she said, not about to back down now. "I say, 'Go big or stay home.' I'll get the money."

"What are you going to do? Rob a bank?" Izzy asked.

"Ha-ha." Cassidy paused. "I'm going to ask my dad for the money."

Izzy, Mei, and Piper exchanged a glance.

"What?" Cassidy asked when no one spoke.

Piper answered. "Nothing, Cass. We just didn't know you were talking to your father again."

"Sure, I talk to him. I mean, we're not best friends or anything, but we talk. He's got the money, so I'll just ask him. It's no big deal."

The tinkling of the bell above the glass doors interrupted them. The Paris High offensive line crammed into the little shop, a veritable tsunami of unruly testosterone in blue-and-white letterman jackets.

The guys spotted the four of them at once. *Crap, here we go*, Cassidy thought.

"Hey, dude, I didn't know they served bacon-flavored yogurt here."

"Nah, pigs don't eat their own kind; they love slop."

"*Suuueeey!*"

Piper looked like she was going to cry. Cassidy jumped to her feet.

"That's real mature, dickheads. I didn't realize the numbers on your jerseys were also your IQs."

"Whoa, Cassidy, I didn't know you liked kissing pigs, too," Jackson Grosbeck, the resident dumb ass, taunted her. "I thought you were only into kissing other girls." He sauntered over to her, trying to intimidate her with his bulk. "'Cause that's hot."

Yuck. She could smell the Copenhagen chewing tobacco on his breath, but she didn't back away. Why would she? Even wearing her Vans she was taller than he was.

He raised one eyebrow in challenge. "Or at least that's what Jason told me."

Cassidy had gone out with Jason Cairns, a varsity baseball player, for two weeks at the beginning of sophomore year. Their relationship had come to an abrupt end when one night in the cab of his truck he'd rounded second base and tried to steal third. She'd almost broken his jaw. He'd told everyone it was because she liked girls. *Ah, life in a small, bigoted town.*

Was Australia really far enough to get away from crap like this? She prayed it was.

"You guys run around in skintight pants playing grab ass all day, so I'd say kissing girls is a better option. Besides, if what Marissa Haliday says about you is true, Jackson, then your height isn't the only thing about you that's small."

That wiped the smirk off his tobacco-stained mouth. The other guys guffawed behind him like the juvenile asses they were. Cassidy took Piper's arm and led her and the others from the shop.

They all loaded into Piper's purple Honda Civic and pulled out of the parking lot back onto Clarksville Street.

"That was epic, Cassidy," Mei said, and laughed.

Izzy joined her. "Yeah, I thought Jackson was going to pee his pants right there."

"Thanks, Cass," said Piper. "You're the best friend ever."

Cassidy sat in the passenger seat, arms akimbo, still fuming. "That, ladies, is why we need to do this. We need a break from Paris, Texas. The sooner, the better."

"Damn straight! I am *so* sick of the guys around here," Izzy agreed.

"What about River?" Piper reminded her.

"Don't you remember? He went to college. We're on a break."

"Didn't look like you were on a break at the party," Mei said.

"Trust me. We're. On. A. Break. So, Costa Rica, here I come. I mean, why not?"

"Well, I'm not going to be the one left behind," Mei said. "I guess I can take the SAT next semester. It's not like it's going anywhere."

"Yay! I can't wait," Piper said. "I promise this is going to be the best thing we've ever done."

Chapter 3
Izzy

Izzy slinked out of her room, hoping to escape to freedom unnoticed by any of the family members she'd rather avoid. Which, typically, was all of them.

She paused outside the bedroom of her younger brother, Shane. She could hear him in there pounding away on his keyboard. Oh, she couldn't hear the music he was playing, of course—he had the headphones hooked up—but she could hear his fingers flying across the keys. She used to love listening to him play, back when he'd merely been very good, back before he was a prodigy. Before her mother had decided to sculpt him into a virtuoso. The better Shane had gotten, the crazier their mother had become, channeling more and more of her energy into her youngest son. No one else in the family seemed to think it was absurd for a teenage boy to spend eight hours a day practicing Liszt, but Izzy sure did.

She skipped down the stairs before she could contemplate breaking Shane out of jail.

The sounds of a football game roared from the den, along with a wash of football-fueled aggression. Her older brother, Linc, and half the football team were in there watching the tapes of their opponent for next week. Probably her father, too, since he was the high school football coach. There weren't enough Jane Austen adaptations in the world to counteract that much testosterone.

Ducking down the hall toward the back of the house, she sniffed the air and caught a whiff of scorched poultry. Five years as a stay-at-home mom and her mother still burned to a crisp anything that passed within six inches of her gourmet cooktop. The woman should have stuck to litigation. Unfortunately, there weren't many job opportunities for high-powered attorneys in Paris, something her father hadn't considered when he resigned from his position as assistant coach for the University of Texas football team, picked up the whole family, and moved them from Austin to the desolate boondocks of northeast Texas. He'd been fostering John Wayne–like delusions of ranching. Her mother had been thrilled to devote herself full-time to Shane-the-musical-wunderkind, so really, Izzy was the only one who hadn't benefited from the move.

Izzy bypassed the kitchen and ducked out through the side door. Once free, she dropped down on the steps outside the sunroom. For a moment, she felt a pang of something in her chest. Regret maybe. She fought against the stupid urge to go back inside to talk to her mother. To tell her everything that had happened with River the other night at the party. Mothers were supposed to be good at this sort of thing, right? True, hers probably wouldn't be, but it was worth a try.

She considered it for about ten seconds. Then the smoke alarm went off in the kitchen. With a sigh, Izzy sent a text message to her mom explaining that she'd be at Piper's for the night. Her mom probably wouldn't check the message for hours. There were moments, like this one, when Izzy didn't quite mind being invisible.

Slipping her cell into her back pocket, she headed for her car but stopped when she saw the overflowing garbage can by the garage. Taking it out was Linc's job, and he'd once again thrown the recycling in with the trash. The jerk.

"It's two feet away," she grumbled as she transferred the aluminum cans into the recycle bin. "Would it kill him to walk the extra few steps?"

Her irritation with Linc made her clumsy, and one of her mother's

Diet Coke cans bounced off the edge and rolled down the driveway, coming to a rest somewhere under Izzy's flaky and unreliable Kia, Brittney.

Dropping to her hands and knees, she peered under the vehicle, then scooched on her belly and started wiggling. She'd just grabbed the can when she heard the rumble of a truck pulling into the driveway beside her.

Great. Someone was here: either a random delivery guy or another one of her father's flunkies. And her father's flunkies were precisely the kind of bully who made fun of a girl for crawling on her stomach for the betterment of the planet. And would possibly take pictures.

"Please be UPS. Please be UPS," she muttered under her breath as she scooted out from under her car.

It wasn't UPS.

She nearly groaned when she saw the familiar bright red of Tanner Colt's gas-guzzling Dodge Ram pickup. Tanner leaned against the passenger-side door, legs stretched out in front of him, arms crossed over his chest, looking for all the world like he'd just settled in to enjoy the show. One eyebrow was arched and a smug smile curved the lips that Piper could rhapsodize about for hours.

"Hey, Isabel."

"Well, if it isn't Tanner Glock," she snarled.

"Careful, Isabel. One of these days you're going to run out of guns to make fun of my last name with."

"Oh, I don't know. With rednecks like you here to fuel the demand, I'm sure the gun manufacturers will keep me in supply. By the way, why are you always at my house? I mean, I know your parents live outside of Paris, but don't you have family of your own around here?"

Ignoring her jab, he nodded toward the car. "You taking auto repair this semester?"

Izzy flashed the aluminum can. "Recycling, actually," she quipped, trying to sound cool and collected. Suave even. As if she hadn't just been crawling around on her belly.

She pitched the can toward the recycle bin, sending up a silent prayer that it would actually make it. It didn't. Once again, the can rolled down the driveway. This time, Tanner grabbed it and sent it sailing straight into the tub. The show-off.

"You going to watch the movie with us?"

"What movie?"

"Your brother invited the team over to watch some slasher flick."

"Absolutely." She smirked, then wrapped her arms around her chest and faked an exaggerated shiver. "That explains the sudden temperature drop. Hell has actually frozen over, and I'm going to spend my free time hanging out with the baboons my brother calls friends." Then she cocked her head and pretended to think about it for a second. "Nope. Still not cold enough."

"Then I guess I'll catch you on Monday." He flashed her a wink and sauntered off into the house.

"I'll be all shivery in anticipation." But he was already gone.

Why was it that she spent most of her time being Invisabel Isabel—the girl no one noticed—but whenever she was doing something embarrassing, the most popular guy in school was there to witness it?

Not that she cared what Tanner Colt thought about her. But she *would* like to retain the last shreds of her dignity.

Still, as much as she wanted to, she couldn't blame her bad mood on Tanner. That rested solely on River's shoulders. The jerk hadn't called her since the party out at Mike's barn. Which might not have been such a big deal, if that hadn't been the night they'd slept together for the very first time.

She was purposefully late to Piper's. She didn't want to be alone with anyone for fear of spilling her guts about River. What would have been the point?

She'd already figured out that sleeping with him had been a pretty stupid idea. Like, colossally stupid. Like, she'd previously thought only cheerleaders-made-mistakes-that-dumb stupid.

And the thing was, when you did something really, massively stupid, you didn't rush out to tell your friends about it.

Even though she knew they'd be on her side—Cassidy would be first in line to break River's nose—it was too soon to talk about. There was a giant raw spot inside of her and she wasn't ready to expose the wound to air.

Besides, this wasn't *ha-ha* stupid, like the time she'd driven from her house to Cassidy's with her iPod sitting on the roof of her car. Or the time she'd locked her keys in the trunk at the state park after dragging Piper hiking.

This wasn't the kind of stupid you could joke about a few days later. No, this was the kind that burned in your gut and ate at your confidence. The kind of stupid that hurt. The kind you were ashamed of.

What good would telling them do? Cassidy would probably lecture her about personal responsibility and girl power. Mei would ask if she'd practiced safe sex, even though Mei would never in a million years sleep with a guy who'd already dumped her. But it was Piper's response that Izzy dreaded the most. Piper would be *supportive*.

Trudging up the stairs, Izzy shuddered at the thought. Supportive was the last thing she needed right now. One word of sympathy and she'd be blubbering like a baby. And nobody needed to see that.

Besides, Piper had enough drama going on for the four of them. As if kissing the pig wasn't bad enough, life with Piper's mother was hell. Izzy wouldn't trade places with her for anything—not even if it meant getting away from the mess she'd made with River. No, she just had to keep her misery to herself for a few more weeks. As soon as they went their separate ways to other countries, they'd forget about River. All of them. Even her. If it was possible to forget the guy who was your first.

She entered Piper's bedroom to find Cassidy already sprawled on the beanbag, her fingers bright red from a bag of Flamin' Hot Crunchy Cheetos. Piper sat cross-legged on the bed, a folder of DVDs open on her lap.

"You're late," Piper chided.

"Sorry. I got distracted by your boyfriend."

Piper perked up. "Tanner was at your house?"

Izzy sighed, instantly sorry she'd brought it up. "When isn't he at my house? Along with most of the football players. It's just one of the perks of my father being the coach."

"Remind me why we're not spending the night at your house." Piper waggled her eyebrows lasciviously.

Everyone else groaned and ignored the question.

Cassidy chuckled. "I'm surprised that Germaine the Vain lets him out of her sight long enough to hang out with the rest of the team."

"She doesn't own him," Piper reasoned.

Cassidy didn't even look up, just continued flipping through the magazine open on her lap. "No, she just controls him with the promise of sex."

"Not just the promise. Or at least not according to Jackson Grosbeck." Mei shook her head in disgust. "When is that girl going to learn to use her brain instead of her body to get what she wants?"

"Easy for you to say. You have the best brain." Cassidy popped a Cheeto in her mouth.

"But only one?" Piper teased. "I thought maybe with all those fantastic grades, you kept a spare one stashed somewhere."

Mei rubbed her hands together like an evil scientist, cackling. "Igor, bring me the spare medulla oblongata!"

"Ah, so that explains why Germaine is so vapid," Cassidy said. "Obviously, her brain is no longer in her head."

"Yeah." Piper giggled. "How dumb do you have to be to not appreciate Tanner?"

Ordinarily, Izzy would have been right there with Cassidy, slamming

Germaine, but today she wanted to kick something. Some girls used sex to get what they wanted from boys. She, on the other hand, apparently used sex to actively drive them away.

How bad in bed must I have been?

To distract herself, she teased Piper, "I *so* don't know what you see in him."

Piper looked truly offended. "What's not to see? The rippling muscles? The silky dark hair? The piercing blue eyes?"

"The ego?" Izzy countered. "The vanity? The subhuman IQ? The ungodly obsession with a sport that worships pointless violence?"

"Last year he was in my honors biology class," Mei pointed out.

"So?"

"Sooo, he was the only other person who got an A."

That gave Izzy pause, but she soon dismissed it with a wave. "Okay, so maybe a few functioning brain cells have survived the numerous blows to the head he's sustained. But you've got to give me the football thing."

Piper crossed her arms over her chest and stared at Izzy. "This is Texas. Everyone is obsessed with football."

"That doesn't make it any less pointless or violent."

Piper smirked. "Objections to football, coming from the only girl in the history of the school to try out for the team?"

Izzy gasped.

Cassidy's head jerked up. "Not cool, Piper."

Freshman year, Izzy had gone out for the football team as the kicker. Cassidy had spent all summer helping her practice. The rest of the football team had laughed their asses off when she showed up for tryouts, but she'd been prepared for that. She *hadn't* been prepared for her father to not even let her walk onto the field. That was the last time she'd tried to win his approval.

"I was just teasing, Cass." Piper paused, head cocked to the side. "I think this is what I'm going to miss the most. Who's going to tease us when we're off in the four corners of the globe?"

"Um . . . a globe doesn't *have* corners," Mei pointed out.

Cassidy snickered. "That's why it's called a globe."

Piper beamed, clutching the DVD folder to her chest. "See, that's what I mean. In France, no one will know me like you guys do. I'm going to miss that." She sniffed a little.

"Don't buy stock in Kleenex just yet, Pipes." But Cassidy smiled as she said it.

"We're going to be apart. For ten whole weeks. Seventy days. No sleepovers. No movies. No Cheetos."

"I'm pretty sure they have Cheetos in France," Cassidy interjected.

"That's *so* not the point." Piper grabbed a Cheeto and threw it at her.

Cassidy—überathlete that she was—dove for it and actually caught it in her mouth.

She held up her hands as if modestly accepting the praise of thousands. "Thank you. Thank you very much."

Izzy flopped back on the bed. "Jeez, Pipes, just pick a movie. We're not vampires who are never going to age, you know? What about *The Princess Bride*?"

It had always been one of Izzy's favorite movies. When she'd first moved to Paris, Piper, Mei, and Cassidy had invited her over for a slumber party. As they huddled around the TV, watching *The Princess Bride* and downing Pixy Stix, Izzy had known that these were the friends who would be with her for the rest of her life.

"Oh, are we back to picking a movie?" Cassidy asked. "I didn't realize Piper was done waxing melodramatic."

Piper gave Cassidy a playful shove. "I refuse to apologize for being woman enough to admit I have feelings. Just you wait until you're all alone in Australia next semester, we'll see who's—"

"Actually," Mei interrupted, "I've been doing research. There's one program we could still get into this semester. We could leave in October."

"Wow, that's so quick." Piper's eyes lit up. "Awesome!"

"But," Mei looked a little sad, "we've seen each other almost every day since the first grade."

"Excuse me?" Izzy protested.

"Okay, Ms. Precise," Mei conceded. "Since the sixth grade. The point is, we're going to be all alone there. We'll be lonely."

"Not me." Cassidy shook her head.

But Mei gave her a piercing look. "No phone calls. No hanging out at lunch. Plus, some of us won't even speak the language."

"All of us except Cassidy," Piper pointed out.

"I'm not sure Australian qualifies as English," Izzy said. "Don't you remember when we tried to watch *Mad Max*?"

"The point is," Mei interrupted, trying to steer them back on course, "are we really prepared to live on texting alone?"

Cassidy froze, seemingly considering it, and Izzy didn't blame her. Izzy had been so focused on how great it would be to get out of Texas for once that she hadn't thought about leaving her best friends. Her head had been full of images of hiking through the jungle, picturing herself like one of those cool chicks in the Subaru ads driving off-road somewhere. Or zipping from tree to tree on a canopy tour. Maybe even being interviewed for some hip ecology e-zine.

She hadn't imagined being lonely. "There's always e-mail," she pointed out.

"No, Mei's right," Piper said slowly. "We should try to keep in touch on Facebook."

"But we're going to be busy. We won't be checking our Facebook pages."

"We could Foursquare our locations," Mei pointed out.

Cassidy groaned. "We'll let you do that, Ms. Vogel, while the rest of us are off doing something fun."

Piper coyly added, "Or some*one* fun."

They all squealed at her bad joke. Izzy said, "Yeah, right. Please tell me that you're not actually considering having sex with guys in France."

"Uh, no, perv. But now that you mention it, a little smooch action might be nice. Preferably something without snout."

"Now there's something for your Facebook page," Cassidy said.

If Piper had been a cartoon, a lightbulb would have appeared in a thought bubble above her head. "Oh my God. I have the most spectacular idea!"

"Yes, yes," Cassidy grumbled. "You want to get some lip action in France. Big shocker."

"Nooooo." Piper drew the word out. "I want us *all* to get a little."

"You can't be serious," Mei chided.

Sometimes it was like Mei and Piper didn't even belong to the same species.

"Of course she's serious," Izzy said. "It's Piper. Talking about guys. And kissing. She's always serious about guys and kissing. Throw in some cute shoes and it's her nirvana."

"Excuse me? Who *isn't* serious about guys and kissing?" Piper asked, genuinely dumbfounded.

Cassidy dropped another Cheeto into her mouth. "You want us to kiss guys and then post about it on our Facebook pages? That's way classy."

Mei's spine stiffened as if she'd only just realized the horror. "On our Facebook pages? Our parents would see!"

"You're Friends with your parents?" Cassidy asked her, chuckling.

"Aren't you?" Mei looked at each of them in turn.

"God, no." Piper shuddered in disgust. "Can you imagine? As if Germaine's cyberbullying wasn't enough. The last thing I need is another forum for my momster to torment me."

"My parents don't even know what Facebook is." Izzy shrugged. "If you're Friends with them on Facebook, wouldn't we have seen them post?"

Mei smiled meekly. "They respect my privacy enough that they don't post on my wall."

Cassidy snorted. "That's so sweet."

"We definitely don't want our parents to see it," Piper chirped, steering them back to the topic at hand. "I doubt they respect your privacy *that* much."

"Couldn't we just create new Facebook accounts? And then make our own private fan page?" Izzy asked. "As long as we kept it completely separate from our real Facebook stuff, no one would ever know it was us, even if someone did stumble onto it."

Cassidy folded over the top of the Cheetos bag and set it aside. "Are we really doing this?"

"Why not?" Izzy asked. "I could use a lip lock or two." Anything to distract her from River's lack of communication.

"So what do we do? Just post if we kiss someone?" Mei asked.

"No no no!" Piper said, perfectly mimicking Germaine's bless-your-heart tone. "These are not going to be your everyday occurrences. We need something bigger than mere posting on Facebook. These are not I've-decided-to-buy-Milk-Duds-instead-of-Jujubes-at-the-movies posts. These are life-altering experiences we're talking about!"

"Um . . . we are still talking about kissing guys, right? Not radioactive spiders?" Mei asked blandly.

Piper groaned. "You have no sense of drama."

"That's because you have enough for both of us."

Cassidy snorted. "As long as this doesn't involve us mailing each other some tacky pair of jeans."

"Like I said, we have way more panache than that," Piper retorted.

Izzy leaned forward as genuine excitement for this distraction began to take hold. "What are you suggesting?"

"Something . . ." But then Piper seemed to flounder, apparently unable to think of anything worthy. "Just something bigger than what we've done here in Paris. Something we can all get excited about."

Izzy cocked her head to the side and considered her three friends. She and Piper would be on board no matter what. She needed the distraction and Piper was game for anything. As for Cassidy and Mei, they definitely needed something to hook them. But what?

They were each driven in their own way: Cassidy to prove she was more than her mother's daughter, and Mei to prove she was as worthy as any child her parents might have had if they'd been able to conceive. It took Izzy only a moment to land on the thing that would appeal to both of them.

"What about a competition?" Izzy offered.

"Right," Cassidy quipped. "One point per guy?"

"And three for a superhottie!" Piper exclaimed, ignoring Cassidy's sarcasm.

Mei banged her head against her palm. "I can hear my mother now. We're setting feminism back to the dawn of the last millennia."

"Come on!" Piper fairly bounced up and down. "How can I ever paint a masterpiece if I haven't embraced my carnal nature?"

"Some of us are nervous enough about embracing a new language."

Once again Piper ignored Mei's comment. "I'm starving for life experiences! We all are! But none of this is going to be fun if it's just me doing it. It has to be all of us. We're in this together."

"Just so long as you can get three points for a superhottie?" Cassidy asked.

Piper grinned. "Why not? Unless you're afraid there aren't any three-pointers in Australia."

"So it *is* a competition, then?" Izzy asked, eager to nail down the details.

"Not a competition. More like a club," Piper said.

"A kissing club?" Mei injected incredulously.

"Not just any kissing club." There was that bless-your-heart tone again. "The International Kissing Club, or IKC for short." Piper paused dramatically, as if she expected a gasp of awe from the crowd.

"Aren't you at all worried that this is the kind of thing Germaine would do?" Mei asked in a wincing tone. "Rating boys like they're cattle? That's so shallow. And you know it would piss us off if guys were talking about girls that way."

"Okay, then." Izzy nodded—after all, Mei did have a point. "Maybe it's not about how hot the guy is." Piper looked ready to protest. And since the last male she'd kissed had been porcine, Izzy couldn't really blame her. If anyone deserved to kiss a hot guy, it was Piper. "Maybe we don't rate the guy, maybe we rate the kiss. Just 'cause a guy's hot, doesn't mean he knows how to kiss."

"Good point," Mei agreed. "John was sure cute enough, but there was zip lip chemistry between us."

Cassidy rolled her eyes. "You're just saying that because he thought Jimi Hendrix was one of the Beatles."

"Jimi Hendrix!" Mei threw up her hands, as if that should have been explanation enough. "The Beatles!" She shuddered in mock disgust.

"The point is," Piper said, picking up the argument, "hot guys do not always hot kissers make. If I want to expand my carnal knowledge base, shouldn't I be aiming for really great kissers? If we're seizing all of life's experiences, then we want these to be transcendent, life-changing kisses."

Izzy nodded. "Exactly!"

Piper's eyes gleamed with excitement. "Okay. One point per kiss. Three points to lip scorchers."

"Okay, well, my mother will still kill me," Mei said dryly, but Izzy could tell she was intrigued.

"We're taking charge of our sexuality," Izzy countered. "She'll be thrilled."

"Yeah, right," Cassidy said. "That's what I'll tell *my* mom when she's attaching the chastity belt."

"Which is why we're not going to tell them," Izzy pointed out.

"That's why we're creating new Facebook accounts and doing it anonymously. They'll never know."

Piper had had a lot of crazy schemes over the years, but this was one Izzy could get behind. Especially if it would help her get over River. Born-again virginity was so overrated.

Chapter 4
Mei

"So, did you get any sleep at all last night?" Mei asked Piper, as they waited outside the counselor's office. The girl was bouncing around like she'd just drunk three double espressos from Starbucks.

"A little bit. Why, does it show?" Piper reached into her voluminous purse and dug around until she pulled out a compact.

Mei rolled her eyes. "You're fine. I just meant that you look like you could orbit the earth under your own power."

And it was true. Piper was always a little high-strung, but ever since Friday night she'd been jumpy enough to make her mother's Chihuahua nervous.

"I just want to get this done, you know? I'm ready to leave for Paris tomorrow."

"Well, maybe not tomorrow. You do have to pack, after all."

"Right. I was thinking about that most of the night. We're going to have to go shopping in Dallas before we leave."

Well, wasn't that just so Piper? Forget the million details that went into planning a trip like this. Forget that they hadn't checked on vaccinations or visas. Forget even that they still hadn't run the idea by their parents. *Let's go shopping for a new pair of shoes.* Anything to get them out of Paris—and away from censorious eyes, even for a little while.

Of course, retail therapy was a time-tested means of overcoming depression, right? Piper's dad must have thought so. It had always been obvious to Mei that he funded Piper's shopping expeditions out of guilt. He must have known his wife was a nightmare. But if Piper was as unhappy with her father's negligence as Mei thought she must be, Piper was too much of a trouper to complain to them about it.

Thankfully, Mei was saved from having to respond about the shopping trip when Ms. Vogel opened her office door. "Girls, come on in," she said with a bright, sympathetic smile.

"The others aren't here yet," Piper said. "Shouldn't we wait for them?"

"We can get started. Unless it's a problem you're all having." She lowered her voice. "Are the kids still bothering you about 'the incident,' Piper?"

Mei ground her teeth together. She knew the counselor was only trying to be helpful, but did Piper really need everyone—even the school staff—to remind her of her problems with Germaine the Stain? It was hard enough to talk Piper out of the house most mornings.

Especially since Jackson had taken the blame for the pig incident and Germaine had gotten away almost scot-free. It was just like last year, when Germaine and her minions stole Piper's clothes out of her gym locker and strung them up the flagpole. They'd gotten away with that, too. It had been just another crushing blow in their campaign to destroy Piper—at least until someone had added beet juice to their self-tanner and the cheerleading squad had walked around bright pink for almost a week.

Germaine was still trying to find proof of who had done it, but Mei and Cassidy had plotted too well to leave any evidence behind.

Once they were seated in Vogel's office, Piper launched right into her spiel. "You know how you were telling us about the international exchange program and how we need to stretch ourselves to reach our full potential? Well, we've decided that that's exactly what we want to do." She paused for dramatic effect, then blurted out, "We want to be foreign exchange students." Then she ruined her one attempt at being serious by shrieking so loudly she nearly broke the sound barrier.

"It'll be so much fun and such a great experience. I've always wanted to go to France. Can't you just see me walking along the banks of the Seine in my brand-new beret? It'll be azure of course, and I'll—"

"We've all given this a lot of serious thought," Mei cut in, taking pity on the counselor, who was currently attempting to massage her aching eardrum.

"That's great, girls. I'm glad to see you so enthusiastic about an *academic* program." Piper seemed to miss Vogel's subtle emphasis on the word "academic," but Mei certainly didn't.

"We talked about it all weekend—"

Mei needed to cut Piper off before she could do more damage. If Vogel heard even a hint of anything related to pigs or kissing, she'd eighty-six the whole plan. This had to seem like genuine, scholastic enrichment. "The exchange program offers unique and varied opportunities that we can't get here in Paris, Texas."

Jeez. She hated to be the cliché of the typical Asian egghead, but really, someone had to be the organized one, and, God love her, Piper just didn't have it in her. "We've put together a proposal that we think adequately demonstrates our goals."

Piper's eyes widened. "We did?" she whispered loudly enough to be heard in the next county.

"Of course we did. Don't you remember, we spent hours on it?"

"I remember Westley's sword fights and too many Pixy Stix, but—"

Mei stepped on Piper's foot, hiding it with her backpack as she reached into the bag and pulled out her leather portfolio, with the twelve-page report she'd printed out the night before.

Vogel accepted the portfolio with raised eyebrows. "Great. Why don't you give me a few days to look this over and we'll see about setting up something for next semester?"

"We can't wait until next semester," Piper cried in horror. "We have to go now!"

"I'm afraid that's just not possible. The program—"

"Well, actually, it is possible." Mei reached across the desk. "If you'll look at the timeline on page three of my report, there are a few programs that don't start until October first. You'll see that as long as we submit the paperwork by Friday, we can be a part of this semester's program. Plane tickets are available to our destinations and there are still openings at all of the schools. Cassidy will need to have her passport expedited and the program in Costa Rica is filling up quickly, so we need to act now."

"Costa Rica?" Vogel asked faintly. "I thought y'all wanted to go to France."

"Oh no," said Piper. "We're going to four different continents." She slanted Mei a mischievous look. "How can we 'broaden our horizons' if we're all in the same place?"

Of course, what Piper really meant was now that she'd committed herself to the International Kissing Club, she wanted all the French guys for herself. Well, really all the European guys. Mei wasn't even sure Piper would leave her any guys in Asia to kiss—the continents were connected, after all.

Not that that was a big deal. She really wasn't in this for the kissing, anyway.

Mei slid the last dish into the cabinet, then leaned against the kitchen counter and stared toward the living room. She couldn't put it off any longer.

Her mom and dad both still had a little wine in their glasses. Good. Mei had the feeling her mom was going to need a drink when she heard what Mei had planned.

All day she'd thought about the right way to ask them, and she'd come to the decision that it was best just to spit it out. The more she practiced the speech, the less likely her parents were to believe that she hadn't been plotting this for years.

She didn't want to hurt them, didn't want them to think she was unhappy with her life or that this was anything more than just an amazing opportunity.

But the fact of the matter was, she'd been curious for years now. Curious about China. And curious about the parents who had abandoned her because she wasn't a boy.

She exhaled a long breath and went to join her mom and dad. A gritty guitar solo from Eric Clapton played in the background while her mom graded papers and her dad worked on his laptop.

"Do you have a lot of homework tonight, sweetheart?" her mom asked as Mei took the seat across from them.

"Not really; I finished it already."

"That's my Doodlebug," her dad said without looking up from his screen.

Mei let the nickname go—it so wasn't the time to fight that battle—then took a deep breath. Clasping her hands between her knees so she wouldn't be tempted to chew on her nails, she blurted out, "Mom, Dad, I need to talk to you."

Her mom looked up at once, concern accenting the tiny lines by her mouth and eyes. "Is there something wrong? Something at school?"

"No, nothing's wrong, but it is about school, sort of." They were watching her expectantly, so she went for it. "I would like to apply to do an academic program abroad this semester . . . in China."

A very long pause followed, then her parents exchanged a glance that was easy to decipher—and that didn't bode well for her.

"What brought this on?" her dad asked. Her mom reached for her wineglass, but seemed to otherwise remain composed.

What brought this on? Well, I've been haunted by the question of my birth parents for the past ten years.

Yeah. That would go over great. Though she couldn't ever remember them saying anything aloud, Mei knew that deep down both of her parents had feared that this day would come. This was going to require a delicate approach to avoid worrying them. "Well, the thing is . . ."

Her mom tipped back the glass and drained it.

Okay, forget delicate. She'd have to lie.

"Mr. Webb had us work on practice essays for the SAT, and the prompt was whether a person's identity is something they are born with or is something people create themselves. And when I started to compose my answer, I realized I don't really have an answer, because I don't know who I am."

How could she know when the only information she had about her origins was the name of the orphanage where she'd been dumped?

"Sweetheart, of course you know who you are: you're our daughter and we love you very much," her mom replied.

Her dad just chuckled. "Doodlebug, no one knows who they are when they're sixteen."

Oh God, any minute now her mom would dig out Mei's Mulan doll to comfort her, and her dad would kiss her on the forehead to make it all better. Sometimes it was easier for them to pretend she was still a little girl who didn't truly understand what it meant to be adopted.

"I know you do, Mom," she said with exaggerated patience. They were never going to get this. "It's not about that. It's just that I realized I want to know more about where I come from, culturally." Though she considered the people in front of her her real mom and dad, she knew nothing about her life before the age of two—and it didn't help that she was the only Asian at Paris High.

"You don't have to go all the way to China to do that. That's why we have the Internet." Mei could tell her mom was doing her best to remain calm, but her fingers gripped the stem of her empty wineglass like a lifeline. "And you haven't even used that Rosetta Stone DVD we got you."

Nothing like a DVD to put you in touch with your cultural heritage. But she didn't say that to her mom. "China's where I'm from,

Mom. I'm your daughter, but I'm also Chinese . . . and you're not. I need to understand what that means."

"You know, Mei, your mother and I planned on taking you to China when you graduated from high school," her dad said. "Why do this now?"

"I feel like this is something I have to do on my own. So, today I talked to Ms. Vogel, the guidance counselor. It's only a ten-week trip, and I would be home in time for Christmas. She said doing this would be a great addition to my college applications." Mei smiled brightly, hoping her parents didn't notice the nervousness underneath. She'd been thinking for a while that she'd like to visit China, and now that the opportunity was right in front of her, she couldn't let it pass. She only hoped throwing in the college application would sway things in her favor.

Not even close.

"You talked to the guidance counselor before you talked to us?" Her mother dropped all pretense of composure.

"Calm down, Susan." Her dad pried the wineglass out of her mother's hand before she broke it. "Mei, what is this really about?" They both pinned her with a searching look.

For the briefest moment, she considered telling them the truth. But . . . she just couldn't. Not yet, anyway. Instead, she pulled out her ace in the hole: the only-child card.

"Piper, Izzy, and Cassidy are all going to be exchange students. We thought it would be fun to do it together—you wouldn't want me to be left here alone, would you?"

"I should have known Piper was the instigator. Ever since y'all were kids she's been the ringleader in one crazy scheme after another," her mom said, exasperation in her tone. "That girl is going to end up just like her mother if she's not careful."

"This isn't about Piper, Mom." Mei clenched her hands in her lap. Had she toed the line so carefully all her life that her mother couldn't even imagine she'd want to step off the path? "This is about me and a great opportunity. Just promise me you'll think about it before you answer, please."

"Of course we will," her dad said. And after he nudged her with his knee, her mom nodded, too.

Knowing she'd done all she could, Mei rose from the chair. "Okay, then. I'm going to go practice now." She gave them both a kiss and climbed the stairs to her room. But instead of playing her guitar chords, she stood on the landing and listened to her parents. They were keeping their voices deliberately low, but if she held her breath, she could hear what they were saying.

"I don't want her to go," her mom said.

"Susan, she has a point: we can't provide her with the answers she's looking for. Maybe this is what she needs."

"Yes, but why does she have to do it now? I'm not ready for this yet."

"You're never going to be ready, honey."

"Rick, what if she's looking for her family?"

"*We're* her family, Susan, and nothing is going to change that. We always said we'd be supportive if she wanted more information about her birth parents . . ."

"I know, but saying that and facing it are two different things. Those people abandoned Mei, and I don't want them to hurt her."

Mei heard a muffled sob from her mother. It made her chest tighten.

"It'll be okay, honey," her dad said comfortingly.

Guilt made her slink to her room and silently close the door. Mei had played down and dirty and she knew it. Part of her wanted to tell them to forget the whole thing, but she didn't. Instead, she sat on the bed and hugged her knees to her chest as tears slipped silently down her cheeks.

This was one time she couldn't be the good daughter.

Chapter 5
Piper

"What do you think of these?" Piper asked, holding up a pair of skinny jeans. They were the exact shade of faded blue she liked, plus they were ripped in all the right places.

"I think they look exactly like the last three pairs you held up," Cassidy answered with a grimace. "I'm so *not* the person to be asking. Come on, Izzy, help me out. Just pick a pair and let's do this. I'm starving."

"That's easy for you to say—you already bought what you needed for the trip."

"Because I'm a normal person." Cassidy held up her lone bag, then gestured to the five Piper had been lugging around for the last hour. "You already have more clothes than anyone in Paris—Texas *or* France. Why do you need more?"

"We can't all get by on a new pair of Vans and a cute sundress, Cassidy."

"You *could*," interjected Izzy. "You just *won't*."

Piper giggled. "Can you even see me in a pair of Vans?" She held up her foot, which was currently encased in her favorite pair of high-heeled sandals. "These are much more my speed."

"I don't think speed has anything to do with those," Cassidy said.

Mei snorted. "Yeah, God forbid you should actually need to run."

Piper looked pointedly at Mei's Doc Martens. "Yeah, because you can win a marathon in *those*."

"I could if I had to," Mei answered with a grin. "Which is more than you can say."

"Seriously, Piper, are you going to get the jeans?" Cassidy asked. "Because I'm going to gnaw off my own arm if we don't get some food soon."

"Okay, okay." Piper dropped the disputed jeans back on the table. "Let's go. I don't want to be the one to cause our star basketball forward to die of malnutrition."

"Thank God," Cassidy said. "Let's hit the food court."

A few minutes later they were all seated at a table, chowing down on chili-cheese fries and chocolate milkshakes. But after a few bites, Piper was all but squirming with excitement again.

She couldn't believe that in just a few weeks, she would be walking along the banks of the Seine.

Strolling through French museums.

Studying art in the place where so many of the masters had lived.

Kissing boys in the city of love.

Her lips tingled at the thought. She *so* couldn't wait for October to get here. In her mind, she was already there, racking up points with one lip scorcher after another. If things went according to plan, it wouldn't be long before she would finally be able to get the feel of that whiskered snout off her lips.

Now, if only Germaine could see it. Stuck back in Paris, Texas, she'd die of envy.

"So, are we done here?" Izzy asked after taking a long sip from her milkshake. "Because it's getting late and I want to hit the REI before we head back to Paris. I need to get some stuff, too."

"Don't you ever get sick of wearing clothes made from recycled bottles?" Piper teased her friend with a grin. "I mean, they look cute on you—especially the hemp stuff—but really, Izzy, it's not like they're the most fashionable things in the world."

"Because fashion is so much more important than saving the environment," Izzy snapped. "God, Piper, could you be a little shallower?"

Piper froze, a french fry halfway to her mouth, feeling a little bit like she'd been slapped. She and Izzy had been bickering back and forth about each other's clothing choices since Izzy had moved to Paris in sixth grade. It was a time-honored event, one no trip to a Dallas mall would be complete without. She hadn't meant to hurt Izzy's feelings—she'd just been following tradition.

But one look at Izzy's face said traditions were the last thing on her mind. For the first time, Piper wondered if something was really wrong with Izzy. She'd been extremely touchy lately, and everything set her off. At first Piper had thought it was because River was gone, but now she couldn't help wondering if something had happened between them before he'd left. Not that she would dare ask right now— Izzy looked pissed, really pissed, and the last thing Piper wanted was for Izzy to jump down her throat again.

As she sat there trying to think of something to say to gloss over the tension, a little shiver of nerves worked its way down her spine. Even as she was looking forward to their international escapades, she couldn't help feeling like everything was changing. Like maybe when they got back from this trip, things would be different. Not just with Germaine, but with the four of them as well.

At first, she'd thought that was a good thing—she couldn't get rid of the Kiss the Pig moniker soon enough, after all—but now she wasn't so sure. She wanted to change everything about herself, wanted to experience all the things she'd missed by being stuck in Paris, Texas, for sixteen years, but at the same time, she didn't want everyone else to change, too. It might be selfish, but after the summer she'd had, she was terrified of losing what little she did have—namely, the three best friends any girl could ever ask for.

She wanted this trip badly. They all did, but now that it was slowly becoming a reality, Piper realized just how much she would miss them.

She'd miss Cassidy's sarcasm, the way she always called things like she saw them. With her long blond hair and lean, athletic body Cass might look like Sporty Barbie, but she was so much cooler than that.

And Mei, who seemed so prim and proper on the outside with her always perfect black hair and flawless skin but who, inside, had the wild soul of a rock star.

Even Izzy, whose behavior had been strange and erratic lately but whom Piper always knew she could count on when she needed her. She had a feeling she would miss Izzy most of all. When she was in France, who would make her laugh so hard she was in danger of spewing?

She glanced at Izzy, realized her friend's chocolate-brown eyes were completely spaced out. Even though she was sitting at their table, drinking her milkshake and twirling a lock of her hair around her finger, she was a million miles away. Maybe she needed someone to remind *her* for once that everything was going to be okay. "I'm sorry, Iz," she said, even though she wasn't really sure what she was supposed to be apologizing for. "I was just joking. You know I love your style."

Izzy sighed, and it wasn't until she relaxed that Piper realized how tense her friend had really been. Reaching out, she rubbed a hand between Izzy's shoulder blades. "I know," Izzy answered. "Sorry—I shouldn't have jumped at you like that."

"This much shopping would make anyone irritable," Cassidy said, though the glance she exchanged with Mei told Piper that the two of them were also weirded out by Izzy's strange behavior. "I'm pretty close to losing it myself."

Izzy laughed and Piper shot Cassidy a grateful look—thank God her friends were so good at smoothing over the rough edges when she stuck her foot in it. Cassidy grinned back and Piper couldn't help thinking that of the four of them, Cassidy looked the least like she was going to lose it. In fact, she was practically glowing, as if just the thought of getting out of Paris, Texas, for a while was enough to light her up from the inside.

Not that Piper blamed her. She'd had it rough ever since the Cotton Festival a few months before, but Cassidy had had it rough from the very beginning. Even though it was the twenty-first century, things in Paris hadn't changed so much that people didn't look down on Cassidy because her mom had gotten pregnant in high school. It was stupid and bigoted and enough to drive Piper crazy, but there it was.

That's how the two of them had become friends, in fact. In kindergarten, one of the older kids had been teasing Cassidy about being a "bastard" while he walked by their table in the cafeteria. Piper hadn't known what the word meant, but there was no mistaking the mean sneer on the boy's face. Plus Cassidy had looked like she was about to cry, and Piper couldn't stand that, so she'd picked up the huge bottle of ketchup on the table in front of her and squirted it all over the little jerk.

She'd spent the next week sitting on the bench at recess, but it had totally been worth it. Especially since Cassidy had sat with her every day. They'd been inseparable ever since, and every once in a while Cassidy still referred to the boy's shirt as Piper's first canvas.

As she looked around at her friends, Piper realized that she wasn't the only one with a semiurgent reason to get out of Paris. Even Mei had a motive for going. Her entire life she'd been on the outside looking in. Sure, that had changed a lot when she and Cassidy had saved Piper from drowning before swim class when they were in second grade (they'd become fast friends), but it was still hard for Mei sometimes. Especially since her parents bent over backward to make sure she didn't feel different—which usually ended up making her feel exactly that.

And Izzy—she'd always seemed like the normal one. Not that it was easy to be the middle child. Being trapped between the football god and the piano prodigy had pretty much rendered Izzy invisible. And things had only gotten worse since her idiot older brother had punched a locker and broken his hand after losing the first game of the season. But Piper wasn't insensitive enough to say anything about that to her friend—she liked her head just where it was.

Mei must have been feeling the tension as much as Piper, because after she finished her fries, she dusted off her fingers and then reached into her back pocket and pulled out her iPhone. "So, I've been thinking about the whole Facebook page. Do we have all the rules for the International Kissing Club laid out?"

"I'm pretty sure," Cassidy said. "I mean, how hard is it? Kiss a boy, get a point."

"Don't forget the three points for a really good kisser," Izzy added.

"Can I just say how much I absolutely love that?" Piper commented. "Three points for a transcendent kiss."

Cassidy coughed. "Transcendent? I'm not expecting an out-of-body experience, Pipes. It's just a kiss."

"Just wait," Izzy said. "When you get a really great kiss, you'll thank us."

"Absolutely," Piper said. "I can't wait!"

Mei scrolled through their page until she found the rules, then asked, "Are there bonus points?"

"Bonus points?" Cassidy asked incredulously. "For what?"

"I don't know. I just thought I'd ask."

"Of course there are bonus points!" Piper nearly bounced out of her seat as an idea occurred to her. "You get five extra points if you kiss two different guys in the same week. Ten if you kiss three."

"Three guys in a week?" Cassidy shook her head. "I thought you were trying to escape Germaine, not become her."

"Oh, please," she said. "I think I have a little more class than that."

"I don't know," Mei said. "You kiss that many guys, things are bound to get messy pretty fast."

"Right," agreed Izzy. "I think we should get bonus points for kissing the same guy twice, too. Or five times. Whatever."

"Why would you want to waste your ten weeks abroad kissing the same guy when the world is *filled* with superhotties?"

"Amazingly, Piper, there are many other things to do in Europe besides kiss hot guys," Mei said with a shake of her head.

"I know that. It's not like I'm planning on kissing twenty-four-seven. But what's the point of getting stuck with the same guy for ten weeks? This is probably our only trip out of Paris before graduation, and I don't plan on wasting a second of it."

"I think Piper's right," Cassidy said out of the blue.

"You do?" Izzy asked, incredulously.

"Absolutely. I definitely have no plans to get serious with a guy. Do you two?"

"What would be the point? We're going to be there less than a semester," said the eminently practical Mei.

Piper leaped on her friend's words. "Exactly! That's what I'm saying. We only get points for kisses from new guys." She giggled.

"I think I've figured out your going-away present," Cassidy smirked. "I'm getting you Chapsticks—a giant box of them."

"Make them strawberry—it's my favorite flavor. And I've got an idea for a going-away present for y'all, too. But you don't get to know what it is until right before the trip."

Izzy arched an eyebrow. "Am I the only one here who thinks that sounds sinister?"

"Not sinister," Mei observed. "Just devious."

Piper ignored them, too caught up in the totally cool thought about the IKC that had just occurred to her. "What if we take the whole privacy thing off the Facebook page?"

"What? And let everyone know what we're doing?" Cassidy exclaimed. "Are you kidding me? I haven't officially gotten permission yet. If my mother saw that, she would flip!"

"So would mine," Mei agreed. "I can hear her lecture now about how girls today just don't respect themselves, yada yada yada." She shuddered. "No, thank you."

"Well, obviously, I don't mean that we should broadcast our identities across the world. That's why we created separate Facebook accounts. But, I don't know, what if we used nicknames or something? Avatars. Something that hides who we are but at the same time lets other people see what we're doing."

"But what's the point of taking the privacy off?" asked Mei. "If we're hiding who we are, anyway?"

Piper shrugged. "Wouldn't it be cool to show just a few choice people how much fun we're having outside of this stupid town?"

"A few people? Or Germaine?" Mei reached over and stole the last of Piper's fries.

"Germaine, of course. Plus all the guys who have spent weeks oinking at me. It'd be nice to show them that the world doesn't revolve around them. That others can have fun, too."

"It *would* keep River from thinking I'm pining for him," Izzy mused, her eyes brighter than Piper had seen them in a while.

"Exactly!" agreed Cassidy. "And it would shut up all those guys who claim I'm a lesbian just because I wouldn't sleep with them."

"Not to mention providing us with the ammunition to one day take down Germaine and her stupid Kiss the Pig page once and for all." Mei's eyes gleamed with approval.

"Well, there is that." The thought had definite appeal to Piper—a whole Facebook page about kissing hot guys was so much cooler than one about kissing a pig. And if the thing took off, it would be awesome. It could be a whole revolution against mean girls everywhere.

"We'd have to be careful," Izzy said. "We don't want a bunch of skeezy guys around the world cyberstalking us."

"Ooooh, yuck," Piper agreed.

"So what do we call ourselves, then?" Mei asked. "I mean, if you want to hide who we are, we need good nicknames."

Cassidy poked her in the shoulder. "I think you should call yourself Mulan."

"Yeah, right."

"Why not? That's kind of cute, actually." Piper tugged gently on her friend's jet-black hair.

Cassidy added, "Yeah, and if we go with something as lame as Disney, then nobody will ever guess who we are."

"It's not lame!" Piper protested. "Especially if I can be Esmeralda."

Izzy choked on a french fry. When she was finally finished coughing, she gasped, "You're cute, Pipes, but you're no Demi Moore."

"Whatever." She paused, her mind racing over the possibilities. "So who should I be then?"

"Ariel, of course. You can't wait to get out of here and be someone else."

"Hmm. That's a good point. And I think it would be kind of sexy to be a mermaid."

"Of course you do." Cassidy glanced at Izzy. "I think you should be Jasmine. Since you love hummus so much. And flying carpets *are* environmentally friendly."

"I can get behind that," Izzy agreed.

"No no no! I've got it!" Piper said with a grin. "You're Jane, from Tarzan."

"You *are* going to the jungle," Mei pointed out.

"And God willing, there will be half-naked men there," Cassidy added.

Izzy nodded, considering. "I have always thought that Tarzan was a sexy hunk of ink."

"Not as hot as Chang." Piper nudged Mei. "You lucky dog."

"What about Cassidy?" Mei asked, blushing. "Is there a sporty princess?"

"Cassidy's Rapunzel," Piper said.

"But don't you think I'm more of a Pixar girl?"

"No, honey, you're Rapunzel." Piper patted her on her hand. "You've been trapped here for sixteen years and are just dying for a chance to let your hair down."

"My hair's already down, thank you very much." Cassidy held up a blond lock.

"Yeah, well, the escape thing still works," Mei said.

Cass thought about it, then said, "It kinda does. You're right."

"Okay, then." Piper held up her milkshake. "I propose a toast. To the launch of the IKC fan page and the hottest Disney princesses to ever walk the planet."

"Or at least the most insane," Mei said as she bumped Piper's cup with her own. Izzy and Cassidy joined in.

A little while later, as they were about to leave, Piper remembered to ask Cassidy, "So, have you gotten the whole money thing figured out yet?"

"Actually, I'm going to ask my dad today," Cassidy said, looking determined and more than a little scared.

Holy crap. And Izzy was the one in a bad mood? If Cassidy had this hanging over her head, she should be the one snapping at people. Even if Izzy hadn't talked to River since he went off to college, that was nothing compared to calling up a scuzzy deadbeat dad and asking him for money.

"Don't worry, Cass, it'll be fine," Piper said, squeezing her friend's hand. "I just know it."

Mei gave an encouraging thumbs-up. And even Izzy smiled with false cheer as they threw away their trash. But Piper could tell by the looks on Mei's and Izzy's faces that her friends were as concerned about Cassidy's plan as she was. Not because of the money thing, but because of what it might do to Cassidy to talk to her dad again. Their relationship was pretty nonexistent and the fact that she was willing to ask her dad for the money showed just how important this trip out of Paris was to Cassidy. She needed a chance to just be herself, to get away from all the jerks who thought she would put out just because her mom had—not to mention the ones who called her names when she wouldn't.

Knowing Cassidy wouldn't want to dwell on anything related to her dad, Piper shifted all of her shopping bags until she had a free arm. Linking it with Cassidy's, she said, "Recycled clothes, here we come!"

Cassidy laughed. "I can't wait."

Piper figured they all knew she was talking about a lot more than a shopping trip.

Four hours later, Piper bustled out of Mei's car and down the walk to her front door, weighed down by all her shopping bags. Who would have guessed that REI actually had some cute stuff? Not a lot, but she loved the new jacket and backpack she'd picked up there. While they weren't made of recycled water bottles, even Izzy had been forced to admit they were cool.

As she opened the front door, she sent up a quick prayer that her parents had already left for their dinner party. The last thing she was in the mood for was a long, drawn out "discussion" while her mom pawed through her shopping bags and criticized everything she'd bought.

But the second she walked in the house, she knew she was out of luck. Her father's cigar smoke—gross—hung in the air, mingling with the scent of her mother's before-dinner drink. Or maybe she should say bottle, as her mom was going through a lot more than one drink these days.

"Piper, you're home!" Her mom came into the foyer just as Piper started up the stairs. "I was hoping we'd catch you before we left."

After running through a number of inventive curses in her head, Piper forced a smile as she turned to her mom. "Yeah. Sorry I'm late—Izzy took forever at REI."

"I don't know why she insists on shopping at that ridiculous store. She's such a pretty girl. She'd look so much better if she didn't dress in burlap all the time."

Though Piper secretly agreed, she felt honor bound to defend her friend. "It's not burlap, Mom. Besides, Izzy really cares about the environment."

"I know, I know. But I don't see why she can't look good while she's caring about the environment." Her mom walked closer to the stairs, her four-inch stilettos tapping out a rhythm on the marble floor. The quick patter told Piper that her mother was a lot more sober than she'd originally thought, though Piper didn't know if she should be happy about that or not. A sober mom meant a nosy one, and she would really like to get up the stairs without a postmortem on—

"Well, don't just stand there. Show me what you bought."

Too late. Of course, it had been too late the second her mother realized she was home. With a sigh, Piper tromped down the scant few steps she'd managed to climb and followed her mother into the family room, where she laid her bags on the couch for inspection.

It didn't take long for the criticism to begin. "There isn't one bag here from Neiman's. Really, Piper, are these stores the best you could do?"

"You know Piper, Mom," Savannah said as she walked into the room. "She thinks she's too good for Neiman's."

Piper shot her sister a glare, but Savannah only grinned evilly as she poked at bags from BCBG and Express.

"Besides, she thinks she's an *artiste*. Neiman's is probably too boring for her."

"I like it just fine, Savannah. But these stores are cooler. Plus, you know my friends aren't crazy about Neiman Marcus."

"Which is one more reason I've always questioned you hanging around with them," her mother said with a disapproving frown. "You always looked so much nicer when you were hanging out with Germaine. Now there's a girl who knows how to dress."

Piper gritted her teeth and tried to ignore the little flash of betrayal that came with the realization that, despite everything, her mother was still on Germaine's side. It didn't matter that she had caused Piper—and her mother—months of untold grief. Nor did it matter that she was a manipulative narcissist who cared about no one and nothing but herself. All that mattered to her mother was that Germaine looked good while she terrorized the halls of Paris High.

And wasn't that just typical? In her mother's world, it didn't matter how things really were as long as they appeared good on the surface. Who cared if Piper was suffering as long as she pretended to be happy? Who cared if her mother was a drunk as long as she looked and acted sober? Who cared if her mom actually loved her as long as everyone thought she did?

Piper could feel her annoyance turning to tears, and she battled them back. It wouldn't do her any good to cry. Her mother would just remind her that crying made her skin blotchy and her eyes swollen—two things she really couldn't afford, especially with her "eccentric" looks.

"Aren't you going to be late to dinner with the Franklins?" she asked desperately.

Her mother glanced at the Cartier watch on her wrist. "We still have a few minutes. Your father isn't quite ready yet."

She reached into one of the bags and pulled out the funky shoes Piper had bought to go with her new sundresses. They had thick heels and were a really cool electric-blue that made her happy just looking at them.

"Oh, Piper, really? Blue shoes?"

"I like them, Mom."

"Which just goes to show how little taste you have," Savannah said with an eye roll.

"Of course you like them, dear. But this color shoe doesn't look good on anyone. And those heels aren't the right shape. They're going to make your legs look short and with your thigh issues, that's not what you need."

Piper swore she could feel her perfectly normal thighs expanding under her mother's judgmental gaze. *Aren't mothers supposed to make you feel better about yourself?* she wondered as she frantically began chewing on a thumbnail. It was a habit left over from when she'd been a kid and one she'd mostly broken—except when her mother was on a tear. Which was more often than not these days, thanks to the whole Kiss the Pig thing.

"And this dress." Her mother pulled out one of the sundresses she'd bought on sale. "Do you really think you need to be showing off your arms in this thing? It's not like you've been going to the gym with your sister and me lately."

"You know what? Forget it. If you don't like what I bought, you can take it all back tomorrow. It doesn't matter to me." Piper headed for the stairs at a dead run, leaving her bags where they were, knowing that she'd lose it completely if she didn't get away from her mom.

"Don't speak to your mother like that, young lady!" Her father's voice boomed from down the hall.

Suddenly, she couldn't keep quiet any longer. "Why don't you tell her not to criticize everything about me?" she shouted back as she ran up the stairs, her mother's Chihuahua, Pookie, nipping at her heels. "I'm sick of her trying to control every part of my life. I'm not Savannah. I'm not going to let her dress me up and parade me around the pageant circle."

Her sister snorted. "Like the pageant circle would want you."

"I don't know what to do with that girl, Tom," she heard her mother say as she ran to her room.

"Don't let her upset you, Mom," Savannah said in a tone that would make Germaine proud. "You know Piper hates that she's the only one of us girls not to win a beauty pageant."

Piper gritted her teeth and swallowed the urge to scream at her sister. That was exactly the reaction Savannah was looking for, and she *so* wouldn't give her the satisfaction. Not now, when freedom was within reach.

"I was just trying to help," her mother said with a sigh. "Doesn't she realize if she looked better, she wouldn't be such a target? No one would ever make Germaine kiss a—"

Piper slammed her door in Pookie's face, then hurled herself on her bed. Yanking her iPod off her nightstand, she slipped it on and then cranked up her favorite playlist. Pink came on and masked the sounds of her parents leaving for the night. But it couldn't mask Piper's thoughts—or the tears that burned behind her eyelids.

She blinked them back. It was bad enough that Germaine had made her cry—she wouldn't let her mother do it, too.

IKC Fan Page

The Official Rules and Guidelines for the International Kissing Club

📑 Info

- Kiss and be kissed
- Often
- Kiss and tell
- One point per kiss. Three points if it really makes you shiver . . .
  - Bonus points: five points for two guys in one week and ten points for three

Chapter 6
Cassidy

"Cass? Earth to Cassidy?"

"Huh?" she said, staring in a daze out of Mei's car window.

"I asked if you thought Izzy was acting weird, but then maybe you're not the best judge right now, either," Mei said.

"I'm sorry." Cassidy shifted in her seat and fiddled with the air vents. "I was just thinking about other things." She sighed heavily. "Just about calling my dad." She paused. "He'll do it, right? Give me the money, I mean. It's not like I've ever asked him for anything before." Not that he'd been around to ask even if she'd wanted to. She knew Mei had no idea whether her father was going to agree to this or not, but when she said it out loud like that it sounded completely within the realm of possibility.

"You haven't talked to him lately, have you?" Mei's question made Cass realize she hadn't been as smooth about hiding this fact as she'd thought.

She was slow to answer. "No. Not since my tenth birthday." She turned and caught Mei's sympathetic gaze. "Don't tell Piper and Izzy. I just . . . just don't tell them, okay?"

"Of course I won't." Mei looked so serious, it made Cassidy smile. She and Piper had been friends the longest of the four of them, but sometimes Mei understood her better. Maybe it was because Mei was adopted and she knew what it was like to have a parent she didn't know.

"So, what are you going to say to him?" Mei asked the question that had been weighing on Cassidy's mind all week.

"I guess I'm going to tell him the truth: I'm going to Australia and I want him to pay for it."

"And what if he says no?"

Cassidy took a deep breath. "Then I'll remind him that my mom stopped taking child support six years ago and he owes me. He's got his own business, and, from what little I've been able to find out, he does pretty well for himself."

"Why did your mom stop accepting the payments? Seems like she'd want him to keep paying through the nose after he left her."

Cassidy shrugged. "You know my mom—too much Barlow pride. She said that if he didn't want to be a real father to me, then we didn't need his guilt money, either."

They pulled into the drive of the little house Cassidy shared with her mom. "Won't she get mad when you tell her?" Mei asked as they got out of the car.

Cassidy had been wondering the same thing. She and her mom had always been close; they'd pretty much grown up together. And this would be the first time she'd ever deliberately gone behind her mother's back to do something. Conspiring with her father no less—to her mom, it would be the ultimate betrayal. She might even try to keep Cassidy from taking the money if her father ponied up. Which was why Cassidy had decided she wouldn't say anything until it was done. If he didn't give her the money, there would never be any reason to tell her mom what she'd done.

"No. Not until after. She's working an extra shift at the lab today, so I'm going to do it before she gets home."

"Do you want me to stay while you call? For moral support?"

It would be good to have someone there in case she chickened out, but Cassidy didn't want to say that. "You don't have to. You know, if you have stuff to do . . ."

Mei smiled. "I can move my guitar lesson to tomorrow. Let's do this."

They walked inside the house and Cassidy dropped her backpack on a chair in the living room. Everything was quiet. "Mom?" she called, just in case. No answer.

"Do you have his number?" Mei asked.

"No, but I know where I can find it. Come with me." Cassidy walked into the back bedroom and went to her mom's dresser. She quashed a pang of guilt as she reached for the drawer handle. She and her mother didn't have many boundaries, and she hated that she was crossing one now. Cassidy slid open the top drawer and dug beneath a pile of socks. At the bottom her fingers hit the edge of a large manila envelope.

"I found this a few years ago," she said to Mei, pulling it out of the drawer. "My mom doesn't know I've seen it." She opened the metal clasp and reached inside, bringing out a collection of papers. One fell to the floor and Mei picked it up.

It was a picture of Cassidy's mom sitting on the back of a late '80s maroon Mustang convertible. Her fuchsia satin dress had big bows on the puffy sleeves to match the riot of blond, poufy curls on her head. She was beaming at the tall, slim guy standing next to her in a tuxedo coat, creased Wranglers, and cowboy boots, with military-short reddish hair and blue eyes as bright as his smile.

"Are these your parents?" Mei asked.

"Yeah, at prom."

"They look *so* young."

Too young, Cassidy thought. "My mom got pregnant that night. They were going to get married, but in the fall my dad left to play baseball at Texas A&M like he'd always planned, and it never happened."

"You don't look anything like your dad, Cass. Well, except the height."

Cassidy stared at the guy in the picture. She'd definitely gotten his tall, lanky frame. Everything else—her wavy blond hair and brown eyes, the smattering of freckles across her nose—was all from her mom.

Sifting through the papers, Cassidy found what she was looking for: a business card. "Conway Brothers Well Digging" it said, with a cartoon of a well gushing water in the corner. Beneath that read "Casey Conway, Co-Owner." She flipped over the card. On the back in a man's messy scribble was a home address and phone number.

Mei looked at the card in Cassidy's hand. "Your dad lives in Tyler? But that's only two hours away!"

Cassidy nodded. "He has a whole new family there, two little boys and a girl. I've never met them, though." And she bet they had no idea they had another sister.

Until her dad's new daughter had come along, Cassidy had held out a secret hope that maybe he just couldn't relate to girls and that's why he'd stopped calling. But a birth announcement had come in the mail when her half sister was born, and she'd seen the look of pride and love on his face as he held his new daughter.

Cassidy put the other papers back in the envelope and hid it under the socks again. They crossed the hall to her room and sat on the bed, staring at the card. Now that she had the number and was actually about to do this, the nervous energy was almost paralyzing, like she'd just shotgunned a Red Bull while wearing a straitjacket.

"Are you okay, Cass?"

"Mm-hmm," was all she could manage.

Mei reached for the phone. "Do you want me to dial for you?"

Cassidy couldn't answer. A kaleidoscope of images flitted across her mind like an out-of-control slide show until it stopped at the picture of her mom before prom. She'd looked so happy, but Cassidy wondered how much she regretted the decisions she'd made that night. Because the fact was that her mom had gotten left behind not only by Cassidy's dad but also by life—stuck in a shitty job, in a nowhere town, forever.

Cassidy would not let the same thing happen to her.

"No. I've got it." She took the phone from Mei and dialed the numbers on the back of the card, ignoring her shaking fingers. The line rang once, twice, three times.

"Hello?" a woman's voice asked. Cassidy hadn't expected his wife to answer. She choked.

"Hello?" the woman repeated.

Oh God. *Hang up, hang up*, Cassidy thought. Mei squeezed her hand reassuringly.

"You can do this," her friend mouthed to her.

Cassidy squeezed her eyes shut and breathed. She could do this. She *had* to do this. "Hello, may I speak with Casey Conway, please?" She was proud of herself—her voice wavered only a little at the end. Mei gave her a thumbs-up.

"Yes, can I tell him who's calling?" the woman asked.

"This is Cassidy. His daughter."

Later that night, the four girls met up again over at Izzy's house for their regular Saturday night sleepover. Izzy had the biggest flat-screen TV for movie watching, and since Linc would probably be home, the chance that Tanner would be with him meant that Piper wanted to hang out there whenever possible.

Izzy and Mei had just congratulated Cassidy on getting the money from her dad. The phone call had been totally awkward, but she'd done it and he had come through. Plus, he'd sounded genuinely happy to hear from her, and had even mentioned that they should plan to get together as soon as she came back from her trip. Cassidy didn't want to raise her hopes too high, because plans with her dad had the tendency to fall through at the last minute, but it still felt good imagining it could happen.

Izzy's door banged open and Piper made her entrance, weighed down with two large Victoria's Secret bags in tow. "Good, you're all here. Because I've brought goodies!"

The change in Piper since they'd all decided to go on these trips was nothing less than manic—she'd been so low since the Kiss the Pig fiasco that Cassidy had really begun to worry for her, but now she seemed to be back to the old perpetually bright and optimistic Piper. Although now that Cassidy looked closer, Piper's eyes were a little red. Another round with her mother? Cassidy had known those blue shoes were a bad idea. She sent up a silent thank-you that her own mother was so laid back.

"Now, I know I said I wasn't going to give you these until closer to the trip," Piper trilled, "but I decided I couldn't wait. A little something from me to y'all for those unexpected, special events." She winked and handed out the little pink boxes like Santa Claus on Christmas Eve.

"You got us underwear?" Cassidy asked. "Um, no offense, Piper, but I like to buy my own panties."

"It's not underwear," she declared. "It's *lingerie*." This in her best French accent.

Mei had already opened her box and was holding up what looked to Cassidy like black polka-dotted tissue paper with two straps, and a pair of matching string bikini panties. Mei's gaping mouth said what they were all thinking.

"I thought you'd like black best, Mei—it's more demure, like you. I got you a camisole, too, so it would be warmer, 'cause I read online it gets pretty cold at night in Shenyang."

Mei examined the garments, the thin straps more like angel hair pasta than spaghetti, obviously wondering how these and "warm" belonged in the same sentence. Also, did Piper not realize that nothing was "unexpected" in Mei's hyperorganized life? And that any special events would not involve underwear purchased by someone else? "Thanks, Piper. That was really . . . thoughtful of you."

Cassidy was now wondering with one part morbid curiosity and another part total dread what she was going to find in her own gift box. Turned out, both feelings were rewarded by what she found underneath the tissue: three pairs of boy-short panties—a hot-pink-and-black-striped pair, a hot-pink cheetah pair, and a hot-pink pair covered in little red cherries. They were all cut so high in the back that her butt would be hanging out of them.

"They're called Cheekies," Piper said, "because they show your—"

"I got it," Cassidy cut her off, looking inside the box again to see if Piper had left a gift receipt. If any "special events" happened on this trip, which they probably wouldn't, Cassidy was more than certain none of these would be the underwear she would want to be wearing.

"What the hell is this?" Izzy cried. Dangling off the end of her finger was a tiny triangle of green lace and a filament of string connecting all three corners.

"It's called a Brazilian thong, and there are five of them because I didn't know how much access you would have to a washing machine in Costa Rica. Oh, and there's a push-up bra, too, for a little extra boost of confidence."

Mei's eyebrows practically touched her hairline as she picked up the bra. "If Izzy has any more 'confidence,' she'll tip over face-first."

"Is that a bra, or a melon catcher?" Cassidy asked.

Izzy pretended to look offended. "Hey, we can't all get by in a sports bra and tank top." They all burst out laughing so hard that Cassidy thought she might have pulled a muscle.

"You think this is an appropriate undergarment to wear in the rain forest, Piper?" Izzy asked, eyeing the scraps of fabric.

"What? It's Brazilian," she replied. "I got myself a sexy black bustier with match—"

The door flew open, and Linc stood in the hall, Tanner just behind him. "What the hell, Isabel," her brother said. "We can't hear our game over y'all's noise."

Linc had been in a pissy mood since he'd stupidly punched his locker and broke his hand after losing the first game of the season. Nice to know he was taking it out on his sister.

Izzy still had the thong in her hand. "Damn, Izzy, put those away. I don't want to see that," Linc said.

"Hey, Tanner," Piper said, all flirtatious smile. "Do you prefer lace or thong panties?" She held up a pair of each that she'd grabbed from the girls' gift boxes.

Ugh. Cassidy wished Piper would stop trying so hard to make Tanner notice her every chance she got. It sucked watching your best friend waste her time on someone who obviously wasn't interested. But at least Tanner was a decent guy—except for his Germaine problem, that is.

Unlike Linc, who commented, "Shouldn't you be asking a pig?" The urge to break his other hand started to bring Cass to her feet.

Luckily, Mei saved her the trouble by saying, "If she'd asked you, she *would* have been asking a pig. That's why she asked Tanner."

Linc's walnut-sized brain struggled for a response. When nothing came, he elbowed Tanner and asked, "Does Germaine even wear panties?"

Jeez, did putting a football in a guy's hand turn him into a jerk, or was it that only jerks played football? It was an age-old riddle Cassidy had yet to solve.

Tanner just grinned. "Nice panties, Isabel."

"Nice gun, Derringer," Izzy quipped, but by then he'd already disappeared down the hall with Linc. "Damn it. Why can't I be quicker on the uptake?" She made a disgusted face before throwing the thong back into the box.

Piper looked disappointed that Tanner hadn't answered *her* question.

"Okay, then," Mei cut in. "We have other things we need to get done tonight."

"I hope so," Cassidy said.

"Me, too," Izzy agreed.

Mei took out her laptop. "We need to come up with avatars to go with our IKC pseudonyms—you know, something unique to each of us, but not too revealing."

"Definitely not pictures of us in our new underwear, then," Izzy snickered.

"*Lingerie*," Piper corrected. She grabbed a camera off Izzy's desk and flicked it on. She panned around the room, focusing on Mei's laptop case resting against her calf. Piper crouched down to shoe level and snapped a couple of shots. Then she jumped to her feet in triumph. She turned the camera around to reveal the picture to the others. The laptop bag dominated the left side of the photo, the toes of Mei's funky Doc Martens extended beyond the edge of the bag. Studious with a dash of edgy. It was so Mei.

"Oooh, I love it!" Piper cried in excitement.

She hopped up and dashed for the pile of junk she carted with her to every sleepover, pulling out her brand-new pair of blue shoes. She slipped them on and gazed around the room. "I don't have a good bag."

"Sure you do," Izzy chimed in. She pointed to the vintage train case that Piper had inherited from her grandmother. It was white with pink trim and looked like a miniature suitcase. Piper stored her ever-growing stash of cosmetics in the chic little bag.

A few minutes later, they had the perfect shot of Piper's Smurf-blue shoes kicking above the cosmetics case.

Cassidy's shot was simpler: her aqua Vans against the sports duffel she usually carried to practice.

Izzy dug in her closet to find her new favorite shoes, her Simple Mary Jane sneakers made from hemp and recycled tires. She posed them on either side of the hiking backpack she'd bought for Costa Rica.

Once Mei had loaded all of the pictures onto the page, she looked up. "That's done," she said. "I can check it off my list."

Good. One step closer to getting the hell out of Paris. Now that Cassidy knew for sure she could pay for the trip, all this other stuff: the Facebook page, the kissing—should there be any—it was all icing.

Especially the kissing. She glanced down at the cherry-print Cheekies—the kissing could be the cherry on top.

IKC Fan Page

The Official Fan Page for the International Kissing Club

4

people like this

🗨 IKC Page

Mulan Testing: 1, 2, 3. Testing: 1, 2, 3.

Ariel Only 6 days until IKC hits international air space.

Rapunzel What's Vegemite? And is it going to make my breath smell bad?

> **Ariel** Oh God, yes! Avoid it at all costs. Wikipedia says it's horrible.
>
> **Mulan** I guess when a country starts as a penal colony, you take what you can get.

Mulan Btw, has everyone confirmed their flights? And selected their seats? I'm in 26C.

> **Rapunzel** Great, now your stalker knows where to find you. Don't post that crap. Remember that's why we're not doing this on Foursquare.
>
> **Ariel** I've been reviewing my airplane dining options. I think I'll order the cheese tray. Very French.
>
> **Rapunzel** Must be nice to fly first class. I'll probably be stuck eating a Vegemite sundae.
>
> **Mulan** Um, I think they serve it on crackers.

Ariel Emergency meeting! Desperate. Need help. My house at 7:00.

> **Rapunzel** Mulan, do you need us to Foursquare that location for you?

Chapter 7
Izzy

If it hadn't been for the word "emergency," Izzy would have ignored the post on the IKC Facebook page. Piper, Mei, and Cassidy had been shooting messages back and forth nonstop since first devising the club. For a while she'd been as excited as they were, but that had all changed this past Monday when her parents had told her the news: there wasn't enough money for her to go on the trip. When her idiot brother had broken his hand, he'd blown his shot at a scholarship from the University of Texas. Unless he had the healing powers of a super-hero, he'd be out for the rest of the season and there was no way UT would give a scholarship to someone who'd spent the year on the bench. Plus, her mom was plotting to send Shane to New York for the qualifying round of some international piano competition that no one under the age of ninety-eight would be interested in. Because of all this, her parents were too broke to send Izzy to Costa Rica. Since then, she'd been dodging her friends at school and online.

Now she felt a faint glimmer of hope. Emergency meeting? Maybe she wasn't the only one. If her parents could overspend, it wasn't out of the realm of possibility that Piper's had, too.

Ten minutes later, she pulled Brittney into the empty space in front of Piper's house. Today, she didn't dare curse at the car the way she sometimes did. Who knew how much longer she'd have a car to curse at?

She found her friends up in Piper's room. Mei lay sprawled across Piper's rumpled bed, flipping through a magazine. Cassidy perched on the back of an armchair, her feet on the seat, her elbows propped on her knees. Piper stood before the closet doors, along the top of which she'd hung a half-dozen hangers of clothes. Two suitcases lay open at her feet.

"What's up?" Izzy asked, sitting on the edge of the bed beside Mei. "What's the big emergency?" She hadn't yet told them her news. Her throat tightened just thinking about it, and she was glad she'd been able to talk without her voice sounding all funny.

"Piper's having wardrobe malfunctions," Mei said dryly.

"It's a disaster! I have no idea what to pack." Piper gestured to the hanger on one side of her and then to the other. "What do you think— the flutter cardigan or the silk-screened hoodie?"

"That's your big emergency?" Izzy stood up. "You don't know what to bring?"

"It can't all be about saving the world, you know." Clearly Piper heard the annoyance in Izzy's voice and just chose to ignore it.

Ever since devising IKC, Piper had been inhabiting her own little universe. Not that Izzy blamed her. It wasn't like she'd want to be a pig-kissing Internet sensation, either. But really, right now, there was only so much giddy joy she could take.

"I mean, it's Paris!" Piper was saying. "Probably the most fashionable place on earth. Nothing I own is going to look right." She crossed to the bed and flopped down backward on it, barely noticing that Mei had to roll out of the way to avoid being squashed. "I'm doomed."

Izzy shoved her hands into her back pockets. "You get to go to Paris. I seriously doubt anyone's going to notice what you're wearing."

Mei looked up from her magazine and cocked her head to the side as she studied Izzy.

Izzy didn't meet her gaze but paced over to the closet, trying— really trying—to consider her friend's clothing options past the haze of her own resentment. So far, not happening.

"You're right," Piper muttered. "Nothing I own is cool enough for Paris—it all shouts small-town reject. Mom said she was going to give me a spending allowance. Maybe I can shop there."

The spending allowance pushed Izzy right over the edge. She whirled around and glared at Piper, and her words came out in an angry rush. "I can't believe you expected us to drop everything and run over here for this big *emergency* and all you're worried about is what to pack. Why are we supposed to even care what color beret you wear?"

As soon as the sentence left her mouth, Izzy clamped her lips shut, wishing she could take it back.

Cassidy's head snapped up. Mei's gaze became more interested. Slowly Piper raised herself up onto her elbows.

"Wow," Piper whispered, her eyes wide. "Where did that come from?"

"I—" But, damn it, how could she explain? "I've just been in a rotten mood lately."

Piper smiled brightly. "I know what'll cheer you up. This morning on Facebook, I noticed that a certain sexy eco-guy has posted new pictures on his page."

"Oh, Piper, I really don't think . . ."

Piper didn't even hear Izzy's protests. She swept over to her laptop and popped it open before Izzy could even finish the sentence.

"You know River and I broke up, right?"

"So?" Piper looked over her shoulder with a quirky grin as she quickly navigated through the maze that was Facebook.

"So, I unfriended him." She'd done it eight days after the kegger, right about the time he left for Lubbock. By then, it was obvious he wasn't going to call her. "I'm not interested in what he's doing."

"That's just because you haven't seen how pathetic and sad he looks without you."

"He looks pathetic and sad without me?" She nearly cringed at the note of hope in her voice. Pathetic indeed.

"Why wouldn't he? He doesn't have you anymore, right? Okay, here's his—"

Mei put her hand over Piper's mouse just before she could click. "Maybe you should let it go. If Izzy unfriended him, then she doesn't want to see the pictures."

"Of course she does." Piper clicked.

"No really, I don't—"

Piper clicked again. A second later, the first of the photos loaded. Silence fell over the room.

It was a picture of a shiny white Cadillac Escalade. Leaning against the bumper was some blond chick with big hair, big boobs, daisy dukes, bikini on top.

The image was labeled, "New college, new toys, new major."

Izzy felt like the world was telescoping down to just that photo. Her peripheral vision faded out, and she could hear Mei, Cassidy, and Piper talking as if from far away.

"Holy crap," Cassidy muttered.

"The bastard!" Piper cried.

After a moment, Mei asked, "Does that sign behind him say, The Department of Petroleum Engineering?"

Izzy ripped her gaze away from Bikini Barbie and found the granite sign River's Escalade was parked in front of. Sure enough. *That* was his new major. Freakin' Petroleum Engineering.

Three weeks ago, she'd had a boyfriend who was completely devoted to her, who she believed valued all the things she held most dear. Yes, he'd been leaving for college nine hours away. And yes, he'd told her they should break up now rather than try to do the long-distance thing. But she'd never—not in a million years—have dreamed he'd run off to Lubbock and do crazy shit like this.

Nausea hit the back of her throat like a ninja. He'd betrayed her. The blonde wasn't even the worst part. He'd lied about everything—about who he was. About everything he believed.

Sleeping with a guy who'd just broken up with you, but who you loved and admired . . . that was almost like saying good-bye. Sleeping with a liar, and an oil-sucking one at that, well, that was just . . . incredibly stupid.

Izzy felt like she couldn't breathe. Unable to swallow the emotion building in her chest, she stormed out of Piper's room and tromped down the stairs, making a beeline for the sliding glass doors leading onto the patio.

The Douglases' backyard was landscaped like a tropical paradise. The kidney-shaped pool dominated the oasis, a rock waterfall tinkling away at one end. Near the back door, potted palms and over-sized umbrellas shaded the elegant furniture. On a table sat a tray with three pillar candles nestled into a base of smooth river rocks.

Her muscles itching to throw something, Izzy palmed several of the rocks and moved to the edge of the pool. For a second she just stood there, staring into the pristine aqua depths. Then she pulled back her arm, let loose one of the rocks, and watched it skip across the surface before sinking into the pool's depths. One for her friends, who hadn't even noticed she was upset. One for her parents, who were always putting her needs dead last. One for the trip she couldn't take. One for the job she'd have to get. One for the guys she wouldn't be kissing.

She was out of rocks. But not out of anger. She slipped her hand into the pocket of her favorite cargo pants. Her fingertips touched smooth plastic—her earrings. The delicate leaves of some Amazonian plant that had been encased in epoxy. The present River had brought back for her from his trip to the Brazilian rain forest last year. For weeks now, she'd been carrying the earrings around, unable to wear them—'cause they kind of made her want to puke now—but also unable to just get rid of them.

Now she wrapped her fist around them, pulled them out of her pocket, and hurled them into the water.

Where they floated.

Ah, crap.

Behind her, she heard the door slide open. Mei, Cassidy, and Piper had made it out just in time to see the last of her temper tantrum.

Double crap.

If they'd been here ninety seconds ago, she wouldn't have thrown the earrings. After all, she'd worn them nearly every day for almost a year. If they knew she'd thrown them into the pool, they'd freak out and demand answers. More in-depth answers than River's stupid Facebook post could explain.

Sink, damn it! But they didn't sink. They'd always been suspiciously light. He probably ordered them in bulk on eBay and gave them to all his girlfriends. The jerk.

Not giving herself time to think it through, she toed off her shoes, yanked her shirt over her head, and then shucked her pants. Fury gave spring to her muscles as she dove cleanly into the pool.

Her body sliced through the cool water, washing away the heat of her anger, soothing the prickling irritation of her skin. She swam to the bottom, the chlorine stinging her eyes as she searched for the stones she'd thrown. One by one, she plucked them off the bottom of the pool until her lungs were burning. Looking up at the surface, she saw the earrings floating just above her head. She kicked off, her empty left hand stretched above her. She snatched the earrings out of the water just before she broke the surface.

Heavy with rocks and disappointment, she swam awkwardly to the steps, climbed out, and sat on the edge of the pool. The limestone pavers were hot through the damp cotton of her underwear. Despite the late afternoon sun beating down on her, an icy shiver chased across her skin. She pulled her legs in to her chest and wrapped her arms around her knees, curling up like a baby chick still in its shell.

Keeping the earrings in her palm, she let the rocks fall from her hand to the ground beside her.

"I didn't want them to clog up the system," she said into the stunned silence.

Someone, Mei probably, draped a towel across her shoulder. She grabbed the ends and pulled it tight, then stood. She could just imagine what they must be thinking: *Oh, crap. Here she goes again.*

Jeez, it was what *she* was thinking, too.

And she could hear them whispering behind her.

"What do you think she's going to do?" Cassidy spoke in a whispered hiss.

"Should we check her for new piercings?" Piper asked.

That had been just over a year ago. She still had a faint scar just to the left of her belly button. That one had hurt like hell. And gotten infected. Which was *so* not sexy.

"Duh," Cassidy muttered. "She's not going to do the same thing twice."

Piper sat down beside her and rubbed a hand across her shoulder in a way meant to be soothing. "Iz, you can stay at my house if you want to run away again. I bet my mom wouldn't notice for—"

"Shut up, Pipes," Cassidy said, cutting her off.

"I'm sure your parents would notice this time," Mei said, but her voice lacked conviction.

Izzy stood up. "I'm fine." Her friends looked at her with serious doubt in their eyes. "Really, I'm fine." She gave her body a quick once-over with the towel and then reached for her pants. As she pulled them on, she slipped the earrings back into her pocket.

"Iz, you just stripped naked and jumped into my pool." Piper, always there to state the obvious. "I don't think you're fine."

The earrings would have been so much easier to explain than jumping into the pool naked. Clearly, she had not thought this through.

"I'm not upset about River."

"Yeah, right," Cassidy said doubtfully.

"I knew it was over when he left for Texas Tech. We broke up weeks ago."

"Why didn't you tell us?" Piper demanded.

"She did," Cassidy pointed out.

"But they hooked up again at the party. If they broke up after that, she should have said so."

"Why?" Cassidy demanded of Piper. "We're her friends. Not her therapist. She can break up with whoever she wants."

"Yo!" Izzy waved her hands between them. "That isn't what I'm upset about!"

They stopped, both turning to stare at her. Then Piper asked the question Izzy had been dreading. "Then what the hell is wrong with you?"

"Isn't it obvious?" Mei asked. "She can't go on her trip."

"What?" Piper leaped to her feet. "That can't be true."

"Huh?" Cassidy's mouth hung open in obvious shock.

Izzy could only nod as she choked back the tears that had been pressed against her eyes for the past week. She met Mei's gaze. "How did—"

"I overheard Mr. Szachowicz saying that if your brother didn't play this fall, there's no way UT is going to give him a scholarship, regardless of who your father knows. I didn't think much of it, but then—" Mei shrugged. "You stopped responding to texts. You never posted on the IKC page. I figured something had to be up."

"What does her brother playing football for UT have to do with her trip?" Piper's voice was thick with indignation.

Mei leveled her practical gaze at Piper. "If her parents were counting on a football scholarship, then this ruined everything. His grades aren't good enough for him to get into one of the top-tier colleges. And maybe they can't afford to send him at all. They have to think about Linc's future."

Leave it to Mei to put the pieces together so succinctly. "She's right," Izzy said. "Without the scholarship, Linc might not be able to go to college at all, even if he could get in."

"It's not fair!" Piper protested.

"You don't have to tell me that." Not fair was pretty much the rules of the road in her house. For her father, football was everything. For her mother, it was Shane. And there she was, trapped in the middle. The only unexceptional member of the family. With her nimble-footed dolt of an older brother scoring touchdowns and her nimble-fingered baby brother storming the competition circuit, there was more than enough talent in the family to satisfy both her parents. Unfortunately, none of it was hers. As a result, anything that had to do with her came in last. She'd thought she was used to it.

Cassidy was shaking her head. "It doesn't make any sense. You live in one of those big old houses near the square. I thought you guys were loaded."

And they should have been. When her dad had left the University of Texas, he'd walked away with a lot of money. The Paris Independent School District had lured her father there with visions of building a state championship team. Her parents had sold their old house in Austin and bought a 1920s foursquare in the historic district of Paris. Even without her mom's salary as a lawyer, they should have been okay. But it wasn't cheap for her mother to cart Shane around to all those competitions, and the price tag would only inch up as he got older.

Still, they might have been fine, if her father hadn't gone and bought the ranch outside of town and started running cattle on it. *Our nest egg*, her father called it. But under her breath, Izzy's mom always called it *the money pit*. Not that Shane's baby grand had been precisely cheap. Still, if her parents were having trouble scraping together money for college, Izzy suspected that damn ranch was to blame. Turned out, beef was bad for more than just the environment.

"I think my parents are just really shitty planners."

We really wanted to send you, honey, her mother had cooed at her last week. *But it's just not going to work out. You understand, don't you?*

Cassidy frowned. "But they already paid for it. They were on board from the beginning. Not going doesn't save anything."

Izzy pulled her shirt back on. She'd gone over all of this with her parents. Again and again. She didn't want to dissect it with her friends, too, like one of those poor frogs in biology class. But she knew they wouldn't let it alone.

"My parents just paid the deposit. So we're only out two hundred dollars there."

"The airline ticket," Cassidy protested. "You've already paid for that, too, right? And that's nonrefundable."

"It's exchangeable." She sighed. "My mom and Shane are going to use the tickets to hit the qualifying rounds of some big competition in New York in the spring. They said there's no money for anything extra. Not the rest of the fees, not the cost of books and supplies. Not any spending money."

"What are you going to do, Iz?" Mei asked, her voice quiet.

"I'm going to stay here and get a job." The resolve in her voice surprised her, because she hadn't thought it through until just this second. One thing she knew: she wasn't going to let this happen again. She was done relying on her parents. "And I'm going to study my ass off for the SAT. If there's not enough money for them to send Linc to college without a scholarship, then you can bet there's not enough money for me, either. Plus, I'm going to need money for gas—if I even get to keep Brittney."

Cassidy sucked in a sharp breath. "Your car. They can't make you sell your car! That's your freedom."

"Forget the car," Piper jumped in. "Screw that! Sell the damn car and use the money to pay for the trip to Costa Rica!"

Izzy nearly smiled at Piper's indignation. "Sorry. It's a done deal. They've already canceled everything."

"No way." Piper poked a finger up in the air like she was leading troops into battle. "We're the International Kissing Club. We're not leaving a member behind while the rest go off to have a grand adventure."

"Really, it's fine. I'll—"

"I'll stay, too," Mei interrupted softly.

All heads swiveled in her direction.

Mei nodded with stoic resolve. "Piper is right. You shouldn't have to stay here alone just because your brother's a dick. I'll stay behind to keep you company."

Izzy's throat constricted and the tears she'd been trying so hard to keep in check finally spilled out. "Thanks, Mei." For a second, she even considered it, how nice it would be to have a friend with her for the next ten weeks.

It wouldn't be Costa Rica. It wouldn't be living in the rain forest, helping the researchers who were—literally—going to save the world someday. It would still be another ten weeks trapped in tiny, boring Paris, Texas, where gas-guzzling SUVs ruled. But at least she wouldn't be alone. She'd have a friend with her. A friend who had given up on her own dream to keep her company.

Finally, Izzy shook her head. "I can't ask you to do that. I wouldn't be a very good friend if I let you stay behind. Going to China is just as important to you as going to Costa Rica was to me."

She studied Mei, who hadn't been back to China since her parents adopted her when she was two. Who rarely got any closer to Chinese culture than the Panda Express in Sherman.

Izzy managed to dredge up a chuckle. "Who am I kidding? Going to China is way more important to you."

Piper sat down beside her and wrapped an arm across her shoulder, bumping her head against Izzy's. "Are you sure? We could all stay."

"Don't be silly." But she had to swallow back another wave of tears. "I'm just not used to being the one left behind."

Then her gaze darted to Cassidy as it hit her. This must be how Cassidy had felt all their lives. All the times they'd gone off to summer camp or to Six Flags in Dallas for the weekend. They'd never meant to exclude Cassidy, but there'd simply been things she couldn't afford to do or work she couldn't get out of. Somehow, Cassidy always bore it with a grin. She'd wave them off with a cheerful good-bye. "Have fun storming the castle," she'd say, quoting *The Princess Bride*.

Now, feeling slightly sick to her stomach, she looked at Cassidy and tried to smile. "Boy, this staying-behind thing really sucks. I'm sorry, Cass. I didn't know."

Cass just smiled, not her normal cheerful smile, but one that was a little sad. "I'm sorry, too."

· · · · · ·✈

Three days later, all four of them loaded up Brittney, and together they made the three-hour drive to Dallas/Fort Worth International Airport. The windows were down to hold the bungee cords strapping Piper's extra suitcase to the roof. At first, Izzy had only planned on driving Cassidy, whose mother had to work and couldn't bring her. Then, since all their flights left on the same day, Piper had decided it would make a fun road trip.

Mei's parents had been the holdouts. Susan cried at the thought of not bringing Mei to the airport to see her off, but Mei's feisty grandmother, Janece, had faked a fall to convince her to stay behind so Mei could make the trip with the rest of her friends.

They spent the drive singing along to their favorite songs and gossiping about the kids at school. Piper's flight was around noon, but Mei and Cassidy would have to hang out at the airport most of the day before their flights later in the evening. Mostly, Izzy tried not to think about them, waiting in the airport, browsing the shops, and eating at the food court. No matter how bad airport food was, she knew they wouldn't mind. It was the start of an adventure. One she wouldn't be going on.

Still, Izzy managed to push down her sadness until the moment they all stood outside the security check point. With their boarding passes in hand and their suitcases already checked, the girls waited to get in line as long as they could. Finally, it was Izzy who said, "Come on, you've got to go. Piper, your flight boards in twenty minutes and you don't know how long this line will take." She gave Piper's shoulder a friendly shove. "Just go already."

"Okay, okay." Piper held up her hands in a sign of surrender. "I'm going."

Mei and Cassidy looked at each other. "Our flights don't leave for hours," Cassidy said. "We'll hang out here with Iz for a while."

Izzy forced a smile. "No, it's okay. Really." She pulled out her phone to check the time. "I've got to get back anyway. I'm stopping by DQ to pick up an application."

Mei cringed. "I can't believe you're going to apply at Dairy Queen."

Cassidy smiled too brightly. "Hey, free Blizzards. You can't argue with that."

Izzy tried again to smile. "It'll keep me busy. Besides, I can start saving for next year's exchange program."

Finally, Piper laughed, pulled everyone into a big hug, and whispered, "You should still kiss as many boys as you can, Izzy. We'll make a special exception for you and allow boys from other counties as well as other countries."

A few minutes later, just before Piper, Mei, and Cassidy disappeared into the crowd of international travelers, Izzy gave one final wave and called out, "Have fun storming the castle."

When the last of them vanished through the metal detectors, she headed out to her car and started the long, lonely drive back to Paris, Texas. North of Dallas, she pulled off the highway into a parking lot and burst into tears. She cried until she almost couldn't breathe. Then, when she opened her eyes, she realized she was in the parking lot of a Panda Express. And she laughed.

IKC Fan Page

The Official Fan Page for the International Kissing Club

15

people like this

🗨 IKC Page

Jane
Just dropped off IKC at the airport. Stopped at Panda Express in Sherman on the way home. Mulan, I envy all the great Chinese food you're going to eat. Off to study SAT vocabulary. Have fun storming the castle!

Ariel
Arrived in Paris. Ooh là là! Am eating French pastries and craving French guys! The shopping is already fabulous and I haven't even left the airport! Seriously, the shops at the airport are better than at Stonebriar mall. I'm at the Chanel counter! In Paris! Paris!

> **Ariel** Paris!
>
> **Jane** Yeah. We get it. I'm in Paris, too. :P
>
> **Rapunzel** I haven't even made it out of the country yet! I'm stranded in LAX hell and kind of wishing I'd brought a toothbrush in my carry-on.
>
> **Mulan** I thought I suggested it. Sorry!

Karrie Meeker
V. cool page. Just Liked it. I kissed a boy in Playa del Carmen. He was muy delicioso. So that means three points for me, right?

> **Jane** Absolutely! Hey, Mermaid girl, you're already behind.
>
> **Ariel** Not for long. I'm prepping my lips now with my new gloss from Chanel.

Chapter 8
Mei

Bleary-eyed and trembling from fatigue and nerves (she wasn't a great flyer), Mei deplaned and trudged up the ramp at the Shenyang airport, rolling her spiffy new Samsonite carry-on with the extra-padded laptop compartment. At the opened double doors to the terminal, she paused. The airport was bustling even at this early hour, not unlike a major American airport. Except that here, everyone looked like her.

Never in her life had she seen so many Chinese people in one place. Of course, this was China, her practical voice reminded her. But knowing something and seeing it were two different things. Mei looked up and down the wide airport corridor and all she saw, except for the American businessmen who had been on her flight, were Chinese people. It was odd, but exciting.

She located a sign overhead with a little cartoon picture of a suit-case and guessed that it pointed the way to the baggage claim. She merged into the throng of luggage-toting people heading in the same direction, and, for the first time in her life, she blended into the crowd. Everything about the outward appearance of these people was famil-iar. Though their rapid-fire, singsong voices sounded completely for-eign to her, and she could barely discern a word here or there, the intricacy of the sound spoke to her on a soul-deep level.

As she made her way up to the baggage return with her plane's flight number on it, she couldn't help feeling a profound sense of relief. Though she hadn't admitted it to anyone—had barely admitted it to herself—she'd been worried about coming to China.

Worried about the fact that she didn't speak the language.

Worried about the possibility that she wouldn't fit in here any better than she fit in in Paris, Texas. But already her fears were going away, the strange connection she felt to China assuaging even the darkest ones. She belonged here.

It took her only about ten minutes to get her luggage, but it took another hour to clear customs and exchange her American currency for Chinese renminbis. By the time she stumbled onto the curb outside the airport, she was nearly catatonic. Sure, being around all these people who looked like her had energized her at first, but that second wind was fading fast. She had left home over twenty-four hours ago, and the lack of sleep had definitely caught up with her.

She'd been a little concerned about catching a cab, but there was a long line waiting to pick up passengers. Some were green, some were maroon, and as she walked toward them she wondered if there was a difference. She had printed out directions from the airport to the Shenyang Secondary School from Google before she'd left home, then run them through Google translator in simplified Chinese. She only hoped they were good enough to get her where she needed to go.

Squaring her shoulders, she headed toward the nearest cab. The driver took one look at her and spoke in Mandarin so fast she could barely distinguish the sounds, let alone understand the words he was saying.

When he finally wound down, she began to recite the phrase she had rehearsed on the airplane numerous times. Despite her practice, the words were slow and halting. "I need to get to Shenyang Secondary School. Can you take me there?"

The driver grinned when he heard her accent, and then it was his turn to speak in broken syllables. "You speak English?" he asked carefully.

"Yes," she answered, relieved. "I need to go to—"

He shook his head and spoke a bunch more Mandarin and she realized, with a sinking stomach, that those three words had exhausted his supply of English. Reaching into her laptop carrier, she pulled out the address and directions she'd printed the day before. She handed the papers to him and he took them, nodding.

Then he said in deliberately slow and simple Mandarin, "You go to school?"

"Yes," she answered.

He opened his trunk and reached for her suitcase. With a sigh of relief, Mei watched as he secured the bag. Then she slipped into the back and rested her head against the seat.

The driver started the car and pulled away from the curb with a bang. As he drove, he chattered at her so quickly she had no hope of understanding. She tried her best, but she was so tired that her concentration was almost completely shot. Finally, she gave up and sat back in silence.

She glanced out the window and watched the city passing by in a blur. Though they were on side streets, the cabbie was driving like a NASCAR racer. Every time a sign came up and she tried to read it, they zoomed past before she could catch more than one or two characters.

They drove into a more heavily populated area, and she was relieved, figuring the presence of pedestrians everywhere would make the driver slow down. But it was as if he didn't even see them. He careened around a corner and Mei clung to the seat in front of her, eyes squeezed tightly shut, as she waited for him to crash into something or someone.

When nothing happened, she risked a look and then almost wished she hadn't. A truck barreled toward them, looming huge in the window. Just as she was certain her life was going to end, the driver took another left then a quick right.

And then things got a lot calmer.

They were on a small, shop-lined side street now, and Mei peered out the window, fascinated by the bright colors and teeming masses. People were everywhere, in the shops, on the streets, spilling onto small balconies dotting the sides of the tall white buildings that stretched far above her. Many of the balconies held four or five people, despite their being no larger than a bathroom stall back home. As she absorbed everything around her, Mei had the fleeting thought that the entire population of Paris could squeeze into this crowded street alone.

The driver said something else to her in Mandarin, and Mei nodded blankly. It wasn't until he pulled the car right up onto the sidewalk and stopped that she realized they had arrived at her destination.

Taking a deep breath, she climbed out of the car and stared at the school that already felt familiar to her. She had spent so much time on its website and Google Earth these past two weeks that she could tell apart the huge, cream-colored buildings with their turquoise roofs. The one right in front of her, with its round turrets and soaring steeples, was the administration building. The larger buildings behind it were where classes were held. The ornate one to the right was the library, and the cluster of squat, square buildings to the left were the dorms.

Her ability to distinguish one building from the next calmed down the last of the butterflies in her stomach, and Mei was grinning as she reached into her bag to pay the cabbie. After he gave her her change, she grabbed her bags and headed through the iron fence and up the long brick walkway that led to the administration building.

Students milled around the beautifully landscaped grounds, dressed in uniforms and carrying books as they chattered to each other in Mandarin. None of them paid any attention to her, and the lack of questioning stares thrilled her as nothing else could. For the first time in her life, she was not "the little Chinese girl," a curiosity in a town populated by descendants of Anglo-Saxon pioneers who had lived there for generations. Her ancestors had lived here for millennia.

Already, deep in her bones she felt a connection to these people and this place.

Her ethnicity wouldn't separate her here; she was part of the same community. Her heritage, her identity, came from this place, and if she was very lucky, maybe she would find a clue to her birth parents in the following weeks.

Either way, she was home.

Or she was in hell. She couldn't quite decide which, but at the moment she was definitely leaning toward the latter. Mei had chosen Shenyang Secondary School after seeing the brochure and reading testimonials on its website. Large, beautiful, and filled with pride in China's long history, it offered a full language immersion program and a strong cultural emphasis that she hoped would really help with the discovery of her Chinese identity.

But now, standing before the school's director—who was in the middle of dictating an endless list of rules and regulations about what she could and could not do during her stay—Mei just hoped she had some identity, *any identity*, left when she got back home. Although, at this point, she'd settle for having a smidgen of identity left when she finally escaped this office.

No nail polish. Mei curled her black-tipped fingers into her fists.

One single pair of earrings at a time. Studs. Mei tossed her hair to hide the multiple piercings along the curves of both ears.

"You will need to purchase a uniform, which you will wear always during class," said Director Song, her glossy black hair pulled into a severe knot, her gray suit tailored with military precision. "Though you may, of course, wear your own clothing for after school hours."

Well, at least that's something, Mei thought—she couldn't even imagine wearing the same navy polo top and matching pants from morning to night, every day of her time here.

"You will be attending ten class sessions a day, including physical education. We can provide you with a tutor to help with your Mandarin during classes. Also, you will have two *hao you* assigned to you, 'buddies' who speak English and who can help guide you through your immersion experience at our school."

The door to Director Song's office opened and two girls, both in ponytails, came in wearing the plain, yet seemingly comfortable uniform.

"Mei, this is Dao-Ming and Bao, they will be your *hao you* while you are here. They will show you to your dormitory and help you find your classes each day."

Mei smiled, eager to make new friends. Dao-Ming's and Bao's smiles faltered almost immediately when they saw her, making her own smile a little less bright. She didn't know why, but she had the distinct impression that they were disappointed by her. Maybe it was the nail polish . . .

Speaking in very slow, very precise English, the girls assured Director Song that they were happy to help Mei get settled in.

Then they left the office, leaving Mei to follow, dragging her suitcase behind her. "Thank you for your help," she offered in English when they didn't speak to her. The two glanced back in unison, then shot each other a look that did nothing to alleviate her initial feeling that they were less than pleased with their charge.

The three of them made their way down the school's long institutional hallways, with doors branching off in both directions. Mei peered into the classrooms, seeing scores of uniformed students seated in uniform rows, each classroom looking almost identical to the one before it. Maybe this was where she got her appreciation for order and organization, she thought—it seemed to be a running theme at this school, anyway.

Across a beautiful courtyard, Dao-Ming and Bao brought her to the dormitory building.

"This is your room," Dao-Ming said when they reached the last door at the end of a long hall on the third floor. The girl unlocked it and then handed the key to Mei. "You will be the only one in this room, as we have no other American students at the school right now."

Mei walked in, her shoulders sagging with disappointment. The room—her home for the next ten weeks—made the school's spartan halls seem positively opulent by comparison. A metal twin bed lined each wall, along with a wooden desk. But that was it. No dresser. No nightstand. No blankets. The place had all the warmth and comfiness of a maximum-security prison cell. Were she Piper, she'd have this place whipped into a charming pied-à-terre by the end of the day, but Mei could see nothing beyond the drab gray walls and concrete floor.

At least the large square window in the room overlooked the courtyard below.

Dao-Ming stood at the window. "There is the cafeteria." She pointed to the east building. "In there is the gymnasium." She pointed to the west building. Then she headed to the door. "Your schedule will have the room number printed next to each class."

"Thank you," Mei said. "Hey, maybe we can eat together? I would very much like to be friends." She hoped that if she reached out to them they would reciprocate.

Dao-Ming gave her a look of unconcealed scorn that bared an uncanny resemblance to one of Germaine's. "You may dress American and act American and talk American," she said, attempting an exaggerated flat accent that Mei supposed was her attempt at "American." "But you're just another Chinese girl. Nothing special here."

"A Chinese girl nobody wanted," Bao added, her English words stiff, but still able to get her point across with a heavy dose of contempt.

"We have enough Chinese friends already, we don't need another one. So I hope your Mandarin is better than Bao's English," Dao-Ming finished, and then they were gone.

Stunned but too tired to respond, Mei sank onto her bed. Part of her wanted to chase after them, to ask why they wouldn't even give her a chance. But one look down at the quad and she knew she wouldn't have a chance of finding the girls. In their uniforms, everyone looked the same. Plus, if she didn't get some sleep, she would lose all ability to function. Her first day had been bad enough without her descending into a drooling, incoherent mess. Besides, she hoped everything would look better after she got some sleep.

By the next day, however, Mei had figured out that hope did not always spring eternal. And here in China, it didn't even spring internal.

Was this how Piper had felt at the height of the pig debacle? Or had she felt even worse? For the first time, Mei wondered if maybe she hadn't been sympathetic enough. Because being ostracized sucked. Big-time. Even for a day.

Not to mention the huge clusterjam that was her academic schedule. Turns out that three semesters of online language courses from Paris Community College and a Rosetta Stone DVD were not enough to get a person through eight hours of school taught fully in Mandarin. Mei spent most of her class time sitting in the back of the room using her phone's translation app to cobble together enough words for general understanding of what was being taught.

Math, at least, was a universal language, and if not for the trigonometry and physics classes, these next ten weeks would be a complete waste of her time, scholastically speaking. If she wanted to put a positive spin on things, she could say it was good she didn't have to consider a social calendar *at all,* leaving her to devote the entirety of her free time to her studies.

As for her tutor . . . it turned out he was Dao-Ming's boyfriend. And at Shenyang Secondary School, nobody crossed Dao-Ming. Which left Mei not only tutorless but completely friendless as well.

When her last class of the day ended, she decided that enough was enough. If she had to spend one more second in this imitation of a Chinese prison, she was going to completely blow a gasket. Maybe even two.

Stopping by her dorm room just long enough to drop off her backpack, change clothes, and grab some money, Mei headed straight toward the huge black gates and ornately cut hedges that marked the entrance into the school. As she walked, she tried to ignore the fact that all around her students had melded into laughing, Mandarin-speaking groups. Looking at them reminded her too much of her life back in Paris and the way she, Piper, Izzy, and Cassidy usually spent their free time.

The second she stepped onto the street outside the school, Mei was assaulted by colored lights from all directions. It was already dark out, and the reds and blues and yellows flashing from every sign and window blinded her. She blinked, tried to adjust, and somehow managed to stumble straight into the path of an oncoming bicycle.

Her eyes focused just in time to see the two-wheeled behemoth bearing down on her and she jumped out of the way, but not before the rider shook a fist at her and screamed. She didn't understand the words coming out of his mouth, but she had a feeling they closely resembled the ones Piper's mother had said after she'd seen her daughter front and center on the Kiss the Pig Facebook page.

Terrific. She'd been off school grounds for all of three minutes and she'd already almost died. She was stressed out, intimidated, and just a little bit scared of Shenyang. It was a small city by Chinese standards, but those standards were relative. In this case, they meant several million people. And she'd thought Dallas was crowded . . .

Another bicycle passed her, and this time its rider knocked her into one of the parked cars hard enough to bruise her elbow. Jeez. This was ridiculous. She glanced behind her at the school, so austere and imposing, and thought seriously of spending the rest of the night alone in her dorm room.

But she hadn't come to China to hide in an eight-by-eight room all the time. Besides, she'd already learned everything about herself that that room could teach her and it hadn't taken long.

Ignoring the insistent throb in her elbow, Mei pushed herself off the car and back into the fairly imposing foot and bike traffic currently taking up the sidewalks. No. She wasn't going back to the school. At least not yet. She was in China. It was time she started acting like it.

Next stop: Chinese music store or bust.

IKC Fan Page

The Official Fan Page for the International Kissing Club

50

people like this

 IKC Page

Jane Where is everyone?

> **Jane** Helloooooo . . . llooo . . . oooooo . . .
>
> **Jane** PE sux sooooo much more without you here.
>
> **Jane** Karrie? You there?
>
> **Idina V.** I'm here. Just got back from Rio. Two points for me.
>
> **Slim Smallwood** Hey, girls. I'm in Alberta and my lips are available.
>
> **Jane** Are you effing kidding me???

 Messages

Between **Izzy** and **Mei**:

Izzy
Get your ass over to the IKC page and rescue me!
I'm all alone over there with Mr. Tinydick.

Mei
I'm in the middle of Shenyang hell. Homeland Security has nothing on the Communists.

Izzy
Fine. Guess I have to do everything. Btw, isn't it cool that other people are chiming in? Well, not the creepy guy, but everyone else.

Jane   Sorry, Slim, you and your tiny package have been blocked.

Lisa Monroe Thank God he's gone. I'm landlocked in Nebraska, but just hooked up with my longtime crush. Squee!!! Can those points count?

Jane Congrats! You're doing better than the rest of us. Deets, please. I'd like to get some vicariously.

Bojana S. Sorry English not so good. I love the long-term crushes. They are the best.

Chapter 9
Piper

Paris was just so . . . Paris! And she didn't mean *Texas*. As they cruised down the Champs-Elysées, it was all Piper could do to sit still when every instinct she had was screaming at her to fling the car door open and step out onto the beautiful, bustling streets of the most romantic city in the world.

"Are you hungry?" her host mom, Marie, asked in heavily accented English as she whipped her little car down the wide, crowded street.

Am I hungry? Piper wondered incredulously. She was *starved*, not for food but for experiences. She wanted to wander the boulevards with their quaint French cafés and markets bursting with fresh produce, to glut her senses on the sounds and smells and feel of Paris as she roved from museum to museum. To immerse herself in the shops and architecture until she couldn't remember a time when she hadn't been there.

"I'm okay," she answered, still full from their breakfast of crepes, coffee, fruit, and cheese. Her mother would've put her on a cleanse after so much food, but Marie just urged her to enjoy herself and eat more.

"My favorite patisserie is right around the corner," interjected her host sister, Simone. "Pull over, Maman. I'll buy some chocolate croissants." She turned to Piper as Marie eased the car to the curb of the nearest side street. "You like *chocolat, oui*?"

"Oh, *oui*! What's not to like?" Piper answered. "Can I come with you?" She would just *die* if she got left in the car.

"Of course." Marie smiled warmly as she handed her daughter some money. "Pick up enough for Papa and Sebastian as well. He said he might stop by later today."

"Who's Sebastian?" Piper asked curiously.

"My older brother," Simone replied. "He's studying at the Sorbonne, but sometimes he comes home on weekends. I can't wait for you to meet him—you'll love him!"

Maybe so, but in Piper's experience siblings were more trouble than they were worth. Still, this was Paris, and everything was better in Paris. Besides, the French don't play American football, and that gave Simone's brother a leg up already.

Refusing to let her unfounded uneasiness ruin her first full day in Paris, Piper listened as Simone spoke to the baker in French so perfect it made chills skitter down Piper's spine. But then, everything about Simone was perfect. From her long, gleaming black hair and bright blue eyes to her creamy, blemish-free skin and incredible fashion sense (her outfit was gorgeous), she all but screamed supermodel. The fact that she was just an ordinary high school junior blew Piper's mind . . . and had her hoping that Simone would decide to come back to Texas for part of next semester, as the exchange program encouraged.

Germaine the Lame would have a stroke if she had to share the halls of PHS with someone as gorgeous as Simone.

As her host sister paid for the croissants, Piper wandered over to the huge picture window at the front of the bakery. She looked out at the color and the conventions of Paris and wanted nothing more than to wrap her arms around the city and gather it close.

Nothing she'd ever done, nowhere she'd ever been, could compare to this. And that she hadn't gotten even one strange look the entire time she'd been here was proof positive that this was going to work. No one in Paris knew who she was, which meant she had a chance to actually breathe for the first time since the Cotton Festival. It was an awesome feeling—especially since Marie seemed so much nicer than her own mom—and it gave her the confidence she'd been lacking for months.

Germaine wasn't going to know what hit her when Piper finally got back home.

"It's a bit overwhelming, *non*?" Simone linked her left arm through Piper's and propelled her from the store. "But don't worry. You'll get used to it soon enough."

Worry? Who was worried? Piper just wanted to get started. She wanted to be out there, doing something. *Anything.*

They climbed back in the car, and as Marie zipped down a few more side streets, Simone pointed to a huge, fancy stone building. "There's our school."

"*That's* the Paris International Academy?" Piper asked incredulously, twisting in her seat to get a better look at the campus. Gothic in design, the school's main building had too many pointy turrets and gargoyles decorating the outside to count. Add in the tall black fence that surrounded the grounds and the huge stained-glass windows, and it looked more like her idea of a haunted house than it did an establishment of learning.

"It is," Simone confirmed. "You'll love it."

"I bet." Already her fingers were itching to sketch it, to try and capture its air of gloomy dissatisfaction. "How long have you been going to school there?"

"For two years. I want to major in international business in college, so Maman and Papa thought it would help me to be at a school that catered to international students."

A little while later, as they walked into her host family's apartment, Piper had a minute to look around. When she'd arrived the night before, she'd been too zonked to appreciate the décor.

Simone noticed her preoccupation and commented, "It's probably not as big as you're used to."

"It's great, though." And it was. Simply decorated, it was as far from her mother's too-fussy house as anyone could get—and Piper loved it.

Loved the bright red couch with its blue and yellow cushions.

Loved the modern art in shades of crimson and black and indigo that hung on the walls and the small sculptures that were displayed in a simple china cabinet.

Loved the plants in their charming cerulean pots that crowded the corners of the living room and half the balcony.

"Not really." Simone tried to look nonchalant, but Piper could tell she was pleased by the compliment. "Come on, I'll help you unpack." Simone thrust open the door to her room. "I cleared out half my closet for you. Although," she looked at Piper's suitcases doubtfully, "I'm not sure that will be enough room."

"I'm an expert at squeezing too many clothes into too small a space. Whatever room you've got for me will be perfect."

The next hour passed in a blur as Piper unpacked, chatting and giggling with Simone the whole time. When her last sweater had been scrunched into her side of the closet, she flopped onto her bed with an exaggerated sigh. "Whew! I was beginning to doubt my abilities. I'm not sure how we got those last few things to fit."

"Don't ask me. I would have given up ten outfits ago." Simone's eyes gleamed mischievously from where she was perched, cross-legged, on her desk. "So, are you ready for a snack? Papa isn't back yet, but I'm tired of waiting."

"Won't your mom mind?"

"Of course not. It's probably taken all of her self-control not to bring a huge tray in here as an excuse to make sure you're settling in okay. She's been very excited about you coming. We both have." Simone stood and stretched, which made her look even longer and leaner. Next to her, Piper was beginning to feel like an ugly duckling with no hope of turning into a beautiful French swan.

"I'll go get the croissants and be right back."

As her host sister left, Piper took the opportunity to really look around Simone's room. It was totally cool—and as far from the turquoise and pink monstrosity her mother had designed for her as it could get.

The comforters on the bed were done in an abstract black and violet print that was stylish and sophisticated. The walls were covered with posters of rock bands—everything from classic American bands like Aerosmith and Led Zeppelin to slightly more modern French ones, like Indochine and Noir Désir—which Piper recognized only because she'd Googled French music a few days before. And the furniture was all smooth, sleek lines.

One whole wall was made of corkboard and on it were hundreds of photos of people she figured had to be Simone's friends, along with a bunch of notes, concert tickets, and brightly colored flyers that Piper couldn't read as they were all written in French.

It was the kind of room she'd always wanted.

The kind of life she'd always dreamed of.

For a few seconds, anxiety assailed her. Who was she kidding? Simone had popular written all over her—it wouldn't take her long to see through the sophisticated image Piper was working so hard to cultivate. And what would happen when she did? Would Piper go back to being the social outcast she'd tried to leave behind?

The thought made her palms sweat, made her doubt the sanity of this whole, grand trip.

What had she been thinking, coming to Paris when she'd all but slept through French class for the last two years?

How was she going to get around on her own?

How was she going to function at school?

How was she going to impress French guys when she couldn't even get any of the ones back home to notice her—at least not in a nonporcine way?

Taking a deep breath, Piper forced herself to push the worries to the back of her mind before they could take over. Sure, things were strange, but she'd figure them out. After all, everything had been great so far.

Reaching for her purse, Piper pulled out her iPhone and started messing with the apps she'd downloaded before leaving America. One was a map of all of France and another was a tourist's guide to Paris and the surrounding areas. She'd studied it—and the old-fashioned guidebook her mom had picked up for her—until she practically had both memorized, but still, she wasn't sure where to start.

There was so much to see in Paris, so much to do. The Louvre, Notre-Dame de Paris, the Eiffel Tower, the Arc de Triomphe. Ten weeks wasn't near long enough to do everything she wanted to, but that didn't mean she wasn't going to give it her best shot.

"So, are you sure I look okay?" Piper demanded later that night, as she and Simone cruised through the brightly lit streets of Paris in her host sister's Mini Cooper.

"You look great. *Très chic.*"

The words thrilled her like nothing else could have, and Piper couldn't resist flipping the car visor down as she tried to decide if Simone was just being nice. But no, the girl in the mirror—with her borrowed silver halter top and wild jewelry—was almost unrecognizable, in the best possible way.

Piper's dark-brown hair had been slicked back, making her face much more of a focal point. Plus, Simone had applied some kind of silver shadow to her eyes—along with some pitch-black liner—that made her look exotic and grown-up and as far from the cute American kid who had gotten off the plane as she could get. This girl looked like she was cool. Even more, she looked like she belonged—in Paris and in a funky nightclub.

Simone barreled around a corner without so much as hitting her brakes, and less than a minute later whipped around another one before sliding almost effortlessly into a parking spot that Piper wouldn't trust herself to park a bicycle in, let alone a car.

Then they were strolling down the street toward a group of teenagers standing on the far corner. Piper felt her stomach tighten. She'd been in Paris just a little over twenty-four hours and Simone was already taking her out to meet her friends. Her lips tingled, hoping that some of them were male. Or all of them. She started school in two days—along with many of the people who were currently studying her in much the same way Germaine *le Paine* and her minions did—and she wanted to make a good impression. The last thing she needed was another two and a half months like the ones she'd just run away from.

Tugging at her purple skirt—which Simone had rolled three times at the waist for her—Piper had a brief moment of panic that her ass was hanging out. She liked short stuff as much as the next girl, but this skirt felt more like a napkin than an article of clothing, and the last thing she needed was to show the group her underwear. Especially since she didn't even have on her fancy lingerie.

As they got closer to Simone's friends, she linked arms with Piper. "You're going to love Le Bataclan. It's one of the coolest clubs in all of Paris. And there's an American band playing tonight, so it should feel like home."

Piper glanced around the crowded, brightly lit streets and could barely stop herself from laughing. Everywhere she looked there was centuries-old architecture, clubs with loud music pouring out of their front doors, and cool arty-looking people in various states of dress— and undress. Yeah, it was just like home—if she lived in the middle of Greenwich Village maybe. Paris, Texas, however? Not so much.

Thank God.

She paused for a moment, took a deep breath. The streets smelled like alcohol and baking bread—an odd combination, no doubt, but one she wanted to remember forever.

"Come on!" Simone tugged on her. "I can't wait for you to meet my friends."

"Hold on a second," she said, then leaned close to whisper in Simone's ear. "Which one do you like?"

"What do you mean?" Simone asked, her voice suddenly wary.

"You totally lit up the second you saw the guys. So just tell me which one you like, and I won't ask him to dance or anything."

It wasn't dark enough to conceal Simone's blush, so Piper reached for her hand, squeezed it encouragingly. "I didn't mean to embarrass you."

"No, it's fine. I've been trying to get Jean-Claude to notice me for what feels like forever."

"Well, introduce me and we'll see what we can do about getting you noticed."

Simone laughed. "You know, Piper, I'm really glad you're here," she said.

"Believe me, so am I."

Simone pulled her forward and the next couple of minutes passed in a blur of names and greetings that Piper could barely keep up with. Raoul was the guy with the black goatee and ripped jeans who was much hotter than his name implied. Maricella was the girl with the almost indecent red tank top. Violet was wearing a pair of kick-ass Doc Martens, or the French equivalent, Piper couldn't tell in the dark. Antoine's clothes were so wrinkled she figured he'd slept in them at least twice before heading out to the clubs. And Simone's guy, Jean-Claude, was gorgeous. Plus, he was wearing a worn black leather jacket that made him look totally cool.

She wanted to make a good impression—needed to make one if she didn't want to spend the next ten weeks as an outcast in yet another Paris—but couldn't help feeling stilted and uncertain. The whole Kiss the Pig thing had robbed her of any self-confidence her mother hadn't previously destroyed.

But no one here knew her lips had ever touched swine, she reminded herself determinedly. She needed to get over it, forget about it, or this whole trip would end up being for nothing.

Smiling brightly, she allowed Simone and her friends to pull her into the club. After handing the doorman her money, she followed her host sister and the others down onto the main floor. European techno-rock blasted through the speakers, and she recognized the group on stage as one from a few flyers Simone had up on the bulletin board in her room.

They were good—better than good—and she felt herself relaxing as the music's beat worked its way through her.

"You like?" Simone shouted to be heard above the pounding music.

"I love!" she answered.

"Good." Simone leaned closer, so she didn't have to yell quite as loudly. "It's still early so the club isn't crowded yet. You want to look around? There're all kinds of cool paintings on the walls."

"Sure, that'd be great." Piper stifled the nervous giggle that welled up in her throat. It was ten thirty and Simone was calling that early. Where she was from, even the Dairy Queen was winding down by now. Perception really was everything, she supposed.

Skirting around the small groups of people scattered throughout the club, she followed Simone and Violet to the back. As they walked, someone latched onto her arm and she turned, surprised to realize Raoul was the one holding on to her elbow so deliberately.

"Mind if I tag along?" he asked with a quick grin that lit up his whole face. In that moment, he went from handsome to drop-dead gorgeous, and Piper felt a few butterflies take off in her stomach. It had been a long time—read never—since a guy this hot had gone out of his way to talk to her.

"No, of course not. Simone was going to show me some of the art on the—"

"Come with me," he said, and started leading her in the other direction.

"But—" Piper looked back, not wanting Simone to think she was ditching her, but her host sister just smiled wickedly and nodded.

Piper kind of shrugged, the universal *what-can-I-do?* move. Simone shook her head and mouthed, *Have fun.*

Like she needed the encouragement? She planned on having the time of her life tonight.

Raoul started up the steps in the center of the club and Piper followed him curiously. The music wasn't quite as loud up there—she could almost hear herself think. Raoul led her to the back of the room and the butterflies turned into pterodactyls. Where was he taking her? What did he want? Simone hadn't seemed worried, but—

"Here," he said, leaning close to her so she could make out his words. His breath was mint scented and hot against her ear and Piper shivered, despite the fact that the temperature in the club was several degrees above comfortable. "These are my favorites."

She followed his gaze and gasped, astounded by the clarity of the paintings as much as by the subject. A series of French entertainment scenes depicted beautiful women in various states of undress. Their faces were heavily painted and while some were onstage, dancing the cancan or performing what looked to be an old-time French follies, others were in dressing rooms, clothes half off, bare breasts displayed for the world to see.

She tried to picture the same scenes in an American club and failed miserably. Which was a shame, because the paintings were gorgeous. Vibrant. Alive. Exactly how Piper felt in that moment, with Raoul's hand warm on her elbow and his dark eyes watching her with obvious interest.

For a minute, her fingers itched for a sketchpad. She wanted to capture this scene, this moment, so she never forgot it. So she remembered forever what it was like to stand in front of beautiful artwork in the middle of a rapidly crowding club, with a hot guy who was looking at her like she belonged in one of the pictures on the wall.

"Do you like them?" he asked, leaning in even closer, so she could smell the dark, musky scent of his cologne.

"I do." She felt disoriented, mixed up, like her body had suddenly forgotten how to process oxygen. "This one—this one is my favorite." She lifted her hand to the painting of a cancan girl with one foot onstage and one on the steps leading up to it. Caught in two different worlds—beautiful, exotic, excited—she was a part of both. A shot of envy pierced Piper's heart. God, she wanted to be like that woman, if even for a little while: leaving the mundane behind for a world filled with lights and colors so bright they were nearly blinding.

"I like that one as well." Raoul interrupted her thoughts as he leaned so close to her that his chest was almost touching hers. He reached out, stroked one long, rough finger down her cheek, and Piper saw stars. "She looks like you."

It was happening, a little voice at the back of her head all but screamed. It was finally happening. *I'm gonna get kissed. I'm gonna get kissed. I'm gonna get kissed.* The taste of swine would be forever wiped from her mouth.

For one second, the voice of common sense intruded. And it sounded an awful lot like Cassidy.

OMG. Are you really about to kiss a guy you just met, like, five minutes ago?

Hell yes, she was. That was four and a half minutes too long. That's what being a charter member of the International Kissing Club was all about.

As Raoul closed the distance between them, Piper barely resisted the urge to do a happy dance right there in the middle of the club. The only thing holding her back was that to do one, she'd have to pull away from Raoul. And that so wasn't happening.

"Does she?" Her voice was breathless, but she couldn't help it.

"*Oui. Vous êtes belle. Magnifique.*"

He'd called her beautiful! Raoul—the hottest guy she'd ever been this close to—had called her magnificent. Piper's heart galloped in her chest, then nearly stopped altogether when he entwined his fingers into her hair.

Tugged her closer.

Lowered his mouth until his lips were barely an inch from hers.

Then he stopped, waited. Piper was afraid to blink, afraid to breathe. Certain that any move from her at all would shatter the moment. Why, oh why, hadn't she taken Simone up on her offer of gum in the car?

Raoul smiled, almost as if he could read the thoughts flying through her mind at a thousand miles a minute. And then he bridged the small distance between them, his lips brushing against hers, once. Twice.

The whole club lit up as colors exploded behind Piper's eyes. She didn't know what to do, what to say, but Raoul didn't seem to care. Nor did he seem to need any direction, because as her hand came up to clutch at his, he lowered his mouth again. And this time he kissed her. Really kissed her.

He tasted like peppermint and wine and clove cigarettes, and when his tongue stroked slowly over hers, Piper grabbed onto him with both hands—partly to stop herself from falling and partly because she was afraid Raoul would pull away. And she wasn't ready for this to end. Not by a long shot.

When he finally did lift his mouth from hers, the room was spinning, like it had when she was a little girl and she twirled around so fast and so many times that everything around her had looked blurry and out of focus.

Forcing herself to concentrate, Piper lifted her eyes to Raoul's dark ones. He looked as amused as she was happy, and then he was tugging her back toward the stairs.

"Do you want to dance, Piper?"

"Sure." She was shocked she could still form words. "But I should probably find Simone."

"Don't worry about Simone," he said. "She probably expects us to be gone for a while longer."

A shiver of unease worked its way through Piper. What did he mean? Had this whole thing been a setup? Did he like her or was he just trying to mess with the American girl?

Or did it even matter? She'd been kissed. By a human.

Besides, wasn't that what she was doing, too? It's not like she was in love with Raoul. This was all about the experience. What was the point of being young and an artist in Paris if you didn't kiss a few hot guys? Look at Picasso. Look at—

"There you are! I was just coming to get you!" Suddenly, Simone was right in front of her. She put her arm around Piper's shoulders and squeezed. "The headliner is about to start."

The brief feeling of unease slid away like it had never been there. "Who is it?" she asked.

"The Black Keys. They're an American band—do you know them?"

"Know them? I love their new album. It's got like three of my favorite songs on it."

"My brother likes them, too." Simone shouted to be heard over the sudden riff of live music that replaced the recorded stuff they'd played between sets. "He's the one who suggested we come tonight."

"Oh. Is he here?" Piper glanced around the suddenly packed club. How long had she and Raoul been upstairs, anyway?

"I don't think so. He'd talked about coming, but then he never called me back, so . . ."

Just then, the first strands of "Howlin' for You" filled the club and Simone squealed. "Come on, let's dance!"

She grabbed Piper's left hand and yanked her toward the dance floor. Piper followed her, conscious of the fact that Raoul still had a tight grip on her right hand. Happiness fizzed up inside her, nearly overwhelmed her. This is what she'd wanted, what she'd hoped for. What she'd spent her life waiting for. And then they were on the dance floor and she let the music take her over. She danced and danced and danced.

Paris, Texas—and the life she had there—had never seemed farther away.

IKC Fan Page

The Official Fan Page for the International Kissing Club

227
people like this

 IKC Page

Ariel   Ooh là là Raoul! Three points for me!

> **Karrie Meeker** Raoul sounds sexy. Spill!
>
> **Ariel** It was très romantic. The paintings. The music. The dancing . . . And now I'm looking for bonus points. Perhaps with a guy who doesn't smoke.
>
> **Camille Fournier** In France? Good luck. If you find one, send him my way when you are done with him. I'm in Versailles.
>
> **Jane** Dang. Eager much?

✉ Messages

Between **Piper** and **Izzy**:

Piper
What's up, sweetie? You sound down. Is Paris even more awful than usual?

Izzy
I just miss you guys a lot. Our table is lonely. I'm actually going to the football game this Friday. Need social interaction.

Izzy
What? No shock and disapproval?

Piper
Do what you need to do. I'm sorry you're lonely. Maybe you could hang out with the art club. Donna's okay, and so is Stacy.

Izzy
Yeah, because I'm so artistic . . .

Jane   Rapunzel, Rapunzel, wherefore art thou, Rapunzel?

> **Mulan** I don't think wherefore means what you think it means. And Rapunzel is probably still over the ocean.

Mulan   Btw, I have a bone to pick with the Texas Education Agency. Did not know the Pacific Ocean was so big.

Rapunzel   JC. I just got off the plane in Sydney, and you're already kissing guys? And, holy crap, there's a hot guy holding up a sign with my name on it. Seriously, people! Why didn't someone make me pack a tooth-brush!

> **Ariel** Forget the toothbrush. Pop some gum and go get him, tiger!

> **Stephanie Richards** Good luck, Rapunzel. Australian guys are the best!

Chapter 10
Cassidy

The tires of the 747 hit the runway with a hard bounce, and air roared through the flaps on the airplane's wings as it raced to a stop.

"Ladies and gentlemen, welcome to Sydney, Australia."

Thank God. Cassidy couldn't wait to stand up and stretch her body to its full height. After twenty hours spent wedged between Mr. Both-Armrests-Are-Mine and the hip-hop stylings of DJ Wannabe and his too-loud tunes, she knew how that last clown must feel when he finally emerged from the miniature car.

As the plane taxied to the gate, she reached into her backpack, pulled out her cell phone, and flipped it on. The international rates were exorbitant, but her mom had asked that she call the instant she landed.

When she'd left Paris, things between Cass and her mom had still been a little tense. Though she hadn't been truly angry when she'd found out Cassidy had called her dad and asked for the money, she hadn't been pleased, either. Cassidy knew she'd hurt her mom by going behind her back; the look of betrayal when she'd told her was not something she'd forget anytime soon. And Cassidy knew from her mom's quiet acceptance of the plan, after she'd explained how badly she wanted to go, that, even more than being hurt, Megan Barlow's fierce pride was sorely battered. That Cassidy's absentee father could provide their daughter with such a once-in-a-lifetime opportunity while she, the mother who'd given up her whole life to keep and raise her alone, could not was more than a bitter pill.

Guilt twinged inside of Cass, freshly sharp, when she thought about it. Somehow, some way, she'd make it up to her mom. She promised. Because given the choice again, she wouldn't change anything. She wanted this trip that badly.

The phone finally connected and her mom answered before the first ring finished. "Cass, are you okay? How was the plane ride?"

"I'm fine, Mom. The flight was fine, just really long."

"Good, good. I've been waiting up for your call. It seems like you've been gone for weeks already. What time is it there?"

"I don't know. Daytime," she answered, looking out the plane's tiny window at the sunlight streaming in. Flying seven thousand miles and crossing the equator had made her mind too numb to do the math.

"Mrs. Gatwick is going to pick you up from the airport, right?" her mom asked. Mrs. Gatwick would be Cassidy's host during the trip. Normally, the foreign exchange agency placed students with families that had other kids about the same age, to help with the transition of being in a strange country. Cassidy, however, had been more than relieved when she'd found out she'd been placed with an older, widowed woman. Not having grown up with a dad or siblings, she didn't think she would've been comfortable in a full-on family setting, anyway. Her only real experience with a conventional mom-dad-kids situation was during sleepovers at Piper's or Izzy's, and if those weekends had taught her anything, it was that the more family members one had in the house, the greater the dysfunction. This two-person arrangement suited her just fine.

"Yeah, the e-mail said she would pick me up outside of the baggage claim. She'll have a sign with my name on it so I'll know it's her."

"Okay, then I'll let you go—don't want to use too many minutes. E-mail me when you get settled and let me know how it is. Be extra careful and have a good time. I love you."

"I love you, too, Mom. Bye."

At last Cassidy staggered off the plane, her legs barely able to function properly. She had the urgent need to pee. After going through customs she found a restroom and saw herself in a mirror for the first time since leaving North America.

Holy crap!

Stale, recirculated airplane air, confined space, sleep deprivation, and crossing an ocean obviously did not do wonders for one's appearance. Not that she usually cared about that kind of thing, but come on. She looked like a creature straight out of the movie *Zombieland*: red-eyed, pale skin, and with a decidedly funky aura. And her hair . . . even under the best circumstances her hair was about as easy to tame as a horde of flesh-hungry zombies.

With a groan she splashed water on her face, wrestled her hair into a braid, and popped three Altoids into her mouth. It wasn't much, but until she had her luggage it was the best she could do. She only hoped Mrs. Gatwick would be understanding enough to take her straight home and to a hot shower.

Cassidy joined the thousands of people navigating the ginormous airport's maze of corridors. She didn't know what she'd expected, but most of the people looked and dressed just like Americans. Well, maybe not Americans from Paris, Texas, but big melting-pot cities like Dallas or Houston, for sure.

She got to the baggage claim to find the hundreds of bags from her flight already circulating around the turnstile. She cringed when she spied her own from a hundred feet away. Unfortunately, there was no mistaking the 1970s guacamole-colored Samsonite suitcase she'd had to borrow from her Memaw. To make it worse, her Papa had strapped two bright red and yellow bungee cords around it to be sure no one would "poke around" in her stuff. It looked like a rejected piñata from a Cinco de Mayo festival.

She slunk to a spot in back where the fewest people stood before claiming it, then walked toward the exit area where loved ones and others stood waiting for arriving passengers.

With nothing more to go on than the description from Mrs. Gatwick's e-mail, Cassidy scanned the crowd, looking for an elderly female holding a sign with her name on it. When she didn't find anyone, she flipped open her phone to make sure there wasn't anything saying Mrs. Gatwick would be late. Then she decided to open Facebook to check the IKC page and let the girls know she'd arrived somewhat intact.

While she was posting, someone bumped into her and she glanced up from her phone. She caught a glimpse of her name scrawled across a white piece of paper. However, the person holding it was neither old nor a lady.

Oh. God.

Those were the only words that formed in her mind when she saw him. Tall and tanned, in a white tee, frayed cargo shorts, and flip-flops, the golden streaks in his tousled sun-bleached hair setting off deep-set hazel eyes to perfection, the guy looked like summer at the beach.

Their eyes met and he starting walking toward her.

"Are you Cassidy?" he asked in a rumbly, Aussie accent.

"Y-yes," she managed to croak.

He smiled, a wide, eye-crinkling grin punctuated by a gorgeous little dimple on his left cheek. "I'm Lucas." He held out his hand, but she hesitated. She *was* a girl by herself in a foreign country. Hadn't she watched enough *48 Hours* episodes with her mom to know the serial killer always turned out to be the guy with the good manners who nobody ever suspected?

As if sensing her nervousness he said, "Mrs. Gatwick asked me to get you from the airport as a favor. Her car is small and she thought you might have a lot of bags. Don't worry—I swear I'm not some weirdo who hangs out at the airport trying to pick up cute tourists." He was teasing her, but it immediately put Cassidy at ease. She laughed at her overactive imagination and shook his hand.

"I'm Cassidy," she said—then remembered the sign he was holding with her name on it. "But you already know that. I'm sorry. It must be jet lag. Sitting for twenty hours on a plane made all the blood drain from my head to my feet, and—"

Cassidy suddenly stopped herself when she realized she was babbling. *Jeez, could I sound more idiotic?*

Luckily, Lucas politely overlooked her sudden onset of verbal diarrhea. "Glad to know you, Cassidy. My car's in the park across the way." He tossed his head, indicating outside beyond the glass doors. "Let me get your bag for you."

"No, that's okay." Cass stayed planted in front of the monstrosity to hide it from his view. "I've got it."

"I insist," he said, and before she could stop him, he reached around and took it. "Hey, my gram has one just like this." *Why, oh why, couldn't the airline have just lost the damn thing?*

Outside, he led her to an open-top, faded-blue vintage Bronco with an orange-and-brown-striped surfboard strapped across the roll bar. *Of course*, she thought. A surfer: as if he could have been anything else looking like he did. When he got into the driver's seat beside her she smelled the clean, breezy scent of the ocean coming from his skin.

"This your first time in Australia, then?" he asked as they drove away from the airport.

"It's my first time anywhere," Cassidy answered.

"So, why did you travel halfway around the world to come to school here? Or don't they have schools back in Texas?" He winked one golden eye at her.

He was so freaking cute her breath caught just at the top of her throat, making her stammer. "D-did Mrs. Gatwick tell you I was from Texas?"

"Yeah. She's a friend of my gram. I've known her since I was a little bloke. Her daughter and grandkids don't live in Sydney, so I help her out from time to time."

"That's very nice of you. Do you live near her?" If he lived close to

Mrs. Gatwick, then maybe he would go to her school. Cassidy imagined the possibility. If Lucas were in her classes, she could actually see herself becoming quite the stellar student . . .

"No. I live with some mates across the harbor in DeeWhy. I graduated last spring. I'm taking a gap year before I decide on university."

"Oh." Cassidy hoped Lucas hadn't heard the deflation in her tone. See, that's what happens when you get your hopes up—inevitable disappointment.

They made more small talk as they blew down the highway into the heart of sprawling Sydney. The skyscrapers in the Central Business District gleamed in the sunlight as Lucas drove through the car-and-pedestrian-crowded streets. Already overwhelmed with flight fatigue and the boy sitting next to her, Cassidy could hardly take in the entire whirl of sights and sounds. But, when they drove north across the iconic Sydney Harbour Bridge and she saw the great stretch of blue water surrounded by rolling green coastline and dotted with the sails of hundreds of boats, she realized just how far from Paris, Texas, she had come.

The tall business buildings gave way to quieter tree-lined streets, and Lucas pulled to a stop in front of a white two-story house.

"We're here," he said. He got out of the car and pulled her suitcase from the back. Cassidy opened her door and stepped onto the curb.

"Thank you for the ride," she said.

"No worries." He smiled and his dimple made a charming reappearance. Cassidy ignored the resultant wobble in her step and reached for her bag, but Lucas moved it out of her grasp. "I'll walk you to the door—Mrs. Gatwick would be on the phone to my gram in a heartbeat if I left you on the curb and didn't stop to say hello."

He saw her into the house and after making introductions between her and Mrs. Gatwick, he opened the door to leave. "Well, I'll see you round," he said. "The swells are supposed to really be going off today and I don't want to miss 'em." Then he looked at Cassidy. "If you need anything or want someone to show you the city, just ring me. Mrs. Gatwick has my number."

"Oh. Thank you," she stammered. Cass knew he was just being polite, but still the idea of seeing him again sent her heart into overdrive.

"Have a good time, Cassidy. I think you'll like it here."

"Thanks for breakfast, Mrs. Gatwick. It was delicious as always," Cassidy said, finishing off the last bite of smoked ham, poached eggs, and toast. Mrs. Gatwick was an excellent cook and, like all grandmothers, believed food a cure-all for whatever ailed a body. It was a good thing Cassidy had the metabolism of a cheetah or she wouldn't be able to fit into her school uniform by the end of the month.

She did wish, however, that Mrs. Gatwick believed in sleeping in on the weekends—seven thirty was on the early side for breakfast on Saturday. Especially when that left at least fourteen hours to fill until she could reasonably go to bed and not be a total loser.

"Do you have plans today, Cassidy?" Mrs. Gatwick asked, pouring herself another cup of Earl Grey. "You should ring one of your schoolmates for a day at the beach. I'm sure all the young people will be out on a lovely spring day."

She could, but there was no one to call. Not that the girls at North Sydney Secondary weren't nice enough—after two weeks at school, she was at least eating lunch with some of the ones she played volleyball with—but being the "American girl," she got the sense they found her a bit of a curiosity and none had made any real overtures of friendship. And she wasn't exactly one to reach out—even if she was so homesick most days that she could barely tear herself away from her laptop screen in case she missed the chance to chat with one of her friends online.

Saturdays back home were always spent with Piper, Izzy, and Mei, even if it was nothing more than hanging out, with Piper bemoaning the cruel fate that had landed them in a town with nothing to do. At least they were doing nothing together. Now, Cassidy was on the other side of the globe and the thought of another eight weekends without them made the distance feel that much more vast.

And she missed her mom. They exchanged e-mails almost every day and Skyped at least once a week, but of course it wasn't the same as sitting at the table together in their cozy kitchen, griping about her mom's job at the hospital and Cass's schoolwork over reheated pizza.

This whole thing sucked, especially considering she couldn't remember a day since she'd turned ten when she hadn't wanted to be as far away from Paris, Texas, as she could get. So, this homesickness was a real kick in the ass.

Irony—it wasn't just a theme for an American Lit paper.

Cassidy gulped down her orange juice and gathered her plate and Mrs. Gatwick's to take to the kitchen sink. "I thought I might make the cliff run from Bronte Beach to Bondi," she said, trying for a bright, excited tone so the older woman wouldn't guess just how lonely Cassidy was. She knew it would only make her worry, and then she'd just feed Cassidy more. "The guidebook says it's a must do, and I feel like some exercise."

That wasn't a lie, at least. A good sweat and sore muscles always made her feel better. Between riding the buses across town, making the 3.5 kilometer run, and getting back, it would take her at least four hours. She could bring her swimsuit and dip into the waves a bit to burn some more time, though she suspected the water would still be freezing this early in spring. But if she played her cards right, she could occupy herself till at least midafternoon, followed by an early supper and a bit of "telly" in the evening with Mrs. Gatwick before bed, and that would be another day down. As Mei would say, success is all about careful planning.

"You should ring Lucas," Mrs. Gatwick trilled. "He'd be nice company for that, I'd imagine." Yes, Cassidy imagined he would—he of the warm-honey-colored-eyes-and-heart-palpitating-smile-and-I'm-pretty-sure-he's-an-excellent-kisser looks. And she *did* have his number—in case she needed someone and Mrs. Gatwick couldn't be reached. Of course, she'd never actually dialed it.

Calling someone like Lucas wasn't like making a three-pointer at the buzzer—*that* she could do in her sleep. Making a move on a hot guy, though, was *so* not her game. She wasn't Germaine, for chrissake. Just thinking about it made her tummy squirm with angst-ridden awkwardness.

Besides, he'd probably forgotten all about her. Or if he hadn't, maybe his offer had expired. He could have a girlfriend, too—guys that cute didn't have to wait around for strange girls to call them.

"Well, I'm off soon to meet Beatrice Farley," Mrs. Gatwick said. "We're having our toes done, then a bit of lunch. And this evening, Mr. Barrington is taking me for supper and dancing." She stood with her teacup and twirled to the sink, the ruffles of her lavender housecoat fanning out over fuzzy slippers, her gray-blue eyes twinkling. Mrs. Gatwick was what Cassidy's papa would call a "handsome" woman: trim, good bones, a nice smile, aging gracefully. Mr. Barrington was a lucky man.

"Help yourself to anything you'd like in the kitchen, m'dear, and don't wait up for me, I may be late." Mrs. Gatwick gave her a saucy woman-to-woman wink. Cassidy forced a closed-lip smile to keep her eggs and bacon from coming back up. Why did older people always get a kick out of making sexual innuendos in front of the children? Yuck.

"I'll be fine, Mrs. Gatwick, you have a good time." Mrs. Gatwick blew her a kiss as she left to get dressed.

Great. Sixty-five-year-old Mrs. Gatwick had a rockin' love life and Cassidy might as well fill out an application at the nearest convent for all the good coming to Australia had done for her in *that* department. Not one guy had asked her out. Not one. Although the guys in Texas had never been subtle about why they wanted to be with her, at least they took a swing. Here, where she had a clean slate, no one would even come up to bat.

Cassidy put the dishes in the drain board and trudged upstairs to the small gabled room that was her home away from home. She flopped onto the twin bed, propped her already open laptop on her stomach, and logged onto Facebook. Maybe one of the girls was online and they could chat for a while, but no. She tried to calculate the time difference in her head, only to realize it didn't matter. Everyone was offline.

She clicked over to the IKC fan page and scanned the updates.

Mei sounded hungry.

Izzy was bored.

Piper was—*Good God!* Twelve points! Piper had racked up twelve points. In just two weeks; three more than yesterday. She was like some lip-locking ninja over there. Chapstick should take out ad space on her lips.

Cassidy shut her computer. This was getting ridiculous—somebody besides Piper had to get in the game. She glanced sideways at the nightstand, where her phone sat holding Lucas's number, so far her only lead to scoring some kissing points. Before she could come up with another excuse to stop herself, her hand shot out and grabbed the phone. She scrolled down to his number and pressed dial.

In her stomach a watermelon-sized glob of nerves formed, then congealed like her Memaw's Jell-O mold when the ring went unanswered. Damn. This was worse than calling her dad to ask for the trip money. After all, she'd had years of experience dealing with her father's disinterest, but this . . . this could be rejection on a whole new level.

It rang a fourth time. If he didn't pick up now it would go to voice mail. Cassidy decided this would mean she'd given it her best shot, but it just wasn't meant to be. She wouldn't leave a message.

"Hello?" answered a groggy, gravelly Aussie voice on the other end.

She glanced at the clock and cringed inwardly: 7:58—she'd woken him up! Smooth. Desperate much?

"Hello, Lucas? This is Cassidy Barlow; ah . . . you picked me up at the airport." There was a pause on the other end, during which

Cassidy was certain her heart beat no less than a hundred and fifty times, and then she heard the rustling of sheets and the groan of mattress springs as if he'd sat up in bed. She had to force herself not to drool over that mental image.

"Yeah, the American girl. I remember you," he answered at last. "You didn't call me. I was heartbroken." Cassidy swore she could hear the smile in his voice.

That was promising.

"Yeah, I'm sorry to call you so early on a Saturday and all, but I was wondering if maybe"—*courage, Cassidy, just spit it out*, she heard Piper's voice say in her head—"I could take you up on your offer to show me around Sydney. Unless you already have plans, then don't worry about it. It's no big deal."

Yay, Cass, you did it! Piper's voice cheered.

"I do have plans—"

Her courage belly-flopped onto her spleen. Screw you, Piper.

"No, no, don't worry," she interrupted him, now wanting to get this over with as quickly as possible and therefore minimize the soul-scarring embarrassment that was even now beginning to travel along every nerve ending in her body. "Like I said—no big deal. Another time—"

"Cassidy—"

"I have, like, eight weeks left, so maybe another time. Or not. Okay, then."

"Cassidy, wait." Lucas laughed at her insane rambling. "Jeez, give a guy a chance. I was going to say I have plans to surf with a few mates, but I'd like you to come."

"I don't surf," she said lamely.

"Just because you haven't, doesn't mean you can't. Whatdya say, American girl? Think you can hang Down Under?" he challenged in his too-sexy accent.

That did it—Cassidy could never back down from a challenge. "I'll be there." After Lucas gave her directions and they hung up,

Cassidy was buzzing. Not only had he remembered her, but he'd invited her to go surfing—it wasn't officially a date, since his friends would be there, too, but it was something. She was off the sidelines and ready to play. She reopened her laptop, the IKC fan page still on the screen, and dashed off a new post: *Ariel, may the best kisser win.*

· · · · · ✈

Three hours later, however, Cassidy was seriously second-guessing her decision.

She disembarked with the other ferry passengers onto the dock and into the covered landing. A sign overhead proclaimed: MANLY... SEVEN MILES FROM SYDNEY, AND A THOUSAND MILES FROM CARE.

Carefree was not how Cassidy would describe herself at that moment. More like on the verge of a total and complete nervous breakdown.

Why was this freaking her out? Any normal girl would be thrilled to be meeting a cute guy on the beach. But not Cass. What was wrong with her?

Chill, Cass. This is no big deal. It was just going to be a friendly get-together on a public beach. Kissing was an option, not a requirement, for the day. And only if Lucas initiated, because the phone call had been enough for her.

Taxis and cars lined the street in front of the landing and people milled along the *corso*, the shop-and-restaurant-lined plaza that led to the beach.

"Hey, Cassidy, over here!"

She turned and saw Lucas jump over the side of his Bronco and come toward her. He looked like a Billabong ad, in his boardshorts and flip-flops—a sun god, descended to walk among the mortals. What had she been thinking? He was *so* out of her league.

She waved and gave him a nervous smile. "Hey, Luc—" but before she could say anything else he wrapped her in his toned arms, lifted her off her feet as if she weren't almost as tall as he was, and hugged her like they were long-lost friends rather than near strangers. Normally, something like this would have put her on her guard. She didn't like people in her personal space, but with Lucas, she didn't mind so much.

"I'm happy you called," he said after he put her down.

"Me, too," she said, enjoying her fluttery excitement.

"Come on, then." He took her hand like it was the most normal thing in the world and led her toward the car. "My mates are waiting for us. You brought your suit, yeah?" He took her backpack and opened the car door. Two surfboards were in the back.

"Yeah, but don't expect too much from me," she said. "I live about three hundred miles away from the nearest beach."

Lucas slid into the driver's seat. He winked as he started the car. "No worries, Cassidy. I'll have ya frothin' by sunset."

Fifty waves later, though, Cassidy was pretty sure she wasn't frothin', unless it was from the mouth after the gallons of saltwater she'd just swallowed.

Coughing and spluttering, she managed to drag the longboard to the beach before she collapsed, exhausted, on the sand next to it. She closed her eyes against the brilliant white sunlight and focused on drawing long, cool breaths into her burning lungs.

A shadow crossed in front of her lids and cold drops of water pattered over the small amounts of skin her wetsuit didn't cover.

"Are you okay, Cassidy?" Lucas asked.

"I think I almost drowned that time."

"Nah, you pretty much had it." She could hear him holding back laughter, though. "You did it just like I said to and you were standing up. You got off balance a bit, that's all."

She cracked open one eye. Lucas was leaning over her, an arm braced on either side of her in the sand, little drops of seawater glistening in his hair and on his grinning face. The smell of zinc oxide clung to him.

"You make it look too easy," she accused him with a laugh. He and his friends, Anthony and Zed, carved the water like Michelangelo through marble, as Piper would say. Their grace and precision and the utter confidence in their play was amazing to watch.

"That's 'cause I'm part shark," he said, and she laughed. "You were doing great, Cass. You're a natural. I know if you can just get up, you'll love it. When you're out there, it's just you and the board and the hum of the ocean—you're totally free from everything and everyone. There's no feeling like it in the world." The tip of his finger moved a wet clump of hair off her face, and he stared into her eyes for a moment before he leaned toward her. "Well, except, maybe this . . ."

Panic set in. Her heart began flip-flopping around in her chest like an Olympic gymnast during the medal round, and she would probably have hyperventilated if she'd been able to breathe at all.

God, she hadn't been kissed by anyone in so long. What if she'd forgotten how? What if she sucked at it? What if—

And then every last coherent thought she had suddenly floated away when his mouth touched hers. Warm and gentle lips slanted across her own, easing all the tension from her body into the shifting sand beneath.

He tasted heavenly, like the salty waves and hot summer sunshine. Cassidy reached up to place her hand on his back, pulling the heat of his body closer, feeling the play of his muscle beneath the neoprene wet suit. She felt him smile against her lips, and he deepened the kiss, still tender and sweet, but just hard enough to make sure every cell in her body came wholly alive. The dizzying sensation made her shiver.

Lucas lingered another moment before slowly pulling away. "Are you cold?" he asked, pausing only an inch or two from her lips, which did nothing to help stop the shivering.

"N-n-no," she stuttered like an idiot and closed her eyes, willing him to kiss her again.

"Cassidy, you don't have a guy back home, do you? No Texas cow-boy that's gonna want to kick my ass for that?"

The thought made her giggle. Jeez, was she channeling Piper? She opened her eyes. "No, there's definitely no boyfriend, especially not a cowboy one."

"Good," he murmured.

"Hey, get a room, you two!" Zed's voice taunted from down the beach.

"Yeah, there're kids out here," Anthony joined in.

Lucas laughed, then kissed her quickly on the tip of her nose. "I'll never hear the end of this. Come on, then." He stood and pulled her limp body up with him. "One more try for you, and this time you're going to ride the wave all the way in."

She didn't need to. Cassidy knew without question that kissing Lucas had felt way better than surfing ever could.

IKC Fan Page

The Official Fan Page for the International Kissing Club

871

people like this

 IKC Page

Mulan　　My stomach is eating itself. Must have food.
Would worry about any guy too close to my mouth.
Shenyang is no Panda Express.
> **Jane** Will trade you Texas barbecue for tofu.

Ariel　　Painted the Eiffel Tower with a cute art student. One
more point. Who says thirteen isn't a lucky number?

Rapunzel　　Scored a three-point field goal. Finally in the game.

Jane　　Enough about the kissing. Is anyone sightseeing?
> **Ariel** I triumphed under the Arc de Triomphe!
> **Rapunzel** Of course you did.
> **Ariel** Well, my school looks like a gothic cathedral.
> So beautiful. I'm planning my trip to the Louvre
> already and thinking of trying glassblowing.
> **Rapunzel** I thought Texas was hot. Down here we're
> about a mile from the sun.
> **Mulan** Boo-hoo. Turns out Shenyang is about a mile
> from Siberia. Something else my inferior American
> education didn't prepare me for. Google Maps fail.
> Am cold and hungry.
> **Bojana S.** When in Siberia, make snow cones.
> **Rapunzel** Snow cones. Yum. Have taken up
> surfers . . . oops. Freudian slip. Meant have taken up
> surfing.
> **Idina V.** No you didn't, you lucky girl.

Jane　　If anyone's interested, it still sucks here.

✉ Messages

Between **Izzy** and **Mei**:

Izzy
I'm sorry you're having a terrible time. I guess I'm not the only one who's miserable.

Mei
Is it that awful? I've met Germaine's Chinese doppelgänger. Am beginning to have a whole new sympathy for Piper. But how are you holding up? You're not just sitting at our table by yourself, are you?

Izzy
At our table? Hell no. Al Gore and I are spending quality time together under the trees in the courtyard.

Mei
You mean his books, I assume. I hope Germaine isn't hassling you now that Piper's gone and she has no one to torment.

Izzy
Are you kidding? I'm not even a speck on her radar. So, at least I'm okay on that front. I just miss you guys.

🗨 IKC Page

Jane
Btw, ladies, quick poll: what's the best way to get rid of a gift from a skanky ex?

> **Bojana S.** Set it on fire!
> **Karrie Meeker** Unless it's big enough you'd get arrested by the fire marshall. Then, I say, run it over!
> **Jane** Trust me. Not big at all.
> **Jennifer Wilson** I'm always fond of a hammer.
> **Jayson** Do you have a blender?

Jayson
Btw, is this page LGBTQ friendly?

> **Ariel** Absolutely, just not skanky-ex friendly.

Chapter 11
Izzy

Izzy still hadn't decided what to do with the earrings from River. In her free time—which she had oodles of, now that Mei, Cassidy, and Piper had abandoned her—she contemplated various methods of destroying them. As delightful as the suggestions on the IKC page had been, most of them were *too* dramatic. In the end, she decided to channel Mei.

Last year, when Mei broke up with her long-term boyfriend, John, she simply gathered the detritus of their relationship and politely dropped off the box at his house. No drama. No emotion. And the dopey expression on John's face had been visible even from the car, where the three of them sat waiting to head to the movies.

Obviously, Izzy wasn't going out to Lubbock. But when Saturday rolled around, she gassed up Brittney and headed for the farmers' market in Sherman, which was where she and River had first met nearly a year ago. His mother had a stall in the back, where she sold beeswax candles and tie-dyed shirts that hung from the awning rafters like brightly colored flags.

When Izzy got there, Autumn, River's mother, was chatting with a customer, but as soon as the woman left, Autumn engulfed Izzy in a big patchouli-scented hug. Autumn was a tiny woman, with long brown hair worn in a braid down her back. As always, she was dressed in jeans and one of the T-shirts she'd made.

Wrapped in Autumn's soothing embrace, Izzy squeezed her eyes shut against the tears prickling the backs of her eyes.

"Oh, honey," Autumn cooed. "I'm so glad you came by. I was worried when you and River broke up that I wouldn't see you anymore. Come sit down. I have a really nice ginger maté tea in the thermos."

Izzy swallowed past her tears, tried to speak, and then just nodded as she sank into one of the chairs at the back of the stall. Autumn bustled around, offering roasted soy nuts and fresh figs, before sitting down beside Izzy and gently patting her hand.

And that was when Izzy knew why she'd really come. It didn't have anything to do with the earrings. She just missed Autumn's gentle maternal air. The way she focused her attention so completely on Izzy. Her own mother never did that. Not when Shane had so much more potential she could be cultivating. After years of benign neglect at home, was it any wonder Izzy had missed this?

A second later, she burst into tears, without ever handing back the earrings or even explaining why she'd come. Autumn just let her cry.

By the time Izzy was cried out, Autumn had sold three more candles but no T-shirts. Apparently the kind of customer who bought tie-dyed T-shirts was easily scared off by hysterical girls.

Once again, Autumn patted her on the hand. "You'll feel better now that you've expressed your grief."

"I guess," Izzy muttered. What she really felt was adrift. She took a sip of the tea. The pungent brew felt like it was stripping the lining from her sinuses. Forcing herself to swallow it, she set the cup aside.

But hashing out the relationship couldn't be any harder than drinking the tea. So she started talking. "On paper, River and I looked like the perfect couple. I thought we were alike in every way."

Autumn nodded sympathetically. "I know, honey."

"And now he's off in Lubbock." She shot a sideways glance at Autumn, not sure how much she could say. "Have you seen his Facebook updates lately?" she asked tentatively.

Autumn's smile wavered and her head bobbed. "He is expressing his freedom uniquely."

"So you've seen his page. Why aren't you freaking out about it?"

Autumn sighed, but the placid nurturing never left her expression. "He has to find his own way."

Suddenly Autumn's unending acceptance grated against Izzy's nerves. "He's betraying everything you raised him to believe," she pointed out.

"Honey, I know you're having a really big experience of anger right now—"

"I'm not having an *experience* of anger." Izzy gritted her teeth. She hopped out of the chair and away from Autumn's touch. "I'm frickin' pissed." Finally she settled on why Autumn's attitude annoyed her. "And I don't understand why you're not pissed, too."

"Honey, did it ever occur to you that you and River were too much alike? Sometimes when people fit together too well, a relationship can become confining. Smothering."

Izzy's eyebrows shot up. "You're saying I smothered him?"

Before Autumn could answer, another customer came over to buy a candle. Instead of waiting for her to come back, though, Izzy left the earrings beside the god-awful tea Autumn had tried to poison her with. Then she slipped out the back of the tent and made her way through the market.

She realized now, she'd honestly thought Autumn would take her side. Which was stupid. Of course Autumn would stand by her son, even if he was going against everything the woman believed in. She wasn't like Izzy's parents.

It sucked that Izzy didn't have any adults in her life willing to defend her no matter what, but that was all the more reason for her to find her own inner strength. When she went off to college, she knew she wouldn't reinvent herself completely. She didn't love everything about herself, but she certainly liked the person she was enough to know that she wasn't going to trade her in for a newer model the second she left Paris. She had too much self-respect for that.

One thing was certain—regardless of what Autumn or River thought, she certainly hadn't *smothered* him. She had more follow-through than that. If she'd smothered him, he'd be dead by now.

Izzy spent a few more minutes wandering around the farmers' market. Now that she wasn't dating River, she wouldn't be coming back anytime soon. She bought a smoothie to chase away the horrible taste of the ginger maté tea, then she wandered over to the gourmet candy booth, needing chocolate therapy. Her relationship with River was truly over. Though after the visit with Autumn, Izzy wasn't even sure she felt sorry about it.

She'd always thought of Autumn as such a kind, nurturing soul. Today, she'd been too laid-back. Too easygoing. Too . . . what was the word for it?

Mei was right. Izzy needed to spend more time studying for the SAT. Her vocabulary was crap if she couldn't think of the words to describe how annoying someone was.

She was nibbling on a spicy mango truffle and contemplating whether she could inflict her mother's cooking on innocent farmers' market vegetables, when she heard someone calling her name. She looked up and scanned the thinning crowd.

At first she didn't recognize anyone. But just as she decided she must have imagined it, he called her name again, and she spotted him coming toward her. Tanner.

"Um. Hi." She popped the last bit of chocolate into her mouth and rubbed at her lips self-consciously with the back of her hand. Then she added, "If it isn't Tanner Smith and Wesson."

"Hey, Isabel." He grinned, stopping a few feet away. Tanner was usually pretty well dressed. He had that all-American clean-cut thing going for him. But today he was wearing a flannel shirt open over a dark blue T-shirt. His jeans were faded. His Dingo work boots scruffy and worn. Somehow she liked him better for looking less like he modeled for Abercrombie & Fitch. She smiled at the thought.

Tanner's grin slowly faded and he seemed to be studying her. Suddenly she was aware that she'd been crying her eyes out not too long ago, and she probably looked all red and blotchy. She didn't particularly mind his seeing her red and blotchy—he was just Tanner, after all—but she hated anyone knowing she'd been crying over River.

Turning back to the vegetable stall, she pulled her shopping bag from her purse and started mindlessly loading it up.

Beside her, Tanner chuckled. "Wow, your family must really love acorn squash."

She glanced down at the bag. Acorn squash? Was that what these things were? "Yum," she muttered. "We love the . . ." And then her mind went blank. The what? The . . . ? The . . . ? "Fiber," she finished lamely.

Note to self: There's a fine line between not caring what someone thinks of you and purposefully making a fool of yourself. Let's not cross it again.

"You need any help with that?" he asked, looking like he was trying not to laugh.

"Don't be silly." But then she could barely lift it. *Okay, study SAT words and hit the gym.* Before she could protest—or more logically, put some of them back—he'd hefted the bulging bag and carried it over to the clerk.

Izzy fished out her wallet and paid the lady, carefully hiding her shock at how expensive eight acorn squash were. Now she really wished she *had* put them back. Her family was not worth emptying out her cash reserves. Plus, now she was stuck with Tanner walking the bag to her car.

Even though he seemed to be at her house constantly, they never talked much. She found herself unsure what to say to him. "So . . . ," she began awkwardly. As if anything could be more awkward than talking about dietary fiber. "What are you doing here?" Then she cringed. That sounded so *accusatory*. "I mean, you don't seem like the farmers'-market type."

"My parents sell fruit here."

She laughed. "No really, what—" Then quickly realized he wasn't joking. "Oh. Fruit, huh?"

"Yeah. Sun Valley Orchards." He pointed to a stall near the entrance.

Izzy glanced at it. "They have great stuff!"

"I know."

"I had no idea. I *love* that jam."

"The apple ginger, right?"

"Yeah. Now that's how ginger should be used." Not in a tea strong enough to choke a horse. "I guess I should have stocked up. I doubt I'll be back anytime soon."

"I guess not." He looked over his shoulder toward the back of the market where Autumn was packing up her T-shirts. "River always was a pretentious douche." Tanner's voice was low and harsh as he said it.

There was something in his tone that surprised her. It must have shown on her face, because when he looked over at her, he smiled again and shrugged. "I'm sorry. I know you dated him for a while. I'm sure he's a great guy."

"No," she said, suddenly feeling better than she had in weeks. "He *is* a douche."

When they'd reached her car, she opened the passenger side door so he could deposit the squash.

"So what's next for you, Isabel?" Tanner asked as he closed the door.

She looked pointedly at the bag he'd carried. "I'm going to go home and eat a lot of squash."

He chuckled. "No, I meant for the semester. With Mei, Cassidy, and Piper out of town—"

"And my idiot ex in Lubbock," she added, just because it felt so good to joke about it.

Tanner let it slide. "You're going to have to find something else to keep you busy."

"Well, since I'm bored and broke, I think I'm going to get a job. If I can knock my self-respect down low enough, I'm going to apply at Dairy Queen."

"Ouch." Tanner gave an exaggerated wince. "If you want a job, you don't have to work there."

"No, I really think I do. Nowhere else is hiring experience-less teens."

"You could get a job working for my parents." He pointed back toward the stall. "I know they could use someone to help out around the farm. With football practice I'm not there much."

"Don't your parents live in Oklahoma?"

He sent her a "well-duh" look. "No."

"Then why do you live with your uncle?"

"So I can go to Paris High. Play ball for your dad."

"Oh." She started digging through her purse, looking for her keys, only to realize they were still in her hand.

"My parents' farm is about twenty minutes from Paris. But it's a one-A district. I could never get a football scholarship going to school there."

She didn't quite know what to say to that. After living in Austin for so much of her life, dumpy little Paris seemed like a place you ran away from. Not a place you ran to.

This odd, uncomfortable tightness formed in her throat. Not pity, exactly. Maybe sympathy? It seemed wrong, somehow, to feel anything so human for Tanner.

"Why are you helping me like this?" she asked.

He slanted a smile at her. The same one that had half the girls in Paris High School crushing on him. "'Cause we're friends. That's what friends do."

She'd spent years harassing and being harassed by football players. She didn't want to be friends with one. Did she?

Of course, she wasn't exactly in a position to be picky.

"My parents are especially busy right now," Tanner was saying. "The apples and jams are doing so well, they're converting the ten acres near the house into organic crops. If you're interested, I'll talk to them about it."

"That'd be great." Was it helping with scientific research in the rain forest? No. But it was so much better than sprinkling jimmies on soft serve. She swung open the driver's door and clambered into the car, feeling upbeat for the first time in weeks.

Tanner had been—dare she say it?—*nice* to her. On a day when she'd really needed it. And he'd offered to help her get a non–Dairy Queen job.

"You know, Tanner," she said lightly, "for a knuckle-dragging purveyor of violence, you're pretty easy to talk to."

For an instant, surprise flickered across his face. Then he flashed her a smile. "It's because I know so few words."

She thought about what Mei had said about him being the only other person in honors biology to get an A. Izzy had barely managed a B+ in normal biology. "Yeah. Right."

She started the car with a shake of her head. Since it was one of those gorgeous warm fall days, she rolled down the windows.

Just before she slipped the car into reverse, Tanner leaned down and poked his head through the window. "You *can* drive a tractor, right?"

IKC Fan Page

The Official Fan Page for the International Kissing Club

1,391

people like this

 IKC Page

Jane Have moved up the high school social ladder. Am now sitting at the geek table during lunch. But have job prospects that don't involve DQ.

> **Ariel** cool!

Ariel One point at this great little sidewalk café. And then three more at the discotheque last night.

Jane Btw, did y'all think that . . . shall we call him Rio? . . . was a douche?

> **Mulan** I always thought you could do better.
>
> **Ariel** He was never enough man for you!
>
> **Rapunzel** Oh God, yes.
>
> **Jane** Why. Didn't. You. Tell. Me??????
>
> **LaTonya Washington** It's standard girl rules. You can't diss your best friend's man.
>
> **Ariel** Right! All you can do is subtly plot to break them up. Which we tried!!!!!!
>
> **Jane** Okay. New rule: if someone is dating a douche, the rest of IKC must tell her.
>
> **Rapunzel** I don't care if my guy is a douche. He looks so hot on a surfboard.
>
> **Mulan** So says the woman lucky enough to have actually met a guy.

Serena MacAfee Do points count if he's not international, but we were across the border when it happened?

> **Jane** I'm so desperate, I'd count them if they happened at a Taco Bell.

Chapter 12
Mei

Mei tried not to feel sorry for herself as she stared at her laptop screen, reading the Facebook updates on the IKC page. It was hard, especially when Piper and Cassidy seemed to be having so much fun.

Both of them had already racked up points—Piper more than Cassidy, big surprise—but still, Cassidy was holding her own with some hot guy named Lucas. She'd promised to post a picture soon and Mei couldn't wait to see what kind of guy had managed to get past the No Trespassing signs Cassidy usually kept at full mast.

Even Izzy seemed to have found her groove. No kissing action, but she'd gotten a new job on Tanner's farm. Knowing her, she'd be knee-deep in compost by the end of the week. And at least everyone in Texas spoke the same language she did, which was a lot more than Mei could say about China. Here, even the girls who did speak English went out of their way to ensure that they spoke Mandarin in front of her. God forbid she should forget—even for a second—that she was an outsider here. Again.

Mei put her head down on her desk and tried to ignore the sadness that beat at her a little more with each day that passed. She was so tired of being the girl who never fit in anywhere. In Paris it was understandable—she was Chinese, adopted, and the daughter of a liberal gender-studies professor and a well-respected journalist. She didn't have a chance of fitting in there.

But here, in China, where she'd been born? She'd thought it would be perfect. Instead, she was as much an outcast here—maybe more—than she'd ever been in Texas.

What did it say about her that she was in a country with 1.6 *billion* people and she still couldn't find even one who liked her enough to talk to her?

Not that they'd given Mei much of a chance. The girls in the dorm had made it abundantly clear that they wanted nothing to do with her—not because she was American, but because she was Chinese. Because her birth parents had given her up for adoption seventeen years before, she was undesirable. Unsuitable. Unwelcome. It turned out, in China the girls who'd been given up for adoption were just above Democratic protestors on the social ladder.

Her stomach growled loudly, distracting her from her misery for a second, but she ignored it—just as she'd been ignoring it for the last two hours. She was sick of going to the dining hall alone and trying to figure out which of the long lines of dishes were edible and which weren't. So far, she'd had singularly bad luck in what she'd picked out and had ended up throwing away most of the food on her tray at the end of every meal, which only earned her more dirty looks. But who would have guessed that authentic Chinese food could be so disgusting? She shuddered. She really was a long way from Sherman's Panda Express.

A glance at the clock told her she had only an hour before the cafeteria closed, and she knew she needed to head over there to try and eat. She'd only been in China two weeks and she'd already lost so much weight that she'd had to buy a belt to hold up her jeans—and punch a couple new holes in it to actually make it small enough to cinch.

Her parents were going to have a stroke when they saw her.

But not even that worry got her moving—it wasn't like her weight loss was the only thing her parents were going to freak out about. She hadn't had much luck in finding her birth parents yet, but her ability to speak Mandarin was getting a little better every day. Soon, she was hoping she'd be able to navigate the public transportation system well enough to get to the orphanage in Dalian.

Mei glanced at her guitar. It was lying on her bed where she'd left it earlier. Part of her wanted to pick it up and play some old Clapton stuff to chase away the homesickness—but it took more energy than she had. Instead, she pulled up the widget she'd been working on in an effort to stop thinking about how hungry she was. It was a silly thing, but cute, and she thought it would give the IKC page a little more panache.

And something more for visitors to do. She was shocked at how many people had Liked the page already, how many girls were visiting and posting about their kisses—international or domestic. Admittedly, the fans were nowhere near the numbers of Piper's Kiss the Pig page, but linking the IKC page through it had really paid off. And it was nice to see how many girls were getting into the International Kissing Club. It made her feel a whole lot less alone in her little corner of the world.

She messed with the widget for a while—it was giving her a little trouble with the whole stick-a-pin-in-the-map thing, almost as if it knew she had no right to be sticking pins anywhere. Piper, on the other hand, was going to turn all of France—maybe all of Europe—red with her little pins.

Finally, Mei got it to work, and she added one red pin in Sydney for Cassidy, and eight around Paris for Piper—at least she thought it was eight, based on the running tally, but by now it could be a lot more. If so, she'd let Piper take care of that.

Still unwilling to leave her dorm room—why should she when everywhere she went she ran into Dao-Ming, who was like Germaine times ten? And her group of followers was a lot meaner—and a lot smarter—than the cheerleaders of Paris High. Instead, Mei fooled around on the Internet for a little while, but it wasn't the same as back home. So much was blocked by the government that trying to surf her favorite sites, or find new ones, was almost impossible.

Finally she gave up and clicked back to the IKC page to update her status—pathetic—and was shocked when she saw a whole bunch more pins on the map widget she'd just put into place. And none of them were around France, so she knew it wasn't Piper striking again.

There was one in Los Angeles, two in Toronto, and five in Miami. New York had a couple pins in it as well, as did Mexico City and Jamaica. She smiled. The International Kissing Club really had gone global.

Logging off Facebook, Mei switched over to the bus schedule and maps she'd downloaded the day before. She was pretty sure she had figured out the best route to the Social Welfare Institute, where she'd spent the first two years of her life. Still, she ran over the different routes again, making sure she wasn't missing anything. When she was satisfied that she wouldn't get lost, she set her computer aside and stretched. Though she wasn't planning on going for a while, it was nice to know she was ready when the time came.

A quick glance at the clock had her yielding to the inevitable. If the food was really bad, she could eat a huge plate of rice, right? By itself, it wasn't the most nutritiously sound alternative, but if it would quiet her stomach, she would go for it.

Grabbing her sweater—Shenyang got cold at night—she headed for the cafeteria. Maybe tonight she'd get lucky and they'd have egg rolls or orange chicken or a vegetable she actually recognized.

As she walked across campus, Mei weighed her options for the next eight weeks in this institution. She could suck it up and grow a thick skin—who cared if she had any friends, after all? That wasn't what she was here for.

Or she could talk to the dean of student life, Furen Guong, about the fact that she wasn't fitting in. But that was pretty much like admitting her "buddies" had completely dissed her, and she wasn't quite ready to commit social suicide of that order yet.

Or, she could go home early. A lesser girl would call her mom and have a plane ticket FedEx'd stat. But failure wasn't an option. Joneses didn't fail. Besides, if she ran away, she'd never know the truth.

She'd picked this school instead of one in Beijing because it was in Liaoning Province. Shenyang was only a short train ride from Dalian, where the Social Welfare Institute (SWI) from which she'd been adopted was located.

No, she was going to stay here and stick it out whether the other girls liked it or not. And if she didn't want to spend all her time in her room she was going to have to get focused. Dao-Ming and Bao might rule the school, but surely there was one person here who wasn't under their spell. One rebellious teenager in all of Communist China. She decided that by the end of today she was going to find an ally. And then—

The next thing Mei knew she was flying through the air on a collision course with a large tree. She hit it hard enough to daze her, and as she sat there, trying to get her scrambled brain to work, she couldn't help wondering if her fellow students had tired of nonconfrontational animosity and were now starting on actual physical violence.

"嘿，你好嗎?" She heard someone speak, but nothing made any sense. She glanced up, completely nonplussed—right into the eyes of the best-looking guy she'd seen since coming to this school.

He was kind of tall, but that could be because she was flat on her back and he was towering over her. His hair was longish, not cut short like so many of her classmates, and he had a small earring in the cartilage of one ear. As she stared at him, trying to gather her scattered wits, he popped his skateboard and rested it against his leg. She blinked, looked from the board to the earring to the hair and back again, and that's when she knew. For once the universe had actually listened. She'd found her rebel.

Then he was squatting by her side, his dark eyes filled with a concern that warmed her. He spoke again, and again the words coming out of his mouth made no sense to her whatsoever. Finally her addled brain regained its senses and she realized he wasn't speaking nonsense—just Mandarin.

"I speak English," she said as clearly as she could manage.

He said something else, still in Mandarin, and she shook her head. "I don't know what you're saying."

Recognition dawned on his face and he switched to barely accented English. "So, you're the American exchange student that has Dao-Ming and Bao in such a tizzy."

Mei pushed herself up into a sitting position. "Yep. That would be me."

"I'm Guiran." He held out a hand and she took it.

"I'm Mei Jones."

"Look, I'm really sorry about running into you. I'm practicing some new tricks on my board and you walked right in front of me."

So that's what had hit her—a guy on a speeding skateboard. Amazing. It had felt more like an 18-wheeler.

"Sorry. I was . . . thinking." Pouting was more like it, but he didn't really need to know that, did he?

"I bet." He was still holding her hand and it felt kind of strange—but in a good way. Of course, that could just be the fact that after two weeks here she was starved for some kind of decent human contact.

Either way, she resisted the urge to tug her hand away.

"Why do you say that?" she asked curiously, pulling at her uniform skirt—which she had just realized was hiked up to the top of her thighs.

"Here, let me help you." Standing, he easily pulled her to her feet. "I just figure, if Dao-Ming is gunning for you, your life couldn't be that easy right about now."

"You have no idea."

"Sure I do. It wasn't that long ago that I was the new kid here."

"Really?" she asked, fascinated. "You're not from Shenyang?"

"Not exactly. We travel around a lot for my dad's job, so for the most part I was raised outside of China. Now that we're back—" He shrugged. "Now that we're home, it isn't as easy to fit in as I'd expected it would be."

"Yeah. Believe me, I know what you mean."

He glanced at the cafeteria, which was currently bustling with students—many of whom had seen her less-than-graceful fall. Mei felt her cheeks burn. Like she didn't already have enough strikes against her, now she looked like a klutz, too.

"Were you going to eat?"

"Yeah." She didn't know why she felt awkward admitting it. "But it can wait—"

"No, you should go. If you don't get in there soon, they won't serve you."

"I learned that the hard way."

Guiran laughed. "Bummer."

She didn't want to leave him. How else could she cross off the one item on her to-do list? After all, she couldn't count on fate to step in twice. It was now up to her. "Have you eaten already?" she asked.

"Nah. I'm waiting for my friends."

"Oh, right." Mei backed away, stumbling over a large tree root and nearly ending up on her butt for the second time in five minutes. Ducking her head to hide her total embarrassment, she said, "Well, it was nice to meet you. Good luck with the skateboarding trick."

Could I have been any more stupid? she berated herself as she started up the cafeteria steps. Of course he didn't want to eat with her—he already had friends.

She passed a group of girls who pointed and laughed. She ignored them as best she could, but it didn't work. She couldn't make her feet reach the top of the stairs. Instead she turned around and ran back to Guiran. "May I join you and your friends?"

He smiled. "Actually I just texted them. They're running late. So if the invite is still open, I'd love to have dinner with you."

She felt herself light up like the Fourth of July. Somebody liked her. Somebody wanted to spend time with her—even if it was just a quick dinner at the cafeteria. They walked through the double doors together, and as they got into line, she was incredibly conscious of the fact that half the school was staring at them. "Although, I'm not sure what having dinner with me will do to your reputation."

"Don't worry about me. I can take it."

"Oh yeah? So you think you're bad to the bone, do you?"

"I try," he answered, pretending to buff his nails against his jacket. As he guided her through the line, cracking jokes, she felt herself relax a little. Feeling optimistic for the first time since she'd gotten to the school, Mei reached for a dish of who-knows-what. Big surprise—every meal was an adventure in gastronomical distress.

"Oh, not that!" Guiran put out a hand to stop her. "Unless you like overspiced octopus?"

Ugh. Octopus. Was that what she'd tried to choke down the night before? "Not really." She glanced at the remaining choices. "I can't read much Mandarin yet, so I don't know what any of this is. Do you have suggestions?"

He studied her. "Do you trust me?"

"Sure."

"That was quick."

"Well, you already threw me against a tree. I'm not sure what you could do in here that would be worse."

"Hmm. Good point." He leaned across her to reach for something and his shoulder brushed against her upper arm. "Here. Try these." He placed two dishes on her tray.

"What are they?"

"One's beef and one's fish. But they both taste good, I promise."

"I believe you."

They worked their way through the serving line, then Guiran snagged a small table for them against the windows at the back of the cafeteria.

The cut-stone and glass buildings of the campus surrounded an intricately designed and manicured garden. In the evenings, lamps along the concrete paths highlighted huge pieces of contemporary sculpture. It certainly wasn't the sloped tile roofs and gilded lions "Mulan" had expected, and again she was hit by how incongruous her preconceived notions of China had been.

She picked up her first bite with her fingers, popped it in her mouth and chewed gingerly, then smiled at the pleasant taste.

"You like it?" he asked with a wide smile that put her further at ease.

"I do, actually."

"Good." He started in on his own food.

Silence stretched between them for a few minutes as they ate. When she was finally full—or close to it—Mei focused on trying to make conversation. She searched for something to say, then remembered what Guiran had mentioned outside. "So, you weren't raised in China?"

He paused, his chopsticks halfway to his mouth. "No. My parents left when I was three and we lived most of my life in Europe."

"Where in Europe?" she asked.

"France and England. We also spent a year in Germany."

"Wow. You've been all over."

"Yeah."

He looked distinctly uncomfortable, so she tried to change the subject. "I have a friend in Paris right now. She's doing the same kind of exchange program I am."

"Paris is a great place."

He sounded so wistful she couldn't help asking, "You don't like China?"

"It's not that. It's just there are a lot of bad memories here. For my parents, I mean. It makes my mom sad to be back."

"Why?"

His eyes were startled—and a little wary—when they looked into her own. "Are you always this forward?"

"No." She paused, a little self-conscious as she realized she was lying. "Yes, I guess I am. I'm sorry. You don't have to answer if you don't want—"

"Well, you tell me. You're a Chinese girl from America and your last name is Jones. You were adopted, right?"

"Yes."

"A lot of Chinese girls are."

That's when it dawned on her—he might know more about her plight than she'd ever expected. She'd always focused on being the abandoned; she'd never thought about what it would feel like to be the one they kept.

"Do you know what happened to her, your sister?" she asked.

"No. My parents never said. But I assume she was adopted by Americans."

"Like me," Mei said quietly. "That's why I came to China, to Shenyang, to find out about my birth parents. But now . . . I don't know. Everything here is so overwhelming and I can't figure out where to start, not to mention I can barely understand anyone or read anything. So maybe I came here for nothing."

Could she get any more dramatic? A couple more minutes of this and she'd morph into Piper. But it felt so good to say it all out loud, to verbalize the fear and frustration she'd been having for weeks now. She took a really deep breath, filling her lungs. It seemed like she hadn't been able to do that in weeks.

Guiran still hadn't said a word, however, and he'd stopped eating altogether. Mei pushed around the last of the food on her plate with her chopsticks—another source of embarrassment for her. She felt like the only person here who longed for a fork.

Guiran's nonresponse to her babbling made her even more self-conscious, and she worried she'd upset him.

Finally she asked, "Guiran? Are you okay?"

"Yes, I'm fine," he said, tossing his head back to move the lock of dark hair that had fallen across one eye. "You know, I've wondered sometimes if my sister has ever come looking for us. If she thinks about my parents, and why they gave her up." Sadness crept into his dark eyes again.

"I think all adoptees wonder about that at some point. But, at least for me, I've never been angry about it—I know my birth parents did what they felt they had to do." She'd worked hard to bury any resentment she felt at being given up.

"I have wonderful loving parents, and I have a good life with them. I'm sure your sister does, too, Guiran." She gave him a reassuring smile. After a moment, the corners of his mouth turned into a lopsided grin. Her stomach jumped a little and she hoped it was from his smile, and not a reaction to what she'd just eaten.

Then again, how dreadfully inconvenient. Here she'd planned to ignore all the IKC stuff. And now, for the first time since John, there was a guy she might want to kiss. On the other hand, for a girl who had been hoping not to become a leper thirty minutes before, she was getting a little ahead of herself.

"Okay," Guiran said. "I'll help you."

"Help me what?" she asked, baffled.

"I'll help you find your parents. If you have the information, I'll do the translating and go with you to the SWI."

"Really?" she asked, unsure what to make of his offer. "You would come with me?"

He shrugged. "Sure. It's the least I can do to make up for running you over."

"Thank you, Guiran." Mei smiled. Suddenly, China didn't seem so lonely.

"No problem. But, hey, before this goes any further, I have to ask. You don't think there's any chance we're related, do you?"

Maybe she wasn't the only one thinking about kissing. "How old are you?"

"I'm eighteen," he answered. *Oh, thank God.* He was older than she was—there was no way she could be his sister.

"Good. No chance we're related." The sister his parents had given away would have to have been born before him.

As they got up to leave the table, she crossed off the first item on her mental to-do list and added a second. She'd found a friend. Now it was time to find her family.

IKC Fan Page

The Official Fan Page for the International Kissing Club

2,397
people like this

 IKC Page

Mulan Who knew walking across campus was a full-contact sport. Have met cute sk8ter guy. Will post pictures soon.

> **Jane** Any lip action yet?
>
> **Rapunzel** Way to sport up.
>
> **Ariel** Is Chinese kissing as good as French kissing?:)

Ariel Just came back from the most divine salon. Finally have my blue streaks.

> **Rapunzel** Your mom's gonna flip!
>
> **Ariel** Mom? What mom?
>
> **Mulan** You are still planning on coming home, right?
>
> **Jayson** I'm a sucker for blue streaks. Just earned my three points on the subway. He had blue streaks, too!
>
> **Mulan** Hello, Ariel? You are coming home right?

Jane Aren't any of you going to school? Tell me I'm not the only one stuck in high school hell.

> **Rapunzel** When we have to. Not much point, as I don't understand a word they say. Who told me they speak English here?
>
> **Mulan** Better than Mandarin. Community College is no Rosetta Stone.

Rapunzel Hit the beach again today. Finally stood up on the board. Was well rewarded for my efforts.

> **Mulan** You're being careful, aren't you?
>
> **Ariel** Mulan!!!!

Mulan I meant in the ocean!!!! The ten deadliest everythings live in Australia.

Adelaide We have a jellyfish the size of your thumbnail that can kill you in five minutes. Btw, put a point on the board for me! He's local so I'm rounding down.

Jane My brother has a brain the size of a thumbnail and can kill just as quickly.

Ariel   Louvre in T minus eighteen hours!

Chapter 13
Piper

Piper stumbled down the hallway in her pajamas, drawn to the kitchen by the amazing aroma of Marie's special blend of coffee. Her mouth was actually watering for the rich, dark liquid, her brain screaming for the shot of caffeine it so desperately needed.

God, when am I going to get used to the late hours Simone keeps? she wondered as she turned the corner into the kitchen. Not that she was complaining. She loved every second of living and going to school in Paris, so much so that lately she'd been thinking of what a great university the Sorbonne was. But that didn't make getting in at three a.m. after a long day of school any easier to bear—especially when L'Académie de Paris started at seven thirty in the morning.

But today was special. She'd been planning it for years, ever since she first became interested in art, and she wasn't going to blow it by waking up too late to do everything that was on her list.

Thinking about the day she had planned, she was on autopilot as she cruised over to the very stylish coffeepot Marie had in the middle of the counter—and the ambrosia of the gods that was currently per-colating away inside it. When she left here in seven weeks, she was taking an entire carry-on full of the stuff back home. And then she was going to ration it—only bring the coffee beans out on the most special of occasions. Because going the rest of her life without it just didn't bear thinking about—and she *so* wasn't sharing with her family.

She had just poured herself a cup, and brought it to her nose for a long, ecstasy-inducing sniff, when she heard someone else enter the kitchen. Figuring it was Marie or Simone's dad, Gus, she turned with a quick smile, then froze as she took in the tall, dark, and absolutely gorgeous specimen of manhood staring at her, an overnight bag on his shoulder.

He was tall, really tall, and she wasn't just saying that because she was in her bare feet. This guy would tower over her even in the very chic, very sexy five-inch-heeled boots she had spent way too much money on while shopping with Simone the other day. He was also really muscular, unlike most of the guys she'd met here, a lot of whom would give a string bean a run for its money. His shoulders were wide, his chest broad, his biceps well-defined where they strained against the dark cotton of his T-shirt.

"You must be Piper." His voice wrapped itself around her like a river of dark, warm caramel.

"I am." She smiled at him and tried to remember if she had washed her makeup off before falling into bed a few hours before. "And you are . . . ?"

"Sebastian."

Oh, right, of course. Simone's absent brother. She could see the resemblance now—he had the same sapphire-blue eyes and ebony hair, but his was styled in a short, suave cut that emphasized his strong jaw, lush lips, and slightly scruffy day-old beard. For a second her fingers itched to sketch him, so much so that she shoved her hands into the pockets of her sweats to make sure she didn't grab the closest napkin and give in to the impulse.

Her strange reaction bothered her, especially considering how perfect he seemed. Not just how he looked, but in the way Simone and his parents all but worshiped him. If she'd learned anything from Germaine it was that anyone who looked and sounded that good probably wasn't. Too bad the lesson didn't stop her heart from thudding painfully in her chest.

"Right." She forced herself to smile. "Marie said something about you making it home this weekend."

Sebastian nodded before leaning against the counter, ankles crossed in a pose so indolent, so self-assured, that she couldn't help thinking he looked like a movie star—more than aware of his impact on the female half of the species, but determined to act as normal as possible under the circumstances.

"I've got midterms next week and it's easier to study at home than in the dorm." His voice was a little bored but the look in his indigo eyes was intense.

"I bet." She took a sip of her coffee, searched for something to say even though she wanted nothing more than to flee back to her room and away from those eyes that seemed to catalogue everything about her. "What classes are you taking?"

"Basic first-year stuff, except I did manage to squeeze in a class on art history and one on sculpting."

"Really? Who are you studying?"

He sighed, a long, drawn-out exhale that somehow managed to sound both condescending and annoyed. And French, so French. It shot the small niggles of unwelcome interest she'd been feeling right into annoyance, and Piper nearly called him on his boorish behavior. But she had been raised in the South, and annoyance—no matter how well deserved—was no excuse for rudeness.

Still, she couldn't just stand here and gape at him like an idiot. She was struggling to come up with a reason to excuse herself when Marie breezed in. "Piper, you're up early! I thought surely you'd sleep until noon after the night you and Simone had."

Before Piper could answer, her house mother turned and saw Sebastian. She squealed and launched herself at her son while Piper stood by, a little nonplussed at the realization that a woman as elegant as Marie could sound so much like a junior high girl.

Sebastian didn't seem to mind, though. He just grinned and swept his mother up into a huge bear hug, as she babbled in French and pressed kisses all over his face. Piper knew she should slip out and let them talk, but she was fascinated by the genuine affection on Sebastian's face when he spoke to his mother. It seemed so at odds with the bored disdain she'd seen on his face just a few moments before.

When their rapid-fire conversation finally wound down—Piper wasn't able to follow the whole thing but she knew there was stuff in there about school and classes and what Sebastian wanted for dinner—Marie turned to her with a huge smile.

"I'm sorry, Piper. Forgive me. Though he lives in the same city, my son does not stop by nearly as often as he should. It's been weeks since I've seen him."

"It's okay. I understand," Piper said, even though she wasn't sure she did. She tried to imagine what her mother's reaction was going to be when Piper got back to Texas. Somehow, she doubted it would be this exuberant, no-holds-barred lovefest. More likely, it would involve migraine medicine, a cool washcloth, and an hour's worth of complaints about Piper breathing too loudly.

"So, I didn't give you a chance to answer me, Piper," Marie said as she poured two cups of coffee, then handed one to her son. "What are you doing up so early?"

"I'm going to the Louvre." Piper tried to sound casual, but from Marie's indulgent smile, she knew that some of her excitement must have leaked through. "I have tickets for today and tomorrow."

"Oh, that's right! I don't know how I forgot—you've so been looking forward to it."

"Definitely. I've always wanted to see the *Mona Lisa* in person."

Sebastian snorted, muttered something in French under his breath that she didn't quite catch. It must not have been flattering, though, because his mother sent him a warning look.

"Of course you do. It's a masterpiece. What else do you want to see?"

"The *Venus de Milo* and the *Winged Victory of Samothrace*—"

Again Sebastian muttered under his breath, and though he wasn't loud, Piper definitely caught the French word for idiot, along with a couple of other uncomplimentary phrases. She felt her cheeks flame with a combination of anger and embarrassment.

"Sebastian!" Marie's voice cut through the sudden uncomfortable silence. "That's uncalled for. Apologize."

"No, it's okay," Piper said, starting out the door, glad that his ridiculously bad attitude had stopped her knees from trembling. "I'm going to go take a shower—"

"It is not okay! I did not raise him *dans une grange*. In a barn!" She glared at her son.

"Of course, Maman. You're right." Sebastian turned to Piper with a smirk. "I'm sorry that I made fun of your pedestrian taste in art. I will try to keep my more informed opinions to myself from now on."

Piper's face grew even hotter, and if Marie hadn't been standing there she would have gone off on the smug jerk. Instead, she gritted her teeth and contented herself with a simple, "That's okay. I wouldn't expect anything better from a pot maker."

"I'm a *sculptor*." His teeth ground together.

"You know what they say. One man's art is another man's . . ."

"You know what—" Sebastian bit off whatever he was going to say as Marie's laugh rang through the kitchen.

"I have a wonderful idea. Why doesn't Sebastian go to the Louvre with you today?"

"What?" Sebastian yelped.

"No!" Piper said at the same time. "That's really not necessary."

"Of course it is. Sebastian has spent so much time in the Musée du Louvre that he practically has the entire place memorized. He can get you wherever you want to go much more quickly than you could get there yourself. It'll be fun."

Piper didn't think the Junior League Mother-Daughter tea could be less fun than having to waste an entire day putting up with Sebastian's snide comments and bored sighs. She'd been planning this trip forever and really didn't want it ruined by some French moron with delusions of grandeur.

"Really, Marie," she said with a shake of her head. "I'm sure I can find my way around—"

"And I have tests to study for, Maman. Midterms are next week."

"They don't start until Wednesday. I'm sure you can take off a few hours to show our guest around. I'll look forward to hearing all about your day at dinner tonight." With those parting words and a look that brooked no argument, she slapped her coffee cup down onto the counter before gliding majestically out the same door from which Piper had spent the past five minutes trying to make her own escape.

Cold silence filled the kitchen after Marie's departure. Piper didn't say anything for a minute, waiting to see how Sebastian would respond, but when he didn't, she muttered, "Don't worry about it. I don't expect you to—"

"My mother told me to take you, I'll take you. It's not worth the hassle otherwise." He drained his own coffee cup before setting it in the sink. "One thing, though."

"What?"

"You might want to wash your face and comb your hair. I'd hate for the tourists to mistake you for a modern art sculpture."

"Like one of yours?" She raised her eyebrows, glad that his obnoxiousness had made her strange reaction to him vanish as quickly as it had come. "But what was I thinking? It's not as if yours will ever be in the Louvre."

An hour and a half later, Piper was still fuming over Sebastian's quip about her looks. Even though he'd been totally right—a glance in the bathroom mirror had shown her chin-length brown hair sticking up in about thirty different directions and last night's makeup pooled unattractively under her eyes—but that still didn't give him the right to make fun of her. She'd experienced more name-calling than anyone should have to at the hands of Germaine the . . . *Is there a word in French that rhymes with Germaine and means psycho?* She wasn't going to put up with it. Certainly not from an arrogant French guy with much better looks than manners. French assholes had nothing on Germaine.

Putting her annoyance aside, she couldn't help the little thrill that shot through her as they crossed the huge courtyard toward the glass pyramid that would be their entrance into the Louvre. She was finally here, had finally made it to the most famous art museum in the world. She couldn't wait to see the Rembrandt room and the Italian Grand Gallery. For months—for years, really—she'd dreamed about seeing the works up close. Now that it was going to happen, she almost had to pinch herself to believe it was real.

"You're shaking," Sebastian said as they stood at the back of the line waiting to enter the Pyramid. "Are you cold?" He started to shrug out of his black pea coat, but then seemed to think better of it. "You should have brought a jacket."

"I'm not cold," she said disgustedly. "Just excited."

His eyes narrowed. "Really? Over a museum and a bunch of old artwork?"

"Oh my God! You did *not* just say that about the Louvre! This place is . . . is . . ."

"Is what?"

"It's the pinnacle of art museums. The collections here are incredible. The Rembrandts, the School of Fontainebleau, the Goyas, and the Rubenses. There are more works of art here than in almost any other museum in the world—"

"Whoa!" Sebastian held up a hand. "I get the point. Why don't we head to the gift shop first, so you can buy your set of French masters refrigerator magnets?"

"Well, that would certainly save you time, wouldn't it? Then you could get back to studying for the midterm for your how-to-be-a-sanctimonious-jerk class. Oh wait; you've already aced that one."

"No, you must have my university confused with your exchange program. I take *real* classes, unlike you, whose only in-depth education seems to be in oral anatomy."

"Excuse me?" Piper asked, unable to think of a better comeback. She couldn't help but wonder who had told him about her extracurricular activities. *Simone?* But she'd thought her house sister was amused by her quest to experience *everything* France had to offer.

Confused and a little hurt, she snarled, "I don't need you here, you know. I know almost everything there is to know about the Louvre. I've spent years studying the databases and the virtual tours and I made a list of everything I want to see."

"You made a list?"

She rolled her eyes. Trust him to ignore her entire outburst except for the one thing that interested him. "So what if I did?"

One dark eyebrow shot up. "Can I see it?"

Her hand went to the back pocket of her jeans of its own volition, though Piper didn't know if it was because she wanted to show him her list or because she wanted to protect it—and herself—from more ridicule. "Yeah, right. Like I'm going to show it to you?"

When he didn't answer, she sighed. "Look, why don't we call it a day? To make your mother happy we'll meet back here in six hours and say we had a fabulous time." With that, she turned her back on him.

The next thing she knew, his hand was digging in her pocket.

"Hey, what are you doing?" She slapped at him, but she wasn't quick enough. Turning, she saw Sebastian smiling that smug grin that made her want to strangle him where he stood. Her folded-up list was in his hand.

"Give me that!"

He held it out of reach as he opened it. His smirk quickly turned to a frown as he perused the fifty-three items she had listed there.

"Really?" he demanded a minute later. "*This* is the art you've traveled thousands of miles to see?"

"Yeah. So?"

He muttered something about God saving him from tourists, and Piper went from annoyed to angry. "Hey, there's nothing wrong with my list," she told him indignantly.

"Except for the fact that it reads like a must-see list out of a ten-euro guidebook?"

"Those are some of the most famous works in the whole world—"

"Exactly. And they're fine for a bus of Japanese tourists trying to make their way through the Louvre before lunch, but Simone told me you wanted to be an artist. I thought you wanted to look at the real masters."

Then, before her disbelieving eyes, he folded the list in half and ripped it to shreds.

"Stop!" she cried, trying to wrest it out of his hands. "I worked hard on that—"

"Which is the most pathetic part of the whole thing," he answered, right before he tossed the mangled remains into a nearby trash can.

He'd thrown her list away.

Piper stared at the trash can in shock.

Sebastian had ripped up her list and thrown it away, like it was nothing. Like *she* was nothing. And now, here she was at the front of the line, and she was about to go into the Louvre armed with only the names of the paintings she remembered. Which was about twelve.

She was so angry that she wanted to punch him. So angry that she nearly did. Only the fear of breaking her hand—and being unable to sketch for the next few weeks—kept her from smashing her fist into Sebastian's smug face as he ushered her through the doorway, past the ticket booth where he presented his yearly pass, and down the elegant spiral staircase that led to the very heart of the museum.

Piper didn't say a word as they descended the stairs, largely because she couldn't think of anything to say that didn't start with a particularly vile curse. But the second they got to the bottom, she wrenched her elbow from his grip and started blindly toward one of the exhibit halls. As far as she was concerned, she wanted nothing more to do with him, ever. He might be the hottest guy she'd ever seen, but he was also a total asshole and she—

"Hey, you're going the wrong way!"

She kept walking, refusing even to look at him. "I'd say that was impossible, considering the only way I'm going is away from you."

"You can't just wander around the Louvre. Not if you have any hope of getting something out of it. Beyond looking at pretty pictures, I mean."

"Isn't that the point of going to a museum? To look at pretty pictures?"

"Again, I thought you wanted to be an artist."

"I do!"

"Then you should know that real art—true art—is rarely pretty. It's shocking, thought provoking. But rarely is it anything so insipid as 'pretty.'"

His words struck a chord deep inside her, the truth in them absolutely undeniable. And for the first time since she'd met him, his voice held no condescension or annoyance. Just a pure, palpable love for the works of art they were about to see.

For a moment, a connection shimmered between them. The understanding of what it was to be transported out of oneself by a great masterpiece.

The knowledge of what it was like to be surrounded by greatness you could only hope to one day achieve.

"Well, what am I supposed to do? Without my list I don't have a clue where to start."

"You don't have to know." He scooted in front of her, blocked her path. "I know enough for both of us."

She gritted her teeth. "God! It's amazing to me your ego actually fits inside the museum. It's gigantic."

"Maybe, but it's also well earned." He reached for her hand, and an odd tingling started where their fingers connected. She yanked her hand away, tucked it in the pocket of her jeans. He might be the only French guy she *didn't* want to tingle with.

Sebastian sighed impatiently. "Come on, Piper. Trust me."

"Why should I? You've done nothing but make fun of me since we met."

"I'll stop, I promise. And I also promise that I'll give you the tour of your life. If you're unhappy when I'm finished, I know where they sell ten-euro guidebooks."

She narrowed her eyes, uncertain if she wanted to spend the next few hours with him. It kind of seemed like she was making a pact with the devil. "What if I don't want to waste the whole day with you? It's not like you've been much fun to be around so far."

"That'll change, I swear. Now come on, let's get going."

He turned away and walked toward the series of galleries that branched off the lobby, as if he just expected her to follow. For about fifteen seconds, she debated ducking into the ladies' room and waiting for him to leave, but she was smart enough to know that if she did, she would only end up wandering around completely lost for the next six hours. With a grudging sigh, she started after Sebastian.

What followed was the strangest, most amazing museum tour that Piper had ever been on. They began in front of Géricault's *Raft of the Medusa*, a huge painting that showed thirteen survivors of a wreck just as they spotted the *Argus,* a rescue ship. When she told him her impressions of the scene, Sebastian nodded enthusiastically and then pointed out a bunch of stuff she hadn't even noticed.

From there, he took her through the sculpture galleries—which were his favorite for obvious reasons—where they studied the tomb of Philippe Pot and the enormous *Marly Horses* statues, along with some smaller, lesser-known works. She really loved an abstract sculpture of a little girl, and when she pointed it out to Sebastian, he laughed and told her it was one of his favorites as well. Then he pulled her to another room, his voice warm and deep as he regaled her with stories and interesting facts about everything she was seeing.

On and on the tour went, hitting a few works in each of the galleries, though not the ones Piper had originally intended. Sebastian even took her to the Rembrandt room for a few minutes before hustling her into yet another gallery. There was just so much to see, and Sebastian kept up a running commentary on every single piece of art they saw. His knowledge was awe inspiring, and more than a little intimidating.

The day slipped away, along with most of the tension between them. By the time they left the Louvre—after being ushered to the door by two security guards anxious to close up—it was dark out and Piper was starving.

"Thank you so much," she said as they walked back toward the nearest Metro station. And she was shocked to realize how appreciative she actually felt. "It was amazing."

"Better than your list?" he asked with a grin that lit up his whole face and reminded her of just how handsome she'd first found him.

"Well, I wouldn't say that . . ."

"No? But you have to admit you enjoyed yourself."

She started to deny it out of principle alone, but one look at Sebastian's eyes, which were dark and strangely serious, and she knew she couldn't. In those moments, when he stood so close to her she swore she could hear not only her heartbeat but his as well, the International Kissing Club had never seemed less important.

"I did."

"Good." He paused for a moment. He tilted his head and studied her with the same intensity he'd lavished on the sculpture gallery. Really looking at her for the first time. "You have a nice smile." He sounded almost surprised.

But not as surprised as she was. Feeling a little uncomfortable, she tried to joke. "So do you, when you're not smirking at me like I'm a lower life-form."

"Yeah. Sorry about that. It's a hazard of the nationality."

"So I hear."

"Now, that's not right," he said. "You're supposed to tell me it isn't true."

"Frenchmen are arrogant. And you're very Gallic."

"I thought you liked things that are French." Sebastian's eyes dropped to her lips.

Piper grinned—she couldn't help herself—then glanced around in an effort to regain her equilibrium.

It didn't work. But then, how could it? The world around her was straight out of a movie.

The heavy scent of flowers perfumed the air.

The remnants of the late afternoon rain made everything shimmer while the big round streetlamps reflected off the glass of the Louvre pyramid at the center of the courtyard, making it gleam.

Sebastian must have noticed her discomfort, because his smile grew wicked. "What? No snappy comeback?" He nudged her teasingly with his shoulder.

The contact made Piper's whole body light up. There was that damn tingle again. Only this time, she almost didn't mind. Not that she would let him know that.

"Hey, back up, buddy. You're exactly the kind of guy who gives European men a bad name."

"Oh, really? Because I was thinking the same thing about you and American girls."

"What's that supposed to mean?" she asked indignantly.

"Simone gave me the heads-up about you before I came home this weekend. Said you've been breaking hearts all over Paris since the first night you got here."

"Me?" she trilled, pressing a hand to her chest theatrically. A thrill worked its way down her spine at the idea that she was some sort of femme fatale. That was a description she could get used to. "Do I look like a heartbreaker?"

"Actually, that's exactly what you look like." He reached up and pushed a strand of hair away from her face. "Raoul still talks about the kiss you gave him at Le Bataclan three weeks ago."

"That was—that was nothing. I was just . . ." For the first time, she wondered what her kissing exploits looked like to everyone else. She and her friends knew it was all for fun, but maybe other people didn't see it that way.

"Just what?" Sebastian crowded closer and Piper took a step back in self-defense. She couldn't think when he was so close, breathing the same air that she was.

"There's this competition. My friends and I . . . we call it the International Kissing Club."

The eyebrow went up again and she almost melted right there, in the middle of Palais-Royal. For the first time since she'd arrived in Paris, she'd met a guy she wouldn't mind kissing again and again. Despite their rocky start, she realized she liked Sebastian. He was smart, funny, and ooh là là . . . she just didn't know enough French adjectives. What was there not to like? And now that she'd found him, he thought she was just interested in a one-point stand.

Before she knew what she was doing, before she could think better of it, she blurted out the rest. "We get points for kissing guys. One point for each kiss from a different guy and three points if—"

The second eyebrow joined the first. "Three points if . . . ?"

"Three points if he's really special," she whispered.

For a second, Sebastian only stared at her, a puzzled look on his face. Just when she was starting to regret her honesty—what guy liked thinking a girl was interested in kissing him because of a competition?—he threw back his head and laughed. And laughed. And laughed.

He laughed so hard and long that she stiffened, a little offended. But he reached for her hand and finally managed to get himself under control. "You Americans . . . always competing. Always wanting to have more, more, more. Don't you realize that the best things in life are about quality, not quantity?"

She nearly swallowed her tongue at the sizzle in his eyes, in his voice, and for the first time since this whole wild adventure had begun Piper couldn't help wondering if he was right. "What's wrong with both?" she asked softly.

"Nothing. But don't you know, just like in art, you need to master one technique before you move on to the next?" He entwined his long, calloused fingers with her own, and Piper couldn't believe how right it felt to be standing there, letting him hold her hand.

"So, tell me, Piper," Sebastian said after a moment. "If I kiss you right now, will that be enough? Or will you kiss me back and then go to a club and kiss some other guy tomorrow?"

She couldn't breathe, couldn't think. Could barely stand upright as heat streaked along every nerve ending she had. "We could—we could try it." Was that really her voice, that high-pitched squeak that practically broke the sound barrier?

"Oh, chérie, we're going to do a lot more than try."

His hands trembled a little as they cupped her face, which surprised her even as it made her intensely happy. And then he kissed her, and it was more amazing, more delicious, more *real* than any and every kiss that had come before it.

IKC Fan Page

The Official Fan Page for the International Kissing Club

3,954
people like this

🐦 IKC Page

Ariel   Finally saw the Louvre! Am in ecstasy!

> **Mulan** Finally ate food! Am in more ecstasy!
>
> **Ariel** I think I need to revise my points down. I just kissed Sebastian, and if that kiss gets only three points, then everyone else is a definite one-pointer.
>
> **Jane** What about Raoul?
>
> **Ariel** Raoul who? I think I'm in love!
>
> **Mulan** That was quick.
>
> **Ariel** You know us artistes. We embrace life and love!
>
> **Rapunzel** Got mono yet? ;)

✉ Messages

Between **Cassidy** and **Piper**:

Cassidy
Down, girl. You've only known this guy two weeks.
Piper
Um . . . it's actually only been two days.
Cassidy
Holy shit!
Piper
But when you know, you know.
Cassidy
What am I supposed to know, exactly?
Piper
Come on, you can't tell me you don't feel anything for Lucas.

Cassidy

Keep your emotions out of my vacation romance.

Piper

I'll keep my emotions out if you can keep yours out.

Cassidy

New topic, please.

Piper

Okay. How about the fact that my art teacher hates me? Nothing I do is good enough.

Cassidy

What is he, an idiot?

Piper

Maybe I'm the idiot.

Cassidy

No way.

Piper

I don't know. I just can't seem to get in the groove over here.

Cassidy

I thought you loved Paris.

Piper

I do. It's my art that doesn't seem to.

Cassidy

Hang in there. It'll get better.

Piper

I guess.

Piper

I have to go now. I've got class. Wish me luck.

Cassidy

You'll do great.

Piper

We'll see. Btw, happy birthday, Cass. Blow out a candle for me. It's the first I haven't been there to celebrate with you since kindergarten.

 IKC Page

Jane   You kissed Sebastian? I thought you told me you didn't even want to meet the "perfect" older brother?

Ariel That was before he showed me the best art ever. I Louvre Paris!

Mulan We're still talking about paintings, right?

Mulan   Btw, happy birthday, Rapunzel. Let down your hair!

Jane Happy sassy seventeen.

Ariel Don't you mean SEXY seventeen? And don't forget to kiss and tell, vacation girl.

Chapter 14
Cassidy

"Rationalists believe that these ideas exist *a priori*, or prior to experience, and therefore transcend experience . . ."

Mr. MacElroy droned on and on while Cassidy leaned so far against her palm she was nearly horizontal on her desk. She stared over the top of his combed-over pate, fixated on the infinitesimal movement of the minute hand on the clock hanging behind him.

Spending the afternoon held captive by the whims of a teacher so clearly bent on using every last second of "his" time, expounding the medieval worldview in terms too mind-numbing to describe, was not how Cassidy had imagined her seventeenth birthday. She looked at Rachel, her athletics teammate, who sat across the aisle and who was currently miming stabbing her ballpoint pen in her eye to end this misery. Cassidy stifled a snort.

Outside the wall of windows, the bright, clear afternoon beckoned. Already those students lucky enough not to have a pedant (ha! take that, PSAT practice exam) for last session were fairly skipping down the building's front steps to sweet, sweet freedom.

Bzzz. Bzzz. Bzzz.

Her cell vibrated in her bag. She looked at Mr. MacElroy to make sure he hadn't heard—cell phone use was strictly forbidden during school hours, no matter how close to the bell it was. When he didn't so much as pause, Cassidy slipped her hand under the bag's flap to pull out the phone. It was a text. From Lucas.

Meet me outside.

She glanced out the window again and this time saw the blue Bronco parked at the curb. She looked at the clock—one minute to go.

Almost a week had gone by since that day on the beach, a week since that kiss. Cassidy smiled all the way to her toes thinking about it.

"Any questions?" Mr. MacElroy finally finished his monologue as the bell rang. Cassidy, Rachel, and the rest of the class bolted from their desks like they were heading for the last lifeboat on the *Titanic*.

Squinting when she hit daylight, Cassidy shielded her eyes to see Lucas leaning casually against the car door, wearing frayed cargo shorts and a banded tee that skimmed his surf-sculpted torso to perfection. She heard a din of curious whispers erupt from the students on the lawn. Cassidy had to force herself not to take the stairs double-time and come to a skidding halt in front of him. *A shred of dignity, Cass. Be calm. Cool. Casual.*

She covered the last ten feet in fewer than two strides.

"What are you doing here?" she said, inwardly cringing at the bubblegum giddiness in her voice. Lucas looked her up and down.

"Cute uniform." He grinned as he took in her white poplin button-down, navy pleated skirt with matching kneesocks, and Mary Janes.

"Ha-ha." She scowled; she hated wearing it—it was like living in a Britney Spears video. Guys, on the other hand, apparently loved it.

"A little bird told me it was your birthday." From behind his back he presented a single white lily. "Happy birthday, American girl," he said, and brushed a light kiss on her cheek.

"H-how did you know?"

"Facebook, of course. Do you have plans for the rest of the day?" He took both her hands in his, and Cassidy couldn't help the wave of happiness that rippled through her from his simple touch.

"Nothing till later; Mrs. Gatwick is fixing me a special birthday dinner," she told him, blatantly ignoring the hours of homework she currently carried in her backpack. What was one night of missed sleep compared to spending her birthday with a supersweet guy who'd driven across Sydney to see her? Wasn't that why they made double-shot espressos?

"Then get in. We'll have to hurry if we're going to make it." He opened the car door and she crawled into the passenger seat.

"Where are you taking me?"

"I told you I'd show you the sights, didn't I?" His grin was mischievous as he asked, "You're not scared of heights, are you?"

"I don't think so, but I've never really been anywhere higher than the Paris, Texas, water tower," she said.

"Good. If we're lucky, there'll still be time for cake when we're done."

"Done with what? What cake?" She was spinning: the flower, the sweet kiss, seeing him again—it was a lot to take in. But the thought of spending her birthday with Lucas was better than anything she could have planned, so she threw her bag in the backseat and buckled up.

He slid on his aviators and they pulled from the curb. "Trust me, Cassidy—it's going to be a blast."

· · · · · ✈

"This. Is. Awesome!" Cassidy had to yell over the keen of the wind rushing through the steel girders.

"I told you I'd show you the city," Lucas said, obviously pleased with her response.

Standing more than four hundred feet in the air on top of Harbour Bridge, Cassidy thought she could see to the edge of the world. Below them the Opera House, the whole harbor out to the sea, the entire city, sprawled around them for miles.

The climb had taken just over two hours, and though they were strapped to a safety line and Cass was more than capable of climbing the 463 steps by herself, Lucas had taken every opportunity to help her. Each time, his soft touch setting off a firestorm along her nervous system.

Now, standing behind her on the walkway, he braced his arms around her on either side of the railing. The whole walk up hadn't scared her as much as having him stand this close. "There's Manly," he said, pointing in the distance, his chin resting on her shoulder. "And over here"—his hand slid around her waist to turn her—"is Bondi Beach. Have you been yet?"

"No," she said, wondering if his fingertips would leave scorch marks on her skin.

"Then we'll have to go—there's great surf over there. I can take you this weekend if you want."

Cassidy could not ignore the thrumming of blood in her ears. This was not good—not good at all. Sure, Lucas was sweet and hot and all, but she couldn't let herself get worked up over a guy she'd known less than a month and wouldn't see again in two more. They could be good friends—well, friends with kissing benefits should the opportunity arise again—but this whole heart-racing, sweaty-palms stuff, it couldn't continue. She had to get a grip and keep this totally casual. That way no one—especially Cassidy—got hurt when she had to leave.

So it frustrated her, hours after they'd returned to sea level and were sitting outside of a charming bakery on Bourke Street sharing a raspberry-and-chocolate-mousse tart, that she couldn't keep the light-headedness at bay. It obviously was not from low blood sugar.

"This is not a proper birthday cake, you know," Lucas commented as he took another bite.

"It's way better," she said. He nodded his agreement, the fork pressed between his lips . . . lips she knew from experience were warm and firm and—okay, new topic.

"When did you get that tattoo?" Cass pointed to the stylized wave design peeking from the edge of his sleeve.

"Two years ago, when I broke top ten in the junior surf rankings."

"Wow, you're that good, huh? How long have you been surfing?"

"Since . . . forever. As soon as I could walk. My parents live by the beach, and I remember watching guys riding waves for hours as a kid. I knew I had to do it."

"That's pretty cool to have known what you wanted out of life when you were so young," Cassidy said.

"Yeah, well, I wish my dad felt the same way," Lucas replied, his dimple disappearing.

"He doesn't want you to surf?"

"That's putting it lightly." He leaned back in his chair. "My dad keeps hoping I'll grow out of this 'rebellious phase,' go to university and get a degree in banking so I can work with him. We have a deal: I have one last year to get a big sponsor—"

"Or go to school," Cassidy said for him, and then chuckled.

"Why's that funny?"

"It's not, for you—it's just, you're running away from school so you can live your dream, and getting to go to school *is* my dream." She finished off the last bit of tart. Lucas leaned forward and dabbed at the corner of her mouth.

"Bit of chocolate there." That should have been embarrassing, if it wasn't so swoon inducing.

Swoon? Who am I? Not even drama-queen Piper used words like "swoon."

"Got big plans for university? Lawyer? Doctor?" he asked.

"Hardly." Cassidy laughed. "I just don't want to get stuck where I am, if that makes sense. I'm from this little town, Paris. My mom's lived there her whole life, my grandparents and their parents were all born there, and I just don't want that to be my story, too. I want more than that. Getting a scholarship to college is how I plan to make my escape."

"So, that's why you came here? To get away from your small town?"

"Well, that, and because of Piper."

"Piper?"

"And Izzy and Mei: my best friends. We all made a pact to become foreign exchange students together. Except Izzy couldn't go, so she's back home. But Piper's in France and Mei's in China."

Lucas looked at her, his honey-colored eyes crinkled at the corners like he found everything she said amusing. "That's a pretty major pact. Do you girls always do everything together?"

"Sort of. It's a long, long story," Cassidy said.

"Tell me on the way. I've gotta get you back in time for your birthday dinner." He stood and held out his hand and, as naturally as breathing, she took it.

Damn it!

This was getting dangerous. All this niceness, all this touching, all these *feelings*, it was too much. *He* was too much. And she was Cassidy Barlow: things this good didn't happen to her; boys like Lucas didn't happen to her. Her mom's mantra ran through her mind: when a guy seems too good to be true, run like hell and don't look back.

Except she didn't *want* to run away. Not this time.

She liked these feelings, liked the way he touched her and talked to her as if he was truly interested in what she had to say, in what made her happy. Not just looking for an opportunity to grope her. For chrissake, he'd come to her school to surprise her on her birthday, planned an amazing afternoon for her, and done nothing more than kiss her cheek and hold her hand. Who did that?

She'd never had a guy do anything like that for her, not even her own father.

Lucas's thumb rubbed lightly along her index finger as they walked to his car, sending ripples of goose bumps up her arm.

You know what? Paris, Texas, was seven thousand miles away and she had no intention of letting thoughts of home spoil this day. Instead, she let excitement and happiness—the things she was supposed to be feeling on this trip—wash over her, all thanks to Lucas.

Besides, she was tired of being on her guard, always waiting for the disappointment around the corner. For the rest of the time she was here, she decided, she would be a different girl—she would be "Vacation Cassidy," complete with a new positive attitude. Open to new experiences and emotions.

She would be more like . . . Piper, only with less theatrics and a better tan.

Besides, what's the worst that could happen in just seven weeks?

Then again, what's the best that could happen? she thought as they pulled up to Mrs. Gatwick's house.

More days like this, she hoped. Of course, considering the state of her weakened knees, more days like this and she'd never have a shot at that basketball scholarship. Though Lucas might be worth it.

"So, let me get this straight: you came all the way to Australia to kiss guys?" Lucas gave her a sidelong glance.

Cassidy came back to the conversation at hand. She heard the incredulity in his voice and was glad it was dark, because pink was not a good color on her, and right now she was covered in a huge blush head to toe. "I told you it was stupid."

Why had she told him anything about the IKC at all? She blamed that damn dimple—it was like Kryptonite; she was powerless against it. He could charm anything out of her when that little divot made an appearance.

He slouched a little in his seat. "So, how many points do you have so far?" For the first time since she'd met him, Lucas didn't sound so surfer-Zen-go-lucky.

"Me? Oh, well . . . you see . . . actually . . ." She fiddled with the zipper on her sweater as she practically glowed red. She should make up some number. What did it matter? He'd never know. God, if he were playing this game, he would probably have twice the points she did in just the time it took to drive over here.

"Tell me. It's a lot, right?"

She sighed. This was so embarrassing. "Three. I have three points."

"So . . . you've kissed three guys since you've been here," he said, his tone deflated. "Are you still seeing them, the other guys?"

What? No. Wait . . . what was that? If she was better at reading guys, she'd say he sounded pouty and a little bit jealous.

She'd never had a guy be jealous over her before. Cassidy didn't know how to take this development at first, but then she considered it. It was way sexy.

The idea that he didn't like the thought of her kissing other guys gave her off-court confidence a supercharged injection. She scooted toward him and in a gesture a complete one-eighty from her usual reserved self, she did something she'd been dying to do since that day at the airport: she touched his dimple with the tip of her finger.

Cassidy let it linger there before trailing it down his cheek to his chin to turn his head toward her.

"No. The rules of the International Kissing Club state that I get *three* points for an amazing, earth-stopping, epic kiss," she said with all the matter-of-fact seriousness she could muster.

It took a moment for what she was saying to sink in, but then a grin broke out across Lucas's bronzed face, crooked and just a little cocky. Her insides turned molten. *Oh. God.* If he kissed her again now she wouldn't be much more than a puddle of mush on the vinyl seat.

"Epic, yeah?" His hand stole around the back of her neck and he nudged her nose with his. "I can live with that," he whispered against her lips. Cassidy closed her eyes and melted.

The International Kissing Club was Piper's Best. Idea. Ever.

IKC Fan Page

The official Fan Page for the International Kissing Club

5,621
people like this

 IKC Page

Rapunzel Best. Birthday. Evah!!!!!!!

> **Manami Etsuko** Deets, please!
>
> **Rapunzel** We climbed the Sydney Harbour Bridge. The view of the Opera House was awesome, but not the best part of the date.
>
> **Ariel** And the best part was . . .?
>
> **Rapunzel** My business.
>
> **Mulan** Please describe the cake. Spare no details.

Jane Still hungry, Mulan?

> **Mulan** You have no idea. But, sk8ter boy took me sightseeing, saw the Tomb of Huang. Amazing seventeenth-century landmark—300-year-old pine trees.
>
> **Karrie Meeker** I thought this was the International Kissing Club page. Not the International Sightseeing Page. Stick to the lips, please!
>
> **Ariel** Can't we combine the two? I did! Last night Sebastian took me to the catacombs beneath Paris. Le sigh.
>
> **Jane** Catacombs? Since when did you go Goth? It doesn't exactly seem like your scene.
>
> **Ariel** Then love be blind, because I only had eyes for Sebastian.

 Messages

Between **Mei** and **Izzy**:

Mei

What are you up to? Are things any better at school?

Izzy

Let's see . . . I've spent the better part of the week converting all our family home movies to digital; I started working on a design for a rainwater collection system for my garden; and I downloaded an instructional video to learn how to weave plastic grocery bags into purses. In other words, I'm bored out of my mind. But I do start my new job tomorrow, so that'll be something different.

Mei

Hope it works out for you! Who knows, maybe you'll make a new friend at Tanner's farm—it's something I highly recommend doing. :)

Izzy

Oh yeah? How's your new friendship working out? Any lip action yet?

Mei

No. It's not like that. We're just hanging. He's trying to get me to skateboard.

Izzy

Oh, Mei. Get your head out of your books. If the boy wants to teach you something, it's because he likes you. And if he wants to teach you to skateboard, it's because he wants to get his hands on you.

Mei

Izzy!

Izzy

Just saying.

Mei

Have to go now. Am late for dinner. Don't know how I'm going to look Guiran in the eye now.

Izzy

I hear it's better with your eyes closed, anyway.

Mei

Izzy! Not helpful. Logging off now.

Chapter 15
Izzy

Izzy drove Brittney up to the Sun Valley Orchard the following Saturday morning, hoping—rather desperately—that Tanner had been joking about the tractor.

Tanner had told her to be there by seven.

Seven was freakin' early. Earlier even than she got up for school. Was this really worth ten bucks an hour?

But it wasn't like she had anything better to do on Saturday. Sure, she could have spent another day at home, resenting her parents' poor financial planning, but she already had that covered. Besides, it had been so long since she'd actually spoken to anyone, her vocal cords were starting to atrophy. It was time to rejoin the world of humans.

So she rolled out of bed at six fifteen, stumbled downstairs, and made herself an espresso before leaving the house. Her parents couldn't afford to send her to Costa Rica, but they could still keep the coffee maker stocked with a nice Costa Rican blend. Glad to know where their priorities lay.

The Google Map directions led her down a long dusty road that ended at an aging ranch-style house crouching low under some oaks. She parked by the trees and went looking for Tanner. Something resembling an airplane hangar sat on the other side of the road, hunkered down in rows of cotton. The fields near the house were planted with something else. Izzy had lived in northeast Texas long enough to recognize the cotton, but she was used to her veggies artfully displayed at the farmers' market, not still on the stalk.

She stopped several yards away from the tractor. The John Deere loomed over her, like the bright green and yellow carcass of a dinosaur. The behemoth was mud splattered and scuffed, rusting out in places, patched over in others. It looked as though someone should have hauled it off to the dump a decade ago in a mission of mercy. Hooked to the back was a contraption straight out of a medieval torture chamber. Massive rods of metal supported a row of disks, each easily two feet across, their edges gleaming wickedly in the early morning light.

In her mind, the theme from *Psycho* played.

Just then, Tanner appeared as if from nowhere. He clapped her on the back in a casual, buddyish kind of way, laughing when she jumped. "Come on. I'll show you around the barn." He walked toward the building behind the tractor.

"That isn't an airplane hangar?" she asked when he started walking.

He shot her another one of those bemused looks. "If we could afford an airplane, the tractors would be newer. And I wouldn't need a football scholarship."

Good point.

She pulled her gaze away from the evil tractor as he walked toward the barn. It was all arching steel and heavy corrugated doors.

Looking from the barn to the tractor, she tried to muster her courage. Tanner had already rounded the John Deere and was several long-legged strides in front of her. "Seriously," she called. "I thought you were joking about the tractor."

"Don't worry. I'll teach you everything you need to know."

Nearly running to catch up, she said, "Um. Just, in the interest of full disclosure, I failed my driving test. Twice."

"That's okay. You don't need a special license. You won't be driving on public roads."

"That's so not reassuring."

He glanced over his shoulder at her. "You sound really worried."

"I *am* really worried."

"Don't be." He stopped abruptly just outside the barn door and turned to face her. She nearly slammed into him but he caught her hands in his, catching her before she fell against him. "I'll be right next to you the whole time."

His thumb brushed the back of her hand before she jerked it away. It seemed like an awful lot of physical contact between farmhands.

Wrapping her arms around her chest, she pulled her hands into the sleeves of her sweatshirt. "Sooo. This is a barn," she said brightly as they walked inside.

This was one of the situations where changing the subject abruptly was socially acceptable. Wise, even.

Tanner slanted her an odd look and spoke slowly. Like maybe she was slightly deranged. And maybe she was. "Yes. This is a barn."

"It's . . . less red than I expected. And there's no silo." The barn where she'd lost her virginity—the one out at Mike Jenkins's place— hadn't really been used as a barn in years. Everybody knew his family had made their money in the high-tech industry and then moved out to Paris. They stabled horses there sometimes, but the Jenkinses' barn was mostly just for show. Not unlike River had been.

She shied away from the memory, focusing instead on what was right in front of her. Tanner's barn was completely different—all big machinery, dust, and motor oil. It surprised her how at home Tanner looked here as he snagged a set of keys from a workbench. "And no cows," she added inanely. "Or chickens." When he still didn't comment, she added, "Or pigs."

Finally—thank God, before she said anything else idiotic—he said dryly, "My parents live on a farm. They don't live on the Fisher-Price farm."

"Right." Again her tone sounded overly bright. "I know that. I mean, of course." Resisting the urge to slap a big *L* onto her forehead, she babbled on. "I guess that means I'm not going to be milking any cows, huh?"

WTF? Why can't I stop talking about farm animals?

Why did her hand still feel warm where he'd touched her skin? It wasn't like he'd never touched her before. So why was she suddenly so much more aware of him?

Looking up at Tanner now, she noticed he had a dazed expression on his face. Like she'd gone so far into crazy he didn't even know how to respond. So she brought up the one topic every football player wanted to talk about. Himself.

"My dad said you're doing a really good job as quarterback."

"You asked your dad about me? Ah, Isabel, I didn't know you cared." A slow smile split his face and he looked extremely pleased with himself.

Of course he would think she'd asked her dad about him. That was jocks in a nutshell. *Me, me, me.* "Don't flatter yourself, Derringer. Football is all we talk about at the dinner table."

Poor Linc had looked miserable the other night, listening to her father talk about how easily Tanner had moved from wide receiver to quarterback. She'd almost felt sorry for him. But what kind of idiot put his entire future at risk by punching a locker? She'd bet good money—if she had any—that he'd done it only because he thought it would make him look cool. God, she hated sharing chromosomes with that moron.

Surprisingly, Tanner didn't seem to want to talk about her family any more than she did. He grabbed her elbow and steered her toward the front of the barn. "Maybe we should skip the tour and go straight to the tractor."

She stopped walking and dug in her heels. "The tractor?" Her gaze darted to the beast looming just outside the doorway. "Shouldn't I at least meet your parents first or something?"

"My parents?"

"I *am* going to be working for them."

"They're not here. They spend every Saturday out at the farmers' market in Sherman."

"Oh. Right." She should have guessed that—she'd seen them there just the previous weekend. But if she'd known that she was going to be all alone with Tanner today, then . . . then what? She wouldn't have come? That was ridiculous. They weren't *alone* alone. Not in an intimate or romantic way. And it wasn't like she cared. She wasn't Piper, after all.

Besides, he was Tanner. Arrogant, obnoxious football star. He was everything she hated in a guy. Not to mention—

Okay, was it even possible for your thoughts to babble? How nervous was she about this stupid tractor anyway?

She sucked in a deep breath and shut up her mind. Gazing at the tractor she said, "Okay. Tractor Driving 101. I'm ready."

Tanner chuckled. "Not for that one you're not. But nice show of bravado." He led her past the enormous beast and around the corner to where a much smaller tractor stood in the shadow of the barn. "This is the tractor I'm going to teach you to drive."

Before her stood the baby version of the monster she'd been looking at just a moment ago. Equal parts red paint and rust, it looked as though it was easily as old as she was. Older, maybe. On the bright side, the oversized back wheels only came to her shoulder, rather than to above her head.

She clapped her hands together with manufactured enthusiasm. "Okay. Where do we start?"

The hand clapping reminded her of Piper, and for an instant she felt a pang of regret. Or maybe just loneliness. Piper would be so jealous if she could see her now, spending the day with Piper's dream guy.

Forget that learning to drive a tractor was about the most unromantic thing ever.

Piper would still be jealous.

On the other hand, Piper was in Paris at the moment. The real

Paris. And she was racking up points faster than Tanner had during the last football game.

Izzy suspected that by the time Piper got back home, she probably wouldn't even remember who Tanner was. She certainly wasn't going to care that Izzy had spent the fall working for his parents.

It was *so* not an issue.

Izzy turned back to Tanner and flashed him a smile. "Why don't you toss me the keys and I'll give it a try." Then she looked back at the tractor with a frown. "Do tractors have keys?"

Tanner just shook his head, his expression a little bemused. "Yeah." He dangled the keys in front of her.

What is it about this boy that makes my IQ drop fifty points every time I'm around him? Maybe that's what happened to Germaine: too much exposure to Tanner Colt.

Instead of tossing the keys to her, he crossed to her side and helped her climb up onto the runner. He narrated as he boosted her into the seat. "This is your basic open-air cab."

"Obviously," she muttered.

"You got your seat. You got your roll bar." He slapped at the black bar arching behind the seat as he hopped onto the runner beside her. And then he started pointing at an array of pedals, sticks, and levers. "Your clutch, your brake, your gas. Your emergency brake. Your gear shift. Your throttle. Your ignition. And don't forget your seat belt."

"Huh?" She'd just sat down on the cracked and worn vinyl. "Was I supposed to follow all that?"

She looked down at him, only to find him climbing into the cab with her.

"Oh, do you need to sit here?"

"No. You're good." He reached across her. She plastered herself back against the seat, but there was barely enough room and his shoulder brushed against her chest. She found herself wishing for a less impressive bustline. There wasn't room in the cab for her, Tanner, and her damn double Ds. "Here's the other end of the seat belt."

She stared blankly at him as he straightened and handed her the buckle. When was he going to get out of the cab? She swallowed hard, then took the canvas belt he dangled in front of her. "Safety first," she said faintly.

"Don't worry. I'm not going to let anything happen to you."

"What about *you*?" She didn't glance over her shoulder as she asked the question, already keenly aware of how close he was.

Tanner stood just behind her, wedged in between her seat and the roll bar. Despite the cramped quarters, he managed to stretch out, filling every extra centimeter of space. His voice dropped a notch, to the husky murmur that had melted hearts all over Paris High. "Don't worry. I know what I'm doing."

Good thing one of them did.

He pointed to the right side of the steering wheel. "Ignition is right there. You'll want to turn the key counterclockwise for a few seconds first, to let it warm up. Then clockwise. Just like starting a car."

She followed his instructions, trying not to notice how good Tanner smelled. Fresh and clean. Like he bathed in catnip for girls. Most of the football players at her house either smelled like sweaty locker room floor or like they'd drenched themselves in cologne. Or worse, some combination of the two. But not Tanner. He smelled like clean soap and line-dried clothes.

She drew in a deep breath and—

"What was that?" he asked.

All she could do was stare blankly in reply.

"You seemed like you were about to say something."

"Oh." Shit. What was she supposed to say? *No, I was just smelling you?* "Is that long enough?" she asked instead, looking back to meet his eyes.

He hesitated. Like he could read her thoughts or something. Then he shook his head. "Sure. Go ahead and start it up."

She cranked the key in the ignition and the beast hummed to life.

"From here on out"—he leaned even closer to be heard over the roar—"it's just like driving your standard."

She settled her foot onto the clutch. The pedal felt huge. Spongier. This *wasn't* like driving her standard. It seemed bigger. More dangerous.

She pressed down hard and felt the gears line up. The gearshift was directly in front of her seat, right between her legs. Just as she reached down to settle her hand over it, Tanner leaned in and put his hand on top of hers. He had one arm resting across the back of her seat and the other practically draped across her left thigh.

"Here's first." He moved both their hands together as he shifted through the gears. "Here's second. Third, fourth. And here's reverse." This one was down and to the far right, so that his knuckles brushed against the inside of her denim-clad right thigh. "You feel that?"

Was he joking? She swallowed hard. "Pardon?"

"The reverse is a little tricky on this old girl." He gave the gearshift another wiggle. "You've got to work to get it in."

She jerked her hand out from under his, moving so fast her foot slipped, so she popped the clutch and killed the engine. "I think I've got it."

He leaned back; a slow smile broke across his face. "Looks like you do."

She narrowed her gaze to a glare.

"You want to try it again?" he asked, that smug grin of his never leaving his face.

Her heart was pounding and her hands sweaty. What the hell was going on? This was Tanner Colt. Tanner! He was not supposed to make her feel this strange mixture of . . .

But her mind shied away from admitting she felt anything. This was all just standard I'm-a-football-god charm. He wasn't flirting with her. He probably didn't even realize he was doing it. Which should have made her feel better, but it didn't at all.

"Yeah. But back up, Winchester." She threw the last name–gun slur in there on purpose, trying her damnedest to rekindle that old animosity she usually felt for him. "I'll try it on my own this time."

He held up his palms in a gesture of innocence. "Hey, I'm just trying to help."

"Right." She fixed her gaze toward the horizon and stomped on the clutch as she turned over the engine. She had to drive a little distance between them. Put him back in his place. "But I should warn you. When Linc taught me to drive a standard, I nearly killed him."

"I think I'll take my chances."

"Remember his black eye last spring?" she asked as she shifted the tractor into second gear. She felt a jolt of satisfaction as Tanner's eyebrows shot up. "That was me."

· · · · · ✈

The morning would have gone a lot smoother if Tanner had kept his hands to himself.

Last spring, Jake Robinsky had taken Izzy to the Valentine social. The guy had been like an octopus. He looked innocent enough at first glance, but he seemed to have eight arms, and every one of them was focused on dragging her closer to his mouth.

This wasn't like that at all. Tanner didn't grope or paw. His touch was never invasive or inappropriate. And he never once tried to grab her ass. But he was just always there. Right beside her. Covering her hand as he showed her how to coax the tractor into third. Leaning close to be heard over the hum of the engine. Brushing against her legs as he showed her how to use the throttle.

His nearness set her on edge. Made her nervous in a way it never had before. She found herself longing for the days when she'd been Invisabel Isabel, the girl no one noticed.

Not that she thought he meant anything by it. Not that she would have acted on it, even if he had. Tanner was Piper's.

Even though Piper wasn't here. Even though she was off kissing half of France—half of Europe, for that matter—it didn't make any difference. Because he was Piper's.

Or rather, he was *actually* Germaine's.

A fact she was reminded of just before noon, when Germaine's white Acura came barreling down the dusty road leading to the Sun Valley Orchard.

After Izzy had mastered driving the tractor up and down the long driveway, Tanner had hooked a tiller to the back of the tractor and had her tilling a fallow stretch of land beside the house. Still, there had been a lot of cringing, head shaking, and exaggerated wincing on his part. At least until they both saw the cloud of dust coming down the road.

At the end of the row, Tanner reached over Izzy and turned off the tractor. Then he nodded toward the car. "We have company."

"Is that Germaine?" Izzy asked, her voiced sounding too loud after riding on the tractor all morning.

"Looks like it."

For an instant, something odd flickered across Tanner's expression—a tightness through his jaw, like he was holding back a comment.

But the expression passed when the car pulled to a stop in front of the house and Germaine climbed out. She was dressed in a short denim skirt, a skimpy white shirt, and turquoise cowboy boots. Izzy would have bet money that Germaine thought the outfit was farm-girl clothes.

Germaine gave a little wave before popping the trunk of her car and leaning far enough into it to show off most of her ass. When she straightened, she was holding a blanket and a picnic basket. Tottering on the heels of her boots, she carried both items over to the tractor.

"Hey, Germaine—" Tanner started, but before he could say more, Germaine had set down the basket and blanket and launched herself at Tanner. She plastered her body against his and yanked his head down. The kiss was long, slow, and deep enough for Izzy's gag reflex to kick in.

Scooting off the seat of the tractor, Izzy lowered herself to the ground on the other side, knelt down, and retied her shoes. Then she took a long sip from the Sigg water bottle she'd brought with her. Then she cleared her throat.

By the time she looked back, they were still kissing. And Tanner's hands rested on Germaine's indecently short skirt.

Izzy coughed loudly, examining her nails. Her new formaldehyde-free nail polish had not stood up to the rigors of farmwork.

Just as she was considering digging through her trunk for the road flares that had come in her emergency auto kit, Germaine ended the kiss and stepped away.

She giggled and waved at Izzy. "When Tanner told me y'all were working out here at the farm today, I decided to bring y'all a picnic."

"Thanks," Tanner said.

When Germaine looked in her direction, Izzy felt obligated to say, "Sure. Thanks. That's really . . ." Obnoxious? Transparent? Insecure? ". . . really great of you."

"Where do you think I should spread out?" Germaine gazed around, a pout on her lips. She picked up the blanket, stalked a few steps toward the house, to a carpet of tiny bright green plants, and started to shake it out. "How about—"

"Not there!" Tanner yelled. "Those are seedlings."

"Oh, sorry." Germaine giggled again. "That was so stupid of me."

"Yes, it was," Izzy agreed dryly.

Germaine glared at her, but Izzy didn't apologize. She had fewer than five hours' farming experience, and even she recognized that anything planted in perfectly spaced rows should not be picnicked upon.

Germaine thrust the blanket toward Tanner. "Why don't you pick a spot, sweetie? I'm going to go wash the farm off my hands before we eat." Then she gave Izzy a scornful visual inspection. After a moment, Germaine smiled.

It wasn't a friendly smile, but it wasn't exactly belligerent, either.

It was the kind of look Barbie would give Skipper if she ever caught Skipper making moon eyes at Ken.

Still, there was something humbling about having Germaine, the most territorial girl in Paris, decide—after only one look—that Izzy was no threat.

As if Izzy needed the reminder that she was coated in dirt and sweat. Tilling land was messy work. Every time she'd slowed down to turn a corner, she'd been enveloped in a cloud of dust. Of course, Tanner had been on the tractor with her, but somehow, he made dust look good. It only enhanced his rugged, chiseled perfection. She was pretty sure that on her it just looked gross.

Germaine was—naturally—dust-free. Dirt wouldn't dare settle on her.

As Germaine tottered off, she turned to say over her shoulder, "Izzy, do you want to start unpacking the basket once Tanner has the blanket laid out? I brought roast beef sandwiches, pasta salad with tomatoes, avocado, and bacon. And for dessert, prosciutto-wrapped melon slices."

Izzy nearly laughed at Germaine's overcompensation.

Tanner just looked sort of flabbergasted. Izzy suspected he'd never even heard of prosciutto. And once he knew it was just fancy bacon, he wasn't going to want to eat it with fruit.

Once Germaine was out of earshot, Izzy asked him, "Does she come over often when you're here for the weekend?"

Tanner shook his head, still looking baffled. "No. She's only been here once."

On one hand, it was hard to picture Germaine on the farm. On the other, there were lots of branches around where she could perch, black wings wrapped around her body while she searched for carrion to pick apart with her pointy beak.

Izzy propped her hands on her hips and turned to face him fully. "You know she's a total skitch, right?"

Tanner frowned and looked like he might protest, so Izzy cut him off. "Hey, if you were allowed to say River is a douche, then I'm allowed to remark on Germaine's personality flaws, of which there are many."

Tanner's jaw tightened. "River *is* a douche."

"Oh, like you know him so well."

"Our parents sold stuff at the same farmers' market for the past five years. So, yeah, I know him. And he was never interested in all that 'green' stuff until you started hanging around him. He used to make fun of his mom for it. Called her hippie-dippy behind her back."

"Oh." Izzy had *not* known that. "Now I'm kind of wishing you'd mentioned that nine months ago. Or, jeez, even two months ago would have made a huge difference." Before she'd been stupid enough to sleep with him. That definitely would have been useful information. "Which just proves my point. If you don't already know that Germaine is a skank, it's my duty as a human to tell you. She may look like a mere high school cheerleader, but she's really a turkey buzzard in a miniskirt and stilettos. Besides, I'm pretty sure she practices the dark arts."

"Whoa," Tanner said, as he stumbled back out of the blast range. "She's really not *that* bad."

Izzy cocked a disbelieving eyebrow. "Why are you with her, anyway?"

The guy she'd always thought Tanner was—the knuckle-dragging purveyor of violence—was the kind of guy who would date Germaine. But she was starting to wonder if she really knew him at all. And if she'd been wrong about Tanner all this time, then how was she supposed to reconcile his crappy taste in girlfriends?

Tanner sent her an odd look. "Why do *you* care who I date?"

She held up her palms in a gesture of benign innocence. "It's purely a matter of scientific curiosity."

He nodded, as if he could appreciate that. "I guess I date her for the same reason I play football. It's what everyone expects me to do."

"I don't believe that," Izzy said, almost under her breath.

His head jerked toward her so fast, she shifted back in surprise.

And suddenly he seemed to be standing much closer than he had been.

"Then who should I be with, Isabel?" he asked, looking her straight in the eye.

For a second her heart stuttered in her chest and she felt as if time had stopped. Then her brain caught up with her hormones and she blew out her exasperation in a chuckle, doing her best to laugh it off. "Holy crap. Piper's right. You can really lay on the charm."

He gave an exaggerated wink. "Hey, I do what I can."

"So that's it? That's why you're with *her*? Because the poor handsome quarterback doesn't have any other options?"

"So you think I'm handsome?"

"Stop dodging the question."

"What do you want me to say? Germaine wants to be with me. She makes it easy."

"What? 'Cause your life is so hard?" Izzy asked.

He shrugged. "No harder than yours."

She thought about that. He had a point: for both of them, life wasn't as easy as it looked from the outside. But she didn't like to think about being that transparent. Or about him being so observant. Suddenly, she yearned for the days when she thought Tanner was just another arrogant football player—one who didn't seem to know her better than she knew herself.

There was something unexpected in his gaze that made her shift uncomfortably. Time to move the convo back to comfortable territory.

"I don't think you do anything just because it's what everyone expects. I've seen you play football. No one that good doesn't love the sport."

"So Isabel," he drawled, "you're a closet fan, after all?"

Of his or of Paris High School football? Either was a question she wasn't ready to answer.

"I'm my father's daughter," she said instead. "I was raised to spot talent the way most kids are taught to watch for cars before crossing the street. So, yeah, I know you're good. And I know you love to play football. So stop acting coy."

It occurred to her then that he'd never really answered her question, the one about Germaine. Which undoubtedly meant, *She's so hot that I don't care how bad she is. Plus, she puts out.*

"As for Germaine, do me a favor and make sure she knows that this"—Izzy waggled her pointer finger between them to indicate their relationship—"is just work."

"But it's not just work," Tanner said.

And for an instant, Izzy's breath caught in her chest. Okay, longer than an instant. Long enough for her to feel woozy.

Until Tanner added, " 'Cause we're friends, right?"

"Right," she muttered breathlessly. How had she forgotten their close and enduring friendship? "Just make sure she knows that. I don't want to end up dead from some unfortunate voodoo ritual."

Tanner had the gall to laugh. "I doubt she's even noticed you're here."

Now it was Izzy's turn to laugh. Hers was more ironic than his. Germaine may have already dismissed her as being completely nonthreatening, but Izzy still didn't want to trust her fate to Germaine's capricious benevolence. "So she normally makes you picnics?"

"No."

"And puts meat in every dish?"

"What?"

"I'm a vegetarian," Izzy pointed out. "Which she knows, because last year in English she and I were paired for the class debate. And the topic we picked was the beef industry's impact on the environment."

Izzy—obviously—had been antibeef. Germaine's platform had been—literally—"No pot-smoking tree-hugger is going to tell me I can't eat a hamburger."

Chagrin flickered across Tanner's face and he opened his mouth to speak, but Izzy interrupted him.

"Don't tell me she's not that bad. She put meat in a *dessert*. Trust me, anything that sneaky is girl-speak for 'Keep your grubby tractor hands off my boyfriend.'" Tanner looked dubious, but Izzy held up her hands. "Just make sure she knows we're only friends. Or even better, that I'm just another hired hand. Now, I'm going to leave you two to your romantic picnic, and I'm going to go home and eat my tofu scramble in peace. I'll be back tomorrow for Tractor Driving 102."

Before Izzy could escape to her car, Germaine returned, her smile bright and cheerful. "You're not leaving, are you?"

Unless Germaine had had some sort of "bitchectomy" while washing her hands, her new friendliness could mean only one thing. She was completely convinced Izzy was not a threat. Which did wonders for Izzy's self-confidence.

With that, she made for Brittney. Kicking up dust as she drove down the road, Izzy could see them in her rearview mirror.

Tanner standing beside the tractor with his hands tucked into his jeans pockets, his head cocked just slightly to the side. Germaine behind him, her arms wrapped around his body like clinging tentacles.

All in all, her first day working on an organic farm had sucked.

On the other hand, she finally understood what Piper saw in Tanner. Which sucked even more.

IKC Fan Page

The Official Fan Page for the International Kissing Club

6,891

people like this

💬 IKC Page

Vivian King Score! Bonus points. Two boys, three days. Put me at nine points, ladies.

> **Jane** Do we need to have the safe-sex talk again?
>
> **Vivian King** Not yet, but I'll let you know. :)

Mulan Jane, didn't you just start a new job? How did it go?

> **Jane** He thinks my tractor's sexy!
>
> **Rapunzel** Who are you talking about?
>
> **Ariel** OMG! I thought you were working for Tanner's dad? That's disgusting!
>
> **Mulan** Ewww!
>
> **Jane** Calm down, pervs. I'm joking. Trust me when I tell you that no one would have wanted to kiss me after I'd been on a tractor for three hours.
>
> **Jane** Btw, need to invest in a new sports bra. No one told me tractors were so bumpy.
>
> **LaTonya Washington** Bumpy? There's potential there.
>
> **Jane** Um . . . No. Zero potential.

✉️ Messages

Between **Piper** and **Cassidy**:

Piper
Cassidy, I need some advice. My art teacher still hates me.
Cassidy
Why am I being singled out for the academic failure questions?

Piper

I can't ask Mei. She'd freak if she knew I was pulling an F. And things still seem weird with Izzy. Do you think she's okay?

Cassidy

Can't tell from her posts. But would you be okay, stuck in Texas?

Piper

That's what I thought. Maybe I should send her some French chocolates. Or a French guy.

Cassidy

So what's up with your art teacher?

Piper

He thinks I'm a hack.

Cassidy

Drop the class.

Piper

Thanks. Very helpful.

Cassidy

You've got talent. So he's obviously a moron.

Piper

But he's not. What if I only have talent in Paris, Texas—when I'm miserable? This glassblowing is kicking my ass.

Cassidy

Keep searching until you find your niche. Spread your wings. Don't be so Paris, Texas.

Piper

I thought I was talking to Cassidy Barlow?

Cassidy

Yeah. I know. Now change the topic before I make myself sick. In other news, I shot a barrel today.

Piper

I don't even know what that means! Thanks, Cassidy.

Chapter 16
Mei

"It's easy," Guiran told her, balancing on his skateboard like he'd been born with it beneath his feet. "All you have to do is trust yourself not to fall."

Mei snorted. "Sorry, but I put my trust in Sir Isaac Newton and a little thing called gravity. There's no way you're going to talk me into getting on that thing. I'll kill myself."

"Come on. Give it a try." His grin was huge, infectious, but Mei refused to let it get to her. She'd come to China to find her birth parents, not play around on a four-wheeled death trap with a cute guy.

Not that there's any reason I can't do both, a little voice in the back of her head whispered. Mei ignored it. She was only going to be here for another month, so what was the point of starting something she couldn't finish?

Guiran boarded ahead a little, then did a one-eighty, with lots of air, before landing a couple of feet in front of her.

"Come on, Mei. Just try it once. I promise I won't let anything happen to you."

Against all odds, and her better judgment, Mei felt herself relenting. "Is it really so important to you that I get on your stupid skateboard?"

"It is."

"Why?"

"Because you look like you've just lived through the most miserable six weeks of your life. I think you could use a little fun."

"Playing guitar is fun. Shopping is fun. Acing a test is really fun. Getting on that death trap, not so much."

"Fine. Tell me the last time you did any of those things and I'll leave you alone."

"I'll have you know I bought a very nice belt a few weeks ago," she answered.

"Wow. A belt. Big spender," he teased.

"I play guitar every day," she said.

"Okay, then. What I meant was, when was the last time you tried something new?"

When she didn't immediately answer, Guiran's smile grew wider. "See, you need a challenge. That's what keeps life interesting." He stepped off the skateboard. "Try it. If you don't have fun, I promise I won't ask again."

She wasn't sure if she was happy about that promise or not. It had gotten to the point that her time with Guiran was the complete highlight of her day, so much so that she found herself watching the clock—and the grounds outside her dorm room window—at least an hour before he was supposed to show up. The practical side of Mei was a little worried about her dependence on him. After all, it was never good to put all your eggs in one basket, and if this friendship didn't work out between them, then she'd be totally screwed. Without his wicked good translating skills, she didn't know if she was ready to tackle the four and a half hours of public transportation required to get from Shenyang to Dalian. The journey had seemed shorter when she was back home planning her trip.

At the same time, though, the impractical side of herself—the one that dreamed of running off with a rock band instead of going to MIT—refused to be concerned. Guiran was a good guy, it told her. She should just relax and enjoy the time she got to spend with him.

That didn't mean she had to like skateboarding, but if it would make him happy . . .

"All right, fine," she said ungraciously. "I'll try it. Once. If you do something for me in return."

"Name it."

"Let me teach you how to play a few chords on my guitar, so you can experience something I love as much as you love your skateboarding."

"That's not a favor." Guiran laughed. "Why would I say no to a chance to spend time with you and an electric guitar?" he asked, a sparkle in his eye.

As the days had worn on, Guiran had been getting more and more flirty, until Mei didn't have a clue where she stood with him. Back home, she would have sworn he was interested, because, as Izzy had said, if a guy offered to teach you something, it was because he had a thing for you. And the more he got to touch you, the better. But other than the flirting, nothing had happened. So she had no clue if he liked her in that way or not.

Shaking off the girly-girl thoughts, Mei stepped up to the skateboard, determined to get her humiliation over quickly. The last time she'd been on one of these things she was in fifth grade and had ended up flat on her back in front of every kid in her neighborhood. She was not looking forward to repeating the experience now.

Sure enough, she was fine as long as she had one foot on the ground. But the second she started to push off, she tottered wildly. Convinced she was going to fall, she was shocked when she found herself leaning against Guiran's warm, hard chest.

"Here, let me help."

Like she was going to turn down that offer? Not when he came up behind her and placed an arm on either side of her waist.

He was talking, telling her what to do, and she knew she should be paying attention. But for the first time in her life, Mei was a lot less interested in mastering a new concept than she was in simply reveling in the feel of the hottest guy she had ever met pressed against her.

He smelled good—really good—like the spiced oranges her mother made in the winter mixed with the dark, earthy scent of the tilled fields she, Piper, and Cassidy had played in as children. She had loved that place, loved the smell of it, and the fact that Guiran reminded her of those times did nothing to calm the chills racing up and down her spine.

"So, are you ready to try on your own?" he asked, and she realized, belatedly, that he'd been talking to her the entire time she'd been taking a trip to la-la land. *Nice, Mei,* she told herself with a grimace. Now she was going to look like the world's biggest idiot when she tried to board.

But he was looking at her so expectantly that she couldn't back out—no matter how much she wanted to. So Mei forced herself to push off a few times, gathering speed, before she brought her left foot up behind her right. She moved along for a minute, whipping through the cold air like she was born to do it—or, at least, born not to make a total moron of herself. When she didn't fall, her confidence increased—perhaps a little too much, because she started to push herself faster on the board.

She could see why Guiran liked the thing. It was kind of fun to breeze along, rolling through a world where everyone else was a few steps behind. In fact, maybe he could teach her a trick or two—

Mei lost focus and suddenly was wobbling, convinced she was going to hit the ground hard. But just as she started to fall, Guiran was there to catch her, his arms wrapping around her as he pulled her to his chest.

"Hey, you okay there?" he asked. His voice was a little huskier than normal.

"Uh, yeah. I'm fine," she answered. But she didn't feel fine. She felt dizzy, like she couldn't catch her breath and the entire world was spinning around her. She focused on his face, tried to stop the whirling sensation, but looking into his deep, black eyes only made the sensation worse.

"Mei."

"Yes?" she whispered, doing her best to ignore the erratic beating of her heart. *Is he going to kiss me?* she wondered frantically as his mouth got a little closer to hers. *He is!* her dazed brain cried. *He really is. Take that, Piper and Cassidy.* The look in his eyes said she was about to rack up some serious points herself.

Guiran's mouth was only an inch or two away from hers, and coming closer with every second that passed. Mei tilted her chin, leaned forward, but didn't close her eyes. She didn't want to miss a second of this—

Her stomach growled, loudly, and Guiran pulled away with a laugh.

Seriously? she demanded of the universe. The first time a guy had tried to kiss her in over a year and her body had to go and betray her? So what if she hadn't eaten anything all day—that so wasn't an excuse for ruining the best thing that had happened to her since she'd gotten to this godforsaken country.

"You've been skipping meals again?" he demanded, brushing a few strands of hair out of her eyes. "I thought you were done with that."

"I was. I am." She cursed herself as she stumbled over the words. But how could she tell him that she'd come to dread the cafeteria when he wasn't with her? How she hated to walk through the full tables and hear the whispers that followed her wherever she went? When they were together it wasn't so bad—they were usually talking to each other and besides, she wasn't sure why, but no one messed with her when she was with Guiran. Ever.

"Really?" He eyed her skeptically.

"I was just busy. I spent most of today in my room, studying. Mandarin is kicking my butt."

"I told you I'd practice with you." He said something in Mandarin, and though he spoke slowly, Mei was only able to understand two words: "go" and "eat."

"We can't," she said in English, not even willing to attempt the other language. "The cafeteria's about to close."

"Amazingly enough, there are other food sources in this city besides the school's lousy cafeteria. Come on," he said, picking up his skateboard.

"We're going out?" she asked, glancing down at her jeans and thick hoodie. "I'm not exactly dressed—"

"You look great." He led her toward the huge gates that marked the front of campus.

"Where are we going?" she asked as they exited the grounds.

"Somewhere I can be guaranteed you'll actually eat."

She didn't have the heart to tell him that it probably wasn't going to happen. She'd been in China long enough to know that most of the food just wasn't her thing.

Still, she felt a thrill of excitement to be going into the city again. She'd almost ventured past the gates on her own earlier that day, but had chickened out at the last minute. In the city, everything was chaotic and messy and frenzied and fast. She'd been born Chinese, but she was finding more and more that she was small-town Texan to the core. Slow and steady was more her pace.

They walked for about ten minutes, Guiran holding her hand with his free one as they strolled down the sidewalk. All around them, the world was a mixed-up blur of colored lights and speeding cars, honking and squealing brakes, and motors revving. And everywhere there were people, the streets crowded with rows and rows of bodies, as if the four million people in Shenyang had given up trying to house themselves and were just spilling onto the streets.

She thought of Paris, of the lazy tree-lined streets that were more often empty than not. She'd never realized how much she liked the solitude of it, the quiet of being alone with her own thoughts. Here, it seemed the only place she was ever alone was in her dorm room.

Suddenly, Guiran started tugging her inside a restaurant. She glanced up at the sign right before they went in the door, and she started to laugh. Hard. Guiran had brought her to Pizza Hut.

She found a table as he ordered a large pizza and a couple of Cokes. As she sank into her chair, she drew the scent of spicy tomato sauce deep into her lungs. Her mouth watered.

Why hadn't she thought of this before? Maybe she *could* handle leaving the school on her own. She might not speak Mandarin, but surely even she could manage to point at the menu and order a cheese pizza.

They spent the next hour talking and laughing and eating until their stomachs were on the verge of exploding. Mei finished off her fourth slice of pizza and reached for a fifth, even though she was completely full for the first time in weeks. There was something about being here, about sharing pizza with Guiran, that made her happier than she had been in a long time. She didn't want the feeling to end, and if it meant she had to eat until she was about to puke, she was more than okay with that.

But eventually their cups were empty and the last slice was gone. Guiran stood up, looking as reluctant as she felt. "So, are you ready to go?" Again, he offered her his hand.

"Yeah." Her hand slid neatly into his, their palms nestling together. "Can we walk for a while, though? I'm stuffed."

"Sure. Where should we go?"

She thought of the long list of places she still wanted to see, started to tell him Beijing Park, then paused. The guy had fed her pizza. He'd earned a little trust. "Surprise me."

"That's my girl," he said with a wink, and Mei tried not to obsess over the words as they strolled down the street, hand in hand.

It's just an expression, she told herself as he regaled her with stories about some of the points of interest they passed.

He hadn't meant it.

They'd never even kissed.

That didn't seem to matter, though, as they walked through some of the back streets of Shenyang, talking about anything and everything. It was strange, really, how comfortable it felt being with him. How *right* it felt being with him.

They paused in front of an ice-cream place and even though Mei'd eaten a ton of pizza, she let Guiran talk her into getting a cone.

"What flavors do they have?" she asked, staring at the Chinese characters in frustration.

"A bunch you've probably never even heard of."

"They must have vanilla, right?"

"I don't think so." Guiran scanned the list posted on the wall, then turned to her with a sly glint in his eye. "Let me order for you?"

Mei looked at him warily. There was trust and then there was trust. Back home, her ice-cream order was sacred. "Well, that depends."

"On what?"

"On whether or not any of those flavors will kill me. The electric purple one is a little concerning." Not to mention the puce-colored one and the one with the unidentifiable chunks in it.

"Aww, come on, loosen up. Live a little," he prodded.

"I just did—I got on that stupid board and almost killed myself."

"Well, you're not dead yet. And admit it: you had fun. I could tell you liked it. So, trust me now, okay?"

"Okay," she agreed, though still a little wary.

Guiran turned to the person behind the counter and spoke in rapid-fire Mandarin. Within a minute or two, Mei held a double-decker ice-cream cone in her hand. As Guiran ordered for himself, she looked at the thing suspiciously. He'd ordered her black ice cream. Black ice cream. She didn't even know such a thing existed. Or if it should.

She sniffed it. It didn't smell like licorice, but what else could possibly turn ice cream that color? She decided to start on the green mint scoop first and work her way around to the black. If it was some kind of funky chocolate, she wasn't sure she could stomach it.

Her eyes started watering with her first lick, and she swallowed quickly. "You got me wasabi ice cream?"

"Do you like it?"

Did she like it? What kind of question was that? Who on earth actually ate wasabi ice cream? She could barely stomach the Japanese horseradish on her mother's homemade sushi, let alone on a waffle cone.

Still, she didn't want to hurt Guiran's feelings, especially when he was looking at her so expectantly. Bracing herself, she cautiously took another lick. Maybe it wouldn't be so bad if she hadn't been expecting it to taste like mint.

"It's . . . interesting."

He laughed, before shouldering the ice-cream parlor's door open. "Now there's a ringing endorsement if I've ever heard one."

"So shoot me. I'm used to my ice cream being made of flavors I would eat in a cake. Vanilla, strawberry, chocolate, Cherry Garcia."

"Ahh, the boring flavors."

"You mean classic, don't you?" She narrowed her eyes at him playfully.

"No. I meant boring." He took a long lick of his own wasabi ice cream. "So, have you tried the black-sesame scoop yet?"

Seriously? Black sesame? Had she skipped China and landed on a totally different planet altogether? One where people didn't have taste buds? "Uh, no. I haven't."

"And you're not going to, are you?"

"I didn't say that."

"You didn't have to." He bumped her with his shoulder. "It's written all over your face. You're a control freak."

"You make me sound so boring."

"Not boring. *Classic.*"

His words hit her the wrong way. "I'm not boring!"

"I'm just joking, Mei." He laughed. "There's nothing boring about you."

"Not boring, then. Just unadventurous. Anal-retentive," she said.

He didn't answer this time and Mei could feel herself getting more and more worked up. It was stupid, she knew, to let Guiran push her buttons like this—especially over a stupid ice-cream cone—but she couldn't help it. John, her ex, used to give her a hard time about how she planned everything out, how she was never spontaneous. How she always had to control things. The fact that Guiran was suddenly doing the same thing really bothered her. Strange, though, how it wasn't him she was annoyed at, but herself.

Looking around, she tried to find a way to prove to him that she wasn't as staid, as predictable, as he seemed to think she was. It had gotten late, and since it was the middle of the week, the earlier crowds had thinned to almost nothing. So it wasn't as if she could just walk up to someone and do something crazy, like kiss them and finally get on the IKC point chart. But maybe there was something else . . .

Her eyes fell on the fountain in the middle of the square and an idea started to form. It was crazy, ridiculous, especially since it felt like it was about forty degrees outside, but once the idea was in her head, she couldn't get it out. A quick glance around told her that the earlier crowd had all but disappeared.

She turned to Guiran, shoved her ice-cream cone at him. "Here, hold this for a minute."

"Where are you going?" he asked, following her as she started toward the center of the square. "I was just joking, Mei. I didn't mean to upset you. Please don't leave."

She didn't answer him. She wasn't leaving, not by a long shot, but after his teasing, he deserved to suffer a little. Refusing to give herself time to think, Mei stripped off her jacket and dropped it in the center of the square. Next she ripped off her shirt and jeans, until she was dressed in nothing but the black stretchy lace camisole and matching panties Piper had given her for the trip. Thank God she'd decided to wear them today as an extra layer of warmth, but now for the extra confidence boost as well. Somehow, she doubted this would have the same effect if she was wearing her regular underwear. 'Cause nothing said wild and crazy like plain white cotton.

And then, with a quick glance at Guiran to make sure he was watching (he was, with his mouth hanging open), she jumped straight into the huge stone fountain and plunged into the water.

Cold. Oh God, was it cold! Siberia cold. South-Pole-penguin cold.

But it was too late to back out now. The only thing worse than freezing to death in this stupid fountain would be seeing the look on Guiran's face when she wimped out. No way. She was staying put in the waist-deep water for the duration.

"Mei, are you crazy? Get out of there!"

"Why? It's nice." She prayed he couldn't hear her teeth chattering.

"It's got to be like five degrees above freezing. I'm sure 'nice' is not the proper adjective." He was shrugging out of his jacket even as he was telling her to get out, dropping it on the rim of the fountain. "Plus, it's against the law to be in there. You can get a major fine."

She looked around. "Do you see any police here?"

"No. They're smart enough to be inside, bundled up. For now." He shrugged out of his shirt, stripped off his jeans. Mei tried not to stare, but he was even better looking with his clothes off. "Unlike us."

"Hey, no one told you to strip," she answered indignantly.

"Well, I couldn't let you get arrested on your own, could I? You wouldn't last a minute in a Chinese prison."

"And you would?"

"Let's hope neither one of us has to find out." And then he jumped over the edge of the fountain, landing with a huge splash at her feet. "Holy shit, it's cold!"

"You're crazy, you know that, right?" she said, looking down at him, squatting in the freezing water.

"That's pretty much like the pot calling the kettle black," he said, standing up. He was so close that his hip brushed against hers. "I can't believe you did this."

She shrugged. "See? You don't know everything about me. I can be spontaneous."

"Yes, but now I'm questioning your sanity."

"You can leave anytime, you know. No one's making you stay."

Guiran stepped back just a little, let his eyes rake over her from head to toe. "Like that's going to happen."

He reached behind him, picked up his jacket. Slid it over her shoulders. Then brought his right hand up to cup her left cheek. "It just so happens," he said with a grin that suddenly made her knees tremble, "that crazy looks good on you. Really, really good."

Mei tried to answer, but her brain was as frozen as her body. If he didn't kiss her soon, she was going to end up with hypothermia and probably frostbite as well. In fact, she could get stuck with—

Screw it. She was done waiting. Burying her hands in Guiran's soft, silky hair, she tugged him forward until his mouth met hers. At the first touch of their lips, fireworks exploded all around her. It looked like Chinese New Year had come early.

IKC Fan Page

The Official Fan Page for the International Kissing Club

9,334
people like this

 IKC Page

Mulan   I finally went out and scored some points! But I'm not really a control freak, am I?

> **Ariel** Yippee! . . . Honey, we think you're fabulous and love you no matter what!
>
> **Jane** You go, girl! Btw, you're perfect.
>
> **Mulan** Neither of you answered. Am. I. A. Control. Freak???
>
> **Jayson** Well, duh.
>
> **Ariel** Hey, that's mean. You don't know her well enough to say that.
>
> **Jane** Watch it, or we'll block you like we did Smallwood.
>
> **Jayson** Sorry, but I've been reading her posts for the past four weeks. I assumed all control freaks were self-aware. But don't worry, some guys love that.
>
> **Ariel** That's right! Three points. Go, sk8ter boy!
>
> **Mulan** I think you mean: go Mulan.
>
> **Rapunzel** We rest our case.
>
> **Mulan** Nice job covering. Hey, Ariel, where are all your points? You're falling behind!

Chapter 17
Piper

"Are you ready to go, Piper?" Sebastian's voice floated down the hallway toward her, along with the sounds of his parents and Simone leaving for their day in the country. They'd invited Piper and Sebastian to go with them, but Sebastian had wanted to spend the day in Paris instead, and Piper had wanted to stay with him.

"I'll be there in a second," she answered, pulling up the IKC Facebook page on her laptop. She'd been so busy lately with school, and Simone and Sebastian, and her stupid, humiliating art classes that it had been a few days since she'd posted anything. She knew her friends would be worried if she didn't at least let them know she was still alive.

Sure enough, Cassidy had posted, "Ariiiiiiiiiiiiiiiiiiiiiiel? Where are yooooooooooooooou?" just the day before.

Instead of answering, she scrolled through the numerous other comments on the page, from girls who had begun tallying up their points and marking their kisses on Mei's widget. There were a bunch of them, way more than the last time she'd looked, and she couldn't help feeling a little proud. She and her friends had sparked a kissing revolution. Girls taking control of their own destinies. How cool was that?

Piper certainly felt like she had seized control of her own fate since coming to Paris—it was easy to do what she wanted here, to do what felt right, instead of always worrying about how her mom was going to react or how Germaine would use her actions against her.

Not wanting to think about Germaine *or* her mother, Piper continued to skim the comments, stopping only when she found one of Izzy's from a couple days before, saying she was keeping a close eye on Tanner. It seemed so strange to see those words, stranger still to think about Tanner when being with Sebastian had completely obliterated him from her mind. Tanner had been a silly crush, while Sebastian was so much more.

She knew that wasn't what the other girls wanted to hear, though, so she typed back a flippant, "As long as that's all you're keeping on him," before continuing to look for Mei's status. She was dying to know what her friend had been up to in China. She really hoped Mei had met a guy as amazing as Sebastian.

But when she finally found Mei's comment—buried beneath a flurry of postings from girls she'd never heard of—it gave her pause. "Hey, Ariel, you look so happy in those pics you e-mailed us! Good for you—does this mean the angsty artist is a thing of the past?"

Piper stared at the words for nearly a minute, absorbing them. Worrying about them. For so long she had needed to force herself to get up in the morning, to pretend that her life wasn't as bad as she thought it was. To ignore the snipes and gibes that came at her from everyone but her three closest friends.

She hadn't done that in France, not any of it. The realization felt strange. But how could she be anything but happy here? The city was amazing. Marie, Simone, and Gus were the family she'd always longed for. Her friends at school were great. And Sebastian . . .

She sighed. Sebastian was amazing: witty, intelligent, and so sexy that she nearly melted whenever he was in the same room with her. He listened when she talked, let her bounce new and exciting ideas off him. He even let her drag him all over the city, to places she knew he'd been to a million times.

And when she didn't have a plan, didn't have any idea what she wanted to do or where she wanted to go, he always had the coolest suggestions. They'd gone to some of his favorite haunts, off the beaten path and not listed in any tour book she'd ever read. The clubs, cafés, markets, and galleries he brought her to had shown her an entirely different side of Paris—one she really liked.

He'd even taken her deep into the city's underground, into the catacombs she had read about for years but never thought she'd have a chance to see. The whole trip was awesome—spooky and dark and, with Sebastian at her side, more than a little hot. Who would ever have guessed that an underground cemetery could be so . . . stimulating?

She never wanted to leave Paris. Sure, she missed her friends, but they were pretty much the only reason she wanted to go home. Her mother, her sister, Germaine—the idea of returning to Texas to be their scapegoat once more was almost unthinkable. She'd tasted freedom, tasted what it was like to be part of a family that genuinely liked and respected her, and she had no desire to go back to the way things were.

Skipping from the IKC page to her personal one, Piper tossed off a quick update on what she'd been doing. Then clicked over to Sebastian's page to see if he'd said anything about her. The last time he'd posted had been the weekend before, after they'd gotten back from Versailles. *"Belle fille. Des moments de plaisir. Intéressant art. Merveilleux weekend."*

Beautiful girl. Fun times. Interesting art. Great weekend. Though she'd read the description before, it still made her grin. He'd called her beautiful and the weekend they'd spent together great! What more could any girl want? She glanced over at his relationship status. Oh yeah, that. Why hadn't he changed it? They'd been dating for weeks, yet his status still said single. She'd changed hers soon after the Louvre, and it was starting to bug her that he hadn't. He probably just hadn't thought of it yet, but still . . .

She sighed, then logged off Facebook and checked her e-mail superquick. She and Sebastian were going to be out most of the afternoon and she wanted to see if her grade was up for the big project she'd just turned in for art class. She'd worked crazy hard on it and was hoping—

Yes, there it was. An e-mail from her painting teacher, Madame Amirault. Closing her eyes and muttering a quick prayer, Piper clicked on it. Maybe this time her teacher would understand what she was getting at. Maybe this time she would actually like what Piper had done— God knew, Piper had poured her newly shiny heart and soul into the piece.

Taking a deep breath, she opened her eyes—and felt all the excitement drain out of her in a rush. A C-. She skimmed the comments— too juvenile, too sweet, too boring. Not enough zest.

Tears burned in Piper's eyes, and she lowered her head to the desk with a thunk. What was she doing wrong? She had given everything she had to this project—to every project she'd done since arriving in France—but it didn't seem to matter. In class, both of her art teachers—Madame Amirault and Monsieur Blanchard—were always on her ass, always saying her attempts were childish, that they lacked passion. Depth. Vitality.

Yet she'd never felt more passionate, more vital. Never felt anything as deeply as she'd felt these past few weeks with Sebastian. And still she'd disappointed them. And more importantly, she'd disappointed herself.

"Hey, are you ready?" Sebastian poked his head in the room she and Simone shared. "The movie starts in half an hour."

"Oh, right. Of course." Shoving her disappointment—and worry—to the back of her mind, Piper sprang up and yanked on her jacket. Then she grabbed the scarf Sebastian had bought her the week before when they'd been out and she'd been freezing. As her fingers fell on the soft, purple cashmere, she realized again just how much—and how quickly— Sebastian had become a part of her life, almost as if he'd always been there.

He'd made the past two weeks the most fantabulous of her life.

And when she was with him, nothing mattered but the way he smiled at her.

The way his eyes crinkled just a little bit at the corners and sparkled with laughter.

The way his fingers felt—warm and slightly calloused from all his sculpting—when they stroked down her face.

Maybe that was the problem. Maybe she was taking all the feelings she'd always had for her art and giving them to Sebastian instead . . .

More mixed up than she had been in a long time, Piper ducked her head and started down the hallway.

"Hey, is something wrong?" Sebastian asked as she passed him. "You're awfully quiet."

"I'm just thinking." She shook her head. "I got a crappy grade on my latest art project, and it put me in a bad mood. I'll get over it."

"That sucks." His mouth twisted in sympathy. "I know how hard you worked on it."

"I work hard on everything, but it doesn't seem to matter, does it? I think I'm hopeless."

"You're not hopeless." He wrapped his arms around her and hugged her against his chest. "Not even close."

"Then why do I feel so useless? I swear, I can't do anything right." She could sense the tears beating at the corners of her eyelids, but she blinked them back.

"You can't think like that, Piper. I've seen some of your work. You're really good."

"I wish my art teachers felt the same way."

He brushed a soft kiss against her forehead, and Piper shivered, despite her misery. "They will. It just takes time to get in the groove with a new teacher. It's normal to make some mistakes as you try to figure out what they want from you."

She pulled back, looked at him, surprised. "Has it happened to you?"

He laughed. "*Oui*. Of course. Even us *pot makers* can mess up sometimes."

Piper blushed at his reference to the insult she'd hurled at him a few weeks before. It was doubly embarrassing considering how gorgeous his work really was.

Shrugging it off, she grabbed her purse and opened the door. "Come on. We're going to be late for the movie."

"You know," Sebastian said, his arms coming around her from behind, pulling her against his long, well-muscled body. Piper felt everything inside of herself go ooey-gooey at the contact. "We don't have to go to the movie."

"Oh yeah?" She grinned. "And what should we do instead?"

"Guess."

His soft, full lips made her shiver as he pressed kisses up and down her nape, and Piper leaned into him, relishing the contact. Relishing what it felt like to be held by a guy who really cared about her. A guy she had truly fallen for. Big-time.

Forget the movie, she'd be happy to stay right here forever.

Turning, she looked up into the deep, dark indigo of his eyes and felt herself melt. Not just her body, which, admittedly, was completely into what was going on, but her heart as well. It had flipped over in her chest at the sight of his smile, at the feel of him against her, and she wasn't sure how she was ever going to get things back to normal again. Or even if she wanted to.

Reaching up, she framed his face with her hands.

Stroked her thumbs over his sharp cheekbones.

Imagined, not for the first time, what his face would look like in charcoal on her sketch pad or in oils on the easel Marie had let her set up in the corner of the living room.

He was so beautiful standing there, his impossibly long lashes casting shadows on his cheeks while a couple days' worth of stubble darkened his jaw.

So different from Tanner or any of the other boys she knew in Texas.

So much more than she'd ever imagined.

She brushed a finger over his lips and he smiled—not the cocky grin she'd seen so much of the first day they'd met, but a soft, sweet curving of his mouth that he reserved just for her. Then he nipped gently at her fingertip and her heart went crazy. It beat a wild, messed-up tattoo that had her nerves jangling and her breath catching in her throat.

"You're so beautiful," he whispered.

She shook her head. "I'm cute. That's a far cry from beautiful."

"Shh." It was his turn to put a finger on her lips. "You're beautiful to me." His voice wasn't as steady as usual, and she realized, in awe, that the trembling she felt wasn't coming from her. It was coming from him, from the strong body he had pressed so tightly to her own.

The realization that she affected him as much as he did her swept through Piper, made her feel powerful and alive. Made her feel as beautiful as he insisted she was.

"Sebastian—"

He didn't let her finish, his mouth replacing the finger that had slowly traced the curve of her lower lip. And then he was kissing her. Softly, sweetly, and finally with an edge of desperation that simply destroyed her.

Her knees trembled, turned to Jell-O, and she grabbed onto the lapels of Sebastian's jacket to keep herself from falling. He pulled away just a little and she thought maybe he would laugh at her inexperience, but there was nothing amused in the deep, wild eyes that stared into her own. Just a darkness, a need that echoed the one spreading through her at an alarming rate.

He shifted a little so that his arms were tight around her waist, holding her up even as he pulled her body flush against his own. Piper wrapped her arms around him in return, relishing the feel of his broad shoulders beneath her hands. The solid warmth of his chest and stomach against her own. And as she did, everything slid into place. All of her worries, all of her fears, all of the uncertainties about what her future—their future—held slipped away, and it was just her and him and the incredible rightness between them.

His lips skimmed down her throat and she gasped, then sifted her fingers through his dark, silky hair and pulled his mouth back to hers. He tasted like Marie's rich, dark coffee. Like the raspberries and cream they'd had for breakfast. Like the smooth, soft chocolate she'd become addicted to her first week in Paris. She couldn't get enough of him.

He must have felt the same way, because the kissing went on and on and on.

Piper didn't know how long they stood there in the hallway, kissing and touching and tasting. Long enough for the grandfather clock in the living room to chime once, and then a second time. More than long enough for her toes to curl and her entire body to start shaking.

Finally, Sebastian pulled away, his breathing heavy and his eyes hot. "I'm okay with skipping the movie," she whispered.

"Are you sure?" he asked, his gaze searching her face.

"Yeah. Absolutely." She reached for Sebastian's hand, tangled her fingers with his as she wondered if there was a way for her to slip out for a few seconds, just long enough to put on the bustier she'd bought weeks ago in Dallas. Then decided it didn't matter. Nothing did but being with Sebastian.

They moved slowly down the hall to his room, and butterflies flitted back and forth in Piper's stomach as she realized they were really going to do this. Five weeks ago she would have said she wasn't ready for it, but that was before she'd met Sebastian, before she'd fallen in love. Now, being with him seemed natural. And if she was nervous, so what? It was normal. Right?

The second Sebastian's bedroom door closed behind them, his mouth came down on hers again. Hard. For the space of one breath, two, before he pulled away. "You make me crazy, Piper," he whispered against her temple.

Everything inside of her went soft. "Me, too," she answered. "I can't think when you touch me."

She crossed to the bed, sat down, completely overwhelmed. By the feelings spinning inside of her, by the way Sebastian was looking at her, by the knowledge of what she was about to do. Her heart was beating so fast it felt like it was going to pound right out of her chest.

Sebastian followed, but instead of sitting on the bed, he sank to the floor in front of her. Took her hands in his and pressed soft, tender kisses in the center of her palms. She shivered even as her nerves settled.

And then he was sliding her jacket off her shoulders, pressing her back onto the bed, stretching out beside her. Piper gasped at the feel of him, tried to ignore the brief flare of panic that shot through her. She'd never been on a bed with a guy before, never let one unbutton her top before, never let one kiss the sensitive skin of her stomach before.

It felt strange.

But this was Sebastian, she told herself. It was okay to let him touch her. Okay to be with him—

"Hey." Sebastian pulled away a little and looked at her. "Are you all right?"

"Yeah. Of course." She swallowed, wrapped her arms around him tightly. "Why wouldn't I be?"

"You're shaking."

"It's fine. I'm just—" Nervous? Excited? Terrified? "Cold."

He didn't say anything, just stared at her for a long time, his eyes so intense that it felt like he could see all the way to her soul. Then he smiled and reached down to the foot of the bed, pulling his comforter over them.

"Come here." He snuggled her against him, one hand cupping the back of her head and pressing her face into the curve between his neck and shoulder while the other stroked her back soothingly.

They lay there like that for a few minutes, not speaking, not kissing, not doing anything but breathing in the scent of each other. Feeling each other's hearts beat. As Sebastian's warmth seeped into her, Piper felt herself relax. It was okay. This was Sebastian. She could do this.

She reached down, rubbed her fingers over his stomach.

He stopped her, brought her hand back up to his chest. "Piper, we don't have to do anything you're not ready for," he said.

She leaned forward, kissed him. "It's okay. I do—"

He kissed her to shut her up, a soft, gentle brushing of his lips against hers. "I know you haven't done this before, and maybe half-way around the world isn't where it should happen for the first time."

His words confused her, since she couldn't imagine being this close to anyone else. Ever. She'd thought he felt the same way. "But I thought you wanted—"

He pulled her back down, rolled over on top of her so that she couldn't hide. Couldn't protect herself from the tenderness in his eyes. "I do want to." He laughed. "Of course I do. But that doesn't mean I want to push you into it."

"You're not!"

"Okay, then, that doesn't mean I want to see *you* push *yourself* into it." He kissed her again. "Let's just relax, see what happens, okay?"

She nodded as relief and love and happiness exploded inside her. The tension and worry she'd barely let herself acknowledge drained out of her, and she wrapped her arms around Sebastian, hugging him as tightly as she could. Back in Texas, the boys she knew would never have thought twice if they'd believed they could go all the way with a girl. That Sebastian cared enough about her, about what she wanted, not to pressure her, was awesome. Amazing. Wonderful. Was there any doubt why she was so crazy in love with him?

He kissed her again, then rolled back onto his side. "So, tell me about this art project. What's your teacher's problem?"

"It's not her problem. It's mine," she said. "I can't seem to get anything right."

"Can I see what you're doing? Maybe I can help."

"What, now?" she asked.

"Not right now," he answered with a smile. "I don't want to let you go yet."

She didn't want to let him go, either. Not now. Maybe not ever. How could she, when he knew her so well? When he'd known—even before she had—that she wasn't ready to make love with him yet, no matter how crazy she was about him.

Instead, she wanted to study him, to learn everything about him. They talked and touched, kissed and cuddled. She told him about the pig incident and Germaine, and even about her mother. Things she'd never thought she could share with another person, at least not without feeling burning humiliation. But with Sebastian it was easy; he just accepted. And when it was his turn, he told her about why he loved to sculpt, about how he was afraid all his knowledge about art was just a substitute for real talent, that he was no more than a hack who'd never live up to the artists who came before him. After a while they got hungry. They went to the kitchen and ate crusty bread with cheese and some round, fat grapes that Sebastian insisted on feeding to her, one by one. Then they went back to his bedroom and cuddled some more, talked some more.

It was the best day of her life, one she knew she was going to hold on to forever. She wanted to sketch what she was feeling, to create a memento of this day that couldn't fade. When she was back in Texas she wanted to be able to pull out the memory and examine it over and over again, to wrap herself up in it so that when the stupid football players started in on her she wouldn't care. Because she would know what it was like to have had this one, perfect moment. But to do that, she would have to move and she wasn't yet ready to give up the warmth of Sebastian's arms.

Eventually Sebastian fell asleep—between school, his sculpting, and spending time with her, he hadn't been getting more than four or five hours of sleep a night. For a while, she just watched him. Brushed his hair back from his forehead. Traced the strong lines of his face with soft fingertips. Trailed gentle kisses over his jaw.

But eventually the need to sketch him grew overwhelming. She slid out from under his arm, grabbed a stray piece of paper and a pencil, and began to draw . . .

The strong curve of his shoulder . . .

The well-muscled line of his back . . .

The heavy roundness of his bicep.

He was so beautiful, so unbelievably beautiful, that she wanted to capture every nuance of him.

As she sketched, she marveled at the strange familiarity of the moment. She'd sketched tons of people in her life, some aware of what she was doing, some unaware, but never before had it felt like this. So personal, so emotional, so intimate. More intimate, she imagined, than even having sex with him would have been. This watching him while he slept, trying to use her talent to record on paper not just what he looked like but how she felt about him as well.

At first, she hadn't been sure she was good enough to express all that. But as Piper worked, she realized that whatever funk had been bugging her in art class didn't extend to her time with Sebastian. Drawing him was easy.

Smiling, she shaded the angle of his jaw before moving on to the curve of his ear and the pronounced sharpness of his cheekbone. He stirred but didn't wake up, so she kept sketching.

She worked for a long time, until her hand ached and her fingers cramped. She knew it was time to stop—past time—but she couldn't make herself put the pencil down. Her time in France—her time with Sebastian—was finite. Limited. With each moment that passed, it was slowly leaking away.

· · · · · ·✈

Sebastian stirred eventually, ran his hand over the spot next to him on the bed. When he didn't find Piper, his eyes popped open and he searched the room for her. Their eyes met and he smiled, a sweet, sleepy curve of his lips that arrowed right through her. He held out a hand and Piper took it, climbing onto the bed beside him and running her fingers lightly down his back.

As she settled next to him, Piper felt her eyes start to close. She fought sleep as long as she could, made herself a promise as she lay there listening to Sebastian breathe. She had four weeks left in Paris—to explore her art, the city, her feelings for Sebastian, and this place that had taught her so much about herself. She wasn't going to waste a second of it.

IKC Fan Page

The Official Fan Page for the International Kissing Club

11,776

people like this

Jane Hey, Punzy, what's going on Down Under?

> **Rapunzel** Lucas's parents have a little sailboat and they're going to take me on it this weekend.
>
> **Mulan** Don't you get seasick when you go out in your Papa's boat at the coast?
>
> **Rapunzel** Don't worry, I've got my patch, I'm prepared for anything.
>
> **Ariel** Whoa, atta girl. Go for the gold, Rapunzel.
>
> **Rapunzel** Simmer down, Ariel. His whole family is going to be there.
>
> **Jayson** You're a creative girl, if you can't find someplace to be alone on the whole continent of Australia, you don't deserve the gold—god or otherwise.
>
> **Rapunzel** Sit down, Jayson.

Mulan Speaking of sailing, the tide has turned. I finally passed a test and my GPA no longer needs CPR.

> **Bojana S.** I thought YOU needed mouth-to-mouth, not your grades.
>
> **Mulan** Hey, I got my points.
>
> **Jane** Speak for yourself. At this rate, I'm not above faking my own drowning in front of the fire station to get some mouth-to-mouth.

Rapunzel What about you, Ariel? Anything new in your hemisphere?

> **Ariel** Eh, not much to speak of.

Between **Piper** and **Cassidy**:

Piper
OMG!!! Who knew sculptors were so good with their hands!

Cassidy
I don't even want to know what that means.

Piper
All I'm saying is OMG!!!

Chapter 18
Cassidy

The boat moored at the end of the marina's wooden dock was huge and sleek. Its hull gleamed fire-engine red in the sun, the mahogany stained wood on its deck polished to brilliance.

"You said your parents owned a sailboat, Lucas." Cassidy came to a full stop on the dock. She reached up and ripped off the motion sickness patch behind her ear. She wasn't going to need it—this thing was the size of a freaking yacht.

"What? It's a sailboat. There's the sail and everything." He pointed to the gleaming white sail that towered into the wide blue sky above them.

"I thought your dad was a banker and your mom stays at home."

"My mom does stay at home, when she's not hosting charity events."

"And your dad?" Lucas looked everywhere but her eyes while Cass waited for him to answer.

He sighed before finally speaking. "Technically, he is a banker—he just also owns the bank."

"Owns the bank? Which bank? Because the family who owns the local bank in Paris doesn't have a hundred-foot sailboat."

"It's more like twenty-three meters, which is about—"

"Stop avoiding the question, Lucas."

"NSW Bank."

"You mean *that* bank?" she asked, pointing to the skyscraper on the other side of the harbor with the letters *NSW* emblazoned across the top. "So when you were telling me that your dad wants you to work with him, it never occurred to you once in the past six weeks to mention that it would be as chairman of the board."

"Why are you upset, Cass?"

"Because you're rich. Very rich."

"No, my parents are rich," Lucas stated matter-of-factly. She shot him a you-know-what-I-mean look.

Cassidy's already frayed nerves unraveled as the wide chasm between their backgrounds expanded to Grand Canyon widths underneath her Payless sandals. All those golden-god quips didn't seem so funny now that she knew he really was made of gold.

"Cass, it doesn't matter."

"That's because you're the one with the money. It matters a whole lot to me."

He frowned. "It's not that I was hiding it from you." He faced her and put his hands on her hips to pull her to him. "It's that"—he bent and kissed her earlobe—"I had other things"—then he traced the curve of her jaw—"on my mind."

No. She refused to respond to such blatant attempts to distract her. She was angry. How had it slipped his mind to tell her, someone he'd seen and talked to every day for the past month, that his family was on the other side of well-off? That he was a friggin' mogul. Or at least the heir to one.

"Don't be mad, Cass. It's nothing, I promise. My family has money. That shouldn't change anything between us, right?" He brushed her lips, and she leaned into him, but caught herself at the last moment and stiffened.

"No, it doesn't. But you should have told me."

"I'm sorry. And I promise, I wasn't trying to hide it—it just really isn't a big deal. So, are we good?"

Finally she nodded and begrudgingly said, "Okay."

Lucas smiled. "Good. Then kiss me." That she was happy to do. Too happy.

"Come on, I want you to meet my family," he said, and led her to the end of the long wooden dock. "Hello!" He helped her step down onto the deck.

A beautiful blond woman popped her head up from below. *Ah, this must be the cruise director*, Cassidy thought.

"Hello, my darling boy," she called out. She wore a pink polo top and white linen pants with silver sandals, and had a figure that would make even Piper's mom green. She crossed the deck to them and wrapped her arms around Lucas before leaving a smudge of lipstick on his cheek.

"Mum, this is Cassidy. Cassidy, this is my mum, Shanna."

"Cassidy." She smiled and before Cassidy could do anything about it, Lucas's mom embraced her as well. "I'm delighted you could join us today. Lucas has told me so much about you already."

Cassidy shifted on her feet, a bit overwhelmed by the welcome. "Thank you for inviting me, Mrs. McCann." Lucas must have sensed her awkwardness, because he slipped his hand in hers and gave it a little squeeze.

Two other girls climbed up top. "Hey, li'l man," said the first, her long pale-blond hair swinging down her back. Lucas caught her up in a hug as well.

"Cassidy, this is my older sister, Kara," he said before pausing to hug the other girl. Her hair was darker than her sister's and cut into a stylish bob swept to the side of her face, a smattering of freckles across the bridge of her nose. "And this is my oldest sister, Julie."

He was so tall and solid, it was tough for Cassidy to imagine Lucas as the baby in his family. But the way all the McCann women fussed over him, she could see he reveled in the position.

"Where've you been? We've waited hours for you, Lucas." Julie flicked him affectionately on the ear.

He ducked. "Am I the only one in this family who likes to sleep past dawn?"

"Past dawn, no; past noon, yes." His mother smoothed down the collar of his green shirt. "You know your father. He was ready to cast off when day broke. If he had his way, we'd live on this boat."

"We will live on this boat," came a booming voice behind them. Cassidy looked over Shanna's shoulder to see an older version of Lucas coming toward them. Tan and fit, in a pair of khaki pants and a wind jacket, with only a hint of silver in his sand-colored hair, Mr. McCann was a striking man. "Just a few more years, and I plan to circumnavigate the globe with her." He held out his hand to shake Lucas's. "Hello, Son," he said.

After the loving exuberance of Lucas's mom and sisters, Cassidy couldn't help but notice the distant formality that existed between Lucas and his father. "Hello, Dad. This is Cassidy."

Cassidy shook his hand. "Nice to meet you, Mr. McCann." The whole family was so stupidly attractive, she almost began to tremble with the thought of her imperfections. The refrain from the *Sesame Street* song "One of These Things Is Not Like the Others" kept replaying in the back of her mind.

"Please, when I'm not at the office, I prefer Charles. Have you been sailing before, Cassidy?"

She stifled a snort. Unless you counted paddling a canoe in the stock tank on Izzy's ranch, then no.

Mr. McCann sailed the boat (named *Charlie's Angels*—a cheeky reference to Shanna, Julie, and Kara) through the harbor, past the iconic landmarks, and out to the Tasman Sea, heading south along the coast. Lucas sat by her side the whole time, pointing out the sights and laughing with her while they watched dolphins surf in the boat's wake.

It was all so overwhelmingly perfect. And she'd never felt more out of place.

His family was wonderful, of course. He and his sisters poked and ribbed each other like they were all still children, not grown adults, and his mother, smiling and laughing with her kids, taking everything they did and said in stride. They brought Cassidy into their circle and teased her as if she was one of their own.

Cassidy, on the other hand, kept waiting for Mr. McCann to pull her aside and try to bribe her to stay away from his son like what happened on the soap operas her Memaw watched. But instead, Charles—as he kept insisting she call him—stood at the wheel all day, except when they'd anchored for lunch in the sheltered cove of a lush green national park. Even then he talked about sailing and the boat—which he loved, the passion for it glittering in his eyes.

The tension was unmistakable, however, between father and son, though neither acknowledged it. Not even when Lucas mentioned over lunch that he would be competing next week at North Narrabeen Point.

Charles had stayed quiet, returning to his position behind the wheel to sail them back to Sydney.

"Can I come watch?" Kara asked her brother. "You won't embarrass me by wiping out on a puny wave or anything, right? 'Cause I only claim you as my li'l brother when you win."

"Can't wipe out—all the big companies will be there to see me. Want to come, too, Mum?"

Shanna shook her head vigorously. "No, sweetheart. You know I can't watch you do that stuff. It's too dangerous."

Later, when his mother and sisters had gone below deck, Lucas sat next to Cass, legs dangling over the side, their arms against the rail. "Will you come watch me compete?"

"I'd love to," she answered. He put his arm around her shoulder and she leaned against him. "You know you're not all that different from your dad," she said. "Look at him." They glanced to where Charles stood. "He feels the same about sailing as you do about surfing."

Lucas shrugged. "Maybe, but he doesn't see it that way. He thinks

I'm betting my future on a long shot. Julie, she's an attorney. Kara is studying medicine at university. He wants me to fall in line. But I have to know I gave my dream everything I had before I give up on it."

"He's only like that because he loves you, Lucas. He wants the best for you. You're lucky. Trust me, having a dad that's a pain in the ass is better than not having one around at all."

"When did your parents divorce?" he asked. Cassidy hesitated. It made her uncomfortable to talk about her whole messed-up family situation when his was so completely opposite. But somehow she knew he wouldn't judge her, wouldn't think less of her for something she'd had no control over. Lucas was nothing like the small-minded people from back home. She took a breath and dove in.

"My parents were never married. My mom got pregnant when she was eighteen and my dad . . . my dad wanted other things. So he left."

"Sounds like a whacker."

Cass snorted. She wasn't quite sure what a "whacker" was, but she could guess at the meaning. "Yeah, I think so, too."

"D'ya ever see him?"

"Not really," she answered, "though he did pay for me to come on this trip, so I have to give him a little credit."

Cassidy was glad Lucas didn't say something comforting or try to make her feel better about the situation with a sympathetic gesture. That wasn't why she'd told him about her dad. She'd told him because it was such a huge part of what made her who she was and she'd wanted him to know. They were quiet for a while after that, watching the whitecaps crest and roll.

"If you don't get your scholarship, are you going to stay in Paris forever?" Lucas finally asked, breaking the silence between them.

"God, I hope not. Piper says I can come live with her in Austin when she goes to college, at least until I can afford tuition or get a loan."

"You could come back here for university. Maybe I could help you with tuition."

For a split second everything in Cassidy's body came to a complete stop. He couldn't be serious. There was no way he was serious. She snorted. "Right—I'm going to move to Australia so you can pay for me to go to college. Ha. Very funny."

"What's so funny about it? In case you haven't noticed, Cassidy, I like you; I like having you around. And I'd help you if you wanted. If you'd let me."

Oh my God, she'd taken the seasickness patch off too soon. The boat had suddenly turned into a Tilt-A-Whirl and everything was topsy-turvy because Lucas couldn't be serious. And *if* he was then . . .

Oh my God.

Oh my God.

Oh my God.

Cassidy couldn't breathe, but Lucas was waiting for a response. This ride was coming to an end, and instead of letting her off safely, it had dumped her into the ocean. She scrambled for the only life preserver she could find.

"I thought you don't have any money—your parents do," she said.

"I don't. But I could if it were really important to me." Now she was slipping beneath the water and drowning.

Panicked by the direction this conversation had taken, she turned away. Cassidy gripped the railing for dear life and stared out at the horizon, trying to regain her equilibrium. She was a state basketball champion, and she hadn't gotten there without knowing how to stamp down her fear and focus on her goal. In this case: getting off this goddamn boat.

Cassidy shut out everything—Lucas, the noise of the boat, the waves, the wind—and just breathed. And breathed. And breathed.

These past weeks hanging out with Lucas had been the best time of her life. But moving here to be with him, putting all of her faith in him, letting him pay for her expenses—that was a level she wasn't ready for. Not to mention, Cassidy could only imagine telling her mother that she was going to move to the other side of the world to be with a guy who would be paying for her college education. Talk about sending someone to an early grave—her mother's head would spin like a hula hoop before shooting off across the room like a champagne cork.

Not that the idea didn't have some appeal, if she was being completely honest with herself. Why wouldn't it? Life would be a lot easier if there really were white knights that rode to the rescue when a girl needed it. But Cassidy wasn't that girl. She didn't want charity. She could rescue herself, thank you very much.

And grand gestures like the offer Lucas had just made were the sorts of things guys did when they wanted something from you. Not that she believed that about Lucas, but there had to be a better explanation for what he'd said than just that he liked having her around.

Love?

Where had that come from? Just thinking the word gave her a brain freeze. She liked Lucas more than any guy she'd ever known, but love . . . no, it was too soon and she was too young to be talking about that.

Cassidy pulled away from Lucas. She took a breath to sort through her rambling, crazy thoughts. She was still Vacation Cassidy, remember? He was talking about University Cassidy. She wasn't ready to open the box on that model yet. "That's almost two years away. I can't worry about it right now. I just want to focus on the four weeks I've got left here, okay? And *you* need to focus on surfing your ass off next weekend."

As soon as the words came out of her mouth she seized the idea. Surfing . . . yeah. He probably needed to practice in the coming week. And God knew she needed a little time to remember that Hot Guy and Monster Sailboat weren't accessories that Vacation Cassidy got to keep when this trip was over.

"Maybe we shouldn't see each other this week. Maybe we need a break." Yes, that's what they needed: breathing space.

"A break?" His face fell, like she'd just stomped on his surfboard.

"You know, so you're not distracted. You'll get more wave time this way."

"You're not a distraction, Cass," he argued, twirling a long springy curl of her hair around his finger.

She scooted another foot away, out of his reach. "Well, *you* are. Not in a bad way, that's the problem. I like being with you, too much. I could stand to put a bit more effort into my classes so I don't have to repeat junior year. And all your energy needs to go into impressing those sponsors."

Lucas looked unconvinced. "That's all this is about, your school and my surfing? Nothing else?"

"Yes, Lucas, really. Nothing else." Nothing else she wanted to talk to him about anyway.

"This isn't some crap excuse because you want to get more points for that stupid kissing club?"

Cassidy laughed out loud. Jeez, guys could be so insecure, even really cute ones. "No. I promise that's not the reason." She scooted back toward him, playfully punching his arm. "And don't knock the IKC, dude. It's the whole reason we started kissing in the first place."

He cocked an eyebrow. "Reason? That was just an excuse. But you're still coming with me next Saturday, yeah?"

"I wouldn't miss it, Lucas. And it's only six days. It'll be over before we know it."

Six days would be a cakewalk. Just long enough for her to get her head—and her heart—back on straight.

IKC Fan Page

The Official Fan Page for the International Kissing Club

13,272

people like this

🗨 IKC Page

Rapunzel	Taking a break. Need some space to focus on my schoolwork—stop laughing, Mulan. I'm serious.
Rapunzel	Physics sucks globally.
Rapunzel	Late night TV Down Under is worse than QVC.
Rapunzel	Is it purl one, knit two?
Rapunzel	Never mind. Screw knitting.
Rapunzel	Where the $%@& are the rest of you????
Rapunzel	Break over in three minutes. Aaaaaahhhhh.

Where the hell was he?

Six torturous days later, Cassidy stood on the beach at North Narrabeen Point, outside Sydney, shifting from foot to foot, adjusting and readjusting her watchband, pulling her hair into a ponytail, then taking it back down.

"Are you okay, Cassidy?" Kara, Lucas's sister, asked.

"What? Sure, I'm fine. Why do you ask?"

She laughed. "Nothing. You seem a bit twitchy, that's all."

"Oh, sorry, that's the double espresso I had before you picked me up," she fibbed. She couldn't tell Kara the real reason she was acting like she'd missed a dose of Ritalin: she'd spent last night waiting, watching the moon cross the sky, instead of sleeping. At all.

When Lucas had called her to say good night, Cassidy had wanted to crawl through the phone. Turned out, not seeing Lucas was a much bigger distraction than seeing him ever could be.

Stupid, stupid break.

God, she'd wasted a whole week not being with him, and now she had only three more left until she went back home.

Lucas had asked Kara to bring her today because he'd had to get here so early. When the poor girl had shown up at Mrs. Gatwick's, Cassidy was waiting on the stoop and had practically launched herself into the car before Kara came to a full stop.

The crowd was already thick on the beach when they'd arrived. Vendor tents lined the high ground, and you could barely walk without tripping over a surfboard. Cassidy scanned up and down the sand, her breath catching every time she thought she spotted Lucas's wavy blond hair among the other surfers.

"Hey, girls, you made it," she heard his out-of-breath voice call. Cassidy whirled to see him coming up from the water's edge several yards away, carrying his shortboard under his arm. Her heart started hop-skipping around in her chest and she ran what had to be her record best in the fifty-yard dash. Lucas barely had enough time to drop the board and catch her as she jumped onto him, wrapping her arms around his neck, not caring that she was getting soaked to the skin. Good thing he was so strong, because any other guy would have been knocked to the ground by her body slam.

"Jesus, I've missed you," he said before he set her down and kissed her. She kissed him back like she was using the air from his lungs to breathe, and she kept kissing him beyond the point of good taste, until the wolf whistles and heckling got too loud to ignore.

A throat cleared next to them. "Can I get a hug and kiss, as well, li'l man? Only not like that one," Kara teased. Lucas shifted away from Cassidy just long enough to greet his sister, but it seemed way too long for Cass. She wanted him all to herself.

"The first heat's about to begin. You two should go get seats in the stands." Lucas pulled her against him again and smiled. God, that little dimple had haunted her dreams for the past week. "A kiss for good luck?"

She gave him a quick peck on the lips. "That's for luck," she said, casting an impish grin when he looked disappointed. "The one for winning, well . . . you'll have to win to find out, won't you?"

So, Lucas did just that.

And after the finals, he waded through all the well-wishers to find her waiting with Kara at the front of the stands. She was almost gushing—okay, yes, she was gushing—with happiness for him.

He gazed up at her, his honey-colored eyes shining. "Hey, American girl, I believe I was promised a kiss for winning. Pay up."

Cassidy bent over the aluminum rail to reach him. "I believe you've earned all the kisses you can handle, Lucas McCann," she said before granting his prize.

Oh, this had gone way past dangerous—she'd taken the corner around dangerous at a reckless speed and gone off into the abyss.

Who cared if she was drowning? There were so many worse ways to go than this.

IKC Fan Page

The Official Fan Page for the International Kissing Club

14,876
people like this

IKC Page

Ariel   Another guy, another point. I'm back in the game.

> **Jane** Knew you couldn't keep a good girl down.
> **Mulan** Do you get bonus points for that?
> **Rapunzel** Hell, no. Ariel, get that test for mono, yet?

Messages

Between **Piper** and **Izzy**:

Piper
I need help. I think I really screwed up.

Izzy
What happened?

Piper
What does it say about me that I accidentally kissed a guy I barely know!

Izzy
It's not you. Others have done far worse than accidental kissing. We know you're fabulous.

Piper
Why does everyone keep saying that? Is that code for "You're so pathetic we can't tell you the truth"?

Izzy
No. It's code for men are stupid, effing idiots. Believe me. I know.

Piper
Is Linc giving you a hard time?

Izzy

He is the least of my worries . . . But no kissing action here. I'll leave it at that. Btw, thanks for the chocolates. They're a great substitute.

Piper

I'd send you a French guy if I could.

Izzy

Back to you . . . Does the new point you posted refer to the "accident"?

Piper

I told you I screwed up. I was colossally stupid. I really screwed the pooch.

Izzy

Please tell me there wasn't an actual dog involved! Just kidding. Trying to lighten the mood.

Piper

Should I tell Sebastian?

Izzy

God, no. Just try to gloss over it. What Sebastian doesn't know won't hurt him. As long as it didn't mean anything.

Piper

Oh God, no. In fact, I think I deserve negative points. Can I take it back?

Izzy

Don't worry, no one will hold it against you.

Izzy

I really miss you, Pipes.

Piper

I miss you, too, but I gotta go. Simone is taking me to a show at Le Moulin Rouge. Thanks for the advice.

Chapter 19
Izzy

After seven weeks of eating lunch basically alone, Izzy had thought she was used to it. For the first few days, she'd put an inordinate amount of thought into where to sit. One table over was where the stoners sat—not that there were many of them in Paris, but every school had some. By the back entrance was a row of tables where all the 4-H types ate. Since she'd gone vegetarian to reduce her carbon footprint, she didn't exactly have a lot in common with them. Near the door, the hardcore geeks congregated. Then along the east wall sat the trio of tables where Germaine held court. In the far west corner sat the now empty table she'd shared with Piper, Mei, and Cassidy for the past two years. She hadn't been able to face sitting there alone.

In the end, she'd followed Mei's advice and sat with the debate nerds and mathletes. Of course, she meant that with a great deal of affection. They were the only clique that had been welcoming at all. But as friendly as they were, they weren't really her *friends*. They had their own lingo, their own set of inside jokes. So she sat at the end of their table, keeping the illusion of being part of a group, without really being part of it.

Armed with her insulated bag full of hummus, olives, and pita bread in one hand and her battered copy of Al Gore's *Earth in the Balance* in the other, she dragged herself to the cafeteria, determined to hold her head high as she claimed her new spot on the fringes of geekdom. She'd tried to keep up with the conversation, until they'd started arguing the top ten episodes of *Battlestar Galactica*.

Izzy had just unearthed her bookmark from the tome when she saw Germaine's evil minions slithering by on their way to the royal dais. The wolves were circling again. Rosemary tittered as she passed. Izzy just gritted her teeth and focused on the fact that the earth had it a lot worse than she did. But just as she was starting to read her book, someone paused by her table.

Izzy tried not to notice, pretending to be engrossed in reading. When the person didn't budge, she finally looked up. Germaine the Lame. Why wasn't she surprised?

Germaine smiled. "I hope you're not mad about my teasing last weekend out at Tanner's farm."

Suspicious, Izzy searched Germaine's perfect features for the near permanent sneer of disdain. For once, it was absent. Suddenly even more nervous, Izzy muttered, "I—"

"Tanner thought I might have hurt your feelings." Then she gave her annoying trilling laugh, even though there was nothing funny about what she'd said.

"Don't worry about it," Izzy said quickly, wanting the conversation to end. If Tanner had put Germaine up to this, she was going to kill him. Why did Invisabel Isabel have to slip out from under the radar *now*?

"Thanks!" Germaine's smile broadened. "You know, you should come sit with us."

"With you?" Izzy stilled.

"Sure." Germaine gave her arm a little tug. "Pack up your lunch and come sit at our table."

Michaela had stopped a few feet behind Germaine. Now she stood with her mouth gaping open like one of the fake fish people mounted on their walls.

"I don't th—"

"Come on," Germaine coaxed. "What else are you going to do, sit here by yourself for three more weeks? Al Gore hasn't written that many books, you know."

Wait a second. Not only was Germaine being civil, but she was also familiar with Al Gore's books? And she knew who Al Gore was? And what books were?

Germaine's eyes held a note of apparent sympathy. What was the world coming to?

But that was it, wasn't it? There wasn't a genuine bone in Germaine's scrawny body. If she was acting nice, she had her own motives. No way was Izzy going to trust her. But she'd read Machiavelli: Keep your friends close and your enemies closer.

Her friends were pretty far away, but Germaine was right here.

"Well, okay, I guess." Izzy put the lid on her hummus and slid everything back into the bag.

A few steps later, Izzy stopped, halfway between her lonely spot at the geek table and the royalty up on the dais.

Was she really about to do this? Was she really going to throw herself in the path of Germaine the . . . Oh, she couldn't think of a pithy rhyming insult. Cassidy was best at those. But Cassidy was off flirting with hot surfers. Damn her.

Germaine glanced back over her shoulder when she realized Izzy wasn't following. The expression of confusion was understandable. Most of Germaine's sheep wouldn't dream of dawdling.

Germaine walked back over to where Izzy stood in the middle of the cafeteria. Izzy glanced away. Though the lunchroom was crowded with hungry students, the seats closest to them were empty and the noise level was high enough that a rhino could have charged through and no one would have noticed.

"Thanks for the invitation"—Izzy had meant to infuse her voice with sarcasm, but somehow that got lost under a hint of genuine gratitude—"but I can't come sit with you."

She couldn't sit with Piper's sworn enemy.

Germaine didn't pretend to misunderstand. She nodded, something almost like regret settling onto her face. She turned back to her throne but paused, then came back to Izzy.

"Have you really thought about what you're doing?" she asked.

The words were precisely the kind of thing Germaine always said, but instead of her normally scornful tone, she sounded sincere.

"This rivalry between Piper and me has gotten out of hand," Germaine continued. "I never meant for things to go so far."

"But they did." Izzy's hand convulsed on her insulated lunch bag. Cassidy would have punched Germaine out by now. But Izzy couldn't even muster the indignation she knew she should feel. "You *destroyed* her life."

"She's done plenty of things to me, too."

"Yeah, just stupid shit," Izzy commented. "Like the beet juice in the tanning lotion."

"Or the time she filled our Chapstick tubes with glue sticks," Germaine countered. "That could have killed us."

"No it couldn't," Izzy scoffed. "Glue sticks are nontoxic." That one had been her idea. And she'd confirmed it before buying the glue.

"Well, it tasted really gross. But then, of course you're going to side with her. You always do."

"Yes, I do. She's my *friend*."

"You were my friend once, too." And with that, Germaine swung away, leaving Izzy alone again, staring after her in confusion.

Germaine had sounded genuinely hurt. And had those been tears in her eyes? Tears? She'd always thought the Wicked Witch of the West would melt when she came in contact with water.

"Wait a second—" Izzy trotted after Germaine, catching her at the base of the stage. "What's that supposed to mean?"

Germaine brushed at something near her face. "When Piper and I had our big fight, you and Mei and Cassidy all sided with her."

"Well, yeah, we—"

"You never even heard my side of the story." Again there was that glisten of something in Germaine's eyes. Perhaps she wasn't a soul-less turkey buzzard, after all?

"I never knew you had a side," Izzy admitted.

She'd been away that whole summer. Piper and Germaine had gone off to art camp for the month of July in Dallas and had some big blow up. Izzy had asked her parents to send her to the same summer camp, but instead they'd shipped her off to a dude ranch in Oklahoma for eleven weeks—to get her out of the way so they could concentrate on Linc and Shane. That one-child-per-parent ratio worked better for her mom and dad.

Izzy had come home the Saturday before school started to find her clique of friends permanently broken. Once seventh grade began, Germaine had clawed her way to the top of the social heap by spreading rumors about Piper and, to some extent, the rest of them, too.

Germaine had been such a believable villain. Was it possible that she was innocent?

Izzy pressed her fingers to her temple, trying to sort through her thoughts. "You've said so many horrible things about Piper. That's *not* okay. Nothing she could have done—"

Germaine cut her off again. "Really? Nothing?" She stepped close, her voice dropping. "She took away my four best friends. Because of her, I went into the seventh grade with no one. I just did what I had to do to survive." Germaine gave her a slow and appraising look. "I would have thought you, at least, would understand that."

Germaine spun on her heel and stalked over to her table. She didn't even look to see if Izzy followed her.

Izzy slunk back to her spot at the geek table. She wasn't ready to betray her friends. Even if they had misjudged Germaine, Izzy sure as hell wasn't ready to trust her—there was no way she was innocent in all this. Still, the suggestion that maybe they'd treated Germaine unjustly didn't sit well with Izzy. She always thought of herself as being fair and open-minded. Was she wrong? Not only about herself, but about Germaine as well?

That night, when Izzy checked Facebook, there were no new messages from Cassidy, Mei, or Piper. There were, however, another hundred new fans of the page. Which was just freakin' fantastic. Instead of not being kissed just in front of her friends, thousands of strangers also knew she was a total loser. Perfect.

She closed her Internet browser and opened up the essay she'd been working on for a scholarship application that was due in a few months. When it came to getting out of Paris next year, she was going to hit every resource she could.

After reading over what she'd written so far, she snarled at the screen. Pathetic. She sounded like a whiny loser, even to herself. She could just see those big red rejection stamps already.

She deleted the previous title, "The Benefits of Being Alone," and typed in "On Being a Whiny, Pathetic Misfit." But even with the sarcasm, she couldn't think of any actual benefits to being a misfit. And as she stared at the essay, the conversation she'd had with Germaine kept echoing in her mind.

Why hadn't she taken Germaine up on her offer? Why had she chosen to exile herself? Out of some misguided sense of loyalty to her friends? Why?

It's not like they were being loyal to her. They were off in foreign countries. Seeing the sights. Kissing hot guys. Dropping pins all over that tiny map of the world. Lots and lots and lots of guys, if the kiss-o-meter was any indication. Steamy kisses for everyone except her.

It's not like any of them were sitting around at home, contemplating *her* situation.

Besides, what if there *was* some truth to Germaine's accusations?

Izzy opened the browser and popped back over to her personal Facebook page.

Between **Izzy** and **Mei**:

> **Izzy**
> What really happened between Piper and Germaine the summer they went off to camp? Are we sure that Piper didn't steal Germaine's guy?

A few seconds later Izzy's mom called her down to dinner. There was a bone-dry hunk of chicken for the rest of the family, and Izzy had to content herself with a side of mushy vegetables. When she returned to her computer, Mei had already answered.

> **Mei**
> Are you insane? Yes, we're sure. Piper would go ape shit if she found out you were even asking. What's up???
> **Izzy**
> Nothing. Just . . .

She paused, fingers resting on the keyboard. Then she deleted the "just."

> **Izzy**
> Nothing. How's China?
> **Mei**
> Great. I miss y'all. I miss even saying 'y'all.' Gotta go to class. Talk later?

By the time Izzy had typed in her response, Mei had logged out. She checked her own wall again. It was depressingly blank. Even though she had nothing to report, she went over to the IKC page. Though more and more girls were posting, it was no one she knew. And right now she needed her friends.

Glancing down, she saw that Piper was also online.

Between **Izzy** and **Piper**:

Izzy
Pipes, you there? I need advice. I need to figure out who I can kiss.
Piper
Take a page from "Twilight" and flirt with the guy who sits next to you in science. Make sure you smell good.
Izzy
That's the best you can do?
Piper
I'm really sorry, Iz. I've got to go. I have glassblowing class. I think I'm finally getting the hang of it!

Izzy stared in disbelief as Piper logged off. Izzy had been late for Shane's concert the other day because she'd been giving Piper advice. And now, when she needed her most, Piper was too busy to even think about it.

Izzy frowned at the screen, something sour and ugly churning in her belly. Enough was enough.

Whatever had happened between Piper and Germaine, what did that really have to do with her? Piper was in Paris, having the time of her life, kissing more guys than even populated the city of Paris, Texas. Izzy would actually have to start kissing farm animals if she wanted to keep up.

She clicked through the Fans of the Paris High School Facebook page until she found Germaine's wall. She typed a message furiously, then jabbed the Send key before she could change her mind.

Between **Izzy** and **Germaine**:

Izzy
Save me a seat at lunch tomorrow.

A second later, Germaine replied:

Germaine
Can't wait!

Izzy slapped down the laptop lid before she changed her mind.

But she wasn't going to feel guilty about what she'd done. Everyone knew high school was a jungle—you did what you could to survive. And she was tired of moping around. It was time to go on the offensive.

Dropping down onto her bed, she pulled out her spiral notebook from History, flipped to a blank page at the back and began to make a list.

Boys I Could Kiss:

She drew a line down the middle of the page. The left column she labeled "Local," the right column, "International." Even though this was the International Kissing Club, she started with the local column. That should be the easy one, right? But when she put her pen to the page, she only jotted down a single name: *Tanner Colt.*

She stared at the name, her pulse racing. Why had she done that? She couldn't kiss . . .

No. That was ridiculous.

She scratched it out. And then went over it in permanent marker. Then tore the page out, crumpled it into a ball, and started over with a fresh page.

If there was one guy in Paris—in all of Texas, for that matter—that she absolutely could not kiss, it was Tanner.

She focused her attention on the international column. Surely not every guy within driving distance and under the age of twenty was a native Texan. Weren't there some migrant workers on Tanner's farm? And what about that blond guy who worked for them during the week? He didn't talk much, but when he did, she thought she'd heard a faint accent. Besides, his name was Pieter Claussen. No red-blooded Texan would name their son that.

By the time she was done, she felt optimistic for the first time in weeks. She'd needed something fun to take her mind off her loneliness. Somehow, learning SAT vocabulary words just hadn't cut it.

But this . . . this was something she could get behind. And she wasn't a football coach's daughter for nothing. She knew how to make a game plan.

Like her dad always said, "You plan the play and you play the plan." She was guaranteed to score.

Better still, Invisabel Isabel would finally be seen.

IKC Fan Page

The Official Fan Page for the International Kissing Club

15,481

people like this

 IKC Page

Jane Heelloo? Anybody out there?

> **Mulan** I'm here.
>
> **Lisa Monroe** Me, too. But I think my points have bottomed out.
>
> **Jane** Mine don't have anywhere to bottom out from.
>
> **Kyle** I'm having trouble, too. So don't feel too bad.
>
> **Jayson** I can help you with that. Are you anywhere near New York?
>
> **Kyle** Sorry, Arizona. And I don't play for your team. But my best friend does. Do you want me to give him your number?
>
> **Jayson** Sorry, my lips don't reach that far.

Messages

Between **Mei** and **Izzy**:

Mei
Hey, Izzy, I'm about to do something that I thought was right, but now I'm not so sure.

Izzy
No! Don't sleep with sk8ter boy!

Mei
Calm down! Not that!

Izzy
Then what? Whatever it is, don't get arrested in Communist China.

Mei

It's not that kind of bad. I just . . . I don't want to hurt anybody, you know?

Izzy

Okay . . . Is not doing it going to hurt you? Sometimes you need to forget about what other people want and do what you need.

Mei

You're right.

Izzy

You know you're killing me here. Can you at least throw me a bone?

Mei

Sorry, Iz. If I tell you, I might lose my nerve. I'll explain it all when I get back. But how're you?

Izzy

Am making long list of kissing prospects.

Mei

Who's on it?

Izzy

Random guys from Paris High.

Mei

Have you considered John?

Izzy

Eew! No. There are not enough degrees of separation. I would never kiss a fellow IKCer's guy. Even if he's an ex. But don't worry, there are some guys who work with me that might be international.

Mei

Good luck. Post the points the second his lips leave yours. Now, I've got a date with a pizza.

Chapter 20
Mei

Mei thought she'd recognize the Social Welfare Institute where she'd lived before being adopted. She'd expected to feel some spark of remembrance. She'd lived there for nearly two years of her life. Surely it would seem familiar.

However, the campus didn't stir even the faintest memories. Situated on the outskirts of town, the Dalian SWI was a series of squat modern buildings surrounded by a gray wall of concrete blocks. From the outside, it was no-nonsense and austere. She would have walked right past it if Guiran hadn't been there with her, navigating via his phone.

In the yard, chickens roamed freely, pecking at the weed-strewn grass. She could see, back behind the main building, an extensive garden and a pigpen. She knew there was a school and a nursing home here at the SWI. Despite the obvious poverty, there were touches of cheer. A row of flowers planted by the door was standing up to the autumn chill better than she was. A cheerful mural was painted at the front entrance. And yet, Mei had to swallow back a lump of sorrow at the sight of the smiling bunny and happy grasshopper.

She and Guiran were welcomed warmly. The nannies offered her hugs and chattered brightly in a stream of Mandarin too fast for her to follow.

And yet nothing about the place seemed familiar. In all fairness, she'd been twenty-one months old when her parents brought her home, and Mei knew most people didn't retain memories from that age. But she'd always considered herself above average. After all, she did remember the stitches she'd gotten on her chin when she was two and a half.

After a few minutes they were ushered inside. They were shown into the director's office and left alone.

Guiran let her sit first and then plopped down in the extra chair, legs stretched out in front of him. Nerves ate away at Mei's control. She sat upright, hands knotted on her lap, legs pressed together, knees bobbing.

The summer she was fourteen, they'd gone to Hawaii for vacation. She still remembered the cliff divers, the way they stood poised on the very edge of the earth, before they jumped off into oblivion, their bodies tautly arching before they plummeted down to the water. Mei felt like that. Like at any second she was going to dive headfirst into free fall.

Guiran placed his hand on hers. He had to force her fingers apart before he could slip her hand into his. He gave it a squeeze. She looked over at him and tried to match his smile with one of her own.

Her lips were still wavering with the effort when the door swung open and the director of the institute entered. The woman was lean, her expression pinched and disapproving. Back in Paris, Mei had read a ton of adoption stories online—it seemed like every family who adopted a child from China put up a blog about it. Everyone had described these kind and generous women who ran the SWIs. Of all the maternal types in China, this was the woman who ran hers? What luck.

Both Mei and Guiran jumped to their feet. There was something in the woman's gaze that made Mei feel instantly inferior. Her spine stiffened as she automatically straightened her posture to deflect the director's disapproval. From the corner of her eye, she saw Guiran do the same.

Seeing that, she nearly smiled. Who would have thought he'd had it in him? Normally there was a rebellious slouch to his posture. She tended to forget just how tall he was.

After giving both of them the once-over, the director spoke in brisk Mandarin. Even though Mei had been in China all this time, she still only caught about every third word. And they were all negative. God, she hoped the ones she didn't know were the upbeat ones.

When Mei didn't answer immediately, the woman arched one inky eyebrow.

"Could you slow down, please?" Mei asked in Mandarin, her voice sounding unusually small. "I'm still learning—"

The woman barked out a retort before Mei had a chance to finish. She turned to Guiran and delivered another speech in tones as icy as the dorm floor first thing in the morning. He responded, his tone respectful but not deferential.

When he paused, the woman frowned, her lips crimped in a line. He turned to Mei. "She says she doesn't have the time to run errands for a selfish girl too disinterested in her own culture to even learn the language."

Mei quickly swallowed her shock, then mustered her determination before meeting the woman's eyes. She would not kowtow to a bully. She didn't do it at home, and she was tired of doing it here. "Guiran, please tell her that I have been working my hardest, but that a language as beautiful and complex as Mandarin cannot be learned overnight. Then tell her I came a long way for this and that I appreciate her cooperation. And that I'm not leaving until she's checked the records."

The director's gaze didn't waver from Mei as Guiran repeated her words, though it did narrow a bit. She was obviously assessing Mei's willingness to make a pain in the ass of herself. She must have realized that Mei wouldn't let it go.

After a moment, she spoke. This answer was longer and more

circuitous than the previous ones. Then with barely a backward glance, she left.

Guiran flashed Mei a reassuring smile and gestured toward the door. "She said her predecessors kept horrible records but that we can follow her and she'll see what she can do."

The director led them down a long hallway and up a flight of stairs. She paused at a door, unlocked it, and let them walk in. Obviously some kind of storage closet, since boxes lined the walls. Another flurry of Mandarin followed, accompanied by gesturing and pointing. Then the woman left Mei and Guiran standing alone in the tiny room.

Guiran flashed her one of his lopsided smiles. "Here are the records. The boxes near the bottom are probably the correct time period, if we want to search through them."

Mei sucked in a deep breath, the air stale with the musty scent of aging paper. Guiran, obviously not cursed with the same anxiety, dug right in, shifting boxes around to get to the ones the director had indicated. A moment later, he had five stacked by the door for them to start on.

As Guiran opened the first file, Mei felt her heart sink. A few of the pages were typed, the ink faded and blurred from an ancient printer. Others were handwritten. All were very difficult to read. She'd made herself a cheat sheet with a few key Mandarin phrases, her birthday, adoption date. Her name. That was about the extent of her ability to read Mandarin. And that was typed Mandarin. Not handwritten.

She stared at the boxes, dread clutching her throat. "This is impossible. It's going to take forever to read through these!"

Guiran just smiled. "You Americans are so impatient."

She glared, unfairly taking out her disappointment on him. "Let me guess, the journey of a thousand miles begins with a single step?"

He smiled, gesturing to one of the boxes. "Or the journey of a thousand files."

She groaned. "That's so cheesy."

He just laughed and flipped open a folder.

Starting on the next box, she was gladder than ever that she wasn't doing this alone. And at least she didn't feel like bursting into tears anymore.

Three hours later, her back ached, her eyesight was starting to blur, and it felt like half the dust in China had crawled up her nostrils. The stack of discarded files in front of Guiran was about five times taller than the one in front of her.

Frustrated, she dropped another folder—this one had been mis-filed and wasn't even from the correct decade—and arched her arms over her head, stretching the muscles around her spine.

She looked at Guiran to find him watching her and she paused, midstretch. He swallowed, then said, "Not it, huh?"

"Nope." Feeling oddly self-conscious, she tugged at the hem of her shirt, which had ridden up. "I think I need a break. My legs fell asleep about two hours ago, and I've lost all feeling below the waist. You want to go find a drink?"

He shook his head. "You bring me back something. I want to get through this box first."

Mei ventured out into the hall alone. The front stairs would take her past the director's office. Hoping to avoid Dao-Ming's adult clone, she went searching for a back staircase instead, which she hoped would lead her straight to the kitchen. She wandered aimlessly for a minute, down one hall, past the windows that overlooked the fenced-in back-yard. From the window, she could see a path leading to another build-ing. There were kids out playing in the yard and she didn't linger too long. Not all the babies were adopted; some lived their whole child-hoods here, until they aged out at fourteen. She couldn't think too long about them. So she hurried past and down the hall. Just as she'd spot-ted another staircase, she heard the sound of a crying baby coming from one of the rooms.

Inexplicably drawn, she followed the sound to an open doorway. The nursery.

A faint smell of bleach hung in the air, along with something sweet and milky. Baby formula, maybe. The scent was so familiar it grabbed her and pulled her into the enormous room.

There were metal cribs in groups of four. Each set was pressed together so the babies inside could see each other. There were thirty-six cribs in all, though right now, only about half of them were occupied.

A nanny had come by to scoop up the baby who had been crying. The tiny woman held the infant close, gently cooing to quiet her. The two cribs nearest the door were occupied. Mei couldn't guess at the babies' ages, but they were old enough to both be sitting up. They stuck their hands between the bars, giggling as they reached for each other and then snatched their hands back.

Mei watched for a moment, then she walked into the room as if in a trance, crossing to the farthest set of cribs. The wide window beyond them overlooked a tree, its branches hanging low and casting the light in a green glow. Mei stopped beside one of the cribs. It was empty, but there was a baby sleeping in the one beside it. She looked out the window, then crouched beside the empty crib and looked through.

She wrapped her fingers around one of the metal bars. It felt small and cold in her hand. Familiar, yet wrong, as if it should have been bigger. Or her hand smaller.

In an instant, she couldn't breathe. She felt her history pressing down on her. A memory she hadn't even known she had until she stepped into the room. It hung just out of reach, vague and ephemeral. Held together by the scent of bleach and the sensation of the metal bar beneath her hand.

This had been her crib. For nearly two years, she'd lain here, another baby in the crib beside her. Like the girls she'd seen when she first walked in, she had held on to the bars, stuck her hands through.

Tormented the other baby with playful fingers. She'd lived her entire life beside that other little girl. And then one day, her parents had come and taken her home. She'd gained parents, but she'd lost the girl forever. Maybe she had also been adopted, maybe not. Mei would never know. One more question she wouldn't find the answer to.

Suddenly, all of it—her memories, her doubts, her fears, her anxieties—came crashing down, dragging her under. She'd dived off the cliff and now she was going to drown under the weight of the unspeakable anguish that came from losing herself to this country she would never truly understand.

Fighting panic, she jumped to her feet and ran. Back down one hall and then the next, until she was panting, out of breath, and facing the storage room. Guiran looked up as she came skidding to a halt beside the open door.

"I can't do this," she gasped out. "I'm not ready. I can't stay. I can't. I'm sorry."

She didn't give him a chance to reply but dashed for the main stairs and the street beyond, plunging into the bustling midday foot traffic. For a second, her panic nearly brought her to her knees. There were too many people here. Too much noise. The chaos of it all swirled around her, making her head spin. And not in the good way that Guiran's kiss had, either. In an about-to-puke-on-the-roller-coaster kind of way.

She started pushing her way through the crowd, walking aimlessly. Almost at the end of the block, Guiran caught up with her and grabbed her arm. She swung around to face him, opened her mouth to explain, but there simply weren't any words.

He must have read the distress on her face—or, hello? Simply noticed that she'd run like a crazy person out onto the road—because he didn't even ask what was wrong, just cupped her elbow and steered her around the corner to a quiet spot under a willow tree.

Ignoring the stares of passersby, he gripped her by the upper arms.

She thought he might shake her. She kinda needed it. But instead he just looked at her with a steady gaze and asked, "You okay?"

She bit down on her lip, then nodded. And then shook her head. "I didn't expect . . ." She blew out a long breath. She was so not used to being the emotional one. Calm. Levelheaded. Logical. That was her. Bolting when things got too deep? That was Cassidy's job. Mei's cheeks were warm with embarrassment, her throat still tight from choking back tears.

"You didn't expect . . . what? That it would be hard?" Guiran asked. "Why wouldn't it be? It's hard for me."

She raised an eyebrow in question. 'Cause it didn't *seem* hard for him. He appeared to be blowing through boxes.

"Each of those files is a girl," he said. "Like my sister. Some of them were adopted. Some were placed with foster families. But I'll never know what happened to my sister. My parents will never know."

"But you could—"

He shook his head before she finished the thought. "No. Looking into it would be too hard on my mom. I'd never go against her wishes."

Mei felt a sharp pang of regret. Her own parents didn't know what she was up to and they'd be horrified if they did. A part of her wished she could mimic Guiran's blind acceptance, wished she didn't want to know. Before she could spend any more time feeling like the worst daughter ever, he said, "This is a huge step. Why wouldn't it be hard?"

"I just thought—" She twisted away from him, suddenly unable to bear his scrutiny. "I thought I'd find answers in China. All my life, there've been these two sides of me, the Chinese side and the American side. The part of me that's thankful I have a family, and the part of me that's smothered by their coddling. The rule follower and the rebel." And now, there was the guilt too, because what kind of monster felt smothered by the love all these other girls didn't have? "And I thought that if I came here, and I found out something about my birth parents and who they'd been, then maybe I'd figure out something about myself and who I'm supposed to be. But that's not how it is at all."

She risked a glance back at Guiran. He was studying her, his lips once again twisted into that lopsided smile of his.

Crossing her arms over her chest, she bumped up her chin. "What?"

"You thought you were going to get all that from some dusty old file?"

"I—" But she broke off, because when he said it that way, it did seem kind of silly.

"You're seventeen, Mei. Maybe you're not supposed to know who you are yet."

She opened her mouth to respond, but could think of nothing else to say. The words were so similar to something her father had said. Yet, coming from Guiran, they felt completely different. She, who was never speechless and who never felt an emotion she couldn't describe with a polysyllabic SAT word, could think of nothing to say. So she just nodded.

"Come on," Guiran said. "Let's head back to the SWI."

After a few seconds of walking, she said, "I think for today I'm ready to give up. Just put all the files back in their boxes and walk away." Her voice sounded small. "Just for today."

As she'd sat in that little room, looking at the files of all those parents who'd given up their children, she'd realized that her birth parents could have been any of them. Knowing their names wouldn't answer the questions that had been plaguing her.

Or maybe she just wasn't ready to know yet.

Guiran nodded, brushing his lips over her forehead so softly that for a second she couldn't be sure that she hadn't imagined it. But the warmth from his touch, the small sense of peace that spread through her, proved that she hadn't. As they walked through the gates of the SWI, he took her hand.

Staring up at the wide red doors leading into the building, she thought of all the girls and boys who'd come and gone from this place and of all the families they'd found. She thought of the girl in the crib, the friend she'd lost forever. And she was glad she had Guiran here beside her, because she knew she couldn't have done this alone.

IKC Fan Page

The Official Fan Page for the International Kissing Club

18,762
people like this

 IKC Page

Mulan   Y'all don't know how lucky we have it.

> **Ariel** Ahh . . . <hugs> Miss you!
>
> **Rapunzel** I'm never coming home.
>
> **Jane** Are you effin' kidding me? My dick of a brother just showed the football team home movies of me puking. Not feeling so lucky.
>
> **Ariel** OMG. I just clicked over and he's got them on his Facebook page! The bastard! Scum-sucking . . .

📨 **Messages**

Between **Cassidy** and **Linc**:

> **Cassidy**
> You are so dead.
>
> **Linc**
> As long as you do me yourself.
>
> **Cassidy**
> Oh, I will. It'll be long and slow, but you won't enjoy it.
>
> **Linc**
> Bring it, dyke.
>
> **Cassidy**
> You're an asshole.

Between **Piper** and **Izzy**:

Piper
Hey, Iz. Are you okay? Your brother is such a jerk. I'd send more chocolate, but I don't think there's enough in all of France to make this better.

Izzy
I don't want to talk about it. What happened with Mr. Fabulous?

Piper
I didn't tell him.

Izzy
I think that's smart.

Piper
Then why do I feel so icky?

Chapter 21
Piper

"That looks lovely, Mademoiselle Douglas. The colors you managed to achieve are quite impressive."

Piper beamed under the praise of Monsieur Blanchard, the instructor for the glassblowing class that had been kicking her butt since she'd signed up for it her second week in Paris. It was a far cry from the watercolor paintings she'd been doing the past few years, but she'd wanted to try something new while in France. How could she have guessed that she would fall in love with making glass the very first time she'd tried it?

It was hard work—exhausting even, because she couldn't just walk away in the middle of one of its stages like she could with painting— but that didn't matter. She adored the arduous process, the brilliant colors, the amazing pieces it was possible to create.

"*Merci*," she answered softly, using every ounce of restraint she had not to jump up and down at the first compliment he had ever given her. After trying and failing to win his approval three times a week for the past six weeks, she had just about given up hope at ever creating something he might deem worthy. But this time he actually liked what she'd done.

Nothing could have thrilled her more, not even if she could have introduced Sebastian to Germaine the Insane and watched her archnemesis's expression upon realizing that Piper had landed a guy Germaine could only dream about.

The only thing marring her happiness was the fact that she'd kissed that other guy in the club. She couldn't remember his name or even much of what he looked like, and she sure as hell couldn't remember why she'd been stupid enough to let him kiss her. But she had, and she was afraid she'd ruined everything.

Oh, Izzy had said it was okay not to tell Sebastian, as long as it was just a one-time thing. And it was—God, was it! She never wanted to feel like this again—guilty and sick to her stomach and terrified that Sebastian would somehow find out what she'd done.

She hadn't set out to kiss that other guy, hadn't even thought about it. But when he'd grabbed onto her in the club and pulled her close, it had seemed like a natural thing to let him put his lips over hers. It hadn't lasted very long—in the back of her head, her conscience had been screaming at her to stop, to go back, to run away. So she had, after a few seconds, but by then the damage had been done. She was the worst girlfriend ever.

And the weird thing was, even as she'd been kissing that guy, *experiencing everything Paris had to offer,* she had hated it. It hadn't been like those fun, flirty kisses when she first got to Paris—maybe because she knew now what she hadn't known then. That being kissed by a guy who really mattered was worth more than a million kisses from guys who didn't.

Kissing that strange guy in the club had felt wrong. Not just because it *was* wrong, obviously, but because he wasn't Sebastian. He hadn't smelled like Sebastian. Hadn't felt like him or tasted like him or made her feel anything like she did with Sebastian. Piper's stomach churned as she tried to figure out what to do. Somehow in the seven weeks they'd been dating, she'd suddenly gone from wanting to gain as much experience as she could to wanting to experience things only with Sebastian. Which would have been frightening if she hadn't felt as though he was the other half of her soul. If she hadn't believed that her heart was completely safe in his hands.

And she hadn't known just how special that feeling was until the other guy had pressed his mouth to hers and all she'd wanted to do was throw up when she'd realized what was happening. Even though it had been a few-seconds thing and she hadn't let it happen again. Hadn't even been *tempted* to let it happen again, not when she felt so icky about its having happened at all.

With a sigh, Piper tried to shove all her concerns back down where she'd hidden them for the past two weeks. She was worrying for nothing, she told herself as she crossed the room to where her instructor kept tissue paper for them to wrap up their glass projects. She had only a little while left in France—surely she could keep Sebastian from finding out about the other guy that long. And once she went home . . . Once she went home, it would probably be months before she could see him again.

The idea was a lot more depressing than she'd thought it would be when she'd been talking to her friends at the mall all those weeks ago. Had she really thought that she could come to Paris, do wonderful, exciting things with amazing, fascinating people and then just go home? No harm, no foul? It was ridiculous. Paris was wonderful, so wonderful that the idea of going back to Texas was almost unthinkable. Now that she knew what it was like to live the kind of life she'd always wanted—now that she'd made friends here, found a guy she really cared about, found the kind of art she really wanted to do—was she just supposed to give all that up when she got on the airplane back to Texas?

Laying the suncatcher she had just finished on the thin white paper, she stared at its vivid blend of colors—every shade of blue and silver in the spectrum, with subtle hints of purple and green thrown in for effect. She'd made it for Sebastian, for the huge picture window in his room that got such brilliant afternoon sunlight. When he was home from college sometimes, she hoped that he would look at it and think of her and everything they shared. A long-distance relationship—especially one over the Atlantic Ocean—would be hard. But it wouldn't be impossible. Not if they didn't let it be.

Her instructor dismissed the class. Piper finished wrapping the small disk made of intricately twisted glass and then slid it into her purse. She was meeting Sebastian for dinner at a small café a few blocks away. She couldn't wait to see his face when she gave him the present. He liked her watercolors, but the first time he'd seen the one she'd done of the Eiffel Tower, he'd told her that the medium wasn't her passion. She'd tried to argue with him, but by then she'd been a few weeks into her glassblowing class and she'd known that he was right.

She made the trip to the café in only a few minutes, reveling in the sights and sounds of Paris in the evening. Night had descended about an hour before and the streetlights gleamed yellow against the black sky. Stores were lit up in reds and oranges and greens, and small bulbs twinkled in many of the trees she passed.

The roads and sidewalks were still slick from the late afternoon rain she'd heard hitting the windows of the glass studio, and ornate lightscapes stretched from one side of the street to the other, rows and rows of them in dazzling golds and whites.

Piper stood on the threshold of the café for a minute, looking back toward the street. Soaking it in. Creating a mental photograph. Trying hard to ground herself in the moment, in the here and now, so that she would never forget what it felt like to stand on a busy street corner in Paris, France. So that she would never forget this perfect sense of rightness, of belonging. So that she would never forget the person she'd been here.

She'd never felt this at home in Paris, Texas, and hated that once she left here she might have to spend the rest of her life without it.

When she was ready, when she knew that she'd be able to call up this exact moment wherever she was, Piper turned and headed into the café. She spotted Sebastian right away. He was seated all the way at the back of the tiny restaurant, a glass of red wine on the small square table in front of him. She bubbled inside with happiness, knowing she was about to be sitting at an intimate little table, holding hands and flirting with her handsome boyfriend. For the first time in her life, she'd felt like it had finally happened. Like she was all grown up.

Swooping down, she gave him a huge hug before brushing her lips across his. She lingered for a second, and he deepened the kiss, just as she'd hoped he would. God, how was she going to go the next few months without this—without him? She'd grown used to seeing him every day, talking to him, kissing him, just being with him.

Ignoring the little sliver of pain that came with the thought of not being with Sebastian all the time, she asked, "How was your art history test?" She settled herself in the chair across from him. "Did you ace it?"

"I'm pretty sure." He reached for his glass of wine with a grin, took a sip.

"That's terrific!" She clapped her hands. "Not that it's a huge surprise. I don't think I've ever met anyone who knows as much about art as you do."

"I don't know. You've got a pretty decent knowledge yourself."

"What is this?" Piper put her hand to her chest in mock surprise. "A compliment from the guy who once offered to buy me the French masters refrigerator magnets? I'm honored."

"Actually, I did get you something." He picked up a bag from the floor next to his chair and handed it to her.

Guilt slammed into her all over again. She was lying to Sebastian and he was buying her presents? Could she get any lower? "You didn't have to do that," she finally stammered, tucking her hands in her lap, so she wouldn't be tempted to reach for the gift. He always gave her the most amazing things.

"Take it, Piper. You know you want to." He reached for her hand, rubbed a thumb over it. "Besides, I made it for you and I want to know what you think."

Excitement thrummed through her. Sebastian had made something, had taken the time out of his overloaded schedule to create something just for her. Guilt or no guilt, she had to know what it was.

Expecting a sculpture, she opened the bag and pulled out a small journal. Shooting him a questioning look, she flipped it open and realized it was a photo album, not a notebook. On the inside cover, in Sebastian's artist's scrawl were the words, *For the girl who showed me a Paris I've never seen before . . .*

Her hands shook a little as she turned the page and saw a beautiful black-and-white nighttime photo of the Louvre courtyard, the beautiful glass pyramid taking up most of the background. The angle on it would have put the photographer right where they'd been standing the first time Sebastian had kissed her.

The next photo was of the park where they liked to walk, followed by one of the catacombs and another of the steps at the Sorbonne, where they'd picnicked a couple of weeks before. On and on she flipped, through pictures of the Champs-Elysées, the Place de la Bastille, the Cathedral of Notre Dame. Beautiful, stark photos of all the places they'd visited and loved.

She had tears in her eyes even before she flipped to the last photo. It was the only picture in the album that was in color, and it was of her. *Is this how Sebastian sees me?* she wondered as she stared, in awe, at the picture. Was this what he meant when he told her she was beautiful? Looking at this picture of herself, wearing a long, flowy dress in shades of purple with the scarf Sebastian had bought her wrapped around her shoulders, Piper could finally see what he was talking about.

This girl with the big sunglasses and blue-streaked hair *was* beautiful. Confident. Happy. Strong. And in love, so in love as she grinned at the guy behind the camera. As she grinned at Sebastian. She'd always worn her feelings on her sleeve, but it still felt strange to sit here and see, in a photo, just how crazy she was about him.

"You haven't said anything," Sebastian said, sipping his wine. "Do you like it?"

"I love it. It's perfect. *You're* perfect." As Piper said the words, the guilt welled up in her again, and this time it was so strong, so overwhelming, that she knew she wouldn't be able to swallow it any longer. She rushed on before Sebastian could answer her, before he could say anything at all.

"I have something for you, too." She reached into her bag and pulled out the suncatcher she had made him. "But before I give it to you, I have to tell you something."

She took a deep breath for courage and then blurted out the confession that had been haunting her for what felt like forever. "I kissed another guy. Two weeks ago, when I went out clubbing with some of the girls from school. I don't know what happened. I was having a good time and then suddenly this guy I'd been dancing with just grabs me and kisses me. I shoved him away."

The words were pouring out of her mouth, tumbling over each other in her haste to confess her duplicity. "But not right away. I let him kiss me for a few seconds first. I'm sorry. I swear, I'm so sorry. It didn't mean anything and I've felt awful ever since. I promise it won't ever, ever, *ever* happen again."

"Whoa, Piper, breathe," Sebastian said, reaching across the table and taking her hand in his.

"I can't. I'm sorry, Sebastian. I'm so sorry."

"It's fine. Really. No big deal," he said with an easy smile.

Relief coursed through her at his calm acceptance, his . . . "Hey, why are you being so understanding?" If Sebastian had kissed another girl, she'd want to claw his eyes out.

One eyebrow went up in the expression she loved so much. "You don't want me to be understanding?"

"Of course I do. I just thought, I don't know. That you'd be mad before you got to the understanding part."

"Why? I thought that's what you came to Paris to do. The International Kissing Club and all that."

At his words, her stomach did a little flip, and not the good kind.

"But that . . . that was before. I mean—I wasn't trying to rack up points or anything, like when I first got here. I wouldn't do that to you." She ran a hand down his face. "I'm sorry if I hurt you."

"I know that. And don't worry, Piper, you didn't."

"Are you sure?" she asked doubtfully.

"Absolutely," he answered with a reassuring grin. "It's not like we're really serious, right? I mean, we've had a lot of fun together these last weeks, but we both knew it wasn't going to last. You go back to America in a few days and—"

Piper knew he said more. She could see his lips moving, hear the low rumble of his voice. But she couldn't make out any of the words over the roaring in her ears. *Not going to last? Wasn't serious?* What did he mean? How could he say that, how could he even *think* it, when she would do anything for him?

"I love you, Sebastian." The words came out fast as she cut him off midsentence. "I love you." She paused, waited for him to say it back, to tell her everything he'd been talking about didn't mean anything because he loved her, too.

Only he didn't say the words back, didn't say anything at all as he stared at her, eyes wide and mouth slightly agape. And that's when she knew. She'd made a terrible mistake.

He didn't love her.

He didn't want to be with her.

He didn't want anything but to have *fun*.

She grabbed his wineglass and drained it in one gulp.

"Oh, Piper." Sebastian shoved a hand through his hair, looking more aggrieved than she had ever seen him—and that was saying something, considering their first meeting. "I didn't . . . I thought . . . Of course, I love spending time with you. You're great. Amazing, really, and—"

"Don't." She shook her head, tried to think of something to say that wouldn't show him how incredibly humiliated she was. But the look of compassion in his eyes when he stared at her told her that ship had already sailed. There was nothing left to do but get the hell out of there as fast as she could.

The walls of the cute, little café didn't seem so cute anymore, especially since they were closing in on her from every side.

She sprang to her feet. "I have to go."

"No, don't." Sebastian stood too, reached for her. "Piper, please. I didn't know . . . I didn't mean to hurt you."

She jerked away from him. "It's fine. No big deal. I'm fine." She was repeating herself, echoing his words from moments before, but she couldn't seem to stop. "I need to go."

He reached for his wallet, threw some money on the table. "Yeah, of course. Let me take you home—"

"No. Stay. Really. You haven't eaten. I forgot I have homework—"

Her voice broke and she knew she had to get out now, before she humiliated herself even worse by crying in front of him. Leaning forward, she brushed her lips gently over his. "Thanks, Sebastian, for everything. I'll never forget you."

"Damn it, Piper." His hands rose and fell, helplessly. It was a strange look on him, when he'd always been a guy who knew exactly what he was doing. "Don't do this. I'm sorry—"

"It's fine. Really. I'll . . . I'll see you around." She reached for her purse, and as she picked it up, it brushed against the suncatcher she'd made for him. The tissue-wrapped packet plunged to the restaurant floor and the suncatcher shattered, the sound echoing within her as her stupid, unreliable heart shattered right along with it.

IKC Fan Page

The Official Fan Page for the International Kissing Club

19,333

people like this

 IKC Page

Rapunzel   Thanks, Ariel, for making me buy the sundress. You'd be so proud of me. I even got a pedicure!

> **Jane** So how're those Cheekies treating you? Or rather, how are they treating Lucas?
>
> **Mulan** Down, girl.
>
> **Jane** What, Ariel? No words of encouragement for Rapunzel as she rappels out of the tower?
>
> **Rapunzel** Just so long as I don't repel him...
>
> **Jayson** You go, girl!
>
> **Kyle** If you repel him, stop by Arizona on your way back.
>
> **Jane** Why can't I ever say "You go, girl" and have it sound right?
>
> **LaTonya Washington** It's a white-girl thing.
>
> **Sammie** Good luck, Rapunzel!
>
> **Ariel** Our little girl all grown up and wearing sexy lingerie. Sniff-sniff. Don't do anything I wouldn't do.
>
> **Jane** Well, that gives her lots of room, doesn't it?
>
> **Ariel** That's my point.
>
> **LaTonya Washington** You go, girl.
>
> **Kyle** What color are the Cheekies? Tell me they're red.

📧 Messages

Between **Jane** and **Kyle**:

Jane
Consider yourself warned, Kyle. Another comment like that and you're blocked.

Chapter 22
Cassidy

The bell rang at Mrs. Gatwick's front door. "There's your young man, Cassidy," she winked. "Go on, then. Scoot. I'll clean up. You just enjoy your last evening."

Cassidy pushed away from the table and gave Mrs. Gatwick a hug. "Dinner was delicious, and you've been awesome, Mrs. G." Her voice cracked a fraction. She'd been on the verge of tears all day, but she wouldn't cry. Cassidy Barlow did not cry.

"M'dear, it has been my pleasure."

Cassidy grabbed her denim jacket and sent up a silent thanks to Piper for forcing her to buy this long sundress and the things to go underneath it. She'd even gone out and bought a pair of delicate, strappy sandals and taken extra care straightening her unruly mane so she could leave it down. She felt a little foolish for getting so dressed up—she didn't want to seem like she was trying too hard—but she did want to look nice, since she was never going to see Lucas again after tonight.

His eyes almost bugged out of his head when she opened the door.

"Wow, you look *so* pretty, Cassidy."

"Thank you," she said bashfully. "Since I didn't know what we were doing tonight, I wasn't sure what to wear. I hope this is okay."

"You're perfect." He kissed her on the nose. Somehow the way Lucas said it, she believed it.

They drove through the streets until they came to the marina where his parents' boat was slipped.

"Why are we here?" she asked as he helped her out of the car.

"Because my apartment is a hole, my flatmates are a bunch of surf bums, and I wanted to be completely alone with you tonight." He stepped onto the boat's deck, then lifted her down.

"I like your apartment—it has a great view of the beach," she said.

"But not like this." The Milky Way had nothing on the Sydney skyline twinkling along the edges of the dark harbor, the bridge and Opera House dramatically aglow against the night sky.

From behind her, his hands stole around her waist. She leaned her head against his shoulder. "At midnight, there'll be fireworks near the bridge," he said. "They do it for the tourists on weekends, but if you're cold, we could go below."

She shook her head. "No, let's stay here." Turning into him, she slid her arms around his neck. "So, what shall we do till midnight?" she asked, running her fingertips through the soft hair at his nape.

"I have an idea or two," he answered, brushing his lips across her temple.

"Mmmm, because I'd hate to be bored on my last night in Australia."

Lucas chuckled, all male cockiness. "If you start getting bored, then we're not doing something right." She did shiver then. "You *are* cold—I'm going down to bring up some blankets."

He made them a pallet of pillows and blankets, and then they both kicked off their shoes so they could cuddle under the stars. "I got a phone call today from Quiksilver," Lucas said after a few minutes.

"Seriously?" she asked, excited. "What did they say?"

Lucas's smile was blinding. "They're going to sponsor me on the circuit."

"That's amazing!" She rolled over and kissed him. "Have you told your dad yet?"

"No, I wanted to tell you first."

She couldn't believe it, but her eyes felt wet and everything looked a bit shiny. "Thank you," she said, and kissed him again.

"Yeah, everything's coming together. Except you're going away," he said. "Are you excited about seeing your friends again, comparing all those kissing stories?" He was on his side now, his head on his palm as he leaned over her and trailed his fingertip along her collarbone. She hadn't known how sensitive her skin could be till this moment; it was as if all those millions of lights in the harbor were glowing within her just below the surface.

"I can't wait to see my friends. I've missed them so much." She laughed. "I've even missed Piper's melodramatics and Izzy's constant lectures on putting my soda cans in the recycling bin instead of the trash and Mei insisting that Jimi Hendrix is better than Stevie Ray Vaughn. They're my family—I don't think I realized how true that was before this trip.

"But I'm going to miss Sydney, too—the noise, the buildings, the beaches, the water—it's all so different from Paris. So much to see and do and experience. It'll be hard to go back to Saturday nights at Dairy Queen and beer busts in cow pastures."

"What's a Dairy Queen?"

"Doesn't matter," she said. "That's the last thing I want to discuss tonight." Lucas bent and kissed the soft hollow at the base of her throat. Cassidy's eyes fluttered closed. She bit her lower lip against the soft moan that gathered at the back of her throat.

"What about me, Cass? Are you going to miss me?"

More than she wanted to think about. Eight weeks ago, she'd been counting the days until she could leave, but now she wished the hours would slow to give her more time. It was true she couldn't wait to see her friends and her mom after so long apart, but the fact that she might never see Lucas again was like a punch in the gut. It was on the tip of her tongue to tell him so, but the words got stuck between her brain and her vocal chords. Cassidy decided showing him would be easier.

Threading her fingers into the waves of his hair, she pulled him down, taking his mouth and putting everything she couldn't say in words into her kiss. Her tongue slid against his, tasting him, while she breathed in his scent—sun, sea, salt, and sand—and tried to burn it to memory. Lucas rolled on top of her and she twined her legs around his, rubbing her bare feet up his calves, wanting her body as close to his as she could make it.

The kiss was tender. Their chests rose and fell together as their breaths began and ended with each other's. Lucas's hand slowly inched up her dress to brush the bare skin of her thigh at the same time her fingers slipped beneath his shirt to skim across the taut muscles of his stomach.

Then his mouth left hers, pressing feather-soft kisses down her jaw and throat to the neckline of the dress, kissing her through its light cotton material. *Oh my God.* The intimate touch burned against her skin. It was almost too much.

She knew she should stop this, that they were going way beyond anywhere they'd been before, but she didn't. She couldn't. She wanted everything Lucas was doing, everything he was making her feel. And she wanted him to feel it, too.

Reaching for the buttons of his shirt, her fingers sure and confident, she began undoing them one by one. He slid her dress straps down her arms, trailing kisses across her shoulder to just below one earlobe. His warm breath tickled her ear.

"I love you, Cassidy," he whispered.

Desire froze in her veins. Of all the beautiful words he could have said tonight, those were the last ones she'd wanted to hear. Her eyes flew open to find Lucas's, shining and heavy lidded, gazing down at her as if she were the most perfect thing he had ever seen. Everything—the night, the moment, Lucas—suddenly seemed *too* perfect.

Too good to be true . . .

NO! NO! NO! NO! NO!

What was she doing? She couldn't do this. She *knew* better. Hadn't she learned anything from what had happened between her mother and father?

Her whole body tensed as her fight-or-flight instinct kicked in. She pushed Lucas away from her, the movement catching him off guard and knocking him back, hard.

"Cassidy, what's wrong?" Bewilderment colored his voice.

She stood, straightening her dress, and searched for her shoes. "I have to go. Now."

He grabbed her hand. "Cassidy, wait. Tell me what's wrong. Did I do something?"

She jerked away from him, turning over blankets and flinging pillows. Damn it, where were those frickin' sandals?

Lucas stood and held her by the arms, bending down until she was forced to look at him. The confusion and hurt she saw in his face made her turn away. "Cass, whatever I did, I'm sorry. If I got carried away . . . I promise I would never do anything you don't want. I love you."

"Stop saying that," she cried. "Guys only say that when they want to get laid. You don't mean it."

Lucas went very still, but he didn't let go of her. The boat rocked beneath them, the mast and rigging jangled, echoing in the silence after her outburst.

"Listen to me, Cass," Lucas said, his voice soft and calm, as if he were speaking to a frightened child. "I love you."

She didn't move.

"I love you," he repeated.

She couldn't breathe.

"I love you."

His face wavered before her as tears spilled over the rims of her eyes. Screw the sandals.

She jerked out of his grasp, ran down the deck, and hopped over the rail before he could stop her. Lucas yelled for her to stop, but she kept running.

There was a ferry dock just down the street, its lights a beacon in the dark. She heard him running behind her but even barefoot she was faster. She ran down to the landing just as the ferry whistle blew.

"Cassidy!" The sound made her pause for a split second at the threshold, but she didn't look back as she quickly jumped onto the boat. The worker closed the ramp behind her.

The boat pushed away from the dock and sailed into the harbor. The flash of the fireworks in the distance reflected on the inky water, their percussive booms covering up the sound of the racking sobs that were tearing from her chest.

· · · · · ·✈

Heavy gray clouds shrouded the tops of the central business district in the distance and rain dribbled down the windshield of the taxicab.

"Hope you're not a bad flyer—it may be pretty bumpy on the takeoff," said the driver. Cassidy stared out the window as he navigated the winding maze of roads that led through the sprawling airport to the international terminal. Her flight didn't leave for another five hours, but she couldn't stand sitting around at Mrs. Gatwick's making small talk anymore. She just wanted to go home.

Bzzz. She didn't have to look at the phone in her hand to know who it was—Lucas had called at least a dozen times since last night and sent twice as many texts. Cassidy hadn't answered any of them; there was no point. What could she say to him? *Sorry I'm such a freak, but the thought of a gorgeous, perfect sweetheart of a guy being in love with me is more than I'm capable of handling.*

She turned off her phone and dropped it to the bottom of her backpack. A few hours from now she'd be over the Pacific on her way home to Texas, to her real life. And maybe, if she were lucky just this once, the numbness that had settled over her body would last until she could crawl into her own bed, pull the covers over her head, and stay there forever.

Cassidy checked her luggage, waited through the endless line at security, and mentally slipped out of Vacation Cassidy mode when she walked through the scanner. On the other side of security, she turned and glanced back the way she'd come, half expecting to see the discarded shell of the girl she'd been here in Australia. But all she saw was the flood of sunburned tourists and impatient business travelers, oblivious to the emotions churning inside of her. So much had changed in the ten weeks she'd been in Australia, it was hard to believe that there was no physical evidence. But then, why should there be? All the changes were inside of her.

Shrugging it off, she wandered up and down the airport corridor, ducking into each store in turn. Not to shop, of course, but to stay one step ahead of her emotions. It almost worked. At last, the PA system announced her flight would begin boarding, so she made her way to the gate and through another round of security for flights heading to the United States.

That's when she saw him, propped against the window, her forgotten sandals dangling from his hand. In a wrinkled tee and pants, his hair damp from the rain and unkempt, as if he'd dragged his fingers through it a thousand times, he had the same dark circles beneath his eyes that she knew she did. His beautiful face sagged with worry and so much dejection that if she'd had any tears left in her at all, she would have broken down right there in front of the hundreds of other passengers waiting in the gate area.

"You forgot these," he said as he approached, handing her the sandals.

"How did you get here?" were the words that tumbled from her mouth.

"I drove."

"No, I mean how did you get back *here*, through security to the gate?"

"I bought a ticket." Her mouth must have popped open in shock because he shrugged, as if it were nothing that he had just spent a couple thousand dollars on a plane ticket. "I didn't have a choice—you wouldn't answer my calls and I had to see you before you left."

This was like some clichéd scene in a movie—the hero racing to the airport to stop the heroine from leaving, turning the female audience into romantic mush. But Cassidy would be getting on this plane and Lucas would not, ticket or no. She was made of sterner stuff than the average American moviegoer.

"You shouldn't have come, Lucas," she said. They weren't the words she wanted to say. So many thoughts, so many phrases, bubbled up inside her that she couldn't keep track of them all. Any more than she could keep track of the regrets. God, how many of those did she have?

Make a clean break, Cass. Smooth and easy. "I'm sorry about running away last night. It wasn't how I wanted things to end with us. But it—us—we're done. I had an incredible time with you, but I'm leaving now. There's nothing else to say."

Lucas made another tentative step toward her, not too close, as if he thought she might run again if he did, but close enough for her to smell that appealing scent that was all his own. She had to put her hands in her jeans pockets to keep from reaching out to him, to let him hold her one last time and make this horrible hollow feeling go away.

"Cassidy, what I said last night is the truth: I do love you. And I think that you love me, and that's why you're scared."

"I'm not scared," she countered, but it sounded like a lie.

"So then why run away from me last night, barefoot? You know I drove all the way to Mrs. Gatwick's house after you jumped on that damn ferry to make sure you got home okay?"

God, why did he have to be so sweet? It flustered her, making her tone more abrupt than she meant it to be. "It doesn't matter. This isn't going anywhere, Lucas. I'm a junior in high school and you live halfway around the world."

"I don't have to—I can live anywhere."

Now she was getting angry. This wasn't smooth, this wasn't easy.

Why couldn't he just let it go? "If that's true, then you definitely don't want to live in Paris, Texas."

"I'm not ready for this to be over, and if you're honest with yourself, Cassidy, you're not, either."

"This isn't real. You don't know the real me. This was just a—a fling. I was Vacation Cassidy and now it's over. That's it, end of story."

She folded her arms across her chest, daring him to argue. Instead, Lucas closed the space between them and kissed her, holding her by the waist so she couldn't bolt. Not that she could have—her legs had rubberized. Even as unprepared for this as she'd been, it took her a moment to realize this was no tender kiss good-bye. No, it was hot and hungry, and before she knew it, she was kissing him back with everything she had. She'd never felt like this before, not even on the boat last night. She'd never felt this unbelievable connection with another human being. Like Lucas had managed to crawl inside of her. Like he would always be there. And worse, like she would always want him to be.

Her fingers twisted in the fabric of his shirt, holding him to her. Holding on to him as desperately as she'd been pushing him away the night before.

Then he stopped, before she was ready, and she stumbled forward into him.

Lucas caught her before she could fall. His gaze searched her face and then, slowly, he gave her a knowing grin. "That's what I thought." He began to walk away, throwing his expensive boarding pass on the ground.

"I'll see you, American girl," he called out. "Don't be catching a ride with any cowboys once you land in Texas. Oh, and I better not see any more points for you on that damn kissing club page, or there'll be hell to pay when I see you. Hell. To. Pay." And then he was gone.

Dazed by the whole scene, Cassidy boarded the plane. Her seat was the middle of three, smack between a good-looking Dutch student from South Africa and a really cute Canadian semipro hockey player—it was a veritable buffet for a founding member of the International Kissing Club.

Cassidy couldn't have cared less. She'd had all the kissing she could take for a while. Her three points would have to stand.

The cab driver had been right . . . it was going to be a rocky flight.

IKC Fan Page

The Official Fan Page for the International Kissing Club

31,765

people like this

 IKC Page

Jane Rapunzel, wasn't your big date with the Golden God last night? What happened? Spill the deets!

> **Jayson** Yes! Need visual confirmation of his awesomeness. Can you describe him in more detail?
>
> **Rapunzel** The landing was rough. Don't try this at home, girls.
>
> **Maki** Who is this Golden God? Where can I get one?
>
> **Jane** Deets! Please! For the love of God, deets!

Ariel Never thought I'd say this, but I can't wait to just be home.

Jane I've decided to reduce my carbon footprint by kissing locally. I'm making my list of local possibilities with international flavor.

> **Serena MacAfee** I didn't know you were that close to the Texas border.
>
> **Jane** I'm not. But I have a few options at the place I work.

Karrie Meeker Please tell me the page will still be up after you guys all come home.

> **LaTonya Washington** Yes!
>
> **Jayson** You can't desert me now.
>
> **Kyle** Can't take the page down. How will I ever see those Cheekies in person if you do?
>
> **Jane** That's it, Kyle. You're out.
>
> **Jane** But yes, we still plan to keep the page going. It has a life of its own now.

Chapter 23
Izzy

Everyone was returning home—soon!—and the closest thing Izzy had come to kissing was her toothbrush.

In her defense, it had been a particularly bad week guywise. Thursday night her brother had invited the entire team over for hot dogs—the one thing her mother rarely burned. After the meal, he'd loaded up a montage of him playing football that he'd been putting together for college recruiters. When none of the other guys were interested in watching—because, hello? who would be?—he'd pulled up the old home movies Izzy had just converted to digital and played all the low points of her life for comic effect. Like her very first attempt at driving, when she'd jumped a curb, knocked over the mailbox, and nearly killed their elderly neighbor. And the time he'd videoed her when she'd had the Norovirus and had spent four days on the sofa puking her guts out. And the shots of the family vacation in Mexico, where she was sunburned and sweaty, practicing her Spanish with the locals. It was like *America's Funniest Home Videos,* for the psychotically inclined.

And now, there were twenty guys who couldn't be bribed into kissing her. Not that she'd wanted to kiss any of the knuckle-dragging apes who thought someone puking was funny.

Turning her attention to more academic types, she followed Piper's advice and tried flirting with her lab partner in chemistry. Poor Cruz had nearly swallowed his retainer, then told Mr. Szachowicz he was feeling sick and spent the rest of the period in the nurse's office.

Was it wrong to hope he was gay? Because if she couldn't get a short, geeky guy to flirt with her, then maybe she really was repulsive.

By the time Saturday rolled around, she was back out at the Sun Valley Orchard and relieved just to be away from school. Most of the guys on the football team had taken to speaking to her in broken Spanish. When Germaine had first heard about it, she'd laughed, then linked her arm with Izzy's. "I think it's cute. They're probably doing it because they like you. In fact, I think I saw Jackson Grosbeck checking you out the other day."

For a moment there, Izzy thought she'd been struck by the Norovirus again and she nearly lost her lunch. Or she would have if she'd eaten any. Germaine criticized the girls at the table who ate more than carrots and celery sticks. Which Izzy might have ignored, if the guys at the table hadn't made so many snide comments about her vegetarian lunches. She'd taken to sneaking her food into homeroom and eating most of it there.

All in all, being one of the popular kids was way more work than she'd been prepared for.

She might have felt guilty for sitting at Germaine's table, if she'd gotten any enjoyment out of it at all. Germaine didn't treat Izzy any different from her evil handmaidens, but she ruled the people she considered friends with a fist even tighter than she ruled her enemies. Being a lifelong fan of PBS's *Nature*, Izzy knew why Germaine acted like she did. The alpha in any pack had to constantly nip at the betas to keep them in place. Nevertheless, the steady diet of insults and manipulation did little for her appetite.

It had gotten to the point where the farm was the only place she could relax. Tanner's parents were no-nonsense and they expected her to work just as hard as they did. They treated her like all their other employees, even though she was just a high school student. She'd fallen in the habit of going by for a couple of hours after school and for most of Saturday and Sunday, doing whatever needed to be done, from turning the compost pile to plowing under the crops that had already been harvested.

She rarely saw Tanner. During the week, he had football practice after school. On Saturdays he sometimes went with his parents to the farmers' market. Carlos, one of the men who worked on the farm, was always around to supervise her.

The truth was, she was glad she didn't see much of Tanner. He'd been there the other night at Linc's film festival of embarrassment. She'd walked in toward the end—she hated to think what humiliating clips of her they'd watched that she didn't know about. Standing there in the darkened doorway, listening to them all laughing at her expense, she'd considered her options. The old childhood standby—I'm going to tell Mommy!—would gain nothing. Their mother wouldn't have time to deal with it. Their father would slap her on the shoulder and tell her to toughen up. Smothering Linc in his sleep seemed like a viable option, but not nearly painful enough. No, if she was going to murder him, she wanted him to see it coming, to experience a great deal of pain, and to know she was responsible. Poison might do the trick.

And then she'd looked across the room to see Tanner sitting on the sofa, watching the screen.

Why that made it worse, she didn't know.

His expression had been grim, his jaw clenched. He'd held a can of Dr Pepper propped on his thigh and the can had dents from where he was holding it too tightly. She'd been seconds away from storming out, when he tore his eyes away from the screen and met her gaze. The bottom dropped out of her stomach.

Something flickered across his expression. Something like . . . pity.

She fled, dashing up the stairs to her bedroom, where she stood with her back to the door, palm pressed to her belly for a long moment.

A few minutes later, Shane came in and found her sitting on the floor with her back against the wall. He slid down to sit beside her and laced his hand in hers.

"Linc is a complete asshole." He gave her hand a squeeze.

"Agreed." Shane normally lived so much in his own head that she didn't think he would have noticed. The fact that he was even aware of Linc's dumb-assery was a sign of just how bad things were.

"If he wasn't so much bigger than me," Shane said, "I'd kick his ass for you."

She stared down at Shane's delicate hands, with their long, elegant fingers. "Please don't. You'd probably break something just punching him, and I think one career-crippling hand injury is all this family can take."

Shane just smiled. And even though she smiled back, having him there was somehow worse. Shane—like their mother—had a gift for drifting in and out of her life just enough to make her yearn for more. At least with her father and Linc, she knew to always expect nothing. They had that emotionally stilted football gene.

But—she wondered once Shane had headed back to his room to practice—if the football gene turned guys into morons, then what was up with Tanner? And why did she want him to be an exception to that rule?

No. She couldn't even think about that.

Okay, so maybe she didn't actually hate him, the way she'd always thought she had. So maybe his knuckles dangled a few inches above the ground instead of actually scraping it. So maybe ever since he'd helped her get the job at the farm and she'd been sitting at his table at lunch . . . maybe he was almost like a friend—or at least the closest thing she had to a friend here in Paris. At least until the girls got back.

If he really was her friend, maybe that was why her chest felt so tight. No one wanted a new friend to see them at their worst—surely that was the only reason she felt this crushing despair. And the truth was, she'd be perfectly happy if she didn't see him at all. For the rest of the semester. Though, apparently, fate had other plans.

Come Saturday, there he was, sauntering out of the barn, his gimme cap pulled down low against the bright autumn sun. Her nerves jangled at the sight of him, and she tried to tell herself that was a normal reaction to facing someone who'd watched Linc's mockumentary of her life.

She'd felt similar the other day when Jackson had cornered her outside the gym and made suggestive remarks to her in Spanish. True, that had been tinged with more hatred and disgust. But surely the feelings were rooted in a similar place.

Then Tanner smiled at her and thumbed back his hat.

Nope. This feeling wasn't the same at all. No hatred. No disgust. Just . . .

Oh God. Had she developed a crush on Tanner Colt? How stupid was she, exactly?

Okay, yes. He was *super*hot. But she'd thought she was immune to that. He'd been hanging around her house since the ninth grade, when he'd first earned a place on the team as kicker—the position she'd gone out for. All these years, he'd been strutting around her house oozing testosterone and charm, but she'd been able to ignore him. Partly because Piper liked him and partly because he was just too . . .

Just too much. Too perfect.

And she never wanted to be one of the girls who trailed around football players like groupies. So ignoring Tanner had been easy.

But it wasn't easy anymore. Out here on the farm, she didn't have to listen to Piper gushing about how hot he was, or see him laugh at some dumb-ass joke her brother had made, or listen to her father brag about how he was the golden boy who would bring them back to State this year. Without all that other nonsense buzzing in her head, it was too easy to see him as he really was. Smart. Funny. And the only person who'd actually been nice to her in ten weeks.

And she thought he was too perfect before.

Shit.

She yelled a greeting and then made her way toward the tractor, quickly formulating a plan. If she could just get on the tractor and start it up, then she could pretend to be unable to hear anything he said over the roar of the engine. She'd almost made it to safety when he reached her.

"Hey, Isabel, about the other day at your house—"

She held up her hands in a hey-I'm-cool sign. "It's no big deal."

Since no one else seemed to take her humiliation seriously, she was doing her damnedest to pretend it didn't hurt that she had the worst brother in history. Intellectually, she got it. Linc was used to being the center of attention. The star of the school. When he couldn't be in the limelight on the football field, he had to invent ways to get noticed. But understanding sure as hell didn't make it hurt less.

Like her dad would have said, though, toughen up—and she was trying. Besides, if Tanner would just act like a normal football player and laugh his ass off at her expense, then she'd be able to ruthlessly squash this stupid crush of hers.

"That home-movie thing," she said, waving her hand dismissively, "that was no big deal. I mean, if I can't take a little teasing . . ."

"I'm going to talk to the guys on the team about it," Tanner said seriously. "It'll stop."

"Thank you." Her voice sounded as weak as her knees felt. Not the reaction she was hoping for. She cleared her throat. "But it's really not necessary."

"Someone said Grosbeck cornered you out by the gym on Friday."

Jackson was the least of her worries. He was easily controllable. "I took the opportunity to correct his Spanish pronunciation."

Humor laced Tanner's voice as he asked, "Is that why he's been telling people in Spanish that his dick is the size of a peanut?"

"Well, it's better than what he *was* saying about his dick," she explained, with no small amount of pride. Maybe there were benefits to toughening up.

Tanner studied her for a second and then nodded. "I guess you can take care of yourself then."

"Yeah," she agreed. "I can."

Being alone for ten weeks had taught her that about herself. She was stronger than she'd thought. She didn't need anyone to take care of her.

She took a few more steps toward the tractor only to realize she'd forgotten to grab the keys from the barn. When she turned around, Tanner was dangling them from one of his fingers, as if he'd been waiting for her to realize she needed them. She grabbed for the keys, but he pulled his hand back, holding them just out of her reach.

"Before you get started, I wanted to ask you . . ." He paused, as if suddenly unwilling to meet her gaze. He thumbed his hat off, gave his hair a scrub, and then yanked the hat back down.

He looked so awkward, she nearly laughed. "What is it?" she prodded.

"Isabel, did you hit on Carlos's son, Jose?"

Her laughter died in her throat. Probably smothered by her heart that leaped up to lodge itself just under her voice box.

"Pfft." She gave an awkward little laugh that came out more like a choking sound. Then she cleared her throat and coolly tucked her hands into her back pockets. "No." She rocked back on her heels. "No. Why would I . . ." She cleared her throat again. "Why would I do that?"

"Carlos just saw something the other day that made him curious. He's very protective of his son."

"Of course," she answered. Like this was a perfectly normal conversation to be having. And not awkward at all. "I mean, why would I flirt with Jose? He's younger than I am," she pointed out brightly. "He's got to be . . . what? Fifteen?"

"He's twelve," Tanner said flatly.

"Twelve?" Surprise spiked her voice. "He's *twelve*?" She felt her cheeks burning. As they should. Twelve was cradle-robbing. And vaguely illegal. "He's . . . a really tall twelve."

Tanner looked amused by her shock. "I wouldn't have thought anything of it, but the other day I noticed how close you were standing to Pieter."

She held up a finger. "You can't tell me he's twelve. He is definitely over fifteen."

"Yeah. He's seventeen. But he's also married."

"Married?" Her voice sounded all high and squeaky again. "What kind of seventeen-year-old gets married? I mean, even in Texas."

Tanner laughed. "He's Mennonite." He gave a shrug of his shoulders that somehow emphasized their width. "His parents own the farm next to ours and Pieter has helped out over here for years. Yeah, they marry young. He's already got two kids."

Her mind boggled. "Christ, I'm a home wrecker!" And a cougar. How much worse could this get?

"So you *were* hitting on him?"

"No! I mean . . ."

Please, earth, just open up and swallow me now!

Nothing happened. After years of protecting and defending the planet, it wouldn't do her this one small favor? She'd given up meat for the earth, and it couldn't even put her out of her misery.

She forced her gaze back to Tanner. He was *not* going to let this go.

"It's complicated," she muttered.

"I mean, I know it's probably too complex for me to understand, given that I'm a purveyor of pointless violence, but if you use small words, I'll try to stay with you."

Whatever. At this point, the only way to go was up. The explanation could not be any worse than this embarrassment.

"With Piper, Mei, and Cassidy out of town, we thought it would be fun to start a little club. Just as a way of making sure we stayed in touch."

Tanner's eyebrows shot up. "And let me guess. This club has to do with flirting?"

"No, don't be silly." She nearly bit the inside of her cheek to keep the blush from creeping up her neck.

"Isabel?" he prodded.

"Flirting would be impossible to quantify." She covered her mouth with one hand and muttered under her breath, "We're counting kisses."

After an instant of surprise, a slow smile broke across his face. "Of course you are."

She propped her hands on her hips. "It's not skeezy or anything. It's just an innocent little game."

"Can I assume you're behind and that's why you're hitting on all our employees?"

"Yes. Damn it. I'm behind. Everyone else has scored points. But not me." The words just tumbled out of her mouth. She couldn't stop herself. "Piper has been kissing her way through the entire European Union. Cassidy has hooked up with some hot surfer. Even Mei—in Communist China!—has scored more points than I have."

"There are points?" he interjected.

"Of course there are points! Not for me—naturally—but everyone else has oodles of them. There's some chick in Paraguay who—"

"Paraguay? Which of you went to Paraguay?"

"Oh, it's not one of us." She quickly explained about the point system, making the Facebook page public, and the fans who had unexpectedly been popping up. "Girls in repressive developing cultures are getting more play than I am."

"You know, Isabel, if you just want some guy to kiss, I'm pretty sure Grosbeck would be happy to help you out."

"*Eeew.* Just because he dips Copenhagen doesn't mean he's been there. The stench of his unwashed body is not international enough for me."

Tanner nodded, as if finally getting it. "So it's not just a kissing club. It's an international kissing club?"

"Well, when you say it like that, it sounds so skeezy."

Tanner held his hands up in the universal sign of surrender, but he was barely holding back his laughter. "Hey, I didn't say it like anything."

She narrowed her eyes and growled at him. "Look, I said it was complicated."

This conversation was so over. She turned, looking for a disk plow she could impale herself on.

"Hey," Tanner said. "I was just teasing." Then his expression darkened. "But I guess you're getting a lot of that these days."

She hated seeing the glimmer of pity in his eyes, so she socked him on the arm and feigned bravado. "Yeah. I am. So back off, buddy. I have compost to turn, and if you're not careful, I'll dump it in the cab of your truck."

"I'm trying to be supportive here."

"Yeah, right," she grumbled. She started to climb back on to the tractor, but Tanner gave her hand a tug as she stepped on the runner.

"You know," he began as she turned to face him, "maybe you're making this harder than it needs to be."

"What do you mean?" Standing on the running board added a good foot to her height, which made her just a few inches taller than he was.

He took a step closer to her. "If you just need to kiss someone from another country, I was born in Germany." Tanner reached up and grabbed a lock of her hair. He started winding it around his finger. "My dad was stationed in Bamberg. I have dual citizenship until I'm eighteen."

Her heart was pounding so hard she had trouble concentrating on his words. Dual citizenship? What did that have to do with anything? Oh, right. International. Kissing. Club. Kissing.

Was he really suggesting . . .

Then he gave her hair one last tug. She felt herself falling forward and braced her hands on his shoulders. Her feet were barely grounded on the runner. Tanner's arms wrapped around her waist. Her lips were just an inch away from his. And then they were on his.

His lips moved gently under hers. Moist and smooth. So divine everything inside of her seemed to go all gooey and shivery in the same instant. Her feet slipped out from under her and he slowly lowered her off the tractor. She felt the strength of his arm muscles as he held her, the hard definition of his chest as her hands trailed down. Finally her feet touched the ground, but her legs didn't feel firm beneath her.

His tongue brushed against her lips and she opened her mouth to his. He tasted faintly of spearmint gum and sweet water. He tasted like pure heaven. Her hands clenched against his shoulders, needing to cling tightly to something.

Somewhere, in the distant corner of her mind, there was an alarm bell going off. Faint and almost indistinguishable. Set off by some part of her that remembered this was wrong. That she had no right to be kissing Tanner. To even be touching him. Or letting him touch her.

But in that instant, she could barely hear the alarm, and she certainly couldn't listen to it, because kissing Tanner was too frickin' delicious. Like the best, finest chocolate she'd ever tasted. He made every other boy she'd kissed seem like a rank amateur.

Had she even kissed any other boys?

Before she could come up with an answer, Tanner slowly drew away from her, ending the kiss. For a second, he just stared at her, his face taut with the same desire and conflict she was feeling. She thought he was going to pull away completely, but then his mouth came back to hers for one more kiss. He ground his lips to hers in a way that felt hungry and possessive. As if he couldn't *not* kiss her.

Then abruptly he stepped back, shoving his hands deep into his pockets. He turned to look down the road. Staring at his profile, she couldn't read his expression. Had no idea how he was feeling. Head still spinning, she followed his gaze. A car was driving toward them, kicking up dust.

"Well," Tanner said, his voice husky and low, his lips curved in a smile that looked almost sad. "Now you've got some points for your competition."

Izzy's mouth dropped open. Before she could close it, Germaine's car pulled to a stop by the barn. She swung open the door on the driver's side and hopped out without killing the engine. She gave a broad wave. "Hey, sweetie!" she called. And then, with an overly perky smile, she added, "Hey, *chica!*"

Supposing she was the *chica*, Izzy gave a halfhearted mute wave.

"You'll put the keys back in the barn when you're done?" Tanner asked, his voice cooler and more distant than it usually was. As if moments ago he hadn't had his tongue in her mouth.

"Huh?" she asked.

"Carlos will be by later tonight to lock up the barn," he said, ignoring the fact that she hadn't really answered. And then he turned away and jogged off in Germaine's direction. "See ya later, Iz," he called over his shoulder.

Izzy couldn't help herself. She watched him carefully—like the turkey buzzard she'd always compared Germaine to. Her breath caught in her chest as he approached Germaine. *Please don't let him touch her. Please let him blow her off.*

But as always, Germaine wrapped herself around him in a predatory kiss. Though Tanner's hands came up between them and it looked—for a moment—like he was going to push her away, in the end, he didn't. Big surprise. Izzy squeezed her eyes closed. When she opened them a second later, it was to see Tanner climbing into the passenger's side of Germaine's car. As if he'd been expecting her all along.

Izzy finally managed to close her mouth. Or more to the point, her jaw spasmed in rage, closing it for her. What was that?

What. The. Hell. Was. That?

Tanner had just kissed her.

For points.

And then kissed Germaine mere seconds later. Dear God. Her spit had just mingled with Germaine's. It was wrong in so many ways, she couldn't even begin to list them.

She felt the black bean taco she'd eaten for lunch crawling back up her esophagus. Even her food was disgusted by her behavior.

She should not have kissed Tanner. Or rather, should not have let Tanner kiss her.

Because he had a girlfriend. Germaine. Who was either her mortal enemy or her sort of friend. And whom he was obviously still with. Or he wouldn't have just kissed her too and ridden off in her car.

Izzy had hated being the only member of IKC who hadn't scored any points. But now, she hated that Tanner had kissed her only for points. Because when he was kissing her, she'd forgotten about everything else. Even IKC. Even Piper.

And knowing he'd kissed her just as some sort of favor to a friend? There weren't enough SAT words in the world to describe how horrible it made her feel.

There were only two bright points to this whole mess of crap. At least she finally had some points. And at least Piper was no longer pining away for Tanner. Lately she'd been so interested in this guy Sebastian, she'd seemed to have outgrown her crush.

Self-disgust and defiant anger warring within her, Izzy whipped out her phone, pulled up the IKC page, and posted her points. She did it fast, before she could talk herself out of it. Before she could regret posting the points as much as she regretted earning them.

IKC Fan Page

The Official Fan Page for the International Kissing Club

41,547

people like this

 IKC Page

Jane	Three points. Don't ask. Don't tell.

Ariel OMG! OMG! Spill!

Jane Let's leave some things to the imagination.

LaTonya Washington You go, girl! <g>

Jayson It's about damn time. I was tempted to come down to Texas and kiss you myself.

Karrie Meeker So who's the lucky guy? Is he really hot?

Jane Yes. Really hot. But I'm thinking he might be a bit of a jerk. Maybe I should revise down for personality.

Stephanie Richards Oh, honey. So sorry! Men are horrible!

Stephanie Richards Not you, Jayson! Sorry!

Jayson No offense taken. Sometimes, men ARE jerks. You think I don't know that? Jane, if this guy's too much of an idiot to realize how great you are, then you should save your lips for someone worthy.

Chapter 24
Mei

Mei sank onto the bed in her dorm room, reviewing her packing checklist and at the same time trying to think of one way in which this whole trip hadn't been a total unmitigated disaster. Yeah, she couldn't find one. Nothing about coming to China had turned out the way she'd planned.

Learning Mandarin—a failure; her greatest success was that now she could order at Pizza Hut.

Academic enhancement—a failure (see above); if not for Guiran's help and infinite patience, she would have bombed all of her classes. As it was, her grades were so depressed and she was going to be so far behind when she got home, she would have to work doubly hard next semester and probably go to summer school if she had any hope of salvaging an acceptance to MIT.

Discovering a link to her birth parents—a complete and total failure. While she'd known this was a long shot to begin with, she'd still held out hope that she'd find something, anything, that could tell her who she was. She owed what little she had found to Guiran, and for that she could never thank him enough.

For a girl who'd always taken pride in her self-reliance, the trip had really knocked her ego down a peg or two.

A light knock on the door interrupted her descent into Piper-like self-pity.

"Guiran," she said, and her tummy fluttered a little when she saw him standing there, his black eyes gleaming as he looked at her. She was going to miss the way he watched her, as if she was the only person who mattered to him.

"Are you all packed?" he asked, nodding to her suitcase, which was lying open on the unused bed in the room.

"Almost. Just the last minute things to add."

"I figured you would be." He chuckled. As always, hearing him laugh made her want to also. She'd never known someone who was as easygoing as Guiran. She envied it. "Then you should be able to give me that guitar lesson you promised." He stepped into the room.

"Here? Now?" she asked, suddenly flustered. "There's not really enough time for a proper lesson. I have to leave in a few hours for the airport."

"Calm down, Mei—so serious all the time. I thought we'd gotten you over that. I'm not saying I want you to teach me to play Hendrix in the next three hours, but I think there's time to get in a chord or two. I bet I catch onto guitar faster than you did boarding."

Mei's eyes narrowed a fraction. "Are you saying you're a better student than I am?"

He smiled and cocked an eyebrow in challenge. "Why don't we find out?"

"You're on."

Two hours in and Guiran had mastered A to D and E. "I told you I was a better student," he said, strumming handily between the chords. "It took you this long to stay on the board for more than ten seconds without crashing into something."

"Which doesn't prove you're the better student, only that I'm the better teacher," she countered smugly.

Guiran snorted. "You *would* think that. Always have to be the best, the first, the most." His middle finger slid off the string, causing the note to go awry.

"Here, like this," she said, scooting closer. She draped her arm around him, putting her left hand over his to show him how it was supposed to be done. "See? Smooth, with no pauses."

But then Guiran entwined his fingers with hers, and the room got very still. Wow. Though it was near subzero outside, the temperature inside seemed to have suddenly risen to tropical highs in a matter of seconds. Izzy had been right—there really was something to this teaching thing.

Guiran turned so that he was looking over his shoulder at her and they were so close she could smell the spicy cinnamon of his breath. "I know you're happy to be going home, Mei, but I wish you weren't," he said.

As she rested against him, the need to flee didn't seem so strong. Even with everything she'd done in China—or maybe because of it—her time with Guiran suddenly didn't feel anywhere near long enough.

"Having you here has made it almost . . . tolerable to be in this hole of a school," he continued. "No, much better than that. It's been fun."

"Guiran, you're the one who made the time I spent here so much better than it could have been." She paused, wanting to say more. Wanting to do more. But ever-practical Mei pulled away. She was leaving in a few hours—now was not the time to let her emotions run away with her. "I would have been miserable if you hadn't taken pity on me."

He shot her a look that said she couldn't be more wrong. "That wasn't pity, Mei." His eyes swept over her and his grin took on a whole new dimension. "Don't forget saving you from prison in Communist China by dragging you out of that fountain." They both laughed until she remembered how that escapade had ended.

"Nobody back home will ever believe me when I tell them that story."

"Why not? You're a guitarist, right? I think it's a prerequisite for all rock stars to dance in their underwear in a fountain—even control freak ones."

"Yeah, but back home, all most people see is the control freak. I'm not some rebel rock goddess there. I'm Mei Jones, future valedictorian of Paris High School—at least, I hope I still am. After my academic performance here, I may be lucky to graduate at all." Then she got very serious, the mirth leaving her voice. "But, Guiran, seriously . . . thank you for helping me search for my birth parents and for going with me to the SWI. Especially because I know it wasn't easy for you, either." She leaned in and kissed him, soft and gentle. His free hand came up and cupped her cheek while he kissed her back. It wasn't like that kiss in the fountain, wild and impetuous and playful, and yet it was somehow better for it.

She pulled back first, gauging his reaction—*why was she always the one kissing him?* "I hope that wasn't a good-bye kiss," he said.

"No, not good-bye. We'll always be friends."

"Ouch." He winced. "Friends."

"Listen, meeting you was the one good thing that happened to me in China, Guiran, and I'd hate to think I'll never get to see you again." This was something she hadn't considered when she'd set out that day to find a friend: at the end of this trip she'd have to give that friendship up when she went home.

Her bonds with Piper, Cassidy, and Izzy were time tested, meant to last all their lives. She wouldn't have that with Guiran, but it didn't make what they'd shared in their short time together any less meaningful. He had been by her side at one of the most personal moments of her life.

"Don't worry about that. They have this thing called the Internet now," he teased, lightening the mood again. "It's an amazing technology people can use to connect with each other across vast distances."

Mei punched his arm playfully, but she hoped he was right, that they would keep in touch. It made it easier to say good-bye.

· · · · · ·✈

Mei's parents were waiting for her as soon as she exited the Dallas airport's secure area. Mei couldn't hold back the rush of tears that came when she saw them. Her mom got to her first and grabbed her into a hug that she thought she'd need the Jaws of Life to pry herself out of.

"My little girl, my little girl," her mom repeated, rocking Mei back and forth like she was a little girl. "I missed you so much."

To her surprise, she found herself clinging to her mother just as fiercely. Ten weeks in China and her parents' attention suddenly felt a lot less smothering.

"Susan, she can't breathe. Let go, honey," her dad said. Her mom finally eased up, but for the first time ever, Mei wasn't ready to let go.

"Doodlebug, what's wrong?" her dad asked.

"I just missed you. I really, really missed you."

And then she was in her father's arms, inhaling the scent of his aftershave. The same brand she'd bought him for Father's Day when she was six and that he'd never stopped wearing. It felt so good to be a daughter again. To just let herself be loved. To—

Abruptly her mother pulled her out of her father's arms.

"You are rail-thin, Mei," her mom said once she got a good look at her. "Didn't they feed you enough over there? Richard, get her suitcase. We're going to eat right now. She looks like one of those Olsen twins."

"I'm fine, Mom. I'm just really tired—you know I can't sleep on a plane." Her mouth started watering at the mere thought of food. "But something to eat would be nice."

"Of course, sweetie, anything you want. Just pick a place."

"Anything but Chinese food," she answered. "If I never eat another sea cucumber . . ."

"Mexican food it is," her mom said quickly.

Mmmmm. The thought of queso, guacamole, salsa, and never-ending baskets of tortilla chips made her stomach grumble with anticipation. Why couldn't she have been adopted from Mexico? She was so glad to be back in Texas.

Once they'd made it to the restaurant and ordered, her parents peppered her with questions about the trip. Funny, so often she'd yearned for a sibling, just so she wouldn't be the sole focus of her parents' scrutiny. Yet now, after missing it for ten weeks, she couldn't help but revel in their attention. The way her mom wanted to know every single detail of the trip. The way her father hugged her to him in the big, circular booth, even as he listened indulgently as she and her mother chattered about anything and everything. Who knew it would be so easy to go from pariah to princess?

Over a huge platter of enchiladas, she told them about Shenyang, the school, her classes. She spoke some Mandarin phrases that she and Guiran had practiced, and they applauded her for learning so much while she was away. Little did they know that most of the Mandarin she recited was just different pizza toppings. But she wasn't going to let them in on that little secret.

Then again, there were lots of secrets she wasn't going to share, and she hadn't been home long enough yet to feel guilty about that. Instead, she was going to channel Piper. What happened abroad, stayed abroad. For now, she would simply enjoy not just the reunion with her parents, but how being away had made being home so much sweeter.

By going to China she had opened a window into the heart of herself, into who she was and what it meant to be Mei Jones, Chinese adoptee to an American family. The girl who preferred guacamole to moo goo gai pan and Joan Jett to Chopin.

"Your friends have been calling, wondering when you were getting home," her mother said. "It'll be fun for all of you to catch up and compare stories now that you're veteran international travelers."

Mei almost choked on a mouthful of pico de gallo when she misheard her mother's words as "international kissers." Her dad patted her on the back and handed her a glass of water.

"Are you okay, Doodlebug?"

"Fi-fine. Swallowed wrong."

Yes, she was sure they were all looking forward to having Piper, the undisputed queen of the International Kissing Club, regale them with the grandiose tales of her salivic study of the Gallic male. Thanks to Guiran, though, she would not be without points of her own.

In fact, now that she was home and away from Dao-Ming, ostracization, and classes she couldn't understand, she realized there wasn't much she would have done differently.

Well, except the food—if she'd known how that was going to turn out, she would have packed some of Izzy's granola bars.

IKC Fan Page

The Official Fan Page for the International Kissing Club

49,886

people like this

 IKC Page

Ariel
Loved Paris. I'm heartbroken.

> **Jane** Are you really that heartbroken to leave?

> **Ariel** The only thing that makes it bearable is knowing that I'm going to be with you soon. I'm so ready to be around people who love me.

> **Jane** I thought you were enamored of all things French, including Mr. Worth-Four-Points-He's-So-Sexy Sebastian?

> **Ariel** Again, I'm heartbroken.

Rapunzel
h8 planes. h8 rain. h8 bumps. LUV land. God Bless LAX.

Mulan
Just arrived at DFW. Am eating my way back to Paris.

> **Jane** Pick me up some Panda Express

> **Mulan** Don't hold your breath. If I never see another grain of rice, it will be too soon.

Chapter 25
Piper

Piper climbed into her car and started the engine, still having a hard time getting used to driving again after spending the past ten weeks taking the Metro almost everywhere. She'd been back in Texas two days now, and it still seemed a little strange. Nothing had changed in Paris during the ten weeks she'd been gone, and yet *everything* had changed. It was an unsettling feeling, one that made her apprehension almost as huge as her excitement to see her friends again.

She had changed. She knew that. France had changed her. Freedom had changed her. *Sebastian* had changed her. Just thinking his name had her hands shaking and her heart crumbling a little in her chest. She missed him like crazy, way more than she ever would have imagined possible when she'd first met him all those weeks ago. What made it worse was that she'd never talked to him again after that awful day in the café.

He'd e-mailed her, texted her, even called a couple times, but she'd texted him back and said she didn't want to see him, so he'd stayed away. And she was glad he had. Really, she was. She couldn't look at him now, not while her heart was still broken wide open. *How could I have been so stupid?* she wondered as she turned the corner onto Mei's street. *How could I have ever thought that he'd loved me?* Her own family had never been able to love her—why had she been stupid enough to think that Sebastian could?

It wasn't a mistake she planned on making again. The only people she'd ever been able to count on were Cass, Mei, and Izzy. She needed to remember that if she wanted to keep herself from being gutted like this again.

Lost in thought, Piper was at the end of the block before it registered that she had driven right by Mei's house. Terrific. Now she couldn't even remember how to get to her best friend's place. Just how much had changed in ten weeks?

With a sigh, she turned the car around and headed back up the street, making sure to stay aware enough to stop at the right house. But after pulling into Mei's driveway, Piper didn't bound from the car, like she'd thought she would. Instead, she rested her head on the steering wheel and tried to pull herself together.

So what if she missed the real Paris and Sebastian and Simone and even Marie, who in ten weeks had mothered her more than her own had in a lifetime?

So what if she missed the trips to the small, out-of-the-way galleries Sebastian had taken her to?

So what if she missed the glassblowing class where she'd finally found the kind of art she wanted to create?

She was back in Paris, Texas, now. Yes, the Sara Lee bakery was a far cry from the little pâtisserie around the corner from Marie and Gus's apartment, their coffee cake nowhere near as good as the chocolate croissants she'd eaten by the bucketful. But that didn't mean she couldn't enjoy herself. Enjoy her friends and the fact that her mother was sober for once. Although she wasn't quite sure what it said that the second she'd gone out of town, her mom had managed to clean up her act. Nice to have it confirmed that she had been completely responsible for her mom's dependence on martinis and prescription medicine.

But sitting here feeling sorry for herself wasn't doing anything but making her more depressed. Determined to get her head back into this reunion thing, Piper climbed out of the car—just as Mei opened her front door and stepped onto the porch.

As Mei started toward her, Piper's mouth dropped open. Piper had gained five pounds in Paris and dyed her hair, neither of which had sat well with her mother. Mei, on the other hand, had lost so much weight that she looked like a strong hug might crack her in half. Her parents must be twice as freaked out as Piper's mom was.

Her own sorrows forgotten, she bounded up the driveway. "Mei! Are you okay?"

Mei threw her arms around Piper. "I'm fine. How are you? The blue streaks look fabulous!"

Tears sprung to Piper's eyes as she returned Mei's hug. After the past couple of weeks of tormenting herself over her mistakes and wondering what things would be like when she returned to Texas, it was so nice to just be accepted for who she was. This moment, this hug, this connection felt much more like a homecoming than meeting her parents at the airport ever could.

"Thanks." Piper returned her hug, still shocked at how fragile Mei looked and felt. "What happened to you? You're—"

"Ugh. Don't you start, too." Mei rolled her eyes. "Let's just say there were no Panda Expresses in China and leave it at that. On the plus side, I'm finally a size zero."

"More like a double zero, and I didn't know you were aiming for that, anyway," Piper said, ushering her friend to the car.

"I wasn't."

"Well, come on, then, let's go get you an extra-large Blizzard. My treat."

"You have no idea how good that sounds." Mei climbed into the passenger side as Piper started the car. " Better than wasabi ice cream, anyway."

"Wasabi ice cream? Sounds disgusting."

"It wasn't all that bad," Mei said. "But I guess you had to be there."

Piper glanced away from the road long enough to throw her friend an incredulous look. "Are you *blushing*?"

"No! Of course not. What possible reason would I have to blush?"

"Oh, I don't know. Maybe those three points on the IKC page?" She poked Mei in the shoulder. "Come on, spill. Tell me *everything*."

Mei sighed. "I don't even know where to start."

"At the beginning, of course. You got off the plane in China and then what?"

"It wasn't at all like I expected it to be, you know? I mean, I thought once I got to China I'd finally feel like I belonged. But it turns out, over there, I'm even more of a freak than I am here."

"You're not a freak!" Piper was outraged at the very idea. "You're the best. Everyone loves you. And if those stupid Chinese girls couldn't appreciate your utter and complete fabulousness, then that was totally their loss."

"Jeez, vehement much?" But Mei looked happy at Piper's defense of her.

"Ugh. Please don't start with the SAT words already! I'm still jet-lagged."

Her friend laughed so hard she nearly snorted. "You know, I really missed you, Piper. How come you can always make me feel better?"

"Because I am almost as fabulous as you." She whipped her car into the DQ lot and saw that Izzy's car, Brittney, was already parked near the front door. The sight of its battered bumper and dinged-up doors, combined with the easy laughter she'd shared with Mei, cheered her up like nothing else could have. Maybe *everything* hadn't changed, after all.

But as they settled around a small greasy table ten minutes later, she wasn't so sure about that. Cassidy was wearing mascara and lip gloss—*lip gloss*—and Izzy looked like a walking advertisement for a Subaru commercial, and the most rugged, outdoorsy one at that. She wasn't sure what to make of all the changes and wondered if her friends were having as much trouble adjusting as she was.

Mei seemed okay, though the gigantic Butterfinger Blizzard Piper had ordered for her was nearly as big as she was. And Izzy looked great, all tanned and toned and glowing. Only Cassidy seemed as lost and shell-shocked as she felt.

Piper waited until everyone had shoveled in a few spoons of ice cream before demanding, "So, who wants to go first?" She made a concerted effort to appear upbeat despite the sadness that trembled just below the surface.

"You go first," Cass said. "You probably have the best stories after racking up all those points."

"Yeah, but Izzy's the one who racked up the most recent points. I think she should start."

"Ooh, that's true," Mei agreed. "Come on, Iz. Spill."

Izzy looked like she'd just been thrust onto a particularly blistering hot seat, and Piper wondered at the panic she thought she saw in her friend's eyes. But before she could comment, Izzy got it together. "It was no big deal," she said with a shrug.

"You kissed a guy in Paris, Texas!" Piper said. "It's a huge deal. Who was it?"

"Umm—"

"Oh God," Cassidy interjected. "Please tell me it wasn't River again. That guy is a total scumbag, Izzy."

"No way! I haven't talked to him once since he went away to school."

"Thank God!" Piper spooned up more ice cream. "I was beginning to get worried. But if it wasn't River, then who was it?"

"Trust me, Piper. You *don't* want to know. It happened on Tanner's farm. There was a tractor and compost." She shook her head. "Bugs. It really wasn't your scene."

"Okaaaaaay. But—"

"My big three points happened in the middle of a fountain in Shenyang," Mei said suddenly.

"Ooh, se-xy!" Piper said with a wink. "I can just see you and Guiran, all wet and see-through and—"

"Freezing!" Mei interrupted dryly. "The water was like three degrees above absolute zero."

"That's insane! I'm so glad it was spring most of the time I was in Australia."

"So, where did you first kiss Lucas, Cass?" Izzy asked.

"At the beach. It was . . . nice." The look in Cassidy's eyes said it had been a lot more than nice and Piper was thrilled for her. "But whatever. There are so many hot guys in Australia you can't help but trip and press your lips against one of them."

Though she said it with her usual bravado, Piper could hear something in her voice that was totally new for Cassidy. A vulnerability that meant Lucas was more than just the guy who had caught her when she'd fallen.

"If he had the good sense to break your fall, he must be a really great guy. Some of them are, you know," she told Cass, not wanting her friend to lose hope. "Maybe he'll surprise you."

If possible, her reassurances only seemed to make Cassidy even more agitated. "Yeah, well, whatever."

Wow. It looked like she hadn't been the only one to fall hard these past few weeks. Piper didn't know whether to curse the IKC or be grateful for the chances it had given her. The only thing she was sure of was that it had completely messed up her life.

No, said the little voice in the back of her head. That wasn't true. *She'd* managed to screw everything up all on her own. The IKC hadn't had much to do with it at all.

Lost in thought, it took her a minute to realize her friends were looking at her expectantly. Oh right, she was the only one who hadn't shared. But where was she supposed to start? Finally, she just shrugged and said, "Well, my points came from—"

"Everywhere?" Cassidy interjected, elbowing her in the ribs.

"Right," agreed Izzy. "Is there anyone in Paris you *didn't* kiss?"

Piper laughed, because her friends expected it of her, but it was hard, especially as Sebastian's face had flashed, unbidden, before her eyes. The last thing she wanted was for her friends to know how much she was hurting over being dumped. But at the same time, she couldn't lie—it felt too much like another betrayal of what she'd felt for him. "The only points that really mattered happened in the courtyard of the Louvre."

"That's a great story. So romantic. You were with Sebastian, right?" Mei asked.

"Yeah. Sebastian."

"Tell us about him," Izzy said. "I mean, the picture you posted was completely hot, but what happened? How did you leave things?"

"I don't—I can't—" Piper shook her head, afraid she was going to shatter if she had to talk anymore about it. But at the same time, she missed Sebastian so much that everything kind of came spilling out.

"He's not like any guy I've ever met before."

"Well, duh. He's French."

"It's more than that, Cass. I mean, at first I hated him. He was so obnoxious and full of himself and rude—"

"Again, he's *French*."

"I know, right? But there's so much more to him than that. He's incredibly smart and talented—his sculptures are beautiful—and once you get past the smug outer shell, he's really tender. And witty. And caring. And—"

"Wow, Pipes, you really fell for him." Cassidy looked a little stunned, like she couldn't imagine Piper actually finding real love. Or maybe Piper just imagined it, since Sebastian's words were still fresh in her head.

"Yeah, well, it doesn't matter. It's over between us." She did her best to look like it was for the best.

"Why?" Mei looked confused. "If you care about him—"

"It was never supposed to be a big deal," she answered breezily, praying they couldn't hear the hurt behind the attitude. "Just something to pass the time while I was in France."

"That doesn't mean things can't change—"

"Oh, come on, Mei. You understand rules better than the three of us put together. You can't change them in the middle of something, even if you want to. It's not fair to the other people involved."

With that, Piper leaned back in her seat and concentrated on her M&M Blizzard like it was the most important thing in the world. And for those couple of minutes, it was. Focusing on it was the only thing that held her together when she wanted nothing more than to scream about how unfair the world was. How unfair Sebastian was. How unfair love was.

But it didn't take her long to realize she'd totally killed the mood, even though she hadn't meant to. Her three friends were staring at her like they didn't recognize her anymore, and she knew it was up to her to get things back where they belonged. Back to the Piper she'd been ten weeks before. So with a flip of her head and a forced grin, she said, "Speaking of guys . . . Izzy, how's Tanner been?"

Izzy stilled, a spoonful of melting ice cream halfway to her mouth. Again, Piper saw panic in her friend's eyes, though she still didn't have a clue what Izzy was so nervous about. "Wh-why would I know how Tanner's been?"

"'Cause you worked on his parents' farm all semester, silly. Duh." She tried her best to sound enthusiastic. It was really hard. Especially since, for the life of her, she could barely remember what Tanner looked like. But she needed something to talk about other than Sebastian. She needed the distraction, and God knew there were only so many Blizzards a girl could eat. "I bet he's better than ever!"

Izzy didn't say anything, just sat there, frozen, as the ice cream dripped slowly off her spoon and onto the table. But Piper was determined to get things back on an even keel, so she added, "I can't wait until Mond—"

"What is wrong with you?" Izzy hurled the question across the table at her. "Tanner is with Germaine. He is. Always. Going to be.

With Germaine. No other girl will ever have a chance. Even an idiot could see that. So why can't you?

"And what kind of girl goes out of her way to steal another person's boyfriend, anyway? It's demeaning. Isn't it bad enough that you kissed about a million guys in France and then bragged about it for the whole world to see? Now you want to fool around with Germaine's boyfriend as well? Don't you have any pride at all?"

Piper felt all the blood drain out of her face. Shock coursed through her, along with a sense of shame she'd felt only once before—when she'd kissed that boy on the dance floor of the club in Paris.

She glanced around at her friends and realized she wasn't the only one who'd been sucker-punched by Izzy's outburst.

"What is wrong with *you*?" Mei demanded, staring at Izzy.

"Nothing's wrong with me. What's wrong with *her*?"

Mei reached out and put a hand over Piper's. "She didn't mean it," she assured Piper. "You know how Izzy gets when she eats too much processed sugar."

"Forget the processed sugar. I think she needs an antipsychotic. So not cool, Izzy," Cassidy said.

"Where did that even come from?" Mei demanded.

Cassidy's arm wrapped around Piper's shoulder, as if to shield her, and Piper felt tears well up in her eyes. She blinked them back. There were some things that made you cry and some things that hurt too badly to cry. Izzy and Sebastian seemed intent on teaching her that lesson.

She started to tell them not to worry about it—she'd had enough drama—but before she could say anything, Izzy was already up and moving toward the door.

"Oh no, she's not getting off that easy. I'll be back in a minute." Cassidy followed Izzy out of the restaurant.

"Don't let it get to you, Pipes," Mei said after they watched the door slam behind Cass. "Being stuck in Paris obviously made her suffer some kind of psychotic episode or something."

Piper nodded, and though she appreciated Mei's and Cassidy's efforts, nothing they did could take the ache away. She'd been trying to play a part, trying to be the Piper she'd been before the IKC, but she hadn't fooled anyone.

For the first time, she wondered if her mom was right. Maybe the problem was with her. Maybe she'd brought this on herself. It was easy to blame Germaine for all the shitty things she did, but now that she'd lost Sebastian—and maybe Izzy—it was hard not to believe that the fault wasn't really her own.

Izzy's words mingled with her mother's until all Piper could hear was the criticism in them both. She'd left Paris ten weeks ago to get away from everything—from Kiss the Pig, from her mother, from Germaine. She'd thought that running away would make everything better, would make *her* better. And while she'd loved her time in France, now that she was home, she was beginning to understand just how stupid she'd been.

Ten weeks ago she'd been miserable, but she'd also had three best friends to help her deal with that misery.

She hadn't had a boyfriend, but at least her heart had been intact.

She hadn't liked her life, but at least she'd known what to expect.

After Izzy's blowup, she couldn't even say that she had that. Any of it. And worse, school started on Monday, and there was no doubt in Piper's mind that Germaine would be lying in wait, a fresh arsenal of weapons just ready to be unleashed. Running away hadn't solved anything. In fact, it had just made things worse.

The International Kissing Club had been her Worst. Idea. Ever.

Chapter 26
Cassidy

"What the hell has gotten into you?" Cassidy demanded as she followed Izzy to her car. "Piper didn't deserve that. Besides, what does it matter to you if she wants to go after Tanner? Since when do we care about Germaine's feelings?"

Izzy looked miserable, but that was no excuse for taking it out on the rest of them. Cassidy was pretty damn miserable herself. She'd been living with a void in her heart since she'd watched Lucas walk away from her at the airport.

Ever since she'd been home, it had been like she was caught in a riptide—slowly being sucked under no matter how hard she tried to break the surface. She'd been pretending, for her mom and her friends, that everything was fine, that she was the same old Cass—quick with a joke and a snappy comeback—when what she really wanted was to stay in bed for the next year to mope and feel sorry for herself. Izzy looked like she was having the same problem.

Climbing into Brittney's passenger seat, Cass said, "Tell me what's wrong with you, now, or I'm going to have no choice but to kick your ass. Because I know something's up."

Izzy deflated right in front of her eyes. "Don't be mad at me, Cass, please," she said. "I didn't mean to snap at Piper, I just . . . I don't know. Sometimes she just gets annoying. It's like she forgets the rest of us have thoughts and feelings, too, that don't revolve around her."

"You really expect me to believe this is about Piper? I don't think so. And it was really crappy of you to take it out on her."

Izzy sighed. "I know. I'll call her later," she agreed. "I thought that when y'all got home from your trips everything would fall right back into place. But I guess that was a little unrealistic, since you guys left hoping everything would be changed." Then she sighed. "Well, everything certainly feels different. Not better, though."

"What do you mean? What's different?" But even as she asked, Cassidy knew exactly what Izzy meant.

Everything did seem different now, and no, it wasn't better at all. This weirdness that was going on between the four of them bothered her. A lot.

"Look, I appreciate what you're trying to do, Cass, but I don't want to go there," Izzy said. "I'll find a way to make things right with Piper, but for now I can't talk about it."

The radio filled the silence for a while as they drove. Cassidy tried to think of something to say, but nothing was there. She'd been through a lot these past few weeks, and she figured the others had as well. It was no wonder they couldn't get their groove back—they'd experienced all kinds of crazy stuff through the years, but they'd always done it together. This was the first time they'd ever faced things alone, and now that they were back in Paris, their pieces no longer fit.

Brandon Flower's "Crossfire" came on the radio, and despite everything it took her right back to Lucas and reminded her of something she'd been wanting to ask Izzy since she'd landed. "Izzy, were you in love with River?"

Izzy did a startled double-take, obviously surprised by the question. "I don't know," she answered after a moment. "I guess I thought I was, but after everything I've found out about him, I don't think I ever really knew him. Why?"

Cassidy exhaled and told Izzy the whole story about her and Lucas: from the beginning at the airport and learning how to surf, sailing on his family's yacht, and finally running away from him like an idiot when he told her he loved her. All the way to the miserable end when he'd kissed her in the international terminal.

"Holy crap, Cass," Izzy said incredulously when she'd finished. "Do you think you're in love with Lucas? Because if you're not, I think I could be."

That was the million-dollar question Cassidy had been asking herself since she'd watched him throw down that boarding pass and walk away. And she still didn't have an answer.

"How do you know if you're in love with someone? I mean, I think about him all the time, so much that I can't concentrate on anything. And when I was with him I felt like I couldn't breathe if he didn't touch me or kiss me, and then when he did it was like everything in my world was focused on that one moment and nothing else mattered."

"And you don't know that you're in love with him? Did you even hear what you just said?"

"I know . . ." Talking about Lucas hurt; thinking about the way she'd treated him hurt even more. "Do you know what I told him when he said he loved me? That guys only say that when they're trying to get a girl in bed. He'd done nothing but be nice to me and I was a total psycho."

"But a lot of guys *would* only say that to get laid. Sometimes it's hard to tell the difference," Izzy said, her tone taking on an edge.

"But this time it wasn't hard. I think that's what scared me the most. I knew he meant it. Now, look at me—I'm not sleeping, I'm not eating—I'm a total nut job because this amazing guy says he has feelings for me. Can you imagine what I'd be like if we'd actually slept together? Being away from him after that would have been the worst thing ever."

Izzy became very still. "No, Cass, sleeping with a guy who loves you—even if you had to leave him—isn't the worst thing that could happen. The worst is sleeping with a guy who never talks to you again and posts pictures of his latest conquests on Facebook for you and the whole world to see."

Shock held Cassidy immobile for long seconds before she said, "Holy shit! Are you saying . . ."

Izzy closed her eyes for a brief second. When she spoke it was barely a whisper. "I slept with River."

"When? Where? Why didn't you tell us?"

"Just before school started, at that stupid keg party. I didn't tell y'all because . . . I felt stupid, especially when afterward he never called. I thought he cared about me. I thought maybe we might even be in love. But I was way wrong. So I'm probably not the best person to ask how you know when you're in love. Because what I felt for him was nothing like what you're describing for Lucas. And if Lucas feels the same way, then he would never hurt you like River hurt me."

The truth of Izzy's words hit Cassidy full on, along with indignation for what happened to her friend. Rage at River and her father and all the guys like them rose up in Cassidy like a hot geyser about to spew. "He's a total bastard. Wait till he comes home for Christmas break—I haven't given anyone a good ass-beating in months, and he sounds like he's next in line."

Izzy laughed, but it sounded rusty. "Thanks, Cass. You don't have to do that."

"It's not for you, it's for me," Cassidy assured her.

"I just have to learn to pick a better guy next time. Anyway, that's why I was acting so weird before you guys left. The whole stripping off my clothes and jumping into the pool, it was because of him."

"Why didn't you say something at the time? I always thought that if one of us . . . you know, lost *it*, we'd tell each other."

"I just didn't want to hash it out with the whole group. I mean, it wasn't at all what I thought it would be. I thought it would be intimate and make me feel important, make River really see me, but instead it made me even more invisible. The next day he went off to college and forgot all about me. Would you have told us?" She shook her head. "No. You wouldn't have admitted that to anyone."

"We love you, Iz. We would never judge you for something like that. We would have been first in line to hunt him down and bash in his Hummer. And if you want, I'll get Mei and Piper on the phone and we can go do it now."

"He drives an Escalade. But thanks for the thought. And I'm not quite ready to share this with the others yet, anyway. You won't tell them, will you?"

"Of course I won't."

They pulled into the driveway at Cassidy's house. Every light was on. "I guess my mom's home from work," she said. "Why don't you spend the night? We can stay up and watch crappy horror movies and sci-fi flicks that Piper always vetoes."

"Sure," Izzy said, "I'd like that." She smiled a little. "I've heard pretty good things about *Battlestar Galactica.* Can we give that a try?"

When they opened the front door, Cassidy's mom was waiting on the sofa in the living room, still in her hospital scrubs.

"Hey, Mom. Izzy's going to spend the night, okay?"

"Hi, Izzy. Great to see you again." Her mom's eyes pinned Cassidy. "Cassidy Michelle, is there something about your trip that you'd like to tell me?"

Cass froze, her mind racing. If her mother was using her middle name, something was wrong. Very, very wrong. International Kissing Club wrong.

"I don't think so." She sniffed. "Hey, what's that smell? Perfume?"

"Take a look in there," her mom said, nodding to the kitchen, "and then think a bit harder about the answer to my question."

Cassidy shot Izzy a WTF look. Izzy shrugged. Together they walked across the living room into the little yellow-painted kitchen and were greeted by a ginormous bouquet of white lilies sitting in the middle of the table.

Oh, crap. It was worse than she'd imagined.

"Wow, those are gorgeous. Are they for you, Cass?" Izzy asked.

"I guess so." She picked through the fragrant blooms to find the card. Not that she needed to—she knew perfectly well who they'd come from. This many flowers weren't in Mrs. Gatwick's budget, after all. Seriously, had he bought out every last white lily in the state?

See you in March, American Girl.

Holy crap. March? That was only . . . three months away.

She tried not to let her confusion show when she told Izzy, "They're from Lucas."

"Who's Lucas?" her mom asked from the doorway. Between the cloying scent of the bouquet and the condemnation radiating from her mother, she suddenly understood how people could be claustrophobic in a completely open room.

"Um, I think I should go, Cass," Izzy said, "I have things to do at home, anyway . . ."

"No, Izzy, please stay." Cassidy grabbed her arm like she was a lifeline. She *so* did not want to be alone with her mother for this conversation. "Lucas is a guy I met in Australia, Mom."

"A boy from your school?"

"No, not exactly. He picked me up at the airport." When she heard the actual words as they left her mouth, she cringed, knowing how her mother would take them. She didn't need to look to know that her mom's chin had almost hit the floor.

"A strange guy picked you up at the airport? My Lord, Cassidy, have you lost your mind? He could have been a serial killer for all you knew, or some pervert."

"No, Mom. Not like that. Mrs. Gatwick sent him. Lucas is sweet and fun and thoughtful, a perfect gentleman in every way." Her voice caught a little at the end as the dull ache in her chest throbbed with each inhalation of the lily-scented air.

"And you were dating him?" her mom asked.

"Yes."

"Then why didn't you say something?" Betrayal rang in her mom's voice. "Not once in the past two and a half months did his name come up when we talked. I thought we were close enough for you to tell me *anything*."

Cassidy chewed on her lip, upset that she'd hurt her mother again. She'd thought it was bad when she told her mom about getting the trip money from her dad, but the look on her mother's face said this was even worse. "I didn't want you to freak out, because it was no big deal." That was a lie. Even she could admit to herself that the reason she hadn't told her mom about Lucas was because it had been a big deal, bigger than she was ready to accept. And she could see her mom knew it, too.

"Hundreds of dollars' worth of flowers doesn't seem like no big deal," her mom said. " 'See you in March, American Girl' doesn't seem like no big deal."

"Oh my God. You read the note?" Cassidy couldn't believe her mom would do that. All her life, it had been just the two of them. The Barlows against the world. They were in it together, and their entire relationship was based on trust. Trust that had never been doubted. Of course, she'd never given her mother a reason not to trust her until this whole trip had come up and she'd called her dad. Still, it hurt. They'd never had a fight like this. "I thought you trusted me."

"You didn't answer my question."

"You didn't answer mine." They stared at each other for a minute, and from the look in her mom's eyes, Cassidy knew she wasn't going to win. But she couldn't let it go, because as she stood here talking to her mother, it really hit home how much Lucas *wasn't* like her father.

"Did you sleep with him, Cassidy?"

"Mom, no. I can't believe you would ask that."

"Well you must have been doing something with him, because a guy doesn't spend this much money on flowers for nothing."

She felt the words like a slap. "Stop it, Mom. He's rich. The money's not important to him."

"If he's got that much money, then why would you think you're important to him?"

"Why would you think I'm not? Because no one ever spent that kind of money on *you*?" Her mother's eyes widened in shock and

Cassidy knew she'd gone too far. She felt her throat close with tears she couldn't shed, at least not until she made her mother understand.

"Don't you think I haven't thought about that, Mom? Haven't you been telling me since the time I could walk that I should respect myself, not fall for the first guy that looked at me twice? Well, I listened. I listened so well that now I can't trust any guy. Not even one who acted like I was the most perfect girl in the world. A guy who would have done anything for me. I treated him like crap and ran away because I couldn't let myself believe what he was saying to me, that he loved me."

The tears ran hot and sticky on her cheeks now. As she swiped at them with the back of her hand, she was painfully aware of Izzy watching every second of her breakdown, but the tears wouldn't stop. She had hurt Lucas, and he'd done nothing, nothing but love her. Remembering the wounded look on his face the night she'd run away, and then the next morning at the airport—that she had caused it made the pain in her heart so much worse.

Then her mother began to cry too, making Cassidy feel even more horrible. "Oh, baby girl," she said, coming to wrap her arms around her. "You're so young. I just want you to make better choices than I did."

"I know that, Mom, but I'm not you. I won't make your mistakes. Whatever happened between Lucas and me, it wasn't a mistake."

"You're in love with him," her mother said. It was a statement, not a question.

Cassidy sighed heavily, exhausted by the whole argument. "I only knew him for ten weeks. That's not a long enough time to fall in love with someone, right?"

Her mom laughed, a sad, cynical little sound. "Honey, love doesn't follow a schedule—it just shows up, usually when you least want it to. Unfortunately, while there's nothing I know of to stop it, there's also definitely no mistaking it when it does happen." Her mom pulled away, kissed her on the cheek, and then, with a sigh, left the room.

"Are you okay?" Izzy asked, her comforting hand on Cassidy's arm.

"I don't know," she answered. She glanced at the little card she still held in her palm. See you in March. March!!!

Cassidy couldn't help the quick jump in her heartbeat when she reread the words. She woudn't let herself believe it—that after everything she'd done to him, he would still come all the way to Texas to see her. She was afraid to get her hopes up.

She didn't know what frightened her more, the idea that he might come. Or that he might not.

Chapter 27
Izzy

It was supposed to get better once her friends came home.

For ten weeks, she'd lived in solitary misery, so lonely she'd started hanging out with Germaine, for God's sake. Having Piper, Mei, and Cassidy back in Paris should have fixed all that. Instead, it was worse.

The fight they'd had the other day at Dairy Queen still hung in the air. They were all miserable, but no one seemed able to talk about it, least of all Izzy.

On one hand, she'd finally told someone the truth about River. That horrible weight had been pried off her shoulders. And better still, Cassidy hadn't leaped down her throat, ripped out her stomach, and used it to beat some sense into her. Which was pretty much what Izzy had expected Cassidy to do.

And how weird was that? Cassidy—the one who'd always relentlessly ragged on any girl stupid enough to have sex in high school, the one friend Izzy had been sure she could never tell—was the one she had told. Weirder still, Cassidy had been understanding—though she had called River's cell and left a message on his voice mail that could earn Cass fifty years to life if he ever disappeared under mysterious circumstances.

But even Cassidy's vivid description of River's mangled body parts couldn't ease the sick feeling in Izzy's stomach as they entered the yogurt shop to meet Mei and Piper. During homeroom earlier that day, she'd choked out an apology for her behavior at their reunion. Piper had accepted it stiffly. But some warning bell in the back of her mind told her that Piper wouldn't be as forgiving if she found out that Izzy had been sitting at Germaine's table during lunch.

Back when everyone was away, sitting with Germaine had seemed harmless. Now, things had changed. And it wasn't just because Piper was home, either. Izzy had kissed Tanner. Germaine's boyfriend.

Now that Tanner's lips weren't looming over hers, kissing Germaine's boyfriend seemed like a colossally bad idea. This was *Germaine*. The girl who'd once keyed the car of a new kid because he'd parked in "her" spot in the parking lot. She had a well-deserved reputation for being a mite territorial. Izzy guessed Germaine didn't yet know about the kiss, seeing as how Izzy was still walking around with all her limbs intact. She wanted to keep it that way. For as long as possible.

Preferably forever.

Which was also how long she hoped to keep the secret about eating with Germaine.

Her plan for keeping all of her secrets? Well, it was simple.

The way she saw it, there were three separate storm systems brewing on the horizon: Germaine, Piper, and Tanner. If all three came in contact with one another, it would be her own perfect storm. Surely in a town of twenty-five thousand people, in a school of almost one thousand kids, keeping Piper from seeing Germaine and Tanner couldn't be too hard. All she really needed to do was make it through the next week. Then Christmas break would start. If she could just keep her head down for five more days, she could hide in her bedroom and relish her sweet, sweet invisibility.

With that goal in mind, she convinced Piper, Cassidy, and Mei to leave school during lunch to eat at Yogurt Worxx. The four of them, all back together, back at the spot that had started it all, where they'd first decided to go international.

This was supposed to be a happy day, so why did they all look like the photos their history teacher had shown them of Texans during the

Great Depression? Except instead of ancient farming implements, they each held massive cups of yogurt. She knew why she and Cassidy were miserable. She just didn't know why everyone else was, unless her mood was catching. Sitting at Germaine's table choking down a steady diet of carrot sticks and criticism had been better than this.

Cassidy was still paying for her yogurt as Izzy approached the table where Mei and Piper already sat. In front of Mei was a tower of mint yogurt, mounded with an equally impressive serving of chocolate chips. The sensible Mei of the past would have gotten a dash of fat-free vanilla and added a topping just so the rest of them wouldn't tease her. Piper had served herself vanilla yogurt. Without a sprinkle in sight.

The tension in the group was too thick for their forced cheer to cut through. Izzy knew it was up to her to smooth things over, and the words were right there on her tongue, but her own misery kept them trapped in her mouth.

Izzy lowered herself into the chair opposite Piper and dug into her bowl of sour green apple drizzled with caramel. The taste of betrayal, she had decided. More tart than sweet.

She looked up and caught Piper's gaze, digging deep to muster a smile.

Piper gave a little nod, as if to say she too was willing to put the tension behind them. After a minute, she said, "You know what I missed about Paris the most? Besides y'all I mean."

Izzy piped up with an answer. "American cheese?"

Piper giggled. "Yeah, right."

Mei plucked a chocolate chip from her yogurt and popped it in her mouth. "Coffee that doesn't keep you up all night?"

Piper snorted in disgust. "Who needs that? I've been so spoiled by French coffee, I may have to take up drinking tea when I'm not at home."

"I know what I missed," Cassidy chimed in, sitting down at the table. "Real Texas guys. Guys who are tough, monosyllabic, and *don't* talk about their feelings."

"Guys who don't all smoke!" Piper added.

"Amen to that." Izzy shuddered in disgust.

Mei didn't have to give it much thought. "Food. And having only one person in the school who hates me." Then she asked, "Piper, you never said what you missed besides us."

Piper's gaze raked over them. She just shook her head as she smiled. "You know what? That was it. Just you guys. That's all I missed."

Izzy felt her guilt rise up to choke her. She was a bad friend. A bad, bad friend. She'd always thought Germaine was a turkey buzzard, but now she knew it was really her, picking over the remains of other people's relationships.

She'd betrayed Piper by befriending Germaine. She'd betrayed Germaine by kissing Tanner. What were her chances of making it to Christmas break without being smothered by her own regrets?

Piper dropped her spoon. "You know what we need?" Her tone was overly bright. "We need to go into Dallas this weekend. Do some Christmas shopping. Maybe meet some guys."

Resentment reared up to give Izzy's guilt a firm shove onto the back burner.

Piper needed more guys? Tanner wasn't enough? Sebastian wasn't enough? Half the guys in France weren't enough? Piper still needed more? Here she was feeling guilty about kissing Tanner, and Piper was planning to extend her kissing campaign to Dallas.

Izzy threw down her spoon and pushed back her chair. "Screw this. I need a burger."

She snatched the still-full yogurt cup off the table and dumped it in the trash on the way out. Even though there was a recycling bin just beside the garbage can. Five inches away.

"What the hell?" she heard all three of her friends squeal from behind her.

Izzy stopped outside the yogurt shop and surveyed the familiar stretch of Clarksville Street. The nearest hunk of charred cow flesh could be had about a hundred yards down the road at the Dairy

Queen. She set off at a brisk pace. She heard Mei, Piper, and Cassidy spill out onto the street behind her.

She wasn't entirely sure if all the exclamations of confusion were coming from them or from the voice of reason in her head. She didn't care.

Naturally, Cassidy caught up with Izzy first. She didn't try to stop her, just fell into step beside her. "Is this going to be another diving-into-the-pool incident?"

"Nope. This is just going to be an eating-a-burger incident. An I'm-tired-of-making-sacrifices-when-everyone-else-gets-to-do-whatever-they-want incident."

"Fair enough." Cassidy stepped forward and opened the door to the Dairy Queen for Izzy.

She marched up to the counter. Ryan, who had graduated from Paris High the year before, was manning the register. She tried to smile at him, but it felt like a snarl instead. "I want a double bacon cheeseburger."

Ryan stared at her blankly for a second, then asked in a nasally voice, "You mean the half-pound bacon Grillburger?"

"Whatever," she snapped. "And I want a side of those fried steak things."

"Those don't come as a side."

"Whatever," she repeated.

Ryan frowned. "So do you want the steak fingers or not?"

Cassidy leaned forward, speaking slowly—since Ryan was clearly an idiot. "Is there some sort of legal limit to how much beef one person can have?"

"Um . . . no," he stammered.

"Then place the order."

In that instant the door swung open and Piper and Mei came stumbling in.

"OMG," Piper screeched. "Is she really doing it? Is she really going to eat a burger?"

"She will if this idiot ever rings it up." Cassidy glared. Ryan started typing.

"A real burger?" Piper's eyes were huge with disbelief. "With beef in it? From an actual methane-spewing cow? Not some hippie, vegan burger made of spelt but an honest-to-God burger? That a real person, with actual taste buds, would want to eat?"

Izzy gritted her teeth and slammed her cash down on the counter. Then she spun to face Piper. "One time I made veggie burgers for you, one time, and you're still pissing about it a year later."

"*What* is wrong with you?" Piper asked, annoyance making her voice low and clipped.

"I just . . ." She blew out a breath. Trying—really trying—to find words to explain. It was really, really hard. "I just," she tried again, "had a hard time being alone. And . . ." Okay. Here it was. The horrible truth about her three IKC points. The points she never should have posted, won from the lips she never should have kissed. She swallowed again. "The thing is, I—"

But before she could force the words out of her mouth, the door to the Dairy Queen swung open and in marched Germaine.

She stopped dead just inside the doors. A bevy of minions followed in her wake, fanning out on either side of her like a league of pom-pom wielding supervillains. Her icy gaze swept over Izzy, and a disdainful sneer settled onto her face. There was something so cold, so dismissive about that look.

Oh, crap. Her desperate bid to keep the fronts separate hadn't worked. The perfect storm was about to make landfall.

Somehow Germaine had found out that she and Tanner had kissed. Germaine knew and she was going to make Izzy pay. Pay big.

Piper and Mei both swung around. Cassidy stepped forward so the three of them stood almost shoulder to shoulder. Only Izzy hung back, dread supergluing her feet to the floor.

"Well," Germaine sneered. "If it isn't Piper. Finally back from Paris."

Piper stiffened. "Don't bother making any pig jokes," she spat. "I think the World Wide Web is past that now."

Germaine arched one perfect eyebrow. "If you're referring to your little kissing club, you don't have to act so coy. We all know about it."

Cassidy took a step forward, but Piper spoke before she could act. "I bet it was really dull around here for you without me to torture. You probably missed us while we were gone. And there I was, off in the real Paris, shopping at designer boutiques and flirting with French guys so hot they make Texas boys look like, well, *pigs*."

For a moment, real annoyance flashed across Germaine's face, and she had to visibly swallow it back. "If you didn't miss us, then you sure went to a lot of trouble to make sure I knew about it."

Piper smirked. "You can't imagine how much sweeter it was being kissed by a hot guy at the foot of the real Eiffel Tower, knowing you were stuck here in *this* Paris. Why wouldn't we have wanted you to know?"

Germaine smiled in a way that sent shivers of dread down Izzy's spine. "It's not me you should be worried about. It's your parents. And the school staff. Don't you think they're going to be concerned when they realize you were kissing all those boys?"

"You wouldn't!" Izzy gasped.

Piper's jaw jutted out in defiance. "Oh, she can try. But I'd like to see her prove that we have anything to do with the IKC."

But in that moment, Izzy knew that Germaine would find a way. She would twist some computer geek around her little finger and get him to hack the page for her. Something. Izzy didn't know how she'd do it, but she would.

"Germaine, please . . . ," she began.

Germaine narrowed her gaze and spoke in that icy-cold voice. "You think I'm going to do you any favors after you kissed him?"

Mei gasped. Of course. The genius IQ would be the first to put it together.

Piper just looked confused. "Izzy, what is she talking about?"

"I'm talking about her three measly little points on the fan page for the International Who-Would-Have-Guessed-You-Could-Be-So-Skanky Club."

Piper looked from Izzy to Germaine and back again. "You kissed Tanner?"

"What, your plucky little sidekick didn't tell you she'd been poaching? Where do you think her three points came from? Tanner heard that she hadn't scored at all." Germaine's confidence may have wavered a moment ago, but she was back. The look she sent Izzy was equal parts pity and disdain. "I can't really blame him for feeling sorry for you. It is pretty pathetic that you couldn't find *anyone* in town to kiss."

Though time had slowed to a crawl for Izzy, it seemed to have stopped entirely for Piper, who was still staring, openmouthed, at Izzy. "You kissed Tanner and you didn't tell us? *He* was your points?"

Tears sprung up in Izzy's eyes. All she could do was shake her head. But she didn't know what she was denying or who she was crying for. Because if Germaine knew about that kiss, it could only be because Tanner had told her.

"You know what's really pathetic about you, Izzy? If you hadn't gone and kissed Tanner, then we could have stayed friends even after they came back. But you chose to earn points for your stupid little IKC page instead. I rescued you from Loserville. I let you eat lunch with us. And this is how you repay me?"

Izzy could hardly hear past her thundering heart. "I . . . I . . ."

Germaine rolled her eyes, feigning boredom with the conversation, despite her obvious glee. "I know he just felt sorry for you. But really," she slowed down to enunciate each word. "I. Don't. Share."

Then, surveying the wreckage, Germaine smiled, looking truly happy. And why wouldn't she? She'd destroyed them all. That pig stunt had only bound them closer together, but this? This would scatter them like the wind.

"Come on, ladies," she purred to her minions. "I've lost my appetite."

And with that, she spun on her heel and pranced out, leaving stunned silence in her wake.

Piper and Mei just stared at Izzy in horror. Cassidy—looking like she seriously wanted to kick some ass—kept glaring at the door through which Germaine the Hurricane had left.

Izzy couldn't meet anyone's gaze.

From behind her, Ryan said, "Um . . . Izzy, your burger's ready."

She turned around to see him holding out a tray, the burger, steak fingers, and fries wedged into red plastic baskets. Suddenly the scent of charred flesh hit her and her mouth filled with bile.

Shit.

This was proof. Karma was real. Nine-hundred million Hindus had it right: you shouldn't mess with cows. The burgers would bite back.

Chapter 28
Mei

After all the times something tiny had thrown Piper into hysterics, all the times she'd cried over a broken heel or a smudged painting, all the times the most innocent slight had her in tears, Mei would have thought that this betrayal would have sent Piper over the edge. Straight into we-need-a-tranq-gun-stat loonyville.

The fact that it hadn't made Mei very nervous.

After one agonizing moment of silence, in which Ryan kept trying to hand a tray of food to Izzy while Izzy actually turned green, Piper merely stalked to the exit in silence. Mei had to run to catch up to her.

At the door, Piper glanced back, her expression distant. Then she met Cassidy's eyes from across the room. For a second, doubt flickered across Piper's face. She waited. Mei's breath caught, but Cassidy didn't leave Izzy's side.

Then they were out the door, marching back down the road to Piper's car parked in the yogurt shop lot.

They'd just reached the Honda when Izzy called out from behind them. "Wait! Listen to me. It's not the way she made it sound."

Piper stilled beside Mei but rather than looking up, busied herself with digging through her purse for her keys. Mei turned around. Izzy lingered at the edge of the parking lot, hands clenched, skin still tinged with green. Cassidy stood just behind her.

That was the weirdest part of it all, seeing Cassidy hang back.

Cassidy, who jumped into the fray faster than any of them. Who'd been leaping to Piper's defense since kindergarten. Was Cassidy actually taking *Izzy's* side?

"Are you just *ignoring* me?" Izzy demanded.

Piper didn't say anything. And Mei couldn't. She and Izzy had always been close, but she couldn't side with her on this one. What she'd done was indefensible.

"So that's it? I don't exist to you anymore?" Still nothing from Piper as she dug through the bag. Izzy stalked a few steps closer. "You know, she said it would be like this." Piper stilled at Izzy's use of the word *she*. "That once someone gets on your bad side, you're done with them. No second chances with you, huh, Pipes?"

Piper swung around, her oversized purse whacking Mei in the hip. "*She* said that? That's what Germaine said about me? About *me*? The person she's tormented since the seventh grade? And you didn't just eat lunch with her, now you're taking friendship advice from her, too? What. The hell. Kind of friend. Are you?" Her purse slipped and she let it fall to the ground unnoticed as she stepped closer to Izzy. "At any point, when you were off making friendship bracelets with your new BFF, did it occur to you that she's my sworn enemy?"

"At any point, when you were off kissing half of Europe, did it occur to *you* that I was here. All alone. With no friends. At all."

"Okay. You were lonely. We get it. But how do you go from *that* to hanging out with Germaine?"

Izzy's jaw clenched noticeably, but then her chin bumped up. "Is this really about Germaine? Or are you just pissed off that Tanner kissed me? That after years of you mooning over him, he picked *me*?"

Piper looked baffled. "I can't believe you said that."

"What?" Izzy demanded. "You can't believe I called you on the fact that your crush on Tanner is stupid?"

Mei frowned, looking first at Izzy and then back to Piper. It was like they were having two completely different conversations, but neither of them realized it.

"You really think this is about Tanner? *This* is about *Germaine*. You betrayed our friendship," Piper shrieked. "What you did was wrong. Don't try to make this about me."

"Why not?" Izzy demanded. "Everything is *always* about you. Nothing ever happens to the three of us without you bringing it back around to you."

"I can't—" Piper broke off, clearly unable to finish the sentence.

In that instant, Mei saw it in Piper's expression. The line Izzy had crossed had just sprouted a forty-foot-high wall. Piper was done.

Piper shifted to look beyond Izzy to where Cassidy still stood. When she spoke, her words were stiff. Almost uncertain. "You coming?"

Cassidy—who hadn't even cried when she'd broken her foot in the fourth grade—looked ready to burst into tears. "I'm sorry, Pipes. Izzy needs me."

Mei was pretty sure Piper actually bit down on her tongue then. She could practically see the scream her friend was smothering. With jerky movements, Piper climbed into the car. Mei had to scramble to get in before she drove off.

Even though the school was only ten minutes away, Piper didn't make it. She pulled off the road and cut the engine, then dropped her face into her hands.

"Germaine? That's what she spent her ten weeks doing? Social climbing?"

Mei thought of how lonely Izzy's Facebook messages had sounded during the first few weeks of the trip. Piper had been so thrilled with Paris she hadn't noticed. But Mei—equally lost in China—certainly had. Then she'd met Guiran, her search for her parents had gotten under way, and she'd stopped chatting with Izzy as much.

"I don't think—" Mei began weakly.

Piper cut her off. "Of all the people she could have sat with, that's who she chose? She chose Germaine? Sit with band geeks or the stoners. Sit with the lunch ladies, for God's sake. But don't sit with

Germaine." Piper's words were pouring out in a white-hot rush and she couldn't seem to stop them. "I never . . . I never would have sided with Linc. I wouldn't have done that. And she . . ."

And then, she snapped her mouth closed. So tightly her lips started to turn white. She shook her head like she couldn't even go there. After a long minute, Piper drew in a few deep breaths and then asked, "And what's *wrong* with her that she thinks this is all about Tanner?"

Mei considered Piper's question, unsure how to answer. There was an ocean of things that needed to be said about Izzy's schizophrenic befriending of Germaine. She thought about the messages Izzy had sent her a few weeks ago, questioning Germaine's role in the split back in seventh grade. Obviously, more had gone on between Izzy and Piper's enemy than Izzy had let on. Mei had a hard time believing that Germaine hadn't somehow manipulated Izzy, but even if she had, Piper wasn't ready to hear justifications.

"I don't know what to tell you," she finally said, being as honest as she could. "Izzy was wrong. She shouldn't have done it. No matter how lonely she was."

Piper drew in a breath and Mei could hear the shudder of tears she hadn't yet cried. "I wanted us to have the best adventure ever. I never dreamed how it would mess everything up once we got back."

Watching Piper racked by sorrow, Mei felt like crying herself. Even if Germaine had taken advantage of her, Izzy was still in the wrong. You didn't throw in with the person who had destroyed your best friend's life—no matter how much your own life sucked. She'd been pretty lonely in China, but she hadn't started texting Germaine.

Mei reached out a hand and rested it on top of Piper's trembling head. Suddenly she thought of her memory from the SWI. Of that little baby girl she'd known. The infant friend she'd left behind when her parents had adopted her.

Through whatever stroke of luck, Mei had been picked. She'd been given a home. A family. Parents who loved her no matter what.

But she'd had to leave behind her companion to get it. At two, the choice hadn't been hers. Now it was.

She wouldn't leave her friend. As long as Piper needed her, she was staying right here.

Chapter 29
Piper

Piper and her friends sat in homeroom Tuesday morning, waiting for the announcements. Normally the girls would be chatting and giggling about any number of things, but today they could barely look at one another. Mei had slid into Cassidy's usual spot, right behind Piper, while Cassidy was sitting two rows away, next to Izzy.

It was the first time she and Cassidy hadn't sat near each other in class since kindergarten, the first time the four of them hadn't sat together since Izzy joined their group, and Piper hated every second of it.

She felt sick, like a huge weight was pressing down on her chest and stopping her from breathing. She wanted to rush across the aisle, to throw her arms around Izzy and forget everything, but she couldn't. Not when Izzy had hurt her so much. And not when Izzy almost seemed to hate her.

And Germaine. How could Izzy possibly have become friends with Germaine? It was insane, mind-boggling, so horrible she could barely comprehend it.

Just then the TV in the front of the room spewed to life. Normally no one in class paid much attention to the daily news and announcements program run by the video-editing class—this was Paris, Texas, after all. It wasn't like anything major ever happened here. And when it did, everyone knew what was going on long before the daily announcements got around to talking about it.

But today, everyone was watching with rapt attention, and when Piper glanced up at the screen, she knew why. Germaine was on TV. She was dressed like a Dallas news anchor in a pale pink sweater set and pearl earrings, her hair curled, coiffed, and sprayed within an inch of its life. The look on her face was positively angelic.

Piper's stomach tightened. Germaine only looked that sweet when she was doing something incredibly awful. She flashed back to the scene at Dairy Queen, to Germaine's promise that everyone would know what they'd done, and felt the entire world collapse around her as she turned to Mei, who was staring at her with a look of horror Piper knew was echoed on her own face.

"Good morning, Wildcats. Today we have a special program for you," said Marc Bradley, the senior in charge of the show. "A story sure to have you thinking twice before you kiss and tell."

"Oh, shit," she heard Cassidy mutter.

Mei's hand reached out and clutched hers so tightly that Piper feared she might never regain circulation in her fingers. Not that she could complain—she had a feeling, after this, she wouldn't need her mouse hand, anyway.

"Welcome, Germaine. It's great to have you here today."

"Thank you for having me, Marc. You've always been my favorite announcer." Germaine fluttered her eyes.

"Is that a purity ring on her hand?" Mei whispered in Piper's ear.

"Of course it is. Because, really, what else would Germaine the— what's a word that rhymes with Germaine and means *whore*—wear when she's in front of the entire school?" And since Marc was usually a pretty decent guy, Piper couldn't help wondering what Germaine had promised him in exchange for the time to do her little exposé. Something that would make a complete and total mockery of said purity ring on her finger, no doubt.

"Sssssh," hissed Mr. Johnson from the front of the room, where he sat grading papers, oblivious to the horror unfolding on the screen before them. "Quiet, girls."

Right. Of course. Because God forbid they didn't sit silently by and wait for their total and complete annihilation.

Piper thought about gathering her things and trying to slip out the back of the classroom—she really didn't want to see this—but at the same time, it was like she was glued to her seat. She couldn't move.

"Fellow students," Germaine began, "I'm here today to remind you of the dangers of the Internet and how the things you post online can and *will* come back to haunt you for the rest of your life." A feral glint twinkled in Germaine's cold eyes while she looked straight at the camera, as if she were speaking directly to Piper. Which, of course, she was.

"We at Paris High have been made all too aware that what's put on social media websites like YouTube and Facebook can take on a life of its own." A video clip of that horrible pig attacking Piper ran in full, see-every-hair-on-its-snout HD. Piper clamped her eyes shut and willed God to take her now before this got any worse.

"Because we can't control what happens to information once it's posted online," Germaine continued, "teens must be especially vigilant about maintaining an online presence marked by maturity and, above all, dignity." Then her smile took on an even more predatory slant as she said, "Take this Facebook page as a poor example of both."

The screen cut to the International Kissing Club Facebook page—and the silly rules they'd come up with weeks ago at the mall—in every perfect pixel of detail.

"Oh. My. God." Mei leaned closer to the TV for a second, then whipped her phone out of her back pocket. A few seconds later her head hit the desk with a bang.

"What?" Piper whispered out of the corner of her mouth.

"This is streaming. She hacked into the IKC page," Mei said furiously, passing her phone over to Piper. "The video is posted on our page—and on the Kiss the Pig page."

Piper watched with disbelieving eyes as the same video played in the middle of the IKC page. "Just shoot me now."

Everything was on display: their avatars, their posts, pictures they'd taken on their trips, pictures of the boys, their point totals. Germaine continued talking in the background and Piper could hear the absolute glee in her voice as she spoke. "Perhaps the four founders of this page—this so-called International Kissing Club—*thought* what they were doing was all in good fun, and that they were being cleverly anonymous when they used what was supposed to be an *academic* foreign exchange program as a front for kissing boys—not to mention the other sexcapades hinted at in these posts—all across the globe." The camera zoomed in on one of the racier entries on the page. "But what they forgot was that on the Internet, nothing is ever truly anonymous."

Then, before all eight of their incredulous eyes (though at this point, Piper didn't know why anything should shock her anymore), graphics of Cassidy's, Izzy's, Mei's, and Piper's yearbook pictures tumbled across the screen until each interlocked like a puzzle piece with graphics of their respective Disney character avatars. And for the coup de grâce, their kissing point totals flashed above each one.

Suddenly, a strangled scream came from the counseling center across the hall. Seconds later, the class watched Ms. Vogel run out of the open doorway and down the hall as fast as her four-inch heels could carry her. Apparently, Vogel was the only adult on campus who actually watched the school news program.

Back on screen, Germaine looked triumphantly at the camera. "After all, you never know who may be watching—your classmates, your teachers, college admission boards, even future employers. The best rule of thumb for teens' online activities is that if you wouldn't want your parents to see it, don't post it."

And it was done. In less than three minutes, Germaine had accomplished what she'd been unable to until now—Piper's complete ruin.

The camera swiveled back to Marc. "Thank you, Germaine, for that remind—" His last words were cut off as the screen went blue.

Mei closed her eyes. "Do you think anyone at MIT will see it?"

"I think the entire world is going to see it before this is over," Piper answered. They were so totally and completely screwed that she couldn't pretend otherwise, even to save her best friend's sanity. And she'd thought the Kiss the Pig debacle was bad.

Piper felt every eye in the classroom on her and her friends. She slumped down in her chair, watched from the corner of her eye as Cassidy did the same. Izzy buried her head in her hands and Mei, Mei didn't move a muscle, unless you counted the fine trembling that was shaking her entire body.

Of course it was Jackson Grosbeck who broke the deafening silence. "Whoooooa, Piper," he said, leaning over in his chair until he was practically on top of Piper's desk. "I didn't know you had it in you. What kind of international sexcapades are you into?"

The entire class cracked up, and the jocks in the back of the room started catcalling and whistling as loudly as they could. Mr. Johnson looked up for the first time, tried to quiet them down, but there was no maintaining order right now. Similar noises were floating down the hall from other classrooms.

And suddenly, Piper had had enough. Enough of Germaine, enough of Paris High School, and more than enough of Jackson Grosbeck and his perverted questions. Pulling her chemistry book out of her backpack, she hurled it straight at his smug, ugly face. It felt good. Maybe Cassidy had the right idea when she led with her fists.

Jackson squealed like a pig and, for the first time in six months, the sound wasn't directed at her. As blood gushed from his nose, Piper tried to work up some concern, but she couldn't. Once again, she was numb. Besides, suspension or not, she was tired of putting up with his crap. What was one more rule broken? At this point, she couldn't help wondering if the principal had any two-for-one punishments going on.

Mr. Johnson shot out of his chair and stormed down the aisle toward her. "Piper, you—" At that moment, Principal Callahan's voice came over the PA. "I'd like to see the following students in my office: Cassidy

Barlow, Mei Jones, Izzy O'Reilly, and Piper Douglas." His intonation was particularly grim when he said her name.

Mr. Johnson froze a few steps away from her desk, scribbling frantically on a referral form. "Take this with you when you go, Ms. Douglas," he said, and his voice was so dark, his look so dire, that Piper figured she would have been afraid if she'd been able to feel anything at all.

She gathered up her things—minus her chemistry book—and then took the referral from his hand. As she walked out the door with Mei, Cass, and Izzy at her heels, all of whom looked like the world had just ended, she couldn't resist asking, "So, Iz, what do you think of your new BFF now?"

· · · · · ·✈

An hour later, the numbness still hadn't worn off. Which was probably a good thing as she was stuck in the backseat with Savannah as her parents drove home in stony silence. How perverse was it that she was almost disappointed they weren't shouting at her? She would so rather get it over with now, before the feelings she was holding at bay suddenly came crashing down on her.

"Can we stop by the pharmacy, Tom?" her mother asked. "I need a refill on my pills."

"Let me get you home, Cathy. Then I'll go back out." The look he shot Piper over the seat was completely inscrutable.

"I'll take care of her, Daddy," Savannah said with a glare of her own directed at Piper. "I won't let Piper upset her anymore."

"I can't believe—" Her mom's voice broke. "I just can't believe you did this to me. Again."

Piper knew she should keep her mouth shut, knew that things would go so much more smoothly if she did. But throwing that book at Jackson had unleashed something inside of her and she couldn't keep silent. Not now. Not this time.

"I didn't do it *to* you, Mom. I did it *for* me. We all did—"

"And what exactly is it that you did?" her father demanded. "Because what it looks like to me is that I just spent six thousand dollars for you to go on a European sex fest." He choked on the last words.

"It wasn't like that. I swear!"

"Well, what exactly was it like, Piper?" demanded her mother at close to a screech. "Because I think you've totally and completely lost your mind! Did you even think about disease or pregnancy or—oh my God." Her mother banged her head against the headrest. "Are you pregnant? Are you going to have some Frenchman's *baby*?"

"No! Of course not, Mom!" The numbness wore off in a hurry and she felt tears pressing behind her eyes. She blinked them back. Germaine wasn't going to make her cry. Not now and not ever again. "I didn't sleep with anyone. I swear. I just kissed a few guys. It was no big deal."

"No big deal?" her father demanded. "No big deal? They're scheduling a school board meeting to deal with this. And at the rate things are going, by nightfall you'll be plastered all over the Internet as a cautionary tale for American parents! That is a huge deal!"

"I have to cancel bridge this week. And my hair appointment. Lunch at the country club. There's no way I can face anyone after this. What will I say?"

Piper stared at the back of her mother's head in abject shock. Why she was surprised, she didn't know, but she was. Even now, in the worst moment of Piper's life, her mother was somehow making it all about her.

Even Piper's father seemed confused as he looked at his wife like she was from another planet. Silence filled the car until he finally pulled into the driveway and said, "Come on, Cathy. Let's get you into bed. Everything will look better after you take a nap." He got out of the car, then walked around and opened his wife's door and helped her out.

"How will it look better? She's a menace. I swear, she does this just to humiliate me. I can't do it anymore. I can't live like this." Piper's mom let her dad lead her upstairs. "I need a drink."

After he got her mother settled in bed, her dad returned to the living room, where Piper had collapsed on the sofa. He looked confused and angry and helpless, exactly like she was feeling. "She's upset, Piper. She doesn't know what she's saying."

"She knows exactly what she's saying." Piper used the back of her hand to dash away the tears she hadn't been able to stop. "She's always been disappointed in me. But then the feeling is completely mutual."

He started to say something else, then stopped. Rubbed a hand down the back of his neck. "It'll be okay, Piper." He crossed the room, pulled her into his arms for a hug. "We'll fix this."

"How?" she asked, wrapping her arms around him and clinging tightly. Even as she did it, she figured her dad was horrified—he was not big on displays of affection—but she couldn't seem to stop herself. It felt like the whole world was collapsing around her.

"I don't know yet." He brushed a quick kiss on the top of her head. "But the important thing is that you tell us the truth. If you did do what Germaine said you did, we'll deal with it. It's done, over. But you need to be tested for STDs and pregnancy and—"

"I didn't sleep with anyone, Dad. I swear!" Piper wanted to die. Wanted to burrow under the couch and just will her heart to stop beating.

"Okay, then." He pulled away, still looking as miserable as she felt. "Then the rest of this, it's just a tempest in a teapot. It'll blow over eventually."

"What am I supposed to do until then?"

"Tom!" Her mother screamed from down the hall. "I need you! I need—"

"Coming, Cathy," he called, then looked at Piper helplessly.

"Go," she said. "It's not like I won't be here when you're done. I'm never leaving the house again."

"That might be a good idea—for a few days, anyway." He reached into her bag and pulled out her laptop. "You should probably keep this off for a while, too."

Piper nodded, but the second he headed down the hall, she pulled out her iPhone and went straight to the IKC Facebook page. If her humiliation had gone global once again, this time she was prepared to meet it head-on.

But to her surprise, all the posts on the page were positive. LaTonya had called Germaine a series of ugly names. Even Jayson had gotten in on the act, telling Piper how proud he was of her for standing her ground and not letting the Kiss the Pig debacle get her down.

As she read the comments, Piper started to feel a little better—at least until she remembered that Germaine had managed to split her and her best friends up forever. It was really nice to get all this support from the Facebook friends she'd made over the past few months. She only wished her real friends felt the same.

Chapter 30
Cassidy

All four of the girls had been commanded to appear in the school's conference room first thing Wednesday morning.

Thank God she'd already told her mother the whole thing about Lucas. Yeah, she was still pissed that she hadn't known about the International Kissing Club, but it could have gone worse for Cass if her mom had found out about everything because of Germaine. A lot worse.

Piper hadn't shown up, though. In fact, Cassidy didn't know if Piper would ever come back to school after this. Not that Cass knew what Piper was doing, since they still weren't speaking. She'd called and called but Piper wouldn't answer. She hated feeling so helpless when she knew Piper needed her more than she had at any other time in their friendship.

Mei, Izzy, and Cass waited in silence for Ms. Vogel to show up. Mei hadn't said a word to either of them, still obviously pissed because she thought Cassidy had taken Izzy's side against Piper.

This was so far beyond bad—actually, bad would be a major improvement. This was catastrophic. If Germaine were ever again within arm's reach, Cassidy might very well end her. A little holy water and a wooden stake was all she'd need.

The principal and Ms. Vogel finally stepped into the room.

"Girls, I'm sure you're aware of why you were called here this morning," Mr. Callahan said. "Besides the poor judgment you have shown in coming up with this *ridiculous* club, that Ms. Vogel was made an unwitting bystander as the arranger of your international exchange trips is a personal disappointment to me. Your parents are waiting to speak with me and the school board to discuss how we are going to handle this. Is there anything you want to add before that happens?"

"I do," Cassidy said, unable to keep her mouth shut for one second longer. "Why isn't Germaine in here with us? She hijacked the school announcement program and tattled like a two-year-old, but that's cool. We did something I don't even think is against the rules, on our own time, and nowhere near this school, and we're going to have to face the board?"

"I'll be dealing with disciplining Germaine and Marc. And you shouldn't be telling me how to do my job—right now, you need to worry about yourself."

Cassidy bit her tongue to keep from telling him off. Before this mess, nobody at school had stepped in to stop what was happening to Piper other than a cursory slap on the hand for Jackson Grosbeck. This wasn't about anybody else but Germaine and her personal vendetta against them. Why no one could see that and do something to stop her was beyond Cassidy's comprehension.

When no one else said anything, Mr. Callahan left and Ms. Vogel spoke to them. "Girls, this room is a safe place, so what you say in here will remain just between us. But first I want to say that you really let me down. You took advantage of my desire to see you girls expand your horizons, and it will take some time for me to get over that." Leave it to someone like Vogel to make this all about her.

Izzy spoke first. "What's going to happen to us?" she said, sounding on the verge of tears.

"Well, since none of this actually took place on school grounds," Ms. Vogel said, "the recommendation will be for all of you and your parents to attend family counseling."

Great. That's just what Cassidy wanted to do—talk about her feelings with a perfect stranger.

Mei jumped in. "Ms. Vogel, it was never our intention to deceive you. I'm sorry for that, but can we have a few minutes of privacy to talk to each other, please?"

Vogel didn't look like she wanted to leave them alone, like they were juvenile delinquents who might even now be plotting a bigger scheme to embarrass her. But grudgingly, she walked to the door. "Only for a few minutes."

As soon as the door closed behind her, Mei pounced on both of them. "What are we going to do?"

"I didn't mean for any of this to happen, I swear. None of it." Izzy's eyes were wide and completely earnest, her voice panicked.

"Why should we believe you, Izzy?" Mei demanded. "You got cozy with the girl who has spent the past four years plotting to destroy Piper's life."

Izzy was speechless, so Cassidy stepped in. "Okay, Mei, let's calm down. This is so past who did what to whom at this point. And besides, we all agreed not only to create the Facebook page, but to make it public, so we're all partly to blame for this." She took a deep breath. "How *is* Piper doing? She won't take my calls."

"How do you *think* she is? Devastation doesn't begin to cover it. Her mother's pretty much catatonic at this point too, and that's just making everything worse."

"What can I do?" Izzy asked them both, misery making her voice deep and husky. "Germaine's pissed at me for the whole thing with Tanner and she took it out on Piper."

"You have to find some way to make this right, Isabel," Mei said.

"Don't you get it, Mei? I don't think I can. I screwed up. Big-time. I wouldn't forgive me, so why should Piper?"

"Because we love each other, Izzy. All of us," Cassidy said. "Look, we don't get to pick our families, but we do get to choose our friends. And the four of us, we chose each other. We did this together, and now we've all got to see it through to the horrible end. You, me, Mei, and Piper. 'Cause that's what you do when you love someone—you stick it out even when it's hard. You don't run away when you get scared. If there's one thing I've learned, it's that. And friends forgive each other. Piper will. Maybe not at first, but she will."

Cassidy looked at her two friends in the room and thought of the one who was missing. Three months ago she would have thought nothing could tear them apart. Now, if they didn't do something fast, they might never be back together.

The door reopened before she could say anything else and Ms. Vogel stepped back inside. "Girls, the school board has decided that an all-school assembly will be held on Friday to discuss Internet safety. It is required that you be present."

Suddenly, Mei's mother swept into the room, Callahan close on her heels. "The school board's involved in this? Why?"

Callahan looked at her incredulously. "Well, uh, given the uh, contents of the page and the underage, umm, promiscuity and—"

"I'm sorry." Mrs. Jones's voice took on the tone she probably used in her gender-studies lectures. "Can you explain to me what they did that was so wrong?"

Cassidy's mind boggled, and as she looked at Izzy and Mei, she realized they were right there with her. Mei's eyes were popping out of her head and Izzy looked flabbergasted.

Only Callahan looked more stunned. "But the kissing and the boys and the Internet—"

"Yes," Mrs. Jones said, "they kissed boys. Good for them. I'm glad they did it. I would much rather my daughter kiss a lot of frogs before she decided some North Texas toad was her prince. Of all the other trouble they could have gotten into, I can't believe we're even having a conversation about this."

Callahan tripped over his tongue a few more times, his face turning redder by the second, but in the end he couldn't stand up to Mrs. Jones's cool logic. And as Mei's mom escorted them out of the conference room a few minutes later, Cassidy decided right then that if she ever got that basketball scholarship, she was majoring in feminist studies.

· · · · · ·✈

Cassidy knocked on the bedroom door. "Piper, it's me. Please let me in."

"Go away," came the low, sad voice from the other side.

"Piper, come on. I want to talk to you." No response. This was not good. But she wasn't going to let Piper stay in her room and brood forever. "If you don't unlock this door, I'll just get a screwdriver and take it off the hinges. You know I will."

At last she heard footsteps patter across the floor. "Are you alone, or is Benedict Arnold with you, too?"

"It's only me, Pipes." *Click.* Cassidy opened the door and peeked inside. The curtains were pulled tightly closed and the lights were all off except the glow of Piper's laptop on the nightstand, making the bright pink walls of her bedroom look like a Hello Kitty tomb. Piper climbed back beneath the lump of blankets on the bed. Cassidy walked over and sat on the edge, looking at Piper's puffy, splotchy face.

"Have you been to school?" Piper asked her.

"Yeah, we went today to meet with Vogel and Callahan. You should have been there. Mei's mom kicked Callahan's ass." She deliberately refrained from mentioning Izzy by name just yet. *Better to ease into this*, she thought. Cassidy didn't want to spook the gazelle.

"I know. My dad told me about the assembly."

"Are you going?"

Piper shook her head. "I don't plan to ever set foot in that school again." She nodded toward her laptop. "I'm researching boarding schools in New England. And I've looked into getting my GED and going away to college early, instead."

"Your parents would let you do that?"

"Are you kidding? My mother would walk me to Vermont in her

Louboutins if it meant she didn't have to look at me for the next two years."

"It'll be okay, Pipes."

"I don't know about that. What did your mom say when she found out?"

"Well, she's not pleased, but she's not going to send me to boarding school, either. On a different note, my dad called and thinks I should start spending more time with him—you know, have a greater paternal presence in my life." Of course, it was a little late in coming, but Cassidy wasn't going to turn it down, either. Getting to know her dad was something she'd always wanted.

"Well, at least that's one good thing to come out of this," Piper said.

"You can't run away this time, Piper. Believe me, I wish we all could, but unless you plan to leave Paris permanently, there's not much you can do."

"No, Germaine and my ex–best friend, Izzy, have made sure of that. Before this I was only an online joke, but now I'm an after-school special. My only hope is that they don't hire Lindsay Lohan to play me in the movie." Ah, now this was the Piper that Cassidy knew and loved—the drama queen. Things just might work out, after all.

"No, she can play your mom," Cassidy told her. They both laughed. Cassidy took the opportunity of her somewhat lightened mood to talk about Izzy.

"Piper, Izzy feels really horrible about what happened."

Piper's eyes narrowed. "Are you taking her side about this too, Cass?"

"I'm not taking anybody's side. I'm always going to be your friend. I've stuck with you this long, haven't I? I just felt like she needed me more at that moment. I can't say very much because it's not my place, but you don't know the whole story about Izzy right now. I'm not saying that what she did was right—far from it. But she had her reasons. She wants to talk to you, Piper. Maybe you should give her a chance to explain."

"No. She hung out with Germaine. She made friends with Germaine, even knowing everything the Wicked Witch of the West has done to me. How am I supposed to just forget that?"

"Deep down, I think you know that Izzy would never want to hurt you. Germaine is a manipulator and she played on Izzy's loneliness while we were gone. Think about it, Piper—Iz was just as involved in setting up and participating in the IKC as we all were. She's been hurt by this as well. Don't give up on her. She loves you."

Piper looked like she was considering what Cassidy had said and Cass hoped maybe she'd gotten to her a little, at least enough to plant the seeds for a future reconciliation.

"Are we okay, Piper? You know I have your back, right? Always."

Piper nodded. "I know you do. And I'm sorry you got dragged into Germaine's campaign for Bitch of the Year."

"The year? I think she's going for Lifetime Achievement." They both giggled. "It's going to be all right, Piper. I don't know how, and I don't know when, but it will be. I promise."

Chapter 31
Izzy

Damn it. Cassidy and Mei were right. She had crossed a line. Kissing Tanner was bad enough, but in everyone's eyes, the real betrayal had been letting Germaine manipulate her. For years, Izzy had sat on the bench, watching Germaine torment one of her best friends. She'd had front-row seats to the spectacle, so she should have known better. Instead, she'd let that witch drag her down into the mud.

God, it sucked being the one to screw up.

All she knew was that she wasn't going to make the same mistakes Germaine had when she'd separated herself from them all those years ago. She wasn't going to let one argument drive her away from her friends. She wasn't going to cling to pride and her own sense of self-importance. Whatever it took, she was going to make this right with Piper.

On the bright side, she finally knew how to do it. That girl loved nothing like she loved drama. And Izzy hadn't spent the past five years watching chick flicks without learning a thing or two about grand gestures.

That afternoon, the second school let out, she raced to the parking lot and waited by Jackson Grosbeck's aging Camaro. Cherry red—naturally—with black racing strips, the car wasn't new enough to be cool or old enough to be classic—it was the perfect vehicle for a douche like Jackson. She recognized it because it was practically a permanent fixture in front of her own house.

When Jackson saw her waiting for him, his face split in a cocky grin. "Hey, Izzy," he said as he swaggered over. *"¿Como esta?"*

Then he shot a tobacco-stained loogey onto the ground near her feet. Oh, yuck. This had better work.

"Hi, Jackson." She tried to swallow back her natural disgust. "I need a favor."

"Anything for you, baby." He stepped over the loogey and edged in on her. "You lookin' to earn some points?"

Points? Boy, he thought a lot of himself. If she had to kiss him, the rest of IKC would probably *subtract* points. And she so couldn't afford to go negative.

She backed up a step. A big step.

"You're the one who . . . um, acquired the pig Piper kissed, right?"

"Yeah." He frowned, his pea-sized brain working overtime. "Hey, I heard you and Piper had some big catfight. You want to make her kiss another pig? 'Cause I was thinking, you might mix it up. Like, make it a goat next time."

"Yeah. Right. You're a real evil genius," she deadpanned. He actually smiled at her, clearly too obtuse to recognize sarcasm. "But I need a pig. The biggest, ugliest pig you can find."

"What about a chicken?" he asked.

"No, not a chicken." Jeez. Couldn't people get bird flu from kissing chickens? "I'm not doing a stage version of Old McDonald. All I need is a pig. Can you get me one or not?"

He looked disappointed for a moment, then he leered at her. "What are you going to do for me in exchange?"

Ugh. Could he be more transparent?

Thank God she'd anticipated his skeeziness and had a response ready.

She smiled sweetly. "For starters, I *won't* tell my dad you asked me to *chupa tu verga.*"

Jackson stared blankly at her for a second, no doubt entranced by a female actually taking about his . . . um, endowments, but then her words sank in and he frowned. "Come on." He gestured toward his car with a surly nod. "I'll take you there."

A few minutes later, they pulled up in front of a decrepit ranch house a few blocks from Cassidy's. They crossed the overgrown lawn to the front porch, where a couple of aluminum lawn chairs sat. The screen door had fallen off and was propped against the siding. If Jackson had brought her to some sort of crack den to sell her into slavery, she was going to beat him to death with a folding chair.

She rang the bell, and a moment later Tanner opened the door. *Holy crap.*

"Isabel?" He looked about as surprised to see her as she was to see him. "What are you doing here?"

"You live here?" The question just popped out of her mouth.

"Yeah," he said, like he was stating the obvious. "Why?" Only then did he notice Jackson standing behind her. "What—"

"Hey, she made me bring her," Jackson hurriedly explained. "She wants a pig."

"A pig?" Tanner asked.

"*The* pig?" Izzy demanded at the same time. "Wait! *You're* the guy who got the pig that kissed Piper?"

"Hey, I'm outta here," Jackson interrupted. "He's the guy. Izzy, are we good? You're not gonna tell your dad?"

"Yeah, whatever," she muttered to him. A bigger fish had just landed in her frying pan. "*You're* the guy who got that first pig?" she asked again, her voice escalating.

Tanner crossed his arms over his chest defensively, then scrubbed a hand across his chin. "Yeah. I'm the guy. But I didn't know what Jackson was going to do with it, I swear. He said he just thought it would be funny to have a pig at the festival. He paid me two hundred bucks to do it, and I needed parts for my truck. I swear to God I didn't know what he had planned."

Izzy swallowed a lump in her throat. She looked at this sad little house, so worn down and miserable. She thought of the farm that Tanner's parents had spent their lives building. The land out there was beautiful, even if the house wasn't in much better shape than this one. It made her sad that Tanner had to live here, away from his parents, just so he could play football for her dad and maybe get a decent scholarship. Suddenly the ten bucks an hour his parents had paid her seemed like too much.

Tanner looked like he wanted to say something else, but she held up a hand to stop him. "Look, I believe you."

He might be a jerk who would kiss one girl while dating another—and she wasn't even going to get started on the injustice of *that* double standard—but there was a sort of chivalry to him. He wasn't a guy who would purposely belittle a girl. Charm her pants off and crush her heart without blinking an eye, yes. Humiliate, no.

But then, this was the kind of thinking that had gotten her into so much trouble to begin with. She'd let herself get taken in by him. She'd imagined they were friends. And for a second, when he'd kissed her in that needy, hungry way, she'd imagined more.

But Tanner Colt wasn't just some aw-shucks, down-on-his-luck cowboy. He was a star football player with more moves than the square dance at the Cotton Festival. Tanner was as deadly to females as the gun that bore his surname.

He may never have intended for Piper to face Internet humiliation, but that didn't let him off the hook for kissing *her*. And then telling Germaine. And he'd had the gall to call River a douche.

Really, between the two of them, Izzy was pretty sure she had the worst taste in guys. Ever.

"Can you get me the pig or not?" she demanded, so ready for this conversation to be over.

Tanner seemed reluctant. How much had he said Jackson had paid to get the pig? Two hundred bucks. She'd socked away at least that much while working for Tanner's parents, right? Good-bye, college fund.

"I can pay you the two hundred," she added as additional entice-ment. "Just like Jackson."

God, she hoped those were words she never had to say again. *Just like Jackson.* What a bone-chilling thought.

"It's not the money." Tanner shook his head, like he didn't know how to phrase what he was going to say. "I feel bad enough about what happened last time. So, I don't want to be a part of it if you're trying to get back at somebody. You're better than that anyway, Isabel."

Shock rocked her back on her heels. "Jesus!" she all but shouted when she got her voice back. "That's not why I want the pig! I'm not Germaine." She sucked in a deep breath. "Which we both already know, or my boobs would be pushed up to here"—she jabbed at her chin—"and my panties would be discarded in the back of your truck." For a second, she wondered if she'd gone too far. Then another shot of resentment spiked through her and she decided she hadn't gone far enough. "On second thought, I can see why you might be confused, since your tongue has been in both our mouths in the past two weeks."

Yikes. Who knew all that repressed anger would sound so nasty when it spewed all over someone?

He seemed as shocked by her words as she was. The second they left her mouth, she felt a flush of embarrassment. She should not have brought that up.

Forgetting momentarily that Jackson had driven her, she spun on her heel and headed back down the front path. "Never mind. I'll find another pig."

Tanner shot off the porch and caught up with her before she'd taken more than a few steps. He wrapped one hand around her arm and pulled her to a stop. He might as well have tackled her, it was that effective. His hand on her bare skin charged every cell in her body.

She'd always thought of herself as being on the scrawny side, but after spending the fall driving a tractor and wielding a hoe, she'd actually developed a few muscles in her biceps. Yet, Tanner's hand was still so large his fingers met on the underside of her arm.

"Is that what this is about? This pig has something to do with the fact that I kissed you?"

He didn't release her arm as he spoke, and it took all her concentration not to look back down at his hand. But, oh, she was totally aware of it there. For the life of her, she couldn't make herself tear her arm out of his grasp.

"Yes, that's part of it. Piper's one of my best friends. And I kissed the guy she's liked for years. I betrayed her."

Tanner took one step closer to her. His voice dropped a notch. "But *I* kissed *you*."

Izzy sucked in a breath at the intensity of his gaze.

"Isabel, you have no idea how long I've wanted . . ." He broke off and scrubbed a hand over his face. "Piper isn't the one I've had a thing for."

What was he implying?

No! She wasn't going to let herself get caught up in this sick little fantasy he kept dangling in front of her. She forced herself to yank her arm out of his reach.

"Yeah, I get that." She'd wanted to sound breezy and cool, but instead, weeks of angst fueled the words. "Germaine is the only girl for you. You've made that abundantly clear."

"Is that what you think? That I'm in love with *Germaine*?"

"We've already had this conversation and you're still with her. Obviously there's something there."

"I told you. I was with her because that's what everyone expected and because you never . . . Christ, Isabel, do you really think I've spent all that time at your house because I liked hanging out with *Linc*?"

"Yes! That's precisely what I thought!"

"And now?"

"Stop. That."

"What?" he demanded.

"That. Implying that there's something between us when there isn't. You gave me some sort of pity kiss. And then the second Germaine showed up you dashed over to stick your tongue down her throat like you couldn't wait to get the taste of me out of your mouth."

"Jesus, Isabel!" He plowed a hand through his hair. "What was I supposed to do?"

She threw up her hands. "Oh, I don't know. Not kiss her in front of me? That would have been a great start."

"A great start to what? You're the one who said over and over again that we were just friends. That you were only an employee. We've known each other for two and a half years, and you've blown me off every time I tried to talk to you. You only stay around long enough to insult my last name or my intelligence."

"Then why did you kiss me?"

He gave her an exasperated look and shoved a hand through his hair. "Because I wanted not to enjoy it. I wanted to find out I'd been wrong since the ninth grade."

Her breath caught in her chest. "And were you?"

A slow, sexy smile spread across his face. "What do you think?"

She didn't know what to think. Every single thought had vanished from her brain. In fact, every single molecule of oxygen had also vanished from her lungs. It was like she'd been zapped by aliens. Or maybe she'd suffered a head injury. That was it. Jackson really had brought her to a crack den. She'd been hit over the head, and she was hallucinating. That explanation made far more sense.

Finally, her lungs started functioning well enough for her to speak. Only one thing popped into her head. "Can you get me the pig or not?"

"What?" His voice rose sharply. "A pig? That's your response? After what I just told you, you want to know about a pig?"

"Tanner, I—" But once again her brain short-circuited. Synapses stopped firing and she just stuttered. "I—" Because it was all too bizarre. "I—" Was she really supposed to believe that Tanner had liked her? For years? And he'd never acted on it . . . why precisely? Because she made fun of his name? "I . . ." And how exactly was she supposed to process all of this in the middle of her current crisis? "I can't think about that now."

"You're blowing me off *again*?"

"I didn't know I'd ever blown you off in the first place!" she admitted. Was she so stupid about guys that Tanner freakin' Colt had been pursuing her—for the past two and a half years—and she hadn't even noticed? Was it possible that after years of being Invisabel Isabel, there'd been someone who'd seen her all along? And she hadn't seen him? Could she really be that stupid?

Of course, given her history with River, then, yeah, she just might be that stupid when it came to guys. Tanner had taught her how to drive a tractor, after all. Hadn't she told Mei exactly what it meant when a guy tried to teach you something?

"I can't even think about this right now," she repeated, partly to convince herself. "It changes nothing. Piper's pissed with me because I kissed you and because she thinks I'm BFFs with Germaine. I have to fix that first."

Izzy's heart shrunk for a second as she considered the possibility that this thing with Tanner—whatever it was—might not be an open-ended offer. Once she'd repaired her friendship with Piper, he might have changed his mind.

But she couldn't let that matter. "Piper's one of my best friends," Izzy continued. "I have to put her first. It's what she would do."

As she said it, she realized she was right.

Piper was fiercely loyal. She would never—not in a gazillion years—have betrayed Izzy the way Izzy had betrayed her. Not for all the guys in the world. Not for all the guys and all the shoes in the world. And all the lip gloss, too.

And suddenly, Izzy understood why Piper had been so hurt.

She looked up at Tanner—into those gorgeous blue eyes Piper had raved about so many times—and instead of saying any of the things she wanted to say, she asked, "So can you get me the pig or not?"

He studied her for a second. Then he nodded, his expression exasperated but resigned. "I'll get you the pig."

Friday afternoon, everything was in place. The assembly was in full swing. Mei was in the front row with Cassidy, Mei's parents' digital video recorder was charged and ready to go. Piper was in the audience, doing her best ostrich impression. Ms. Vogel was out onstage, discussing Internet safety in tones as serious as her perky voice would allow.

But there was no pig.

Tanner hadn't shown up.

Izzy was pigless. Anxiety knotted her stomach. Where was he? He'd sworn he'd get her some swine. What was wrong with him?

Then she saw Tanner, making his way through the ropes and pulleys for the stage curtains. But he was still pigless.

She hurried to him and whispered, "What happened? You were supposed to bring me a pig."

She was afraid Vogel might be wrapping it up before she'd have a chance to get out there. It was the third time she'd mentioned her office hours.

Then Tanner smiled at Izzy and she forgot to listen to Vogel. "Where have you been? I was about five seconds away from making a cardboard snout out of a toilet paper roll, taping it to Jackson Grosbeck's face, and dragging his ugly ass onstage."

Tanner smiled at her, gazing into her eyes for a second before saying, "Then thank God I got here in time. I'm not letting you kiss anyone else." Before she could process that, he swung his backpack over his shoulder and held it out to her. "I told you I'd come through."

The backpack was heavier than she'd have thought it would be. And it squirmed. And then oinked.

She unzipped a corner and out poked a tiny pink snout, no bigger than a Twinkie. The snout snuffled and wiggled until the hole was big enough for the piglet to look through. It was possibly the cutest thing she'd ever seen. Unfortunately.

Still, you had to work with what you had.

Before she could march out onto the stage, Tanner stopped her. "Isabel."

He didn't even touch her, but something in his voice made her insides tingle with warmth. She stopped and turned back toward him. "Yeah?"

"Before you go out there," he began, and despite herself, she stepped closer. "You said you needed to take care of this first"—his voice dropped lower—"but I need you to know, I broke up with Germaine. The same day we kissed, I ended it. I never should have been with her in the first place. Not when I felt this way about you."

Izzy's mouth was suddenly dry. She couldn't talk. Couldn't even breathe. All she could do was just stare at him, mouth slightly agape, simultaneously wishing that this moment could stretch on forever and that she could rewind it and play it over and over again in her mind.

He raised his eyebrows, clearly waiting for a response from her. After an endless second, he grinned as if enjoying her stunned silence. Then he reached out his hand and gently nudged her jaw to close her mouth.

Finally, she said, "You broke up with Germaine?" She swallowed past her suddenly dry mouth. "Because of how you feel about *me*?"

Tanner's lips twisted into a smile. "Yeah."

"Why didn't you say that the other day?"

He ducked his head, his expression suddenly sheepish. "I think I was hoping for a little more enthusiasm on your part."

"I—" The backpack gave a wiggle in her arms. She glanced out toward the stage. "I need—"

"I know. You need to get out there. Just know that I'll be here when you're done."

Suddenly, the assembly could wait. Not forever, but surely long enough for one kiss.

She rose up on her toes and pulled Tanner's mouth down to hers. His hand slipped into her hair to cradle her head as his lips moved slowly over hers. The feel of that kiss was everything she'd ever wanted. Sweeter and more poignant than their first kiss had been, because this wasn't about points or the IKC. Because this wasn't getting over River or being noticed. Because this was only about him and her and the sweet possibility of a thousand more kisses to come. And because this time, there was nothing between them. Nothing except . . .

The backpack gave a sharp squirm.

Nothing except the pig.

Tanner pulled back, smiling. Trailing his fingers down her arm to her hand, he gave it a little squeeze. "Go get 'em, Isabel."

Before she could talk herself into ditching the pig and just spending the rest of the day kissing Tanner, she charged out onstage, the pig in the backpack banging against her hips as she dashed for the microphone.

Ms. Vogel gasped as Izzy pushed her aside. Izzy scanned the audience, squinting against the glare of the stage lights. After years of being Invisabel Isabel, here she was up onstage for the whole school to see. For the whole world to see, since Cassidy had the camera rolling.

She even had her father's attention.

"I had a big speech written out about how I betrayed a friend and now I'm really sorry," she said into the microphone. "I was going to tell you about how I was one of the popular kids for a couple of weeks, and it wasn't worth it. I was going to tell you that loyalty and honesty and fairness aren't things they can teach you at school." In the far back of the audience, she could already see some of the teachers starting to respond. She recognized her father's silhouette as he elbowed someone aside and made his way down the auditorium aisle. Better get a move on. "But I don't think I'm going to have time to say all that. So let's cut to the chase."

She unzipped the bag, scooped out the piglet and held it up to the audience, turning so both she and the piglet were in profile for the entire school and all the Facebook fans to see. And then, she kissed the pig.

Chapter 32
Mei

Watching Izzy up onstage, putting lips to snout, Mei couldn't help but feel a burst of pride. It took some kind of guts to kiss a pig in front of the entire school on purpose, even a tiny and cute one.

Beside Izzy, Ms. Vogel gasped. Hands in the air as if to ward off a monster, she backed away. But other teachers were less squeamish. Principal Callahan elbowed his way past the other teachers and headed for Izzy. Izzy saw it as well and hopped down off the stage and into the audience. Mei followed suit. They converged on the spot where Piper and Cassidy had gathered in the front row.

A smile on her face for the first time since the showdown at Dairy Queen, Piper looked from Izzy to the piglet. "I kinda thought it'd be bigger."

Cassidy snorted. "Women all over the world say that."

The four of them burst out laughing. As funny as the quip had been, there was more than humor underlying the sound. There was relief. Their friendship was going to make it, after all.

Piper reached out and scratched the piglet behind its cute floppy ear. She met Izzy's gaze over the pig's head and smiled at her.

A second later, Izzy's father reached her. Anger radiated through his stocky frame and his voice rose furiously. "Isabel . . ."

Izzy practically tossed the pig to Piper. "Return this to Tanner for me?" she said with a wink.

Piper caught the piglet in her arms. "You know you didn't have to do this."

"Yeah, I did."

A second later, her father was leading Izzy away. Cassidy said, "Is it just me or does she look a lot like Heath Ledger being dragged off the bleachers in *10 Things I Hate About You*?"

Piper turned to Mei. "Did you know she was going to do this?"

"Me? No. I would have tried to talk her out of it," Mei admitted. "I love you, but I wouldn't wish pig snout on anyone."

Cassidy just shrugged. "All I knew was she wanted me to tape it for the IKC page. She refused to tell us what she had planned."

Before they could say anything else, Tanner walked up to them. He flashed Piper a friendly but distant smile.

Piper handed the pig over to Tanner, who slid it back into the backpack.

"Thanks," she told him, and when she smiled at him, Mei didn't see even a glimmer of the old adoration. *Thank God.* They'd had enough guy-related drama to last a lifetime.

"So what do we do now?" Piper asked, turning her attention back to her friends without a backward glance. Then she giggled. "We could break her out of detention like Julia Stiles."

"Too bad she's the only one with a good rack," Cassidy muttered.

"Umm, I think we've gotten in enough trouble with our clothes on," Mei said. No one mentioned her skinny-dipping in China, and she wasn't going to be the one to bring it up.

Perhaps it was only natural that they ended up at Mei's house. The tension was still thick as molasses at both Piper's and Cassidy's, but their parents trusted Mei's enough to consider her house an appropriate location for lockdown. "Mei, your mom is such a badass!" Cassidy said, popping a Cheeto in her mouth. "I would have thought your mom would chain you up in the kitchen."

"Are you kidding? My mom, the feminist professor, is applauding my attempts to shatter the double standard. And I think deep down they're just relieved I didn't go to China to search for my birth parents. Next to that, the IKC seems so normal and American."

Cassidy just scoffed. "Yeah, like you would do that."

Mei sucked in a breath. Why was it harder to admit this to her friends than it had been to tell Guiran? "Actually, I did."

Piper bolted upright. "Holy crap! Did you find them?"

"Right," Cassidy quipped. "'Cause in a country of one point six billion people, she's just going to order up her biological parents. I bet they were waiting for her at the airport with a sign in their hands."

Ignoring Cassidy's sarcasm, Mei admitted the truth. "I went there hoping to find some shred of information about them. I didn't find jack."

She didn't tell them about what she *had* found at the orphanage. The mood tonight was celebratory, and she didn't want to ruin it with stories from the SWI.

"Wow," Piper said, leaning back against the pillows stacked on Mei's bed. "You should have said something. Are you okay?"

"You know what? I think I am. For a while, it really tripped me out. But now, I'm thinking it's not so bad the way everything happened. Barring your indefinite grounding."

A moment later, Piper snatched up a throw pillow and whacked Mei's arm with it. "But no wonder you only earned three points while in China. I knew a hot chick like you could have gotten more if you'd really put your lips to it."

"Lacking focus and direction. That's me," Mei joked.

A second later the doorbell rang and then Izzy showed herself in. Piper all but launched herself at their friend. "What happened? Did they infringe on your rights? Abuse your civil liberties? Should we call the ACLU?"

"Or PETA?" Cassidy snorted.

Izzy chuckled, prying herself from Piper's protective embrace.

"Well, I finally got some quality alone time with my dad. It was very touching. Too bad I can't repeat any of the words he used."

Even though Izzy was making light of it, Mei could tell she was working hard to hide the hurt. After years of bending over backward to earn her father's approval, this was the thing that had finally gotten his notice. "So what *really* happened, Iz?"

"Well, let's put it this way. One of you will have to drop me at home. I no longer have a car. I no longer have a life. I no longer have anything." And yet she didn't sound nearly as depressed about the prospect as Mei would have thought.

"What?" Piper gasped. "Linc punched a locker and ruined his entire life and he gets sympathy. All you did was kiss one animal. Or two, if you count Tanner."

Mei added, "Maybe if you're lucky you can convince your dad to release you to Tanner's recognizance. For employment purposes only, of course."

"So are y'all together now?" Cassidy asked.

Izzy gave a vague shrug. There was just the faintest hint of smugness in her smile. Like maybe, just maybe, she had hope. But the kind of hope that was so fragile and new you didn't want to talk about it yet. "I don't know."

"Did he and Germaine . . . ?" Piper let the question dangle there.

"Break up?" Izzy bit down on her lower lip and nodded. "They did. Hey, Pipes, don't be mad, okay?" Izzy seemed determined to change the subject. "But I called Germaine and tried to apologize."

Piper gasped. "You didn't!"

Izzy rushed on. "Regardless of everything else, I still kissed her boyfriend. She may be a backstabbing skank, but I knew I'd been one, too. I wanted to . . . you know, be the bigger woman and say I was sorry."

Piper gazed at her through narrowed eyes before finally nodding. "I can see that."

"So did she accept your apology?" Mei asked. Because that was something she'd have liked to see; since it probably qualified as a once-in-a-million-years statistical anomaly.

"I think she was about ready to choke on her own bile. So, no. She didn't. I'm still glad I tried. She did happen to mention—about fifty times—that he was a total loser and that I saved her the trouble of destroying his heart when she broke up with him. So,"—she blew out a breath and ended it with a shrug—"that's everything I know about Tanner."

"Hey, Izzy, check this out," Mei said popping open her laptop. If Izzy was determined to be vague, then the least Mei could do was give her the easy out. "We already put the video up on the IKC page."

"Let me see it." She plopped down on the bed beside Mei and turned the computer to face her. "Hey, I can't find it. What the . . ."

Cass sat down behind her and looked over Izzy's shoulder as she scrolled down the page.

Post after post after post had supplanted the video they'd put up just hours before. There were so many, it took Mei a few minutes to process what she was seeing. Pictures—even a few videos—of girls kissing animals. In a show of solidarity, girls from all over the country, all over the world, were kissing their pets, their stuffed animals, any animal they could get their lips on. And of course, Jayson and Kyle had posted, too. Though, where Jayson had found a lemur in New York City, no one could guess. There were even a bunch of posts from fellow Paris High students, other kids who were tired of Germaine's reign of terror.

For several long minutes, the four of them crowded around the computer, scrolling through the pictures.

"Dang," Cassidy muttered. "We've started a revolution."

"Again," Piper added, with no small amount of pride.

"Jackson would be disappointed," Izzy joked. "There are no chickens and only one goat."

Mei started reading the comments out loud. "IKC rocks. Don't let the yatches get you down!"

"We love you guys," Cassidy read from Jayson's post. Then she laughed as she read the next part. "Hope that skank chokes on her own purity ring." And finally, "You've got to kiss a lot of pigs before you find your prince."

Piper ahhed. "That's my favorite! Who's it from?" she asked, looking up.

"Oh, I don't know." Mei feigned ignorance. "Some guy named . . . Sebastian."

Piper sank back onto the bed. One by one, the other girls turned to look at her.

"What?" asked Cassidy. "You're not pushing us out of the way to get to it? I thought this was your guy. You should be thrilled to hear from him."

"Yeah, well, I'm not."

"What does that mean?" Izzy asked. "What's going on, Pipes?"

"We broke up."

"Then why is he posting here?"

"Because I wouldn't answer his e-mails." She looked away.

"You wouldn't?" Mei stared at her, confused. "What happened, Piper?"

"Wait a second. He just posted again," Izzy said. "I miss you, Piper. Did you get the package I sent?"

"What package?" Cass demanded. "Did you get something from him?"

Piper blushed, then hesitantly reached for her purse. "I did. I just didn't have the nerve to open it."

"Well, give it to me. I'll do it." Cassidy held her hand out for the envelope.

Piper gave it to her, and the three of them crowded around as Cass ripped into it. She pulled out a box with pictures of French paintings all over it, staring in mute horror. Then she said, "Refrigerator magnets? That's the most unromantic gift ever."

Mei didn't want to say anything, but she kind of agreed. Piper didn't seem to mind, though, judging from the huge smile on her friend's face. "It's the French Masters collection. And actually, it's perfect."

Mei wanted to know what she meant, but the look in Piper's eyes said she wasn't going to explain. So she settled for asking, "What are we going to do now?"

"Well, not all of us have found our princes, so I guess we're going to keep kissing frogs," Piper answered with a philosophical shrug.

Izzy groaned. Cassidy fired a pillow at Piper's face. Piper caught it and pretended to fall to the ground. And that's when it hit Mei. She didn't have to travel halfway around the world to find her family. They'd been right here all along.

IVY ADAMS

Ivy is the pseudonym for three friends and writing partners: Emily McKay, Shellee Roberts, and Tracy Deebs. Though *The International Kissing Club* is their first novel together, they have written more than thirty novels between them. They shop, gossip, and watch movies in Austin, Texas.

www.internationalkissingclub.com

Acknowledgments

While writing this book was the most fun we've ever had in front of a keyboard, it was still a lot of work and there are a lot of people who helped make it what it is today.

First and foremost, our fantastic agents, Jessica Faust and Emily Sylvan Kim, who saw the potential as soon as we mentioned the fateful words, "International Kissing Club." It's been a long road and you have been wonderful. We couldn't have done this without you, so thank you, thank you, thank you.

To the people at Walker Books, who gave us a chance to tell the story we wanted to tell—and also gave us the perfect cover—and especially to our fabulous editor, Stacy Cantor Abrams, whose vision for the book, infinite patience, fun-loving spirit, and attention to detail have somehow managed to make the ramblings of three very different writers into one coherent story. We're sure at times it was like herding cats, and we appreciate you more than you will ever know. Thanks for sticking with us!

To Sherry Thomas, for throwing the delicious dumpling party where the idea for *The International Kissing Club* was born (and for all those mornings you spent at la Madeleine, feeding us a steady stream of gossip and fashion news, when we were supposed to be working).

To our husbands and children, who put up with late dinners, no dinners, and bad dinners (not to mention dirty socks) as we struggled to give Piper, Cassidy, Izzy, and Mei their voices.

To the random teenagers we chased through Austin, Texas, with our cell phone cameras as we tried to get our vision—and our characters—just right.

To our beta readers: Abby, Rebekah, and Dakota.

And finally, to each other, because how else could we have had this much fun and learned this much about collaboration, friendship, and lip gloss?